LOVE'S BATTLEFIELD

Leanna placed quick, light kisses upon his mouth, trailing down to nip his chin. His breathing was hard, a low rasp in the quiet of the room as she buried her face in his neck, kissing him again and again. He placed his hands on her hips and pulled her closer. Instinctively she pressed against him, moving in an unpracticed seductive way. It was more than Alex could withstand. He was amazed at her innocent expertise, at her lack of inhibition.

"You're so beautiful," he murmured against her skin. "I've never wanted anyone the way I want you, Leanna . . . never."

Harper
Monogram

CLARA WIMBERLY

Kentucky Thunder

HarperPaperbacks
A Division of HarperCollinsPublishers

HarperPaperbacks *A Division of* HarperCollins*Publishers*
10 East 53rd Street, New York, N.Y. 10022

Cover illustration by Renato Aime

First printing: July 1993

Printed in the United States of America

HarperPaperbacks, HarperMonogram, and colophon are trademarks of HarperCollins*Publishers*

10 9 8 7 6 5 4 3 2 1

All ladies beware of the gay young knight
Who loves—and who rides away.

Diary of Mary Chestnut
January 1862

Preface

This story and its characters are fictional, but it has been interwoven with history as well.

The village of the United Society of Believers, or Shakers as they're more commonly called, has been restored and stands in the beautiful bluegrass country of Kentucky, near Lexington. The first time I visited the village years ago, I was overwhelmed by its beauty and by its peace and serenity. The spirit of the quiet, gentle Shakers still dwells there, and it is felt at every turn.

Pleasant Hill calls me back again and again; I never grow tired of it. And if there is such a thing, Shakertown at Pleasant Hill has become the home of my heart.

I hope this book is a tribute to the kind, industrious people who once lived there—and to the ones who work there now and are so dedicated to showing us the sweet, simple joys of a life well lived.

1

**Lexington, Kentucky
January 1862**

The wind howled through the huge bare-limbed trees that surrounded the house. There was a feel of snow in the air, and the thin strip of remaining light near the sky's horizon was swiftly being replaced by scudding black clouds.

The tall, dark-haired man glanced for a moment toward the house, noting the festive glimmer of lights in all the long, narrow windows. Then he nudged his horse around the side of the house toward the barn at the back.

He felt the first wet flakes of snow on his face and looked up at the gathering darkness of the sky. His black eyes narrowed, and a shiver of disquiet ran along his spine. The storm would bring nightfall early, and he hoped his meeting with Senator McNairy would not take long.

As he approached the barn he saw the huge door open and a figure carefully slip out toward him.

"In here, Major Slayton, sir." The young man spoke quietly as he opened the heavy door wider and motioned the rider and horse inside.

The barn was well built, Alex Slayton noted with a touch of admiration. But then, he should not be surprised. The senator was a man of order and one who took care of what was his. That undoubtedly included his horses as well.

Once inside, Alex relaxed for a moment amidst the warm scent of horses and fresh hay, enjoying a quiet respite from the howling wind.

The boy led his horse to the back of the barn and waited for Alex. He lit a lantern that hung near a door at the back, and its light shone dimly upon the nearby walls.

"Shall I unsaddle your horse, Major?" the boy asked.

"No need for that, Thomas. I hope I won't be here that long."

The boy pointed toward the door where the lantern hung. "The senator had me bring some clothes for you. They're in the back room there, if you'd like to change now."

Alex swung the long cape from his broad shoulders and tossed it across one of the stalls. The brass buttons of his uniform glittered in the dim light as he moved toward the back room.

"Thank you, Thomas," he said with a nod of dismissal toward the young man.

"Come through the back of the house when you're ready. I'll be waitin' there to take you to the senator."

Alex nodded and stepped into the small room just at the end of the barn's wide corridor. One small kerosene lamp spread its soft glow on a plank table against the wall.

Alex smiled as he saw the black formal suit hanging upon the wall. The senator had thought of everything.

It was unlikely that anyone would see him here tonight. But if that should happen, he wouldn't like to have to explain his uniform to the guests of a Kentucky senator.

Unconsciously Alex slid his fingers down the front of his Union jacket. Being out of uniform was hardly a hanging offense, although it might raise serious questions if he were caught. He wondered if his superiors would believe him if he said that the senator was only an old family friend.

Once again Alex felt a prickle of uneasiness as he wondered what had prompted the senator to summon him to his home. Then he quickly began to unbutton the jacket of his uniform.

Leanna McNairy laughed as she looked up at the young man before her. She felt a slight twinge of guilt at the look of hurt in his pale blue eyes. She knew Tyler Jennings was in love with her, but for goodness' sake, she had told him often enough that she did not feel the same. Why did men always have to be so serious?

"Oh, Tyler, darling," she drawled, trying to tease a smile back to his lips. "You know I like you. You're my dearest friend. But I don't understand why you insist on being so serious about this. It's my nineteenth birthday party, and I just want to have a little fun tonight. Please don't spoil it with all this talk of marriage." She widened her green eyes at him and, with a practiced motion of her head, brushed her reddish gold hair back over her shoulder.

She glanced away from Tyler as they heard footsteps coming toward them from the front of the house. When Mrs. Macky, the housekeeper, spotted the two of them talking in the shadows of the long, curving stairway, she frowned.

"Leanna McNairy! 'Tis not seemly for you to be out here in the hall alone with young Mr. Jennings. Your papa will have a fit!"

"Oh, Macky," Leanna said. "You know Papa's fits never last for long, not where I'm concerned, anyway."

"Yes, and more's the pity."

The older woman could hardly suppress the sigh that came to her lips. The girl was a handful, that was for sure. And she had the senator wrapped around her little finger, just like she had every other male that came within sight of those green eyes and full pink lips. Leanna was hardly serious about anything except having a good time. Macky doubted that the little saucebox knew that the war was coming to Kentucky, or would even care if she knew, for that matter.

"Nevertheless," Mrs. Macky said, glaring at Leanna, "you'd best come back inside before you create a scandal you can't talk your way out of."

"Oh, all right. We'll be right there."

Leanna and the young man watched silently as the plump housekeeper moved away from them and down the hallway toward the kitchen.

Tyler didn't miss the gleam of defiance in Leanna's lovely eyes or the stubborn tightening of her lips.

"Do . . . do you think we should go back inside, then?" he asked.

"I'll go when I'm ready."

"I want to talk to you tonight, Leanna. Alone. When am I going to have a chance with all these people around us?"

Leanna smiled, and her eyes sparkled with mischief. She took his hand and pulled him toward the back door. What a splendid joke on Mrs. Macky. No one would ever think of looking for them in the barn, not on such a cold night. Besides, she knew that for all the housekeeper's bluster, she wouldn't dare mention Leanna's behavior to her father.

Alex Slayton heard a noise near the front of the barn. His fingers halted in midair near the last button of his shirt. He held his breath and turned his head to pick up the sound.

He heard the distinct whisper of voices and the unmistakable giggle of a woman.

"Damn."

In one swift move he blew out the lamp's flickering light and stepped back into the corner of the room. His right hand moved instinctively to the Colt Dragoon that rested in a holster secured against his hips. With one deft flick of his thumb, he loosened the narrow leather strap that held the gun in place.

"I'm not so sure about this." The boy's voice was just loud enough for Alex to hear.

"Oh, Tyler, you're as bad as Macky! First you say you want to be alone with me and now you sound like a fidgety old woman." Her teasing laughter rang through the quietness of the barn.

"But what if someone comes in? I'd hate to . . ."

"Oh, come on," she said.

Alex stiffened as he heard them coming nearer. Hell, this was all he needed, to have a laughing Southern belle and her amorous swain trip over him in their search for privacy.

He could see them very well as they entered the room with the light from the barn behind them. The girl was petite, though he could not make out her features in the darkness of the room. But he could see the bright halo of her hair and the way the lights turned it into a shining mass of golden spun sugar. And he could smell her perfume, sweet and tantalizingly close to him.

The young man pulled the girl to him and with a low moan kissed her quickly before she pulled away and danced out of his reach.

A little tease, Alex surmised with a sardonic smile.

"Oh, Leanna," the boy whispered, going again to take her into his arms. "You are so beautiful, I can hardly bear being near you like this without . . ."

Alex frowned. Leanna? Senator McNairy's daughter? She'd been only a skinny, long-legged colt of a girl last time he was here.

"Tyler, please. Let's don't be serious. Life's too short for always being so earnest."

"For once I agree," he said quietly. "Life *is* too short. That's why I want to marry you . . . now! You don't seem to understand that I might never come back. I . . ."

"Don't say that!"

The girl's voice had grown serious for the first time, but Alex wondered if the little sob he detected in its tone was real or staged.

"Of course you will come back, Tyler. Everyone

knows our Confederate troops will whip those Yankees quickly and send them running straight back to Washington."

Alex's eyebrows shot upward, and he bit his lip to keep from laughing aloud. He almost wished his men camped outside town could hear the little Rebel baggage.

"I love you, Leanna. God, I hate to leave you." Tyler spat his words out in a rush, anxious to make her understand. "If only I had some reason . . . something to take with me into battle to remember you by. Something more than a kiss . . ."

By God, what a young scoundrel, Alex thought, though he grinned in the darkness.

"Like what?" Leanna asked. "A lace hanky, perhaps? A ribbon from my hair?"

"Dearest," he groaned. "Please, just tonight, right here. Let me love you. I promise I won't hurt you . . . I'll be . . ."

Alex rolled his eyes and wondered what he would do if forced to witness such an eventuality. He was beginning to grow quite impatient with young Leanna and her overzealous suitor.

"Tyler Jennings! How could you even suggest such a thing? I thought you were a gentleman and that I could trust being alone with you. And now I find you're just as bad as all the rest! Oh, I can hardly believe it." She put her hands to her face and began to sob loudly.

"Oh, Leanna . . . my darling love. I would never do anything to . . . I wouldn't think of behaving in a manner that would be offensive to you. Please say you'll forgive me and I promise I will never speak of it again."

"Well . . . all right." Her voice sounded breathless,

and she made a sobbing little sniff. "I just want us to be friends, Tyler, dear. And maybe someday . . ."

"Someday?" His voice was so full of hope that Alex actually felt sorry for the boy. "Oh, what sweet words, what promise you give to take with me to battle. It's all I'll ask for now, all I'll think about until I come home again."

He bent his head and kissed her again, being careful not to touch her with his hands or hold her too close.

"Thank you, Tyler, dear. Now why don't you go on back to the party. I'll follow in a few minutes, so we won't rouse suspicions."

The boy almost tripped on his way out as he turned to look back at the woman he loved. For a short moment, Alex wondered if he'd ever been that green or that lovesick in all his twenty-eight years.

Leanna's laughter began the moment Tyler was out the door. It started as a rippling little giggle, building until she could contain herself no longer. Finally she threw her head back and hooted with laughter, a hardly genteel sound, Alex thought, but one with no inhibitions whatsoever. For a moment he envied the girl her youth and spontaneity. Then he stepped out of the dark corner.

"A touching performance," he said.

The deep voice coming from behind Leanna took her completely by surprise, so much so that she let out a little yelp as she turned.

"Who's there?" she gasped as she backed toward the doorway.

A match flared, releasing the pungent scent of sulphur into the night air. At that moment Leanna was aware of every sound around her, of the muffled wind outside and the quiet stamping of the horses in their stalls. She stood perfectly still as she looked into the blackest eyes she'd ever seen.

Alex bent slowly and lit the lamp, keeping the girl in sight out of the corner of his eye. She was still staring at him as if she'd seen a ghost.

"Who are you?" she demanded in a voice that had suddenly lost its volume. "And what are you doing here?"

Had she seen this man before? Somehow she thought she recognized his dark chilling gaze beneath the slash of black brows. His hair, straight and full and curved over his collar at the back of his neck, was as dark as his eyes, and as black as the wings of a raven. His skin was almost too beautiful for a man's, smooth, and even now in the dead of winter burnished to a dark golden brown. Only the slight curve of his aquiline nose kept his handsome face from being perfect.

She lowered her gaze, taking in his unbuttoned jacket and shirt. He made no effort to cover himself but rather stood boldly before her with an amused look on his face as she stared at him.

His chest was the same golden color as his face. She noted its muscled contours and the smooth flawlessness of his skin. It took a moment for her to pull her eyes away, and when she did she gasped and took a step backwards. The blue uniform he wore and the brass buttons seemed to leap forward into her vision.

"You're a Yankee!"

"An astute observation."

Without conscious thought Leanna made a move to turn and run from the barn. But she was stopped by two strong arms reaching forward and wrapping around her slender waist, pulling her completely off the ground.

Alex could feel the tightening of her dress as she took a great gulp of air. In anticipation of her screams, he clamped his hand over her mouth. His action only caused her to thrash more wildly against him.

For a moment he considered dropping the girl, leaping onto his horse, and riding away. Forget the meeting with the senator. He felt like a fool, hiding in someone's barn and skulking about. And now he found himself in a tangle with a wild, unreasonable female.

"Hold still," he said. "Just be still a minute and let me talk to you."

But she continued to kick at his shins as she strained to open her mouth far enough to sink her teeth into his hand.

Suddenly Alex released his grip on her and stepped away. She fell onto the hay-covered floor and sat in stunned silence. She glared up at him with bright eyes as she struggled to her feet.

"What are you doing here? And how dare you manhandle me this way, you . . . you . . . ."

Alex stepped closer but stopped when she leapt away from him. Lord, he hadn't intended to frighten the girl out of her wits. He took in her blazing green eyes and her defiant stance. The senator's daughter had grown into a beautiful young woman, although her manners could certainly use some improvement.

"Look," he said quietly, hoping to soothe her, "I'm not here in an official capacity. And I certainly mean you no harm. I'm here at the request of Senator McNairy."

"You're lying! My father would never receive a Yankee soldier, not now with all that's happening. . . ."

"I can't help what you believe, and I really don't have time to stand here debating it with you. For the senator's sake I would suggest that you keep quiet about having seen me here. I'll be gone within the hour, and you, ma'am, will never see me again."

He turned away from her as if dismissing her and began to pull his shirt from his trousers. Did he intend to undress right in front of her? Well, what could she expect from a Yankee? The only ones she'd ever met were rude and overbearing, interested only in money and getting things done in a hurry.

"Wh-what are you doing?"

"If you'll excuse me, I'm changing clothes." His voice was slow and patient, as if she were incapable of understanding the simplest English. "The sooner I meet with the senator, the sooner I can be away from here. That is what you want, isn't it?"

"I suppose you think I won't yell for help? I suppose you think you can just waltz in here like this and do as you please?"

"That's right." With a soft grunt he pulled off his boots, and then looked at her as he began to unbutton his pants.

"Now, I assure you I'm not at all shy, and I don't mind in the least undressing under your beautiful, watchful eyes. But from your little conversation with young Tyler, I'm afraid a quiet, maidenly girl like yourself might faint at the sight of a man's naked body."

"Oh! You are a crude, odious man and I'll . . ."

"You'll what?" He directed his black gaze at her, the humor completely gone now from his face and his manner.

"I'll get Tyler, that's what I'll do. You won't be so smug then."

She whirled around and hurried from the room, her footsteps making soft crunching noises in the hay.

"A frightening thought indeed," he muttered beneath his breath as he quickly pulled on the clothes Thomas had brought. Major Slayton would make sure that Leanna's young hero found only an empty room if he did return.

2

As Alex walked swiftly to the back of the house he could see the shimmer of coach lights at the front. Several carriages had entered the driveway and were slowly making their way through the snow up the sloping hill to the house.

His lips curved into a disdainful smile. Not even a vicious and dangerous storm, it seemed, would keep the McNairy girl from her indulgences. A party in the midst of war did not sit well with him at this point.

Thomas met him outside the kitchen and ushered him down a hallway and into the study.

Senator McNairy rose immediately from a chair near the fireplace and came forward to greet Alex.

"Alex, my boy. Thank you for coming so promptly."

Alex had not seen the man in a while, and he was shocked at the senator's appearance. His round face was dark red, and even the act of getting up from a chair seemed to tire him easily.

"I'll get right to it, Alex. I know it was dangerous for you to come here tonight, and I won't take much of your time." The older man motioned to one of the chairs near the fireplace.

Alex sat down and stretched out his long legs.

Senator McNairy stared into the flames as if hypnotized as he spoke. "I'm in trouble, son, and I need your help."

"What can I do?"

Before the senator could reply, the door to the study burst open. Alex was aware of swirling green skirts and a wealth of reddish gold hair as Leanna McNairy rushed toward her father.

"Father! There's a man in the . . ." Then she recognized the man who sat with her father. "You!"

Alex slowly stood up, the intensity of his black eyes taking in every inch of the girl before him. Here in the light he was able to see that she was even more beautiful, more vibrant than he had first thought.

Senator McNairy looked from his daughter to Alex Slayton. "So you remember Alex, then? I wasn't sure you would."

"Alex?" she asked with a puzzled frown.

The senator chuckled and pulled her to his side. "Alexander Slayton, darling. You remember he often came to visit when you were a little girl. The last time I believe he was . . ." He looked at Alex questioningly. "What, twenty or so?"

"I was nineteen, sir," Alex replied. "And your lovely daughter, I believe, was . . . ten." He smiled, enjoying the flush of color that remembrance brought to her face.

"Yes," she said abruptly. She knew she had seen those black eyes before though she had not remembered them being so cold.

"You're a major now, I believe Father has told me . . . with the Union army." There was no mistaking the definite chill in her voice. She deliberately ran her gaze over the front of his evening jacket, letting him know that she had not forgotten his rude behavior earlier.

"That's correct." He smiled at her, knowing quite well what she was thinking.

At the sound of his deep voice a chill rippled down her neck. He didn't like her, she could feel it and could see it in the glint of his eyes. She was not accustomed to meeting any man she could not soon bring into fawning submission.

"My dear, it might be best if we do not mention Alex's presence here tonight. Some of our guests might not understand."

"Oh, don't worry, Father. I have no more wish than you for my friends to learn we have a Yankee officer in the house. Especially not tonight, when Tyler and his friends are preparing to go to war, perhaps even die defending the rights of our Southern states." She stared hard at Alex as she spoke.

"You mean defending slavery?" Alex Slayton's voice was deceptively soft and polite.

"*We* have no slaves, Major! And neither do many of my friends. And if you had any decency—"

"Leanna!" the senator scolded, looking at her with surprise. "That's enough. Alex is a friend of the family, and I will not have him treated this way in my own home."

"And I, Father, would prefer not having him in my home at all!"

"Leanna, dear, please listen—"

But the senator's words were too late. His daughter had already whirled around and stalked out the door, slamming it heavily behind her.

"I'm sorry, Alex. I've left Leanna alone too long without the calming grace of a mother. She really is a sweet, loving girl."

"I'll take your word for that."

"Well, I'm afraid her behavior only makes my request more awkward."

Alex tried to hide his growing impatience. He was aware of time slipping away and of the storm's growing intensity. He needed to get back to camp.

"I'll do anything I can," he said to the older man. "Just name it, sir."

"If anything happens to me, I want your word that you will take Leanna to Pleasant Hill, to the Shaker village. She'll be safe there. And you are the only one I trust to take her."

"Safe? What's this all about?"

The senator sighed. "The Rebels are compiling a list of names . . . people who have aided the Union. I have reason to believe my name will be on that list, sooner or later."

"You?" He struggled to comprehend what the man was saying. "But why you?"

"Because it's true, my boy. I have aided the Union, and I make no apologies for my actions. I did what I thought was best."

Alex looked at him for a moment in stunned silence. "But what of your neutral status? I thought you and my father both took an oath when you left the Senate that you would remain neutral. . . ."

"We did . . . I did. All the more reason the Confederates will come for me." He leaned forward in his chair, looking into Alex's eyes. "Leanna has no one except me, no family here. There's only my sister in Philadelphia, and Leanna would never agree to go there."

Alex stood and began to pace before the fire. "I don't know how I can . . ."

"Please, Alex. You're the only one I can trust. When they come for me, her life will be ruined in Lexington. Her friends will turn their backs on her, and she might even be in danger."

Alex shook his head. It would be risky. But how could he refuse this man who was his father's closest friend?

"I'm sorry," the senator said. "I'm imposing . . . asking too much. . . ."

"No, of course it isn't asking too much, sir," Alex said quickly. He knew with a sinking feeling that whatever decision he made it would likely be the wrong one. "But I suspect that your spirited daughter is not going to like the idea."

"Oho, you can be certain of that. But I know you can handle her. And I trust you as an officer and as a friend."

Alex extended his hand to the senator. "Then I'll do my best."

The older man stood, sighing with relief and gratitude.

"Your best will do, son. It will certainly do. I feel as if a tremendous burden has been lifted from my shoulders." He turned toward the door. "I know you must go. The storm is worsening by the hour. I'll send word to you if the worst happens."

Just as Senator McNairy was escorting Alex into the hallway, the door across from them opened. A group of young men and women burst through, their laughter ringing loudly in the hall. The senator's daughter was at the head of the group and seemed to be the center of all attention.

It was too late for Alex to turn back, and the senator moved toward the front door as if to escort his guest out properly.

They were halted by the young man that Alex had seen in the barn with Leanna. His gray uniform, resplendent with gold buttons and braid, was obviously new. He stepped forward rather stiffly, and with a soft Southern drawl addressed the senator.

"Senator McNairy, sir. I was hoping to see you, hoping you'd attend the Havelock ceremony later this evening."

Alex smiled slightly at the fervent pride that flashed in the young man's eyes. He looked to be no more than nineteen or twenty, with cheeks as smooth and pink as a young girl's. His blond hair was combed to one side and held stiffly in place with pomade, and there was a slight hint of a mustache above his lips.

The senator hesitated a moment, looking impatient to get Alex away from the group, even though his attire would not give away his Union loyalty.

"Of course, my boy," he said rather loudly. "Be happy to. Soon as I've seen my guest out I'll be right with you."

Leanna linked her arm with Tyler's and glared at Alex.

One of the other girls spoke up. "Why, Senator, you

surely don't intend to send this handsome gentleman out into such a raging storm. Not when we're in desperate need of dancing partners." Although she addressed the senator, she never took her eyes off Alex's tall, well-proportioned frame.

Leanna's eyes snapped immediately toward the blond girl who was batting her eyelashes. "I'm sure the gentleman needs to be on his way, Carolyn. It would be a shame if he became lost in the storm on such a cold night."

Something in her patronizing manner made Alex want to shake her, but he could not suppress his smile. What a self-righteous little piece of baggage she was. He wondered if she had ever been denied anything in her young, privileged life. It was obvious that she was accustomed to being the center of attention.

"Why, Miss McNairy," Alex said, deliberately putting a mocking drawl into his own voice. "I'm certain you promised me a dance before I go."

Her beautiful full lips clamped together into a thin line. If she were to keep her father's secret she could not graciously refuse. She also knew that was exactly the reason he did it.

Senator McNairy mumbled something under his breath and frowned at Alex, but Alex ignored the warning and offered his arm to Leanna.

She gave him a withering glare and then placed her hand lightly upon his forearm. Alex thought she might just as well have touched a viper.

3

When the doors to the ballroom opened, strains of music reached out to beckon them inside. The dancers whirling around the room moved aside when Leanna and her entourage entered. As Alex led her out to the dance floor, the others parted, and there was a smattering of applause. There were also more than a few sighs of admiration as the tall, handsome stranger took the belle of the ball into his strong arms.

Leanna was surprised as he moved her smoothly around the floor. Alexander Slayton had the lean muscular look of an outdoorsman, yet his touch and his step were graceful and light. She would not look up at him, would not give him the satisfaction of showing her annoyance. But she was well aware of his steady gaze on her face, and she knew he only did it to mock her further. It was bad enough that she had to dance with the odious man; she certainly would not engage him in conversation.

"You're light as a feather, my dear," he whispered. Again his voice carried an affected Southern drawl.

"You can dispense with the niceties now, Major Slayton. No one can hear you except me, and I assure you I am not the least bit interested in anything you have to say."

His sarcastic groan of pain irritated her even more. She felt like kicking his ankles, but she remembered his reaction the last time she'd done that. Instead, she smiled up at him as if she enjoyed being in his arms more than anything.

"You didn't seem so uninterested when I was here last time. Why, as I recall, a certain little girl with bright curls left numerous small letters and cards under my door. Letters that declared a fervent admiration, I believe."

"I did no such thing! And even if I had, it is ungentlemanly of you to mention it. I was a mere child!"

As he guided her around the floor he pulled back and looked down at her. His black gaze raked her from head to toe suggestively. "That much has changed, I'll admit."

Her cheeks flushed, and she tried to pull away from him, but his hands tightened around her like a rope. Leanna knew that she could not afford to make a scene. She could only hope that he would leave as soon as the dance ended.

But even as the music stopped, Alex held her against him for one last disturbing moment. It was long enough for her to feel the taut muscles of his thighs pressing against hers. He allowed her to pull away from him only when Tyler made his way across the floor to them.

Alex nodded toward the boy. "If you care about your young beau there, you should convince him to stay here in Lexington. I'm afraid his noble ideas about war will vanish with his first battle."

"Wh-what do you mean? Are you implying that Tyler is a coward? How ordinary you are, Major, to think everyone but your own kind is a quitter."

Once more, he tried to control his urge to shake her. Then, without a word, he turned and walked away, leaving her alone on the dance floor.

It was time for the ceremony, and Leanna, for all her teasing ways, did not wish to spoil Tyler's last evening at home. So, with a brilliantly calculated smile, she turned toward the young man who stepped to her side.

Leanna and Tyler, along with several other couples, went to the center of the room, and all the rest moved away. Leanna could see her father nearby, smiling proudly at her. She was also all too aware that somewhere near the door, another man stood watching as well. She had no doubt there was an irreverent smile upon his lips, but she was determined not to let him spoil her birthday party. Besides, she hoped she'd never have to see him again after that evening.

The man in her thoughts did indeed watch as he leaned casually against the door frame, but she was wrong about the smile, and she had mistaken his words about Tyler. It had not been conceit that made him caution her. There was no triumph in his heart, and certainly no smile of mockery. All he felt was a deep, wrenching sadness for the young men who held such proud and glorious ideals about the war—such naive, unrealistic ideals that Alex had seen shattered for many men the past two years.

Alex watched the ceremony, one that had grown

popular on both sides of the war. The Havelock was a white linen hat with separated flaps that hung down in the back and on both sides of the head. The hat was placed upon the head of the soldier by his sweetheart, symbolically sending him with honor to the glorious service of his country.

Leanna pulled a silk flower from the bodice of her iridescent green gown and placed it on Tyler's cap. A shout of exultation rose from the young men and was quickly echoed by the guests about the room.

Leanna didn't know what made her turn toward the door to meet the gaze of the man standing there. She wondered for a moment at the odd look on his face. Had she not known what kind of man he was, she might have thought it was one of sadness.

She watched him turn on his heel and go into the hallway. She saw him swing a long black cape around his shoulders and heard the sound of the howling wind as the front door opened. Surprisingly, she felt empty and alone. She seemed to be surrounded by a great still silence, even though the room was filled with laughing, chattering people.

Outside, the snow was already piling heavily upon the grass and roadway. Alex pulled his hat down and lowered his head against the numbing wind and stinging flakes of ice and snow.

Strange as it seemed, he actually welcomed the cold and the bite of the wintry wind. Holding Leanna McNairy so tightly against him a few moments ago had elicited a quick and unexpected flash of heated desire in him.

He didn't understand how a willful, spoiled girl—not

at all the type he preferred—could so easily arouse this powerful response. For all her outward sophistication, Alex suspected she was an innocent, at least a sensual innocent. His reaction to her puzzled and irritated him at the same time.

It was nothing, he told himself. He'd probably been without a woman far too long, and that could be remedied easily enough. There was a tavern in every small town now, filled with women only too happy to accommodate a soldier. If they were not the virtuous, ladylike creatures one would introduce to one's mother, what of it? They were warm and soft and more than willing to do as a man wished.

Alex had to admit that these women were not generally to his taste. In fact, the men under his command often kidded him when he'd forego that particular pleasure. But perhaps they were right. Perhaps a warm, willing body was exactly what he needed.

What else would explain the jolt that passed through him tonight, that even now brought the vision of flashing emerald eyes and voluptuous pink lips to mind. What else would cause his fingers to grip the reins so tightly as he imagined sinking his hands into a cloud of golden red hair.

Alex forced himself to think of Senator McNairy. He could hardly believe the dignified gentleman had turned spy for the Union. He was curious to know exactly what he had done. One thing was certain in his mind: if the senator's name was on an arrest list, then it was indeed a serious charge, and McNairy was right to believe that his daughter might be in danger once the news spread.

What on earth was Alex getting himself into, promising to come for her and take her to the Shaker village?

He imagined the feisty green-eyed minx in the staid confines of such a place, and he knew it would never work.

He suddenly nudged the horse's sides, urging him into a fast trot through snow that threatened to blind both of them. He wanted to get back to the shelter of his tent and away from the glittering mansion on the hill and the haunting music that he seemed to hear even now.

Major Alexander Slayton rode with a mind-clearing fury, as if the wind were a howling demon that chased at his heels.

Leanna McNairy sat before the fireplace in her second-story bedroom, watching the flames jump around the hickory logs. The house was silent except for the crackling of the fire and the whistling wind that raced about the eaves.

Her guests had left soon after the Havelock ceremony because of the heavy snowstorm. The McNairy mansion sat on a small rise on the northern outskirts of town, so the guests had only a few miles to travel to get home. Otherwise Leanna would have cancelled the party altogether.

It had been a good party, she thought, even if it was a solemn occasion for Tyler and his friends. It would have been even better had it not been for the arrogant Alexander Slayton and his dire warning about Tyler's going away to war.

Why her papa had allowed that man to come to their home puzzled her. A Yankee soldier, of all people. Even if her father and Alex's were old friends, he should not risk being seen now with a Union officer. Some of the stories Tyler and the boys told about the brutal Union soldiers were simply horrifying.

Of course she had been enchanted with Alex Slayton when she was a girl, even if she denied it to him tonight. But she'd been a child then who knew nothing of war and the damage the Yankees were intent on wreaking upon the Southern states. She was thankful that now finally she could see him for what he was—an arrogant, overbearing marauder who wanted only to force the North's biased policies on her people.

Oh, her father often told her she did not fully understand the war, and she supposed she could not blame him for sometimes defending the Union position. After all, he was a senator and had spent almost as much time in Washington as he had in Kentucky. And, as he so often pointed out, his grandfather had fought with General Washington to establish the Union. Still, she knew more than he thought. Tyler had enlightened her about many aspects of the war.

Why, then, could she not seem to forget the way that infuriating man had looked at her before he left? And why was it that every time she tried to recall Tyler's sweet face, an image of piercing black eyes appeared instead?

Even now the vision of Alex Slayton's tall, muscular body in the barn's dim lamplight burned in her mind. She could still see the contours of his dark-skinned chest, tapering to a flat, rippled stomach. She wondered what it would be like to slide her hand over his smooth skin.

She jumped up from the chair near the fire and paced the floor, her soft, white robe flaring behind her. She went to the window, but an icy chill rattling the glass sent her shivering back to the warmth of the hearth.

She didn't like feeling the way she did. In fact, she hated feeling unsure about anything. She'd felt that way often as a child, when she was alone and confused about whether or not anyone would ever love her. Of course she knew now that her father's absence had not meant that, but when she was younger she'd often felt abandoned whenever he was in Washington.

She'd discovered that laughter and diversion—any kind of diversion—would chase away those feelings, and she'd decided that having fun was the ultimate balm for almost any sorrow.

She'd hardly been without pleasurable diversion since that decision. Oh, she knew that as a result she was regarded by the household staff and her friends as a cheerful, carefree sort of girl who took nothing seriously. No one, not even her father, had ever been able to see through that careful facade. Indeed, she even believed it herself at times.

But not tonight. Tonight that old, uneasy melancholy had returned. And she did not know why.

She thought of Alexander Slayton and the feel of his arms around her. An odd excitement fluttered in the pit of her stomach when she remembered the intensity of his gaze. He'd told her she was no longer a child.

No man had ever looked at her the way he had then, as if he knew everything about her. It made her quiver with a strange but not unpleasant sensation. She remembered the feel of his hard body against hers. She'd been surprised at the scorching warmth she felt through her clothes, as if he were aflame.

Her face flushed at such thoughts. It was odd that she'd never felt these emotions with Tyler, with someone she cared about, and not even with the boys she'd allowed to steal quick, forbidden kisses in the summer garden.

But shouldn't there be love with such feelings? She certainly had no love for Alex Slayton and his overbearing ways. Then what had caused these odd, disturbing feelings in her that made her melancholy and restless?

"Leanna McNairy," she muttered as she paced before the fireplace, "what on earth is wrong with you?"

She only hoped she would never have to see that arrogant man again, for the feelings he evoked in her disturbed her deeply. In fact, they shook her complacent little world and frightened her more than anything had in years. She simply would not have it!

4

In late January news came that General
Grant had moved into Kentucky and that Union gun-
boats on the Tennessee River had reached toward Fort
Henry. A few days later Union troops closed in on the
Confederates at Mill Springs and Somerset, less than a
hundred miles from Lexington.

For a while Senator McNairy was hopeful that the
Rebels would not risk coming for him, with such a
powerful Union buildup occurring nearby. But they
were determined, it seemed, and willing to risk death to
capture a man who, as a fellow Southerner and a sworn
neutral, had betrayed them. To them it was the worst of
all crimes.

He awoke suddenly in the middle of the night, not
sure what had awakened him—a noise, perhaps, the
barking of a dog somewhere in the distance. He felt

himself inexplicably drenched with sweat while his heart pounded furiously in his chest. They were coming for him—he could feel it.

Without lighting a lamp he quickly went downstairs to the servants' quarters and woke the young man sleeping on a narrow cot near the door.

"Thomas!" he whispered. "Thomas, wake up!"

The boy sat up. "Is that you, Mr. McNairy?"

"Thomas, do you remember the note I gave you before and the instructions I told you?"

"Yessir, Mr. McNairy." The young man's sleepy voice sounded frightened.

"It's time. I want you to go to Harrodsburg as quickly as possible and give the note to Major Slayton, just as we discussed before."

They could hear the pounding of hooves outside and see the movement of lights through the windows of the house.

"Hurry now, you must hurry. And don't let anyone keep you from finding the major, do you hear me?"

"Yessir. But . . . but what about you, Senator?"

"Never mind about me. I'll be all right. Now hurry, Thomas."

Footsteps sounded on the front steps and across the porch. Then there was the sickening thud of wood against the front door as the soldiers battered against the lock.

With shaking fingers Senator McNairy lit a lamp in the hallway and stood, waiting for them. From the floor above came the sound of bedroom doors opening as others came to see what was happening.

Leanna, clutching her robe tightly around her, stepped out on the top of the landing just as the front door splintered open. Several rough, unshaven men in dirty worn gray uniforms, holding rifles menacingly across their chests, burst through to the entry hall.

Leanna stood motionless, the sight before her quickly dashing the sleep from her eyes. It was like a nightmare. She couldn't seem to understand why the Confederates would intrude into a sympathetic household in the middle of the night.

She saw her father standing still and straight in his nightshirt and robe. A tall, thin Confederate officer stepped to the front of the group of men and stood before her father. He was not young, perhaps somewhere near her father's age. His face was worn and haggard, but he looked not unkind, nor did he appear angry. There was instead a resigned sadness on his worn features, as if what he was about to do troubled him. In his hand was a worn-looking piece of paper.

"Senator McNairy. I suppose you know why we're here."

"Pierce . . . Pierce Hamlin. I . . . I never expected you to . . . I didn't think it would be anyone I knew who came for me."

Leanna's eyes widened, and her hand flew to clasp the lapels of her robe. Come for him? But what on earth did he mean?

"No," the Rebel officer replied, his quiet voice ringing in the hallway. "And I never thought I'd be coming here to the home of an old friend. It's always easier, isn't it, when we can't see the face of our enemy?"

His eyes glittered accusingly in the lamplight. He cleared his throat, then stepped forward to stand within two feet of the senator. His right hand, clasping the paper, moved outward as if to show his authority.

"As an officer of the Confederate States of America,

I arrest you, Senator McNairy, for treason against the Confederacy and against your fellow citizens."

Leanna gasped, and the blood in her veins seemed to stop. "No!" she murmured as she started down the stairs.

The senator looked up, noticing his daughter for the first time. Her reaction was what he had dreaded most. Fear and confusion clouded her lovely face, and he knew it would not be long until they were replaced by disgust, perhaps even hatred. He would have to leave the explaining to Alex. Perhaps by then Leanna would be calmer and more able to understand, if she ever could.

"You're making a dreadful mistake!" Leanna shouted as she moved toward her father. "My father would never do anything treasonous against the Confederacy."

The tall officer looked at her with a tinge of sympathy in his tired eyes.

"Father, tell him it's a mistake." She went to the senator and clutched at his sleeve. Her eyes shimmered with tears.

"Colonel Hamlin, may I have a few moments with my daughter, privately?"

Pierce Hamlin nodded and stepped away, but he went no farther than the door, where his men still stood with rifles ready.

"Papa?" She looked up into his face, the face of the man she loved more than anyone in the world, the man she considered the most honorable she'd ever known.

"Leanna, my darling, you must listen to me carefully, for we have only a few moments. I should have warned you, but I hoped it would never come to this."

"What are you saying? How can you take this so

casually? You would never do anything against our friends, our neighbors. Would you?"

He took her by the arms and shook her gently. "Just listen to me. You must go away from here now, until I can . . ." He swallowed hard. "Until I can come home again. It won't be safe now for you to stay. Your friends might . . . Alex is coming for you. Just be ready, Leanna."

"Alex? Alexander Slayton . . . coming for me? No, Papa."

"Leanna, will you just listen to me for once and do as I ask? He will take care of you. You'll be safe with him."

Colonel Hamlin stepped forward. "It's time, Senator. We've not much darkness left till daybreak."

The senator kissed Leanna and took her face between his thick hands. "I'm sorry," he whispered.

"Get dressed, Senator."

Leanna stood there shocked, unable to respond as her father complied with the man's orders. Then with a silent resignation he walked outside in the darkness, never looking back at his daughter.

Leanna felt someone's arms around her shoulders and turned to see Mrs. Macky.

"Let me get you some tea, Miss Leanna."

Leanna put a shaky hand to her forehead. This was some terrible nightmare from which she could not waken.

"No. I don't want anything, Mrs. Macky. Do you know what this is all about? Am I the only one who's totally surprised by all this?" Her eyes, filled with fright and confusion, looked pleadingly into the older woman's pale blue gaze.

"I don't know much more than you do, my dear. But

I'm sure your papa will be all right. Just as soon as Mr. Alex gets here . . ."

"Alex! Why him? And why was he already aware of this when I was not?"

"All I know is Thomas left just before the soldiers came in. We knew only that he was to fetch the major if anything happened to your papa. And when they get back, I'm sure we're all going to feel a lot better."

Leanna couldn't believe it. She'd hoped never to see that self-centered man again, and now it seemed she was to be *rescued* by him.

"We'll see about that," she said under her breath.

Alexander Slayton rode swiftly to Lexington with young Thomas following as closely as he could on his slower horse. The boy had come to him in the middle of the night. Alex was acutely aware of the time that had passed and would pass before he could be at the McNairy home. He had no idea what he would find there. Thomas had left without seeing what happened when the soldiers came for the senator, and it had taken almost two days for the boy to get to Harrodsburg.

Alex had left Private James Anderson at the Kentucky River in charge of his handful of men. He hoped it would not be a mistake. They were a small tactical group, involved usually in the planning and execution of troop maneuvers, especially night movements.

Since the war had not yet fully come to Kentucky, they'd had relatively light duty. But that was changing rapidly day by day, and Alex could not be sure when they would be called upon to become actively involved. He only hoped it was not now.

It was well past midnight when Alex reined in his

horse before the large brick house with its columned front porch. Thomas took the reins from him as he stepped down from his horse.

"Thank you, Thomas," he said. "You did a fine job of finding me."

Thomas ducked his head shyly, and Alex could see his pleased grin in the darkness.

Alex went into the house and bounded up the stairs, moving so gracefully that his boots made very little noise. He went to the room that he remembered had belonged to the young daughter years before, when he had last visited for more than a few hours. Perhaps it would have been best to rouse one of the servants to fetch the girl, but there was no time for that. His purpose was to get her away from here quickly, to the shelter of Pleasant Hill, as the senator had asked him to do.

He opened the door slowly and stepped into the dark room. There was a hint of perfume in the still air, the sweet linger of roses and lavender. One small lamp burned near the bed, its wick low. The light flickered on the motionless figure in the bed.

Alex stepped forward, and his breath caught painfully in his chest at the sight of the woman before him. Her face was turned away from the light, and one arm was thrown up above her head, resting on the pillow. Reddish gold hair fanned out about her and seemed to shimmer in the dim light.

She looked so sweet, so innocent with her pink lips parted and the long dark lashes of her closed lids lying against her ivory skin.

She was breathtaking, he had to admit. There was nothing of the spoiled, frivolous girl in her now. He had to force himself to remember what she was really like. But this proved difficult as he continued to gaze down at her perfect loveliness. Her fragile, untouched appearance made him want to imagine things he knew he should not.

It had taken the last few weeks to erase her from his memory and finally get a peaceful night's sleep. He did not intend to let that happen again.

He shook these thoughts from his mind before he stepped closer to the bed. Before waking her he allowed himself one last indulgence. He reached forward and touched a soft, shiny lock of hair that lay spread upon the pillow.

The dark lashes fluttered and flew open to reveal emerald eyes that were bright with fear.

"Shhh," he whispered. "It's only me, Alex."

In one quick motion she sat up in bed, pulling the covers up over her breasts with one hand and with the other hand reaching beneath a layer of quilts and producing a pistol, pointed straight at Alexander Slayton's heart.

The man before her clenched his jaw. His black eyes glittered dangerously at her. Slowly he straightened to stand to his full height.

"There's no need for that. I've only come to take you to the Shakers. It's what your father wants."

"I'm not going anywhere with you," she said firmly, her voice still husky with sleep. "So I suggest you leave my bedroom and go back to whatever it is you soldiers do."

"And if I do, what will happen to you?" His voice was slow, calculated. "How do you expect to manage here on your own? Or would you have me believe your faithful Confederate friends have already rushed to your aid?"

She frowned slightly, her eyes darkened with pain.

She did not want him to know how hurt she felt that none of them had come. For days she had been alone, discarded, it seemed, by nearly everyone she knew. It was as if Leanna McNairy had disappeared from the face of the earth.

"They will!" she said. "As soon as these ridiculous false accusations against Papa are proven untrue. If you want to help, why don't you use your authority for that?"

He sighed and placed his hands on his hips. He didn't have time for these little games. His fingers itched to grab her and shake her thoroughly, to shake some sense into that stubborn, beautiful head.

Leanna watched him carefully. The palm of her hand was sweating beneath the handle of the small derringer. She licked her lips nervously and allowed her eyes, only for a second, to follow the movement of his hands and on down the long muscular length of his thighs.

But that second was all it took for Alex to move, as quickly and as fatally as a striking copperhead. With a deft flick of his wrist, he whipped the gun from her grasp and tossed it away from them. It fell on the soft covers at the foot of the bed.

When she lifted her other hand to lash out at him, he was ready for her, catching her wrist in his hand and holding it firmly between his body and hers.

She struggled futilely for a moment before realizing she would not be able to escape his powerful grasp.

"I won't go with you," she said. "I won't."

"Yes, you will," he said through lips that hardly moved. His voice was steely and quiet, almost a whisper in the stillness of the room.

"You can't . . . you *wouldn't* force me." Her words

held a question that died on her lips as she met his hard, determined look.

"Oh, yes, I could and I would." His grip on her wrists loosened, and he stepped away. "I want you to get dressed. Now."

Alex didn't know why he bothered to insist. It was certainly nothing to him if she wanted to stay. And at this point he wasn't sure if it was loyalty to the senator or his own stubbornness.

Leanna glared at him and pressed her lips together tightly. Then a small light flashed deep within her beautiful eyes. "I hate you, Alex Slayton! I should have shot you when I had the chance."

Alex was exhausted from his journey, and he felt his patience and his control snap. His hand shot to the foot of the bed to retrieve the derringer.

"Here!" he said, slapping it into the palm of her hand. "Go ahead. Do it."

Leanna was stunned, and for a moment she could not force even a sound from her throat. "Don't . . . don't think I won't," she finally whispered.

But her words did not move him, and he did not blink as he stood glaring at her.

She could not believe this man. He didn't seem like the same person she'd encountered in the barn that night. Then there had been a hint of flirtation in his look, an air of insouciance. She realized now, too late, that she had misjudged him. This was no boy to manipulate or to toy with. He was a deadly serious man.

She stared at his blazing eyes and the ebony hair that fell over his forehead. He looked like a madman. There was absolutely no fear in him. Everything about him dared her to shoot.

A shudder passed over her, sending chills up her

arms and the back of her neck. She could not look away from him, and she could not pull the trigger. Her breath was coming in small furious gasps. Her lips trembled, and her eyes glistened with hot tears. She was not used to losing her pride, and that infuriated her more than ever.

Slowly her hand fell to the bed, loosening the gun from its grip. She lowered her eyes from his stare, shaken by his quick, violent flash of temper. Suddenly she was afraid of him.

"We'll leave within the hour. I'll wait outside your door while you get dressed." His voice was quiet and controlled now, with no hint of the rage she'd just witnessed.

She nodded but she refused to look up at him again. She felt like a hurt, dejected child.

Alex stepped to the bed and placed his fingers beneath her chin, forcing her head up. His eyes were frosty in the dim lamplight as they stared into hers.

"I'll say this only once, Leanna. I don't like being threatened. Don't ever do it again." His voice was a low husky growl of warning, and she knew he meant it.

After he left her room, she sat for a moment, her body trembling so much that she wasn't sure she could even stand. She stared at the door as tears ran down her cheeks.

"Damn you, Alexander Slayton!" she whispered. "You're going to regret this night, I swear it."

5

"*God, I have* a feeling I'm going to regret this night," Alex Slayton said to himself as he ran his hand tiredly over his eyes and then lit a small oil lamp in the hallway. He leaned against the wall outside Leanna's room to wait.

What in heaven's name was he doing here, playing nursemaid to this spoiled, willful child? He'd be lucky if he managed to get her to Pleasant Hill and himself back to his quarters without being caught and court-martialed.

He straightened as he heard the sound of an opening door down the hallway. He watched the person who moved through the shadows toward him.

"Mr. Alex? Is that you?" He recognized Mrs. Macky's voice as she approached him, walking heavily on slippered feet.

"Yes, ma'am," he said, keeping his voice low. "I've come to take Leanna to the Shakers." There was a note of impatience in his voice.

"Not an easy task." Mrs. Macky's blue eyes twinkled.

He gave a low growl. "Hardly."

"You're doin' the right thing," she said. "It's not safe for her here. I didn't let on to Leanna, but there's been rumblin's in town about her daddy. It didn't take long for the news to get around, you know."

"No, I'm sure it didn't." His words were quiet, but his eyes had come alive in the glow of the lamp. "What have you heard?"

"Just rumors about what kind of justice some folks think a traitor deserves. And his family along with him. It's mighty thankful I am that you've come in the night this way. No one will know where she's gone. And maybe the talk will all die down before long."

Alex sighed. "I'd like to believe that, but I'm afraid the war is only going to get worse, and with it the tempers of people on both sides."

Mrs. Macky made a clucking noise, and her nightcap wobbled atop her gray hair as she shook her head.

"What about you, Mrs. Macky? Perhaps it would be wise if you came with us."

"Oh, no," she said. "The locals won't bother me none, nor the rest of the household help. They know we're only poor workin' folks, just the same as them."

He moved closer to the elderly woman. "If ever you change your mind, or need anything, send word to me and I'll come as soon as I can. Thomas will know where to find me."

"Thank you for that, Mr. Alex. I will surely do that if need be."

The door behind them opened, and Leanna stepped out, carrying a small carpetbag in her hand.

"Well," she said, "I see you've even managed to wangle Mrs. Macky to your side."

"Now, Miss Leanna . . ." the older woman began.

"Don't bother explaining, Mrs. Macky. I understand completely. Anyone can see the major is an absolute charmer where women are concerned. They undoubtedly flock to him in droves."

"I'm sure you do not include yourself in that number," Alex said.

"Indeed, I do not!"

"Good."

His stare raked her from head to toe, noting the fashionable dress she wore. It would certainly have been appropriate for an autumn ride in the park, but it was near the end of January, and the temperature was close to zero. Did the girl have no sense at all, or was she simply badgering him again?

He pursed his lips and looked down his nose at her. "Perhaps you are not aware that we will be on horseback, and not in the comfort of a carriage."

Her eyes flashed at him, and her face grew flushed as she allowed the sarcasm of his remark to make her even more furious than before.

"I assure you, Major, that there is no need to worry. I am an excellent horsewoman. And I'm certain Thomas has already seen to the saddling of my own horse."

"No doubt," he drawled. "But the wind will cut you to ribbons in that outfit. I suggest you change into something more suitable."

"I will not. You are only doing this to try and tyrannize me. Perhaps I am to assume that I am your prisoner, then?"

He stared at her for a moment, his teeth grinding together. "No, of course you are not."

"Well, then, if my dress does not suit you I suggest there's nothing you can do about it. It is what I'm wearing whether you like it or not."

Mrs. Macky raised her brows, noting Alex Slayton's menacing stare at the girl. She coughed lightly. "Perhaps, Miss Leanna, you could wear a woolen cape over your dress and—"

"Oh, all right," Leanna snapped. "It's not as if I intended to go out without a wrap, for goodness' sake."

When Mrs. Macky brought a royal blue cape and placed it around the girl's shoulders, her hands lingered for a moment. "Miss Leanna, everything's gonna be all right. This is for the best. You'll see," she whispered.

Leanna had not the heart to argue with her now. The woman was the closest thing to family she'd ever known, and she did not know how she could bear to leave her or this house, where she'd spent her entire life.

Against her will tears came to her eyes. "Oh, Macky, I wish you could come with me."

"So do I, child, though I certainly wouldn't relish the hard life of the Believers. No, it's best I stay here, in case we hear from the senator. And soon as we do, I'll send Thomas to you at Pleasant Hill. And I'll write to you."

Leanna stepped forward and took the plump woman in her arms. She did not glance at the dark-haired man who stood silently watching them. She did not want him to see the tears in her eyes or the fear she tried so desperately to hide from him.

"I've just written a letter to father's lawyer asking

him to make funds available to you while I'm gone. And if there's anything you need, you've only to ask him."

"Thank you, missy," the older woman sniffed. "You take care now and try to do as the Shakers ask so you won't get in any trouble."

Leanna managed a laugh. Mrs. Macky was probably afraid she'd destroy the whole village with her pranks and high spirits.

"I will probably have little choice about that." Her lips clamped together as she glanced resentfully at Alex.

Mrs. Macky turned to the tall man before her. "And you, Mr. Alex. You best take good care of this little girl here."

Impulsively he bent forward and placed a quick kiss on the woman's rosy cheek. "You have my word on it," he said.

He turned to take Leanna's arm, but she moved swiftly ahead of him as if she could not bear his touch. She walked down the stairs and without a backward glance marched through the door and outside to the waiting horses.

Alex noted that the air felt even colder than before and that the wind had risen, blasting from the north with a fury that stung the skin and eyes.

As Leanna expected, Thomas had already placed her English saddle on the small frisky mare. He stood waiting in the cold to help her up onto the horse. Then he strapped her bag behind the saddle and handed the reins up to her.

"Thank you, Thomas," she said, bending down to take his hand. "You take care of the place and Mrs. Macky. And if anything goes wrong, you come for me right away, do you hear?"

"I will."

Alex pulled himself into the saddle and watched Leanna urged her mare down the drive, not waiting for him. Her cape flew out behind her, offering little protection from the bitter cold. Her skirts flapped in the wind, revealing layers of white petticoats that seemed almost iridescent in the darkness. At this rate the little fool would probably freeze to death before they ever reached the Kentucky River.

He reined his horse around sharply and away from the house. "Damn stubborn little . . ." His words were lost in the biting wind as he concentrated on catching her before she became lost in the dark.

For the first time in her life, Leanna McNairy was afraid, deathly afraid. She'd always been protected, always had someone to take care of her. Even though her father had often been gone, she'd at least had the security of her home and Mrs. Macky and Thomas.

Now she had nothing. Those men had taken it from her just as surely as they had taken her father. She had only the dress on her back and the few necessities she could cram into her small traveling bag.

She longed to see her father, and she had exhausted herself the past few days with worry. The tears that stung her eyes felt hot against the cold air, and they seemed suspended on her lashes as if they might freeze there.

Where was her papa, and why had those men accused him of being a traitor to the South? These questions tortured her every waking hour. It had to be a mistake, she told herself. But Alexander Slayton had known what was about to happen and had come for her very quickly.

That only confused her. How could he have known if he were not directly involved? Had he come here the night of her party to warn her father or to betray him?

Whatever the truth was, she had the misfortune of finding herself in the protective custody of this Union officer. Family friend or not, she did not trust him. His brutal behavior to her tonight only confirmed what she'd been told about the Northerners' cold and unfeeling ways.

She kicked the sides of the small mare and speeded on, heedless to the freezing bite of the wind or the sound of pounding hoofbeats that grew closer and closer.

She had been riding only a few minutes, but already the stinging wind whipped through her and made breathing difficult. Her eyes, even though still filled with tears, felt dry and cold, and her hands were growing numb from clutching the reins tightly.

She could hear Alex's horse as it pulled nearer and could almost feel its breath on her back. She knew the man in the saddle would be furious with her for the way she was acting, but she didn't care. She was so hurt and confused, so unsure of what the future held, that she wanted only to run and never stop.

When a hand plunged forward and took the reins from her cold hands, she was not surprised. Almost in the same instant she felt a steely arm wrap around her waist and pluck her from the saddle, pulling her hard against his heavy wool coat. She could feel the icy brass buttons dig into her back through the thin material of her clothes. He held her unyieldingly against him as he reined his horse to a stop.

The noises around them assailed her ears—the blowing sound the horses made as they labored against the cold, and the muffled sound of hoofbeats on the frozen ground. These mingled with the loud pounding of her heart as she felt herself suspended in the air above the ground.

After the horse had stopped and stood stamping its feet impatiently, Alex slowly lowered her to the ground and then followed, grasping her arm immediately with little gentleness or sympathy.

"You little fool! What are you trying to do, kill the horses? Did you ever once, in that selfish little mind of yours, consider what it does to a horse, being ridden full out in weather like this?"

Immediately she felt a pang of guilt at his words, for she knew it was true. She had never wanted to hurt any animal, especially her own little mare, Windspry. She said nothing but attempted to pull her arm from his painful grip.

Alex held her fast and practically dragged her to the side of the road and into the shelter of a towering beech tree. There were a few dried leaves still clinging to the branches that rattled in the furious wind.

"Let me go, damn you!" she shouted above the roar. She was crying now, not trying to hide it but rather letting the tears loose to wash over her as the wind moved over them.

"Listen to me," he said, shaking her gently as one would do when trying to gain the attention of a child.

"No!" she screamed. She began to fight him, pushing at his chest as he held her and venting all her frustration and fury at him.

For a moment Alex was stunned at her unexpected

assault. He sensed that the anger was not entirely for him.

"Stop this, Leanna," he said in a voice that was soft and low.

His hands grasped her shoulders and pulled her body to within only inches of his. She felt the warmth that the shelter of his broad shoulders provided against the wind and felt an inexplicable compulsion to move into his arms, to seek the comfort of another human being's closeness.

She was keenly aware of the disparity of her thoughts. This man was her adversary, and yet she felt the need to seek his comfort—something she had not felt for anyone in a very, very long time.

Slowly, within his arms, she quieted, the fury in her spent as she gave in to hushed, shuddering sobs. She could not seem to control herself or the pain that came from somewhere deep inside her.

She was aware of his hand cradling the back of her head and the feel of his chest beneath her cheek as he pulled her against him. She could not fight him any longer, was not even sure she wanted to, even though she hated him and everything he stood for.

Choking back her sobs, she let her body go limp against his, unable to do anything else. Even as she did, she despised herself for remaining in the dangerous embrace of her enemy.

She could feel the strong steady beating of his heart and smell his cool, masculine scent, the faint lingering of some spice-scented soap. Just as when they danced, she was acutely aware of his body touching hers, of his long legs pressing against her own. She could feel the strength of his tensed muscles, and yet he held her surprisingly tenderly, waiting for her sobs to quiet.

Self-conscious, Leanna stepped away from him. Her quiet hiccuping sobs mingled with his quickened breathing and the sound of the wind about them. If he expected his offer of comfort suddenly to change her feelings about him, he was wrong. He was still a Yankee, still the enemy she'd learned to hate, and still the man who had bullied her into coming with him against her will. Perhaps he was even the one responsible for her father's troubles.

Alex sensed her withdrawal keenly, was aware when she stiffened and moved away as if he'd struck her. Damn the girl. Let her freeze, then! Why should it bother him if she did?

"Look," he began slowly, not attempting to touch her again. "I've been on the road for two days, it's freezing cold, and I'm damned tired. We have a long way to go before we get to the river, and if you keep punishing your horse this way, we'll never make it." His voice was weary, but there was an edge to it that would have scared most people.

"Now I suggest that you get back on your horse. The sooner we get to Pleasant Hill the sooner you can be away from me. That should sweeten your disposition immeasurably."

She wiped her eyes with an angry defiant little gesture. "For once I must agree with you."

She walked away from him to her waiting mare and stepping on a nearby rock, pulled herself back up onto the saddle. Alex moved to stand beside her and hand the reins to her. When he reached up toward her, she pulled away, unsure of what he intended to do.

With a small grunt of disgust at her obvious fear, he pulled the sides of her cape together and tucked it beneath her to keep the icy wind from invading its depths again. Then, without further comment, he mounted his horse and moved ahead to make sure that this time she followed him.

6

By *the time* they reached the outskirts of Lexington, Leanna felt as if her entire body was frozen. She was shivering almost uncontrollably and wondering if she'd ever feel warm again. At times she would lean down close to the little mare's neck just to feel the heat from its body.

Her skin felt chafed even through her undergarments by the layers of stiffened skirts she wore. She secretly wished she had listened to Alex about wearing warmer clothes, but how was she to know what it was like to ride in such weather in the middle of the night?

Alex's voice interrupted her thoughts.

"We're coming into town. Although I doubt anyone will be out at this time of morning, we'll take the road around the outskirts. I want to be well away from the city by daybreak.'' Having said this, he nudged his big gray horse into a canter.

Leanna urged her mare forward too, but she was now so cold she wondered how long she'd be able to stay in the saddle. She could not feel her fingers or her toes, and she was beginning to feel a bit dizzy from trying to balance herself in the sidesaddle and at the same time see through the darkness that surrounded them.

She wasn't sure how long they had ridden. It seemed interminable, but she suddenly began to feel better. In fact, she was surprised at how sleepy and relaxed she felt; she could hardly hold her eyes open. She loosened her hands on the reins, and the mare, feeling her response, began to slow its gait. Sleepy, she was so sleepy. Perhaps if she could just lay her head on the mare's neck, only for a moment's rest. It was her last conscious thought.

"Leanna." The voice seemed to come from a great distance, but even so she did not miss the urgency in it, or the annoyance.

"Hell!" Alex muttered with frustration as he pulled back to ride beside her.

Why had he let her go on, he silently berated himself. To teach her a lesson? He was supposed to be the mature one, the responsible one.

"Just let me sleep, Alex. I'll be all right if only you'll let me sleep." Her voice was slurred, and she swayed atop the little mare as if she might fall off at any moment.

Alex cursed again beneath his breath. The girl was dangerously close to freezing. He wondered when she had last eaten a substantial meal.

They were miles from town or even from the nearest

farmhouse, and they had left the rolling hills of the farmlands a long while back. Now they were approaching the long craggy deserted stretch that led into the bluffs along the river.

They were little more than halfway to the Kentucky River, where his men were camped. He knew Leanna would never make it that far. She needed a fire and something warm to drink, and she needed it soon.

He knew of some shallow cavelike outcrops of rock suitable for shelter, but in the darkness he was not even sure that he could find them. Still, he knew he had no choice. This would be the girl's best chance.

He reached over and pulled Leanna from her horse, placing her across his lap. Her body was cold, and even her hips and legs through the material of her dress and cape felt like ice. Holding her with one arm, he reached back into his saddlebag and pulled out a rough woolen blanket. Then he wrapped it around her as best he could in the awkward position and tied the reins of her mare behind him. Now, if only he could find one of the rock overhangs soon.

Somewhere in her misty dreams, Leanna seemed aware of warmth beneath her and of arms that held her securely. But she could not seem to open her eyes or rouse herself from the dreamy state she was in. She was aware of feeling safe and completely free of worry. It was as if her prayers had all been answered, and she would never have to worry about being alone again.

She snuggled against Alex, murmuring under her breath as she drifted in and out of a strange stuporous sleep.

Alex could feel the small indentation of her waist and the hardness of its constricting corset. He swore again. It was no wonder she was in such a state. Not only was her clothing inadequate, but she had bound herself so tightly that she could hardly breathe properly. As far as he was concerned, it was more evidence of her foolish, capricious nature.

"Damn."

"Ummm?" She was aware of the rumble of a voice beneath her ear that threatened to disturb her delicious sleep.

"Women," he muttered.

The sky to the east was beginning to lighten. Alex was grateful for that, at least. Soon the white outcroppings of limestone along the roadway became visible, and the long sparkle of icicles that hung from them as well. Then he spotted a dark circular spot along one of the wall-like formations and he knew he'd found the shelter he'd been seeking.

Alex slowly urged the horses up the narrow ledge above the road, coming to a halt at the entrance to a small cave. Holding Leanna firmly in his arms, he stepped down from the big gray horse and carried the girl toward the dark cavern.

He placed her on the ground at the entrance until he could light a match and see what, if anything, was inside. When he found nothing, he quickly gathered branches and bits of wood and heaped them into a blackened ring of stones, which someone before him had left. It was close enough to the entrance so that the smoke would not fill the cave, and once a fire was lit, its warmth would act as a barrier against the outside cold.

Soon he had a nice fire blazing. He looked around the walls of the small cave. Someone had placed some large rocks to the side, out of the wind, where it would be near the fire ring. Alex picked Leanna up and placed her in a sitting position with her back against the huge rocks. He wrapped her again in the blanket and took an extra shirt from his saddlebag to place behind her head and neck. Her skin was very cold, and her hands looked pink and raw.

He pulled icicles down from the overhang of the cave to melt for water. Soon it was boiling in his tin cup over the crackling flames. When he dropped pieces of beef jerky into the steaming water, the air was immediately filled with a pleasant, meaty aroma.

He had not brought much food with him, since he expected to be back at camp before dark. He knew that Private Anderson would begin to wonder about him. The important thing was to get the girl out of the freezing wind, though, and get her some warm nourishment.

He poured some of the broth into another cup and walked over to the half-conscious girl. He knelt beside her and looked for a long moment at her.

She looked as innocent and sweet as a kitten, nothing like the spitfire he'd seen earlier. He felt a twinge of guilt as he looked at her, knowing that he could have prevented this if only he'd been firmer with her and insisted that she dress properly. He hated to admit it, but he was just as stubborn as she. In fact, it was one of his worst faults, and this time it had gotten him in more trouble than he had bargained for.

He watched the play of light flickering across the smooth ivory skin of her face. Her brilliant green eyes were closed now, and still except for a brief flicker when small tremors moved over her body. He needed to loosen the ties of her corset so that she could breathe more easily. Then he would try to get some of the warm broth down her throat.

He reached forward and pulled the blanket off her shoulders with a quiet, detached efficiency that might have surprised her. His long deft fingers unfastened the small buttons as all the while his black eyes watched her face and the movement of her lashes. The soft blue velvet dress she wore was flattering, accentuating her golden red hair and displaying a small but voluptuous figure.

When he moved the jacket away from her shoulders, she moved and made a small sigh of protest as the cold air touched her skin. She took a deep breath, causing her pale breasts to swell above the low-cut lacy top of her white chemise.

Alex's hands stopped in midair, and he stared hard at her, trying to ignore the tightening warmth inside him. He had not expected to be so disturbed by the sight of her. She was certainly not the first woman he'd undressed, yet something about her affected him as no one else ever had.

He knew she was young and selfish, knew she was spoiled beyond any reasonable understanding. And yet this morning when she had flailed at her horse and run away from Alex, he had understood. And when he'd held her as she fought against him, he'd sensed almost instinctively her need to be comforted.

What he couldn't understand was why she resented him so much. And yet even her dislike of him could not stop the slow curl of desire he felt for her.

He didn't like the feeling. Hell, all he needed was one more soul to care about, to be responsible for. He already had eight back at camp, some of them not even old enough to shave.

Still, he had promised the senator he would take care of Leanna, and he would. Whether she believed it or not, Alex Slayton was a man of principle, a man who let nothing stand in his way once he had given his word.

With hands that were not quite steady, Alex reached behind her to untie the strings that held the corset so tightly together. This willful, opinionated girl was annoying as hell, and he'd be glad to get her off his hands. But there was one thing he could not deny as he took in every inch of her luscious body: she was all woman.

He quickly pushed such thoughts aside. Once he'd untied the corset and loosened the garment all the way to her waist, Leanna gave a sigh, as if even in her semiconscious state she felt the immediate relief it gave her.

Alex refastened a few of the buttons on her jacket for warmth and pulled the blanket back around her. Then he sipped the warm broth to make sure it would not burn her. Settling himself beside her, he put an arm around her shoulders to support her and then moved his hand to her neck to tilt up her chin.

"Leanna," he whispered. "Can you hear me? You need to wake up and drink this."

"Sleepy . . ." she murmured. "Just let me sleep."

"You need to drink something. Can you hear me? Leanna?"

His voice, firm and determined, cut through her unconscious haze, pulling her out of pleasant drowsiness. With it came a burning, tingling ache in her fingers and toes where her skin had begun to warm.

"No," she said, shaking her head and trying to pull away from his strong hands. "Leave me alone. Why can't you just leave me alone?"

"You're going to drink this, girl, if I have to pour it down you."

He shook her a bit until she opened her eyes. Then he smiled as he saw the flash of anger in their depths.

"Damn you," she muttered. But she obediently

reached forward to sip from the cup he held beneath her nose.

She had begun to shiver again, but he thought perhaps that was a good sign. At least now her body was trying to fight the freezing cold. She drank more of the broth, and when she finally looked at him, he thought her eyes were clearer and more alert. And when she closed her eyes with a quiet little sigh and snuggled against him, he knew it was a healthier sleep.

Alex himself was tired and cold, but he held Leanna for a long while, not yet allowing himself the pleasure of sleep. Every few minutes he would force her to drink until finally the cup was empty.

Hours later she woke and looked around the cave and the flickering shadows created by the fire. "Where . . . where are we? Why are we here?"

"We're in a cave near the bluffs. And we stopped because you were in danger of freezing. I should never have let you leave in that flimsy dress you're wearing."

She stiffened a bit, aware for the first time of his arm around her. "It was my choice to make . . . not yours." Her voice was still defensive.

"Exactly my point," he said. "How are you feeling?"

"Horrible," she said. "I'm still freezing, and my hands and feet ache terribly."

"Let me put more wood on the fire, then I'll see about getting you warm. Drink some more of the broth." He poured the remainder of the hot liquid into her cup.

He walked outside and brought in bigger pieces of wood to place across the fire. Soon the flames were leaping high into the air, throwing bright sparks and illuminating the recesses of the shadowy cavern. He paused and looked up at the sky. It was well into morning, yet the light was still dim and gloomy. The sky was filled with black, rolling storm clouds. He hoped it would not snow.

Leanna watched the man who'd brought her here. She noted the worried look on his face and its trace of weariness. He needed a shave, and there was a smudge of dirt against the sharp planes of his cheekbone.

She wondered about him. What kind of man was he? What did he think of her? Then again, she felt she already knew the answer to that. He disliked her as much as she did him.

He seemed very tall in the closeness of the cave, and the bulky coat he wore hid what she knew was a lean, hard body. He looked very different here from in her ballroom—seemed even more rugged than before. She remembered the stories Thomas had told her about him and his sobriquet, the Nighthawk. A relentless hunter, and a name earned, no doubt, by his exploits in his service to the Union.

It was fitting, she thought. Here, away from the niceties of polite society, he seemed more alert and cautious, with the watchful instincts of a wild animal. Suddenly he turned as if sensing her eyes on him.

"What?" he said.

"I . . . nothing. I was only wondering how you got the name Nighthawk."

He gave a low grunt and placed the last piece of wood on the fire. "Where did you hear that?"

"From Thomas."

He still did not look at her. "It's a name. Men have a tendency during war to find names for everyone and everything."

"But this one . . . it sounds different, as if it has some special significance."

"Well, it doesn't."

He had placed the last log across the fire and turned to glance at her cautiously. There was no doubt as to what his look meant to convey. He had no intention of explaining anything about himself, not to her, anyway.

"I . . . I just thought perhaps you'd like to tell me about it." She glanced up at him almost shyly.

"I don't."

Leanna wondered why he didn't. She couldn't believe it was modesty that kept him from recounting all his exploits. She was certain that was the basis for the name. Most men she knew liked nothing better than to boast about their adventures. She wished she could see into his thoughts.

"How long are we going to stay here?" she asked.

"Until I've rested and you're warm."

"Is it far to the river?"

"No."

"You're certainly not very talkative this morning," she said, frowning at him.

He looked at her as if he had not heard correctly and wondered what the purpose of her change of tactics was.

Last night she had not wanted to speak to him at all. He remembered the anger that had flooded over him when she'd pointed the derringer at him.

Leanna saw his look and lifted her chin. Oh, she knew what he thought of her. But for some reason his coolness toward her disturbed her, and she could not understand why.

Alex moved toward her, and she looked up, her body stiffening as he came nearer. When he sat down so close that they were touching, it was all she could do not to jump up and run away from him.

"Wh-what are you doing?"

"I'm going to get you warm." His face was totally serious, and there was not so much as a twinkle in his black eyes.

"No . . . I . . ."

"Will you be quiet for once? I'm tired, you're cold. The sensible thing to do is to sit close together so we can both be warm. Don't you agree? Now give me your hands."

She frowned, not knowing what to make of him. But she moved her hands forward obediently.

He pulled the blanket around both of them and took her hands in his larger ones, massaging them gently. He leaned his head back against the boulders and closed his eyes.

"How are your feet?"

"Still burning. But I think they're beginning to feel more normal." She stretched them toward the roaring fire.

"Good," he murmured, his eyes still closed. "Go to sleep."

Her mouth parted slightly in surprise as she gazed at him there, so close beside her. Within seconds he was asleep, but his hands still held hers firmly, and she could feel his warmth spreading into her own flesh.

She studied every inch of his face—the lean, angular bone structure beneath his dark skin, and the long, thick black lashes that were closed now. Her eyes lingered on his mouth. It was as beautifully shaped as a girl's, and for some inexplicable reason, just looking at his lips brought back that funny, quivering feeling in her.

She closed her eyes and leaned back against the shirt that was wedged behind her head. What was wrong with her that she could be drawn for an instant to the looks of such a man?

She knew what he was, and she couldn't ignore it. He was the man who wanted to destroy her home, the land she loved, and the people in it. And he might even be the one responsible for what had happened to her father.

No, she didn't care what he looked like or if other women might find him attractive. And she didn't really care how he'd got the quaint name Nighthawk. She'd only asked to make polite conversation. All she really wanted now was to be rid of him once and for all.

7

Leanna could feel the warmth slowly moving back into her body as she lay, staring into the hypnotic dance of the flames. The warm broth and the fire had brought her back to life. *And the man beside you,* her conscience whispered. Regardless of how she felt about Alex Slayton, he had saved her life.

Slowly she closed her eyes, and she slept, her hands still clasped by the man who lay next to her.

She wasn't sure how long she slept, for when she woke and looked past the cave's entrance, the sky and the light looked the same as before. But the fire had died down to smoldering red embers that emitted a pleasant warmth into the cave.

She turned her head slightly to see Alex. He was so still, and his breathing so deep and slow, that for a moment she was afraid. Then he stirred and turned his face away from hers.

She noted the corded muscles of his neck, the smooth leanness of his jaw, and the way his lower lip was more pronounced than the upper. She found herself wanting to touch the thick ebony hair that curved over the collar of his coat.

She forced herself to look away from him. Then she pushed the blanket off her shoulders and rose quickly to step away from him and his disturbing warmth.

It was only when she stood up that she became aware for the first time of the disarray of her clothes. With a gasp she reached behind to the unfastened corset.

"What in . . ." She discovered the unfastened buttons of her skirt and the fact that the corset was unlaced all the way to her waist.

She spun around and stared at Alex, only to find him awake and watching her with a look of amusement.

"You . . . you've undressed me!"

"It was for your own good," he drawled, his voice touched with laughter.

"Oh! You almost had me convinced you wanted to help me. To . . . to bring me here where it was warm."

"Well, of course. Why else would I bring you here?"

A devilish smile curved his lips. He made no effort to stand, but instead lay watching her languidly as if they had all the time in the world. His black eyes moved slowly to the front of her jacket.

"Your jacket's unbuttoned, too."

She glanced down and saw that although some of the buttons were fastened, several near the top were not. The sound she made was a low, muffled shriek.

"I should have known I couldn't trust a man like you. A . . . a . . ."

He stood then and moved his arms and shoulders backward to loosen his cramped muscles. "A what?"

"A damn Yankee!" she shouted, unable to think of a more insulting word to use.

He grunted and moved past her to gaze out into the gloomy sky. Casually he pulled a gold watch from his trousers and held it in the palm of his hand.

"Three o'clock," he said. "We'd better be on our way or we'll be caught in the dark again."

"But . . . but aren't you going to explain this . . . to apologize?"

"To you?"

"Yes, to me!" She fairly spat the word out, hardly able to believe his cavalier attitude about what he had done.

He turned and looked straight into her flashing eyes. "No, why should I?"

"Why should you? You undressed me . . . took advantage of me when I was asleep and—"

"Now, wait. Let's get this straight." His voice was patient and maddeningly indifferent. "I did not undress you . . . completely. And I certainly did not take advantage of you."

"But you . . . you saw me. You . . ."

"True," he said. "Very nice, but hardly worth getting myself killed for."

She could not believe it. After what he'd done, now he had the nerve to pretend that she was not even worth his time and effort. "Well, you're right about that at least," she snapped. "My father will kill you when he hears about this!"

"Oh, I hardly think so," he replied as he moved

about the cave, picking up various items. "Not when I tell him how much you enjoyed it, how you snuggled against me and—"

"That is a lie. You are a lying devil!"

"I've been accused of worse. If you'd like a few moments to make a trip to the bushes, I'll wait." He seemed to pay absolutely no attention to her fury.

"A trip to the . . ." She stared at him for a moment, so angry she thought she might cry. "Not only are you a liar, but you are also a crude, hateful, conniving . . ."

"Watch it, little girl," he said. "I warned you once not to threaten me again."

She remembered his anger in her bedroom when he had told her that. His capacity for violence frightened her and made her clamp her lips tightly together.

She took a deep breath and buttoned the rest of her jacket with shaking fingers. She was furious and felt an overwhelming desire to slap his smug face. But she knew he had the upper hand. A man always did. So she bit her lip and marched outside as he suggested, hoping that the cold air would help dissipate her anger and frustration.

When she returned he was already in the saddle and holding the reins to her horse in his hand. The blanket lay across the mare's neck. Alex nodded toward it.

"It's a little warmer than it was, but you'd better wrap the blanket around you. And here are some gloves. They're big, but maybe they'll help."

She would not look at him. One moment she found herself hating him, wanting to hit him for taunting her so unmercifully. The next she felt grateful to him for helping her.

The gloves were so huge that she could do nothing while wearing them except hold onto the reins. When the hood of her cape fell backward, she could not even grasp its edges with her clumsy fingers.

Alex bent forward and pulled the hood up for her, pausing for a moment to tuck several unruly wisps of reddish gold hair back into the hood. He watched the changing expressions on her face until finally she had to look up into his eyes, out of curiosity if nothing else.

He ran a finger down the side of her face and smiled as she shivered. She glanced quickly at him with a look of puzzlement in her emerald eyes.

He smiled.

"That's a good girl." She could have been a child for all his patronizing tone implied.

As he pulled the reins of his horse and turned down the rocky ledge that led back to the roadway, he heard Leanna muttering under her breath.

"I hate you, Alex Slayton," she said. When she saw him glance back at her, she knew he had heard her.

She stared at his broad back and vowed that she would not let him make a fool of her again, would not give him a chance to use her for his own hateful amusement.

They rode for miles in complete silence. Even though the day was still bitterly cold, Leanna began to enjoy the spectacular scenery around her and was glad for its distraction. She found the limestone bluffs simply breathtaking with their thousands of icicles hanging down from the ledges. It was like a picture in some fairy tale. She eagerly took in every new bend in the road.

Sometimes Alex watched her, studying the look on her lovely face. She actually seemed to enjoy the ride, and that was something he would not have expected from a girl like her.

They stopped only once to rest the horses. Alex

pulled a small loaf of hard crusty bread wrapped in white cloth out of his saddlebag. He took their tin cups and walked along a short, well-used path to a natural spring that trickled down from beneath the limestone.

He handed the frosty cup of water to Leanna and broke a large piece of bread for her as well. They ate in silence, she still stinging from his treatment of her and he simply enjoying the quiet.

After they finished eating they rode on, still not speaking. Soon they began to move downhill, and Leanna sensed they were nearing the river. The air here was much colder and touched with a moisture that she could smell and almost taste.

"How much farther?" she asked.

"We're almost there," he said. "I want you to wait here while I make sure everything's all right ahead. A river crossing is always a strategic spot, and I'd hate to run into a gathering of Johnny Rebs."

How strange it seemed to hear someone say that. To Leanna, the term meant friends, not enemies. But she waited, as he asked, not bothering to remind him of their differences.

A few minutes later he returned and signaled that it was safe to continue. They moved downward, rounding a long curve in the road. Now she could hear the quiet ripple of the river and smell the smoke from the campfires.

Then the broad, shining Kentucky River, the mother of the lush rolling farm country, lay before them. Leanna took a deep breath, enjoying the sight. She had not been here since she was a girl.

A flatboat was used to cross the river whenever there were passengers. There was even a permanent cabin where the ferryman lived, perched high above the river, away from flood level.

Along the banks of the river, beneath towering bare-limbed trees, were several tents, which Leanna assumed belonged to Alex's men. In the shadow of the limestone bluffs, darkness had already come, and the men were busy preparing their supper.

Lights shone forth, from the little house on the bluff, reflecting in the rolling river. Leanna thought she heard shouts of laughter from there, and if she was not mistaken, they were coming from women.

As Alex led the way into camp, the men all moved forward, greeting him and looking curiously past him at Leanna. They all looked so young, she thought—too young to be serving in the army.

Alex introduced her, although she knew she would probably forget their names. There were two men, though, who for some reason seemed to stick in her mind.

"This is Private James Anderson, Jimmy we call him." Alex said. "And this is Trey McCord. At twenty-two, the old man of our group." He smiled at McCord, but the black man did not look at Leanna or return her polite smile.

The small encampment was totally silent. No one so much as moved. It had been a long time since they'd seen a girl like Leanna McNairy. Even as tired as she obviously was, they seemed mesmerized by her, unable to take their eyes off her.

Alex's mouth quirked with amusement as he scanned their slack-jawed faces and bedazzled eyes. "Excuse me, gentlemen, but I believe you can return to your fires now."

"Yessir," several muttered, some gazing back at the

flame-haired beauty as they walked away. Their murmured words and quiet laughter drifted back to Alex.

James Anderson stepped forward to help Leanna from her horse. He was obviously not as shy as the rest of the men.

"Thank you, Jimmy."

The young man turned to Alex and took his horse as well.

"I take it the barge is closed for the night, Jimmy?" Alex asked.

"For the day," the soldier said. "And maybe for tomorrow as well."

Alex closed his eyes and rubbed a hand across them. Life did not seem to be treating him fairly today.

"What's the problem?" he asked Jimmy.

"River's froze! At least it is partway on each side. Old man Ramsay tried to force the flatboat across this morning, but it got hung up on some ice and broke the cable. Now they've got repairs to do before we can get across."

"Wonderful," Alex muttered. "Let's just hope General Crittenden's Rebs don't decide to pass this way before it's repaired, or we might find ourselves making our new home in Andersonville prison." This newest obstacle was taking its toll on his patience.

"Yessir, Major. Yessir, I hope not."

"Find Miss McNairy something warm to eat, Private, and then we'll make arrangements for her sleeping quarters. Who's on guard duty?"

"I am, sir," the boy said.

"Good, then I'll count on you to deliver us a quiet night, Jimmy."

"Yessir," Jimmy said with a smart salute.

With no further acknowledgement of Leanna, Alex

moved into a nearby tent. She could see the glow of a lantern illuminating his tall shadow against the canvas.

Jimmy turned to Leanna. He was not much taller than she and surprisingly slender. Of course she realized that some soldiers had a hard time finding enough to eat, but the aroma of fresh fish wafting across from the campfires smelled delicious. Even as her stomach rolled and grumbled, though, she knew she could not take food from the soldiers if they were hungry.

"It's mighty nice to have you here, ma'am," Jimmy said. "Would you like to walk with me to the picket line? Then I'll fetch you and the major some supper." As soon as Jimmy saw the look on her face, he knew she was reluctant to take food from the soldiers.

"Had nothin' to do most of the day except fish," he said. "We've got plenty."

He was sweet, and Leanna liked him right away. This opinion of a Yankee surprised her, but he did not seem so overbearing as his commanding officer. In fact, he was much more like her Confederate friends at home.

"In that case, Jimmy, I confess I'm quite hungry. And I'd love to walk with you. I feel so stiff after today's ride." She followed along gingerly as the feeling gradually returned to her cold feet.

He did not miss her limp. "Hard ride today? We been lookin' for you most of the day." He looked at her curiously.

"Yes, well, I'm afraid that was my fault. I slowed your major down considerably." There was a tightness in her voice that caused the young soldier suspicion.

"Major does seem a mite testy tonight," he said.

"I would imagine the major is usually a mite testy, as you say."

"Why, no, ma'am. He's usually cool and calm. Real

considerate for an officer. The men would do most anything for him. He's about as fair and honest a man as you're likely to meet."

She could not hide her surprise at his words. Fair? Honest? The man who laughed at her, bullied her, and even undressed her while she slept? Surely they were not speaking of the same person.

"You'll excuse me, Jimmy, if I find that a bit hard to believe," she said.

"Yes, ma'am," he said, letting the subject drop.

"Where are you from Jimmy?" she asked him.

"Ohio, ma'am. Same as the major. Huh . . . sorry."

She laughed. "It's all right. I'm not usually so disagreeable. And don't feel you have to walk softly around me where the major is concerned. We're just two very different people who seem to grate on each other's nerves."

"I don't understand that, Miss Leanna. Especially the part about you gettin' on his nerves."

Leanna laughed again, the sound rippling softly across the open ground around them. "Jimmy, I think you and I shall get along splendidly together."

After he'd seen to the horses, he led her to a small fire, obviously his own camp, not too far from Alex's tent. The black man, Trey McCord, was holding a long rod in his hands that he turned from time to time over the flames.

"Supper ready yet, Trey?" Jimmy asked with obvious enthusiasm.

Trey made a low sound, still not looking up to acknowledge Leanna's presence in any way. She supposed it was only natural that a black Union soldier would

dislike Southerners. It was all she could think of that
might explain his cool behavior.

"Trey's a little shy," Jimmy whispered. "He'll warm
up to you once he gets to know you. Here, have a seat
near the fire. I'll go fetch the major."

His words took the pleasure out of her anticipated
meal. She was tired and hungry, and she could think of
nothing pleasant about sharing her meal with the taci-
turn major. When he returned with Jimmy and took a
seat next to her, she said nothing.

As they ate, Alex asked many questions of Jimmy and
Trey. They spoke of things she did not understand—
maneuvers, bivouacs, and various officers whom they
called only by last name. She paid little attention, being
content to sit and enjoy the crisp, mouth-watering fish.
The item she'd seen spitted on the long rod had turned
out to be a crusty, golden brown bread. As the bread
melted in her mouth she could not keep from murmuring her approval.

"This is wonderful," she said. "But I don't understand how you cooked it on that stick."

"Well, we just make a heavy dough, ma'am, and
wrap it around the ramrod—"

"Ramrod . . . from a rifle?"

"Yep," Jimmy answered.

"How ingenious of you," she said.

"Why, thank you, ma'am." The boy beamed.

Alex looked from Jimmy to Leanna with a wry expression upon his handsome features. He wondered
what she was up to now. How very agreeable she'd
become all of a sudden. For some reason that irritated
him.

She and Jimmy had certainly become friends quickly.
He'd been surprised to hear her soft laughter a few

minutes ago. It was something he'd not been privy to himself, nor should he have expected to under the circumstances. But he could not help wondering what Jimmy had said to cause such a delightful sound.

Leanna yawned. The warmth of the fire and the filling meal were taking their toll. Alex noticed and nodded to Jimmy.

"Miss McNairy will sleep in my tent tonight." He only grinned at her when she jerked around to glare at him.

"And since you're on guard duty, Private Anderson, I'll take your cot, if you don't mind."

"Yessir. Don't mind at all."

Leanna rose and glanced toward Alex with a look of displeasure. She wondered how much longer he expected her to endure his irritating sense of humor.

But she was sleepy, and the mere mention of the word cot sounded like heaven after her uncomfortable experience of the previous night.

"Good night, gentlemen," she said.

The three men rose politely, even the silent Trey, and bid her good night.

Normally, she would have been very curious about the quarters of the man who so infuriated her. She might learn a lot about him from the possessions he carried. What would a man like him bring to the field? Pictures of a loved one perhaps? She did not even know if he was married, not that she cared.

Soon all such thoughts vanished as she snuggled sleepily into the narrow cot under a heavy layer of army blankets. And Alex Slayton was forgotten, for the moment.

8

Leanna woke suddenly, not quite sure what had disturbed her sound sleep. She knew instinctively it was still the middle of the night. There was no light, and the inside of the tent was so black that for a moment she felt disoriented. She lay there, listening to the noises around the tent, letting her eyes adjust to the darkness.

Then she heard it, the noise that had undoubtedly wakened her. It was a woman's laughter, shrill and raucous, like the sound she'd heard earlier coming from the ferryman's cabin.

She quietly rose from the cot and stepped toward the tent closure to unbutton the flap and peer outside toward the campfires. To her surprise, the fires were still burning brightly, illuminating the figures gathered around them. She saw that this time the soldiers were not alone.

There were women with them, women who spoke in loud, strident voices and laughed with high-pitched abandon. The flicker of lights illuminated gaudy clothes and glittering jewelry.

Some of the women clung to the men, dancing around in a drunken manner and kissing them brazenly. They made no attempt to hide themselves or what they were doing.

Leanna quickly jerked the tent's canvas opening back into place. Her heart was beating rapidly, and she was now wide awake. She could hardly believe that Alex was allowing such a thing. He had even warned Jimmy that he expected a quiet, peaceful night. Was that only for her benefit?

Leanna knew the women were prostitutes. She'd heard the whispered rumors of how they sometimes visited the camps at night, but she could not believe that Major Slayton, such an imperious disciplinarian, would allow it in his own camp.

Obviously they would not be there if the commanding officer did not approve. She peeked through the opening again, quickly looking toward the tent where she'd eaten supper. It was dark and quiet, with no signs of activity inside.

Then it hit her like a bolt of lightning: Alex Slayton was probably inside right at this moment with one of those vulgar, loud-mouthed women. Why that surprised her, she could not say.

She was angry—angrier than she'd been with him earlier. It was not Alex Slayton who angered her so much, though, she told herself, it was men in general.

Were they all such animals with no sensibility where women were concerned?

"Despicable," she muttered as she flounced back onto the cot. She could hardly ignore the shouts of drunken laughter that came from outside.

The Shakers of Pleasant Hill were beginning to look more appealing to her with each passing hour. At least there she could be among civilized people and able to get a decent night's sleep.

She pulled the blankets up around her ears, then rearranged them again. It was no use. She doubted she'd be able to sleep at all for the rest of the night, more because of the anger that boiled inside her than the noise that kept her awake.

It was not long until the camp quieted down, and she realized with disgust that the soldiers had taken the women to their tents. Did Alex Slayton have no decency at all, to allow this perversity right under her nose? But of course he didn't. Why would she ever imagine he did?

Finally Leanna slept, even as dreams and strange visions flashed through her mind and caused her to move fitfully in her slumber.

She did not wake again until morning, when the sound of hoofbeats pounded on the frozen ground outside her tent. She sat up, nerves on edge as she wondered who was there. Moments later she heard soldiers' voices nearby as they moved through camp, going about their morning chores.

She rubbed her eyes and sat for a moment, cautiously moving her aching muscles. She thought with longing of a warm bath and a change of clothes. She wanted to wash her hair and brush it until it shimmered. Knowing that she would be deprived of these necessities for probably another day irritated her all the more.

After scrambling through her bag for a hairbrush she managed to tie her thick hair back into a bit of order. She took a towel and stepped through the doorway of the tent, intending to go the river, where she could at least wash her face.

She did not see Alex or Private Anderson as she moved past the nearby tent. The other soldiers, busy with chores, looked her way but made no attempts to speak or to approach her.

The clear morning air was still and cold, but the sun was shining through the bank of trees to the east. It promised to be a more beautiful day than yesterday and, she hoped, a warmer one. Leanna felt better just being outside and breathing the clean, crisp air.

Alex Slayton was at his shaving stand just inside Jimmy's tent when he saw Leanna walk by. Alex had been summoned to General McClernand's camp before midnight and had only ridden back to the river a few minutes ago.

He stuck his head outside to see which direction Leanna took. He decided to give her a few moments of privacy while he finished shaving and then join her to make sure she was safe. With the various passengers waiting for the ferry to be repaired, he was wary about the girl being out alone.

Minutes later Alex shook his broad shoulders into his heavy blue coat with its brass buttons, picked up a towel, and walked down to the river.

She was sitting on a rock near the water, tossing small pebbles out onto the ice near the bank. Alex was intent on the girl and did not see Jimmy also approaching her until the boy almost ran into him.

"Mornin', sir," Jimmy said with his usual brightness.

"Good morning, Jimmy."

Leanna turned at the sound of their voices. Seeing the man beside Jimmy, she stared at him coldly for a moment and then turned back to the water and continued to toss rocks across the ice.

When the two men came to stand beside her, she looked up. The sun made a halo around Alex's dark head. She resisted ironic laughter, knowing that he was anything but an angel. She moved her hand to her eyes to shade them from the bright sunlight.

"Mornin', ma'am," Jimmy said.

"Good morning, Jimmy." She ignored the taller man beside him.

With a slow, curious smile Alex moved away and down toward the water, where he broke a small hole in the ice to be used as a makeshift washbasin.

Leanna noted the smooth, cleanshaven look of his dark face, but she also did not miss the tiredness in his eyes and the dark circles underneath. She thought with disgust of the likely reason.

Jimmy did not miss the tension between the two. Squatting down beside Leanna, he motioned silently toward his commanding officer. "You and him have more words this mornin'?"

"No, we didn't," she said. "In fact, we haven't spoken at all."

"Oh."

As Alex slowly walked back toward them, drying his face and neck, Leanna could not deny the powerful air of masculinity about him. She'd never really met a man like him in Lexington. Somehow, his confidence irritated her.

"You look tired this morning, Major Slayton," she said with an insincere smile.

"Do I?"

"Yes, you do. You look as if you hardly slept at all last night."

Alex frowned at the accusatory tone of her voice. She was looking at him in that smug little challenging way of hers. This time, for the life of him, he didn't know why. Obviously she was simply in the mood for another argument.

"Jimmy, I'll watch after Miss McNairy now if you'd like to go on about your duties," Alex's said.

"Uh." The young man hesitated and looked at Leanna as if he were in distress.

"Is something wrong, Private?" Alex asked. What was going on here this morning?

"Uh, no, sir. Nothing. Except . . . could I have a moment with Miss McNairy sir . . . alone?" He barely managed to get the last word out, and his voice actually cracked as he spoke.

A small grin pulled at the side of Alex's mouth as he finally understood the boy's intentions. It was obviously a budding infatuation. He nodded and watched with amusement as Leanna followed Jimmy out of earshot with a puzzled look on her face.

"Miss McNairy," Jimmy whispered. "Did you sleep all right?"

"What?"

"I hope nothing woke you during the night . . . did it? No . . . noises or anything?" His pale blue eyes were wide, staring straight into hers as if to make some point.

She sighed, finally beginning to understand. "Oh, I

see. Yes, Jimmy, I did hear some . . . noises as you put it." She looked over at Alex.

"Miss McNairy, I beg you. If the major finds out what went on in camp last night, he'll have my hide. He . . . he trusted me, put me in charge. Please, ma'am . . ."

She stared at him, still not quite able to believe what he was saying. "Jimmy, what on earth are you getting at? And what do you mean, he put you in charge?"

The young man lowered his voice even more and bent close to Leanna. "Major Slayton was called out last night around midnight, ma'am. To General McClernand's camp. The . . . the voices you heard . . . the, uh, ladies, well, they came after that and—"

"Oh!" she said with surprise, finally realizing what had happened. Luckily she had said nothing to Alex. "The major knows nothing about this . . . about their being here?"

"No, ma'am, of course not! He don't allow such distractions while we're on duty." He frowned at her, wondering why she would even ask such a question.

"I see," she murmured.

"This is real embarrassin', ma'am," he said. "I wish I could explain it to you . . . how the men are and everything. But it wouldn't rightly be proper, I guess."

She laughed then. It was so ridiculous, her standing in the freezing cold and a young soldier trying to explain about the sexes to her. She couldn't help it. She began to laugh, finally bending forward and holding her waist. She laughed more heartily than she had in days. In fact, she could hardly bring herself to stop.

Jimmy stared at her for a second as if she'd lost her mind. But then he smiled, and a snicker of laughter hissed through his teeth, followed by a falsetto giggle until soon he was laughing just as hard as she. When they finally managed to control themselves, Leanna patted Jimmy on the shoulder.

"Don't worry, Jimmy. I won't breathe a word of it to the major."

"Thank you, ma'am," he said with a sigh of relief. Then with a definite jauntiness to his step he walked away, whistling cheerfully.

Leanna turned back to Alex, who, by the look of annoyance on his face, was completely baffled. What on earth must he think after all the giggling?

She had a hard time keeping a straight face after that, and not once she did allow herself to think she was smiling with relief.

"What was that all about?" Alex asked her.

"Oh, nothing important. Just boy-and-girl stuff."

His face was unreadable as he stared at her with fiery black eyes. It was if a shutter had been pulled over his face.

Leanna moved down toward the edge of the river. Suddenly she was feeling so good. She walked across the rocks to the water, and with the toe of her boot tapped the ice-covered water.

"Leanna, I wouldn't . . ." Alex moved behind her as he spoke the warning.

She turned to look at him, smiling broadly. "What?" she asked with a hint of mischief in her voice. "Oh, don't be such an old fogy, Alex. I can't remember the last time I ice-skated. Don't you ever laugh? Don't you believe in having fun?"

Ignoring him, she stepped cautiously onto the ice. It seemed firm and solid enough. After all, if it had stopped the ferry, it surely would hold the weight of one person.

"Leanna, don't do that. The ice is . . ."

Just as she stepped onto the ice, holding her arms out wide for balance, there was a keen cracking sound, splitting the quiet morning air. First one foot went through the ice, then the other, until Leanna found herself standing in numbingly cold water that reached well above her knees. She threw both her arms back to keep her balance, then fell with a quiet thud onto the ice behind her.

"Oooh," she could only gasp, as the frigid water seemed to take her breath from her lungs.

". . . too thin," Alex said, stopping within arms' reach of where Leanna had fallen.

The water slowly moved out of the icy cracks to wash over Leanna's hips. She jumped up from the freezing river with a loud shriek and turned to glare at Alex, who was making no move to help her.

"Well, are you just going to stand there? Aren't you going to help me out of here? I could freeze to death." Her teeth had already begun to chatter.

Alex knew it was not funny. It could have been quite serious, in fact, had the water been deeper. But the look on her face was worth all the trouble she'd caused him. He threw his head back and laughed, his deep voice rumbling with delight.

Leanna stared at him incredulously as the water dripped from her hands and numbed feet. She made her way to shore, and Alex reached out his hand to help her.

His hand felt wonderfully warm as he pulled her up the bank toward him. He was trying to make an effort to stop laughing, she could see by the way he bit his lower lip, but his shoulders shook, and a quiet chuckle still rumbled through him as he looked down at her.

"When I mentioned laughter, I did not mean you need become hysterical, Major Slayton."

"I'm sorry," he said, still trying to contain his laughter. "I tried to warn you. But it seems you're intent on freezing to death before I can get you safely to the Shakers."

"I just wanted to have a little fun, for heaven's sake." She kicked at her skirt, which was so heavy with water she could hardly walk.

"Here, you need to get back to the tent before you become a living icicle."

Without another word he scooped her up in his arms as if she were a child. Her soggy skirt slapped against his legs, getting him almost as wet as she was. With only a few effortless strides he carried her up the hill to the warmer interior of the tent and then placed her on his cot.

Leanna leaned back gingerly, resting her weight on her hands. Feeling a sharp pain in her right wrist, she winced and held it up before her eyes. It looked all right, but there was a stabbing pain from her wrist to her elbow.

"What's wrong?"

"Nothing," she gasped.

"Oh, I can see that," he muttered as he ran his fingers lightly over her wrist.

"Ouch! Do you always have to be so sarcastic?"

"No. Do you always have to be so stubborn?"

She frowned at him as he continued to examine her arm.

"Probably only a sprain. Not so deadly as pneumonia. You'd better take off that wet skirt." Even as he spoke he moved to pick up her small canvas bag, ignoring her quiet protests.

He rummaged quickly through the contents, pushing aside intimate undergarments with little notice. He finally pulled at a lace-covered dress from the bottom and held it up, staring at the thin delicate material as if he held some unidentifiable creature.

"What's this? Is this the only dress you have?" He glared at her with disbelief.

"Well, I . . . I knew the Shakers would probably provide me with something . . . practical to wear, so what was the point of bringing anything else?"

"And just where did you hope to wear this?" he asked, tossing it aside with disdain.

"Well, I . . . I don't know."

He sighed. "If you don't change your clothes you'll likely find yourself in the same state as yesterday, except this time it might be more serious."

"Well, I can't change with you standing there like some . . . some . . ."

"I'm going," he said. "In the meantime wrap yourself in one of the blankets. I'll send one of the men up to the ferryman's shack. I believe there were some ladies waiting there to board the flatboat. Perhaps one of them . . ."

He stopped at the insulted look on Leanna's face. "I will not wear the clothes of a . . . a . . . one of those women!"

He sat down on the cot beside her and looked at her for a long moment with a puzzled expression. "What?"

"I said, I will not wear the clothes of a . . . a harlot!"

"Why, Leanna," he said innocently, "what makes you think those women are harlots, as you so charmingly put it?"

"Oh, I don't know. I just have a feeling they are."
She had almost forgotten her promise to Jimmy.

"A feeling," he said quietly. "How very odd that you
would think that, since you have never seen these
women."

She wondered if he had an idea of what had happened in camp last night after he left. After all, how
many men would resist such temptation? Still, she had
promised Jimmy, and she did not want to break her
word.

"I heard them laughing from the cabin. I guess I just
assumed . . ."

"Hmmm." He clearly didn't believe her, but he let
the subject drop and moved out the door. "I'll be back
soon with something for you to wear."

Leanna's wrist ached badly, and the cold seemed to
make it worse. As quickly as she could she removed her
wet skirt and draped it across a nearby table. She
wrapped herself snugly in one of the blankets and
crawled back beneath the covers of the cot. Still, she
found herself trembling almost uncontrollably, and this
time she knew it was not entirely from the cold.

She could still feel the imprint of Alex's warm arms
where he'd cradled her against him and carried her to
the tent. Still feel his breath against her hair. All the
while the vision of his black eyes, so hard to read, invaded her thoughts and would not seem to go away.

She could not understand the man. Sometimes he
was so hard and cold with her. And yet moments ago he
had touched her wrist gently, and his eyes had been
dark with concern. He'd made her feel things she did
not want to feel.

She was becoming aware of senses she never knew
she possessed and feelings she did not know even ex-

isted. The strange thing was that they were not unpleasant, not at all. Shouldn't they at least be unpleasant? she asked herself with growing alarm. After all, why should this man, this overbearing Yankee, evoke such feelings in her? He often mocked her and made her feel foolish.

She frowned and shook her head, wondering at all the disquieting feelings she'd experienced since meeting Alex Slayton. What on earth was wrong with her?

9

A few minutes later Alex's voice stirred Leanna from her reverie.

"Leanna, I'm coming in."

She made no protest, and he entered the tent carrying a small bundle of clothes.

"I'm afraid this is all I could find. Perhaps it will do until we've dried yours." He unfolded the clothes, revealing a pair of men's trousers and a long-sleeved shirt of soft white material.

For all Leanna's reluctance to wear those women's clothes, she wished now that she had agreed. What on earth would everyone think of her if she wore men's trousers? It was simply unheard of.

Alex was well aware of Leanna's hesitancy. For all her stubbornness, he was surprised at how unwilling she was to adjust to unusual or adverse conditions. His own sister had been a wild little thing, running and roughhousing with the boys as if she were one of them. Then again, he told himself, Leanna had probably led an entirely different kind of life from his sister's.

The senator himself had regretted the absence of a nurturing mother. Leanna had been alone for a great deal of her young life. Perhaps she was more afraid than her fiery, tempestuous behavior suggested.

He supposed it was the surge of pity within him that kept him from teasing her again. That and the thought of his own sister Virginia—Gina, as he'd always called her. If she were here, in such a position as Leanna, he would certainly like to think a man would treat her with respect.

So, without a word, he took Leanna's wet skirt outside to the fire and left her in peace to adapt herself to the clothes as best she could.

At Alex's restraint, Leanna began to feel a little sad, ashamed even. Only a little while ago she had felt a moment's happiness and had been ready to return to her games and laughter. Now she felt completely defeated.

She'd never been exposed to any hardships, except that of being alone, but she could not possibly explain that to Alex. Humiliation was a new feeling for her. She felt dirty and degraded, scrounging around in a tent, surrounded by men she hardly knew, being forced to wear someone else's clothes—and men's clothes at that.

She took a deep breath and gritted her teeth. She would get through this. After all, she kept telling herself, it was hardly a tragedy, only an inconvenience. She would not let herself sit and cry like some lost child when everything did not go her way. She had to face the unpleasant fact that her life had changed suddenly and drastically, and that she had no idea what fate would bring next.

She was not the only person to discover that the war had turned her world upside down. She would try not to whine about it. Somehow, a strength within her, some stubborn determination she did not even know she possessed, took control.

Finally she slipped her arms into the large shirt. Even if she did need a bath, the feel of the material, so dry and clean, seemed like a luxury. She wondered about the shirt and who it belonged to, for it was smooth and fine, obviously not a soldier's, but rather one of excellent quality.

She laughed softly as the tail of the shirt fell below her knees, and the sleeves several inches past the tips of her fingers. But she quickly rolled up the sleeves and decided the length of the shirt might help keep her warm.

The trousers were a different matter. They were small for a man's, and although they gapped around her waist, she found that the seat and thighs fit snugly. They too were a bit long, so she tucked the bottoms into the top of her boots. The pain in her wrist became almost unbearable as she tugged and pulled at the boot tops.

It had been difficult enough dressing with her sprained wrist, but she soon found that brushing her long hair was impossible. She transferred the brush to her left hand, but she wasn't strong enough to untangle the thick mass of long, snarled locks.

"Leanna?" Alex's voice sounded from outside the tent.

"Yes, you can come in," she said, frowning at herself in the small mirror and trying to pull the hairbrush free.

Alex laughed at her.

"What? Do I look that ridiculous?

"No," he said quickly. "Not at all. I was laughing because you look like an angry little girl with your hair tumbling down about your face that way." He broke off and stared at her. Then, with a quick shake of his head, he stepped forward. "Here, let me."

"No . . ." she began, feeling awkward. "I can do it." She pulled harder on the hairbrush, yanking it free at last with a force that sent it sailing through the air to land on the other side of the tent.

Alex went to retrieve it, smiling at her obvious nervousness.

"I'm embarrassed to go outside looking this way," she said, looking up at him almost shyly.

"There's no reason for you to be," he said, surprised at the hint of sweetness he now detected in her. His voice had grown deep and warm, and he looked at her with growing curiosity.

"Really? You're not just saying that?"

"Really," he said softly. "Actually you look kind of . . . sweet."

Sweet? It was hardly the compliment she would have expected from him, and she didn't know how to react. She found herself unable to meet his eyes as a slow flush crept up her neck and cheeks.

What on earth was wrong with her? She had certainly never been the fluttery, blushing type of female. Yet now, in front of this man with whom she'd spent some of her most intimate moments, she found herself feeling positively bewildered.

Alex only smiled at her discomfort and moved closer to her, poising the brush above her tangled hair.

She looked at him cautiously, her emerald eyes wide

and hesitant. "You . . . you really don't have to do this," she stammered.

"I know that. But I don't mind at all, unless you're afraid I'll bite or something."

He was teasing her again. Still, she felt vulnerable and awkward with him standing so near, ready and willing it seemed to perform such a personal task as brushing her hair.

She looked away from his steady gaze and shrugged her shoulders as if she did not really care one way or another.

Alex pulled the brush through her long golden hair and smoothed it with his left hand, letting his fingers slowly run down the length of the shining strands.

Leanna could feel herself relaxing, enjoying his touch against her will. She leaned her head back and closed her eyes, basking in the feel of such luxury and gentle care.

For a while, neither of them spoke. Alex seemed intent on what he was doing as he slowly and patiently brushed the tangles from her hair.

"You seem to have done this before," she murmured, more curious than she wanted him to know.

He smiled but did not reply.

Alex couldn't decide what it was about her hair that fascinated him so—whether it was the brilliant color that gleamed with sparks of gold or if it was the luxuriant texture. It was soft beneath his hands, crisp and clean and healthy. As he ran the brush through it, the faint scent of summer flowers rose up to tantalize him.

Leanna sat very still, her head leaned backward, almost touching his thigh. Her eyes were closed and the thick fan of her lashes splayed across her velvety skin.

Alex allowed his gaze to wander freely across her

features. She was beautiful, even in his large shirt and Jimmy's trousers. Her face looked scrubbed and clean, and there was the slightest trace of freckles across her nose.

His breath caught as he watched her lips, parted now as she tilted her head back. They were soft and pink, and he could see the glimmer of white teeth just beneath her upper lip.

Being so close to her was wreaking havoc on his senses, not to mention what it was doing to his body, but he could not bring himself to step away.

Her hair, now free of tangles, fell soft and loose about her face and down on the white shirt she wore. Alex's eyes moved further, past the red-gold locks, to the full breasts that rose and fell with her quiet, steady breathing.

She looked as untouched and enchanting as the beautiful Kentucky country in which they found themselves. And just like the land, Alex sensed a wildness in her that could match the rage of a Kentucky storm.

He felt he knew that about her, and yet he doubted she was even aware of it. But that wildness, waiting mysteriously behind her haughty, cool exterior, fascinated him and drew him to her against his better judgment.

And yet there was something else, some soft feminine vulnerability in her, that made him want to hold her, to protect her. He could not remember ever feeling such a dangerous surge of feelings about anything or anyone.

His heart was beating hard as he continued to study her. His hands had stopped, holding the brush motionless in the air. Even his breathing seemed suspended as he felt a stirring within him, a ripple of heat that rose from the pit of his stomach and brought perspiration to his brow, even in the cold.

Leanna opened her eyes and found herself staring into the black depths of Alex Slayton's. His lids were lowered, allowing only a glimpse into those disturbing eyes. He was looking at her strangely, as if something bothered him.

"What is it?" she asked. "Is something wrong?"

"No," he answered quickly. "Nothing." He handed the brush to her and tried to compose his thoughts and still the heavy thudding of his heart.

"Thank you," she said. "It feels much better."

His face changed then, becoming impersonal and closed as it had been before. Leanna continued to stare at him, wondering what she had done now to displease him.

Alex knew she could not tell that he was only angry with himself. He had not admitted, even to himself, his other feelings. He had known all along what the tension between them meant, what the fighting and bickering was all about, even if Leanna did not. It signified something that he could not allow to progress any further. Even as the sweet scent of her hair tantalized him, he cursed himself, reminding himself of all the reasons he could never have this girl.

He was a soldier in a war that might last a long time, and he could not let himself become involved with anyone until this damnable business was ended—certainly not an innocent like Leanna McNairy. She was his responsibility now, and he was older and much too jaded for a girl like her. He hoped to make her see eventually that he was not her enemy, but right now she had to hate him and all he stood for.

He frowned. Nothing on this list of grievances

seemed to matter, and he felt his desire for her even more strongly than before.

"Excuse me," he said abruptly, turning to leave the tent. "I have work to do. Jimmy or Trey will see to your breakfast whenever you're ready."

He hurried made his way outside and took a deep breath of cold air before going across to one of the fires.

Leanna was puzzled. Why was he so changeable? And why she should even care?

She sat for a long while, looking through the tent's door toward camp. She'd seen Alex move to one of the fires. Now a young soldier approached him, speaking rapidly and gesturing up the hill toward the cabin and the ferry crossing.

She watched as Alex turned and strode away with the young man.

It would be good, she told herself, if they had finished the repairs. Perhaps she could be in Pleasant Hill before another night fell.

She wrapped her blue cape around her shoulders and walked out into the sunshine. There was no one else in camp except Trey, who was seated before a campfire.

As she approached him, she glanced off to her right and saw the other men converged at the river. She could see Alex's dark head and broad shoulders in the crowd of people.

She approached Trey cautiously, not knowing exactly what she should say to him. She had had very little opportunity in her life for a conversation with a black man.

He looked up at her from the corner of his dark eyes and then quickly glanced back down to the pot he was stirring.

"Good morning, Trey," she said in what she hoped was a friendly tone of voice.

"Mornin'," he said, his deep voice so quiet that she could hardly hear it.

"Something smells awfully good," she said.

"Yes, ma'am." He handed her one of the metal plates.

"What is it?"

"Squirrel stew."

Obviously she was not going to be able to get much conversation from him. As awkward as she felt in his presence, this disturbed her. Had she made him feel badly about something? After all, she was on the opposite side of the war from him. Did he and the others know that? She had assumed all along that they did.

The stew was thickened with corn meal and spicily seasoned with some peppery ingredient she could not readily identify. She thought it was one of the most delicious things she'd ever eaten.

"This is good," she mumbled with her mouth full, still savoring the stew.

Trey looked at her noncommittally but did not answer. For some reason, his reluctance to become better acquainted made her even more determined that they would.

"Trey, I wish you would talk to me."

He looked her in the eye, then, and she saw that it was not fear that kept him silent. It was pride, perhaps even anger. His eyes were hard and his jaw set with a stiff determination.

He was a handsome man, with brown eyes that slanted upward at the corners. He was burly and muscular not as tall as Alex, but with a thick neck and the evidence of bulging muscles beneath his jacket.

"If you wish," he replied.

"I . . . I suppose you must hate me," she said impulsively.

"Hate you?" he asked. "Why would I hate you?"

"Me being a Southerner and everything. . . ." Her voice trailed away self-consciously, and she took another bite of the spicy stew.

"I'm a Southerner, too, from Statesboro, Georgia, near Savannah."

Her eyes widened, then she frowned at him. "Oh, I see. Then you were a . . . I mean, I suppose . . ."

"Yes, ma'am," he said, his dark eyes burning at her. "I was a slave, but I ain't one no more, and I ain't never gonna be one again once this war is over."

Her face flamed with embarrassment. She did not really know how to communicate with someone like Trey. Tyler and his friends often said that the Negroes weren't like white people, that they had no real feelings. But they had to be wrong about this man.

She was beginning to see that none of the long, heated debates in her comfortable parlor had prepared her for the anger and emotion in Trey's eyes.

"I . . . I can understand how you feel," she stammered.

"Can you?" he snapped. "I doubt you've ever been whipped till you can't see. Or watched your parents dragged off to God knows where 'cause they been sold to someone who don't want you. Have you ever heard the screams of a young girl in the night because the master or one of his sons has decided she'd old enough to—" He stopped and stood up suddenly.

"I'm sorry, I shouldn't be speaking about such things to a lady." He began to walk away.

Leanna's eyes were filled with horror at his blunt words, and her heart with an indescribable ache.

"Trey, wait," she said, standing up to follow after him.

He stopped, probably only because she was a lady, and a white one at that. His shoulders and broad back looked stiff, though, and she could hear the sound of his quick, angry breathing.

"I'm . . . I'm sorry. Truly. Please forgive me for being so ignorant and for insinuating I could ever understand your people's suffering." She placed her hand on the back of his arm for only for a second, then turned to go back to the fire.

Trey drew in a breath and then moved away in the direction of the others. Leanna sat back down to finish her breakfast. As hungry as she'd been, she no longer had an appetite, and in spite of her earlier vows to be strong, she felt the sting of tears in her eyes. For once, they were not for herself.

10

From the camp Leanna could see the flat-boat at the landing and the men milling around it. Soon she saw one lone figure heading back toward her, followed by several others clad in the blue uniform of the Union army.

Jimmy was the first man to reach her.

"Got the ferry repaired. Major said for us to break camp and prepare to cross." He was slightly out of breath, and there was excitement in his voice. Obviously he had not liked being confined to one spot any more than Alex had.

"That's wonderful. Do you think I will be at the Shaker village before dark?"

"Oh, yes, ma'am. I think so, if we leave soon, that is."

"Is there anything I can do to help?"

"No, ma'am. All you got to do is get your things. I'll see to your horse soon as I pack up."

After thanking him she started back to Alex's tent.

"Oh, by the way," Jimmy said, making no move to leave. "You look much better in my trousers than I do." He was grinning widely as he spoke.

"Oh," she said. "Are . . . are these yours?" She felt self-conscious again but could hardly resist a quick smile back at the young soldier. He had a way about him that made it impossible not to be friendly. It was odd how he could tease her and not evoke the same disturbing feelings as Alex did when he teased her.

"Yes'm, they are. Can't claim the shirt, though. It's much too fancy for me."

She looked down at the shirt.

"Belongs to the major. You didn't really think a poor enlisted boy like me could afford such a fine shirt, did you?"

"Don't tell her that, Private," Alex called as he approached them. "I'm sure she'd avoid it like the plague if she knew it belonged to me."

Jimmy laughed. Leanna blushed, feeling awkward again and unsure of herself. Somehow the thought of his shirt next to her body, the touch of the fine material against her naked skin, disturbed her.

"Well, I . . . I should get my things."

Within the hour the soldiers had cleared the camp, packed up, and were ready to move across the river. To Leanna's surprise it was not Jimmy who brought her mare to her, but Alex. Upon Windspry's back was a man's saddle.

"How's your wrist?"

She had managed, after Alex left, to wrap her injured wrist. She held it up now for him to see.

"It feels better."

"Do you think you can ride? Or would you prefer to sit in the wagon?"

She didn't want to be stuck in the wagon where she couldn't see anything, and even though her wrist still ached, she would not admit it.

"I can ride, but where's my own saddle?"

"It's safely tucked away in one of the wagons. If this is a problem, if you can't ride—"

"Of course I can do it," she cut him off. She had noticed the way his black eyes raked her trouser-clad figure, and she wasn't going to give him the opportunity to say anything else.

Alex moved very close to her to help her into the saddle. Once again he pulled her cape around her and tucked it beneath her as she sat down. This time, when his hands slid quickly beneath her, she felt an odd sensation move through her.

She looked down at Alex, at the glint of sunshine on his black hair and the way the shadows lay along his chiseled cheekbones. He bit his lower lip as he concentrated on tightening the cinch beneath the mare's belly, and she found that looking at his mouth made her skin tingle with unexpected pleasure.

He lifted his eyes to catch her looking at him. A slow easy smile curved the corners of his mouth, and his black gaze held hers.

"Are you ready?" he asked in a low voice.

"Oh, yes." Her voice was only a whisper as she stared at his lips. "I am."

He seemed to know what she was thinking as his eyes sent sparks of warning. A puzzled frown crossed his face, and he held her gaze for a long moment before returning his attention to the saddle gear.

His silent dismissal of her was like a splash of cold water. The spell was broken. Leanna was troubled by the odd feelings his looks gave her. Lord, but he must think her a fool.

As they rode across to the landing, Leanna saw a small group of passengers waiting to board the ferry. There was a black-covered carriage beside which stood four gaudily dressed women. They wore gowns of satin and silk in colors as bright and varied as the rainbow. Their clothes were certainly not appropriate for cold weather, either, but she doubted Alex Slayton had questioned them or made them feel inadequate.

She heard the women's shrill laughter as she drew nearer. Why did women like that always laugh so loudly? Were they never tired or solemn? Did they never grow weary of laughter and partying with drunken men?

She turned her attention to the men waiting to board and found them all staring at her. Then all of them looked politely away, except one, whose gaze moved over her slowly, insultingly, as if she too belonged with the group of other women.

Leanna thought she'd never seen a more grotesque man, with long skinny legs and enormous stomach. His dyed hair was an odd, greenish black color, plastered tightly across the top of his balding head. There seemed to be more hair in his curling mustache than on his head.

Leanna lifted her chin and stared at a spot on the river above the man's head as she waited for Alex and his soldiers behind her.

"I guess I can tolerate a ride across the old Kentucky with a bunch of damned blue-bellies, as long as it's quick." It was the man who'd been staring at her who spoke. The sneer across his ugly face made Leanna feel sick. "But I'm damned if I'm goin' across with a sorry no-good nigger!" He spat tobacco juice on the ground and wiped the back of his hand across his mouth.

Leanna gasped at his ugly words. She did not know this man and had never been exposed to his particular brand of hatred, but she knew instinctively that he was dangerous.

She thought at first that Alex had not heard the man's words and that she should warn him somehow. But it was too late. Alex stopped right in front of the man, with Trey and Jimmy on each side of him.

Leanna held her breath as the big-bellied man stared up at Trey. Some of the other men murmured angrily, and she knew it would take only one word or one move to start a fight. The four women were quiet now, and, at the motion of a tall blond-haired woman, who seemed in charge, they stepped back out of the way.

Alex's black eyes glinted in the sunlight like the barrel of a gun and were leveled on the ugly man before him. He had removed the heavy coat he'd worn earlier. Now Leanna saw the black leather holster at his side and the glisten of white across the knuckles of his dark hand, where it lay upon the handle of his army pistol.

The other man saw the dangerous look on Alex's face. He shifted his large frame and turned with a nervous laugh to the men behind him. He whispered something beneath his breath, and they all laughed. The air suddenly felt as thick and frosty as the ice that covered the river.

"Didn't know the Federals were so hard up they had to recruit women," the man drawled.

Leanna was stunned as he shifted his target from Trey to her.

"This lady is a Shaker, whom we're escorting across the river," Alex said.

"Damn, she don't look like no Shaker I ever seen!" The man snickered crudely. "And I never seen one wearin' britches afore. Not that I'm complainin'." His smirking look at Leanna left little doubt as to his meaning.

The men behind him laughed and shifted uneasily.

"I'd advise you to shut your filthy mouth, mister," Alex said, his hand tightening on the pistol at his side.

Jimmy's face was hard and alert, and his hand was clasped on the long-barreled rifle he held across his saddle.

From the flatboat, Mr. Ramsay, the ferryman, called. "We'll take the passengers first, Major Slayton. Then we'll come back for you."

Leanna breathed a sigh of relief. They were about to leave, and Alex's words had hit their mark. The man lowered his eyes and stepped backward.

"No offense, Major. Name's Rollins." He stepped forward as if to offer his hand to Alex.

Alex stared at him as if he'd not even heard him.

"What's the girl's name?" the man asked, looking at her again with a hungry look in his eyes.

"Move aside, Mr. Rollins," Alex said quietly.

"I don't mean nothin', Major. I think I know this little lady. You're from Lexington, ain't you, gal? Just bein' friendly to a fellow Kentuckian, sir."

"My name is none of your business, sir," Leanna answered sharply. "And I am not from Lexington."

"Why, ma'am, I believe you are. Don't rightly recall where I've seen you, but I do know you're a pretty big deal in Lexington's upper crust. Senator McNairy's daughter . . . ain't that right, now?"

There was a low murmur of disapproval as the men around Rollins looked with new intensity at Leanna. Senator Andrew McNairy's name was not a favorite one nowadays in Kentucky.

"Oh, for heaven's sake, Rollins," the blond woman called. "Leave the girl alone. Let's get on across the river. Ain't none of your business anyway who she is."

Leanna heard a loud click and turned around to see Alex's pistol pointed straight at a spot between Rollins's eyes.

"Mr. Rollins," Alex said, "you're a damned nosy bastard, you know that? Now this is the last friendly suggestion I'm going to give you. You step onto the boat, and when you get across to the other side, you get on your horse and keep right on riding. Don't even look back. Do I make myself clear?"

He pulled his horse closer until the end of the pistol was practically touching Rollins's skin. Alex's eyes were hard and black, and he seemed to grow more furious with each word he spoke. Leanna was afraid he would shoot the man then and there. She closed her eyes, not wanting to see the outcome.

"And never let me hear words coming from your filthy mouth again about this lady. You understand?"

Leanna opened her eyes and saw Rollins's lips trembling and his face turning crimson with anger. He didn't like being made a fool of in front of his friends. Leanna had the feeling that he wanted to challenge Alex, but his eyes shifted nervously from the pistol to the boat ramp.

Alex saw his look, too, and smiled coldly. "That's right, Mr. Rollins. Better make it now."

Suddenly there was a scurry for the boat. The men,

including Mr. Rollins, pushed past the carriage and the four women to get aboard.

Leanna might have found it funny if she had not been so frightened. She did not stop shaking until the flatboat was almost across and she was certain that nothing would happen. Still, she hardly took her eyes off the man called Rollins, afraid he might decide he could catch Alex by surprise now and shoot from the boat. He did not, although he watched them with dark, resentful eyes until he was halfway across the river.

The soldiers began to murmur, some of them laughing at the encounter. There were whispered compliments and nods of admiration toward their major.

Alex was still visibly angry, looking for all the world as if he might rip someone's head off. This was a different man entirely from the one she'd seen earlier, the one who had brushed her hair and seemed interested only in her comfort.

She wanted to thank him for defending her, but she didn't know what to say.

"That man insulted Trey," she whispered to Alex.

"I know that," he said between clenched teeth.

"Do you think we'll see him again?"

"Oh, yes," Alex said. "We'll see him again. And more like him as well." His look at her was cold and disdainful. "So these are the Confederate comrades of whom you spoke? The ones who fight for the honor and glory of the South?"

"You know they are not!"

He reined his horse sharply and rode away to sit alone staring into the river, waiting for the ferry to return.

"Why is he angry at me?" she asked Jimmy.

"He ain't," he assured her. "The major, he hates this war. And he hates men like Rollins."

"I just don't understand him."

"He's hard to figure sometimes," Jimmy said, shaking his head wisely.

"Honorable's the word." It was Trey's deep voice that murmured beside Leanna. She was surprised that he would even address his words to her after their earlier conversation.

"You've known him since before the war, haven't you, Trey?" she asked.

"Yes, ma'am. When I was younger, the master of our plantation died. In his will, he left us all free. But his son, he had different ideas. Said he'd kill any buck nigger, free or not, that left Statesboro. I ran away on the underground to Ohio. Mr. Alex's daddy took me in. Mr. Alex there, he taught me to read and gave me a job keepin' accounts on his farm. One day a man come to do business, a man a lot like Rollins. He didn't like doin' business with a black man. Said I was uppity and he was goin' to horsewhip me good, put me in my place. Mr. Alex, he stepped in about that time and the man slashed him with the whip across his shoulders . . . sliced him clean open . . . called him a nigger lover."

Leanna gasped and looked toward Alex. "What happened?"

"Mr. Alex, he still thrashed that man. Beat him almost senseless before we could pull him off him. And all the time he was bleedin' somethin' awful. He was laid up in bed for nigh on a week. And he did it for me, ma'am." Trey's voice trembled, but his dark eyes were clear as he looked toward Alex. "Ain't never in my life had a white man fight for me."

"I understand," she said, even though his words about Alex's fury had made her shiver. "You owe him your loyalty, then, and your friendship."

"I owe him everything, miss," he said. "And I joined the army to die for him, if necessary."

Leanna and Jimmy fell silent as Trey seemed lost now in his own memories. She was sure that all of them were thinking about the enigmatic man who sat quietly staring at the river. What a strange, fierce man he was, as wild as the river that he watched. She doubted she'd ever be able to understand him.

She was beginning to see that she really did not know the man hidden behind that handsome, hawkish face.

11

Leanna watched the flatboat make its way back across the river toward them. As it approached the shore it sent waves of clear green water splashing over the frozen ground. Most of the ice that had formed during the past two or three days was melting.

The ferryman let down the ramp, and the soldiers drove the wagons up and into the boat. The others followed on horseback.

As soon as everything was secured and the barge began to move away from shore, Leanna stepped down from Windspry and walked to the bow. Here, on the water, everything was still and silent except for the lapping of the water and the occasional stamping of the horses' feet. The high limestone cliffs that lined the river glistened in the noonday sun.

Leanna glanced toward Alex, who was still stony

faced and silent. He had walked to the opposite side from her and stood watching the water with a closed look on his face.

Across the river on the far shore, Leanna noticed that the carriage still sat where it had rolled off the flatboat. She wondered why.

Jimmy came to stand beside her. "I wouldn't worry about the major, Miss McNairy. He can be downright moody at times. I guess he has a lot on his mind."

"Why should I worry? His disposition is nothing to me."

"Oh, yes, ma'am," he said, ducking his head with a smile.

"I suppose your company will be going on to Harrodsburg once you've deposited me at the village?" she asked.

"Well, that's our official location, but we're actually headquartered near where you'll be, ma'am."

"Jimmy, would you do me a favor?"

"Sure, ma'am. Anything."

"Please stop calling me ma'am. We're probably close to the same age, and it makes me feel quite silly to have you call me ma'am."

"What shall I call you, then?" he asked.

"Why not call me Leanna? It is my name." She flashed him a teasing smile.

"Oh, I don't know 'bout that. The major—"

"The major does not run my life!"

"Yes, ma'am, uh, Leanna."

"That's much better. Now, what were you saying about your headquarters?"

"We were offered the residence of Mr. Sutton. His only son was killed in the war last year, and he said he wanted to do something to help. He and his wife live on this big farm all alone, and I think he enjoys our company. The major uses a guesthouse out in back for his office, and we have the outbuildings, although some of the men prefer sleeping in tents to sleeping with the cows."

"Sounds very unusual."

"I suppose it is, compared to the regular army. But we're kind of a special unit, planning night maneuvers and plotting routes for other companies moving into the area. And since the Union controls Kentucky now . . ." He stopped and looked at her sheepishly.

"What is it?"

"I suppose I shouldn't be tellin' you all this stuff. The major . . ."

She stiffened. Not only did his words insult her, but they hurt her as well. She had almost forgotten they were on opposite sides of the war, but evidently Alex did not feel they could trust her.

"Under the circumstances, I can't really blame you for that," she said. "But I assure you, Jimmy, that even if I were inclined to tell someone, which I'm not, I haven't the faintest idea who I would tell."

He clamped his lips together and glanced at her uneasily. Then he nodded silently but offered no other information.

They had almost reached the shore. Leanna glanced back one final time at the place they'd just left, to the large elm and sycamore trees where they'd camped and the bank of the river where she'd stepped through the ice.

A faint smile flickered across her face as she remembered how Alex had carried her to the tent, his good-natured teasing, his gentleness as he brushed her hair. She glanced toward him now. He was already astride his gray stallion, seeming anxious to be off the water and onto solid ground once more.

Leanna pulled herself into her own saddle and watched Alex disembark first, moving toward the carriage that sat waiting for them.

The blond woman walked away from the carriage and moved to greet Alex. He stepped down from his horse and met her halfway. Even as Leanna walked her mare carefully down the ramp, she hardly moved her eyes from the couple, wondering what this woman could possibly have to say to Alex.

The woman was looking up into Alex's handsome face. Her hands were clasped behind her back, causing her bosom to thrust forward provocatively. She swayed slightly as she spoke in a coquettish way.

Leanna was surprised at Alex's low, muffled laughter and strained even harder to hear their words. She stopped some distance behind Alex and looked in the opposite direction, as if she had no interest in what they were saying.

"I really doubt you're moving there because of me, Maggie, my love," she heard Alex say.

"Oh, but it's true!" the woman said. "Since I rarely saw you when I was in Lexington, I thought Harrodsburg would be just the place for a new start."

"And I suppose it has nothing to do with the fact that the Lexington Ladies' Society had you thrown out of town."

"Why, Alex Slayton! You are very ungentlemanly to bring up such a matter." She tapped his shoulder playfully and then threw back her head and laughed. "You know, if Major Jenkins's wife had not been the president of the society, I'd still be there."

"I suppose Mrs. Jenkins is the jealous type," he said.

"Well, my dear, aren't they all?" She laughed loudly again. Then she lowered her voice slightly. "Alex, my dear, seriously. That man on the barge, that Rollins. He's a loudmouth blowhard, I'll grant you, but he's dangerous. He knows men who can cause you lots of problems. I would take him very seriously if I were you, especially after today."

"Don't worry about me, Maggie. I can handle Rollins."

"I hope you can. He had some pretty nasty things to say about you and your black soldier as we came across. I just wanted to warn you."

"I do appreciate it," he said in a sweet tone of voice that he never used with Leanna.

"I only wish you could be persuaded to show me just how much," the woman said.

Alex laughed. "Soon, perhaps."

"Well, you never were one to waste words," she said with a wistful little sigh. "But then I do so love a man of action."

Alex laughed again, and Leanna found herself irritated by the sound of it.

"What about the girl?" Maggie asked. "Anything personal there? You seemed quite possessive of her back there while ago."

"I promised her father I'd protect her, and I intend to keep my word," Alex said.

"I see. You would have me believe that a big, handsome, virile man like yourself kept a beautiful redhaired girl in your tent all night and nothing happened?"

"Believe anything you like, Maggie, dear," he said. "But just between the two of us, a kick in the head by a mule would probably be less painful than tangling with that one."

Leanna felt a jolt of humiliation rush through her. If she had any doubts before about whether he disliked her, she had none now.

Maggie laughed again, and Leanna moved Windspry slightly away before Alex turned back toward her.

"I'll be expecting you and the boys in Harrodsburg soon now, Alex Slayton," the woman called as her carriage pulled away.

All the while the other three girls had been sitting in the carriage, waving and smiling at the soldiers. As they moved past they called some of the men by name. Jimmy looked at Alex sheepishly, but Alex made no mention of it and moved to the head of the group as they started up the road.

Again Jimmy moved to ride beside Leanna. "Whew!" he said. "I thought for sure Maggie was goin' to tell the major about last night."

"I think the major already knows."

"You . . . you didn't . . ."

"Oh, no, not me. I didn't say a word. I didn't have to. Perhaps Major Slayton knows you and the others better than you think."

"Hmmm . . . now there's a frightenin' thought," he said, looking toward his commanding officer. "'Cause Major Slayton never forgets anything! He'll get me when I least expect it."

Leanna's laughter echoed off the cliffs that surrounded them as they moved along the road.

Alex turned his head at the sound and allowed himself only a brief glance at the two riding behind him. He hoped that Private Anderson would not be hurt when he found out what a notorious flirt Leanna McNairy was. He hated to see him made a fool of as her young beau Tyler had been. Jimmy was a good boy, and a good soldier, and Alex did not want his attention diverted by some unrequited passion.

Leanna noticed Alex's stormy gaze back at them. He looked quite dangerous there with the shadows of the high cliffs cast on his rugged features and black hair.

"Jimmy," she began, "I asked Alex . . . Major Slayton about a name I've heard him called. The Nighthawk. Have you heard of it?"

"Heard it? Why, we're the ones who gave it to him, I reckon. Us and the other Kentucky troops hereabouts. Ain't nobody in Lincoln's army knows more about night strategy than Major Slayton. He's penetrated the enemy lines more often than any other officer there is. He's quiet and smart, and they say he has the vision of a nighthawk. So we just started calling him that, amongst ourselves at first. The major there, he don't like it much. Says it only draws attention to us and our missions, makes the enemy want to bring us down real bad."

"Yes, well, I can see his point about that,"

"I guess. But it's too late now. He's done got the reputation and the name. Guess he'll just have to live with it."

Leanna studied the dark-haired man who rode ahead of them. It seemed that everything she learned about Alex Slayton only made him more mysterious.

She began to notice the scenery again. It was much like the other side of the river, except that where she and Alex had moved downhill yesterday, they now moved up, winding in and out of the curves and rough rocky ground. Soon they exited the canyon, and the land leveled off into beautiful rolling hills and wide dense stands of hardwood. It was even lovelier than the land near her home. The day was still cold, but the warming rays of the sun felt good.

Her mind had been too preoccupied with Alex to think much about the place where she was going. Now she began to wonder about the Shakers. They were a stern, industrious people. Would they be cruel and exact hard standards she couldn't meet? If so, what was she to do then? It was a frightening thought. At least she'd made one friend in Jimmy, and he would be near enough to help if she needed him.

It was midafternoon when they stopped to rest and water the horses. They moved off the road, down to a nearby creek. The men seemed friendly and more at ease with Leanna than before, partly, she supposed, because they were away from the confinement of camp.

Some of them gathered around her, opening knapsacks and offering to share their provisions with her. Jimmy brought her a cold tin of water, and even Trey sat nearby, watching the men's antics and sometimes smiling at their efforts to impress Leanna.

All the while Leanna was conscious of Alex's gaze upon her. He stood alone beneath a huge oak tree, with one muscular arm against the trunk of the tree as he drank from a metal cup. He caught her glance at him and lifted his eyebrows in response.

Leanna looked away, determined that he would not spoil this last afternoon with the young men whose company she'd begun to enjoy.

One of the soldiers, a young boy named Steven, told Leanna that he was from Pennsylvania. She learned that he had the honor in the small group of being the farthest from home. He seemed fascinated by Southern women and asked her numerous questions about their lives until she had to laugh.

"I assure you, Steven, Southern women are no different from the ones you grew up with. We're just like your sisters, your mothers, and your sweethearts."

"Oh, ma'am, I don't think so," he said with a grin. "The women down here seem to know how to treat a man . . . how to make him feel special. And the voices! I thought I'd died and gone to heaven the first time I heard a Kentucky girl speak to me."

Leanna laughed and shook her head.

Alex dashed the water from his cup onto the ground and called to the men, "If you boys are finished with your afternoon tea, we'll ride on in to headquarters now." Then he moved to his horse and mounted up, waiting impatiently for them to follow.

Alex didn't know why he couldn't shake the anger he felt. Hell, he didn't even know for sure who he was angry with. He only knew that Leanna's behavior with his men was entirely different than with him, and that it irritated him. He was tired, weary of the dust and the road, and anxious to be back at the farm. After he delivered Leanna to the Shaker village he hoped to have done with this whole inconvenience.

Leanna was aware of Alex's anger. She could see it in every flash of his black eyes, and she had not forgotten his scornful words to Maggie about her. She should remind him that she had not asked to come with him, but had sworn, in fact, that she would not. He was the one who had practically dragged her here against her will, and now he had the nerve to act as though everything was her fault!

As they began to move again, and for the remainder of the afternoon, she could feel resentment building like a fire in her blood. How she wanted to tell him what she thought of him and his self-righteous attitude, not only toward her but toward his men. If he said one more sarcastic word to her, she was sure she would not be able to control herself.

They began to pass cultivated fields and pastureland that even in winter looked green and lush. She looked around with pleasure and heard Jimmy's voice beside her.

"We're on Sutton property now, but his land goes for miles. We'll reach headquarters soon."

As they rode, Alex dropped back beside her for the first time since the ferry crossing. "If you'd like we can stop at headquarters and let you change into your own clothes. I'm not sure the Believers will appreciate your present attire." Normally his words might have been teasing, but now she thought them stern and accusing.

"How considerate of you," she said demurely, but the look she gave him was anything but that.

Soon the house appeared ahead of them. It sat on a long, sloping hill, a good distance from the road. The straight drive to the house was lined with locust trees, their limbs bare now. In springtime, Leanna thought they would provide a spectacular setting for the plantationlike house.

The house itself was of red brick, two stories with a painted white porch and long white shutters at all the windows. From the wide steps, a brick walkway curved outward like gracious welcoming arms to greet visitors coming up the drive. It looked like heaven to Leanna, especially after the long, exhausting ride from Lexington.

The men rode around toward the back to a carriage house that was separate from the main house. The drive between the main house and the smaller one was paved with brick.

Leanna felt a wrenching sadness as Jimmy came forward to say good-bye. Many of the soldiers waved to her as they passed by the carriage house. Some of them rode to a fenced pasture, while others headed toward a large black barn that stood several hundred feet from the house.

Alex opened the door to the carriage house and stood aside as he motioned her in. The large room was dark, and a pleasant smell of soap and leather lingered in the air.

She stood very still, hardly breathing until the flare of a match brightened the darkness as Alex lit a kerosene lamp. He turned then to face her, and she was suddenly all too aware of the tension between them. She thought of that moment in her father's barn, when they had met for the first time since her childhood.

She did not look away from his penetrating gaze or the appealing slant of his angular features. Her eyes lingered for a moment on the curve of his lips, and she felt a longing sadness stab at her heart.

In that strange moment Leanna felt as confused and as lost as she'd ever been in her young life. For she hated to part with this man, whom she had sworn was her enemy.

12

Alex turned and threw open the curtains at the front of the room to reveal a view of the main house. The only other window looked out on a rock fence and an expanse of green pastureland.

"The bedroom is upstairs. If you'd like to rest for a while, I'll have someone from the main house bring hot water for a bath."

His thoughtfulness surprised Leanna. With a muttered thank-you, she took her skirt, which had dried as they rode, and made her way up the narrow stairway.

There was only one bedroom upstairs, although it was very large, and well lit. Leanna's curious gaze took in the low slope of the ceiling that dipped toward a row of windows facing west. The winter sun hung low in the sky, and the wispy clouds stretched across it glowed gold and pink.

She sank onto the cushions on the windowseat and pressed her forehead against the cold panes. How beautiful it was here, and how very peaceful. In the comfort and coziness of this room, it seemed impossible that there was a war, or that someone had arrested her father. What was she to do without him?

She shook off the thought and looked around the room, noting the touches that Alex Slayton must have added. Above a small walnut desk was the American flag and a picture of President Lincoln. Her eyes moved to the bed, gleaming brass with intricate scrollwork. It was hardly masculine, she thought, but she supposed that Alex had had no choice in the matter. The room was surprisingly neat, decorated only with some pictures and personal mementos that brought a strange tug of affection to her chest.

Leanna moved to the desk and picked up the pictures there. She recognized Alex's father; he had visited their home many times before the war. And of course the woman with him was Alex's mother. Leanna could see where Alex had gotten his striking good looks. His mother was as dark as he, with the same slanting cheekbones and piercing black eyes. Leanna's hand moved to another picture encased in a silver frame. Here was a beautiful dark-haired girl, not much older than Leanna. She was smiling at a young man with fair hair and pale eyes. Leanna was surprised to see that he was wearing the uniform of the Confederacy.

With a small frown, she put the picture back on the desk. Who was the girl, and why would Alex Slayton have the picture of a Confederate soldier in his room?

She heard a thump on the stairway and turned at the sound of a light tap upon the door. When she opened it she found Jimmy Anderson standing there with two buckets of water.

He nodded toward the corner of the room.

"Bathtub's over there, behind that screen."

Leanna quickly moved the screen and stood aside as he poured the water for her. "I didn't expect to see you again," she said.

"Well, there was a message for the major, and so I just brought the buckets along with me," he said, smiling at her. "Well, I best get back . . ."

Suddenly, from below, they heard a muffled noise and the sound of a man's voice. It was not words, but a low growl, like the anguished sound of a wounded animal.

Jimmy ran to the stairs. "Major? Something wrong?"

Leanna was right behind the young soldier, following him down the narrow stairs to the large room that was now flooded with light.

Alex stood at a table near the front window. His outstretched arms supported him as he leaned on the table, and in his right hand he clutched a piece of yellow paper as if he would crush it into nonexistence. His dark head was lowered, and he did not look up.

"Sir?" Jimmy stood still at the bottom of the stairs, making no move to approach the man. It was obvious something was terribly wrong.

Slowly, Alex straightened, leaning his head back as if to look at the top of the window. "It's all right, Private. You can go on about your duties." His voice was low and husky, and he still did not turn to face them.

Leanna felt she could hardly breathe. She did not know what to do, but she knew something was wrong.

She could feel it in the room like a blast of cold air. Was it her father?

Unable to take her eyes off the man at the window, she stood mutely as he turned and handed the yellow paper to Jimmy. He didn't look at her, but ran his fingers wearily through his tousled black hair.

Jimmy's face paled as he read the message on the paper. "Major Slayton . . ." His voice cracked. "I'm very sorry, sir. Is there anything I can do?"

Alex looked up at Jimmy, his eyes still avoiding Leanna. "Thank you, Jim. I'm afraid there's nothing anyone can do. I think I'll ride across the west border. If you would, please see that Miss McNairy, at her convenience, is escorted to the village. I've already made arrangements, and they know she's coming."

Only then did his eyes dart toward her, then move away quickly. Without so much as a good-bye, he turned and walked from the room.

She moved to Jimmy, who still clutched the yellow slip of paper.

"Jimmy, what is it? Is it his family?"

"It's Gina's husband, Lieutenant Hampton. He's been killed." Jimmy's lips trembled slightly and he shook his head in disbelief.

"Gina?"

"The major's little sister, Virginia. Her husband is . . . was in the Confederate army."

Leanna hardly knew what to say. She thought of the fair-haired soldier in the picture upstairs and it made her heart ache, not only for the young couple but for Alex as well. He had obviously been very hurt.

"A Confederate?"

"From what I understand, she visited the major a few summers ago here in Kentucky. He taught school here, you know. She met a young man, a student of Major Slayton's. Him and Gina fell in love. When the war broke out and Hampton decided it would have to be his Southern homeland that he fought for, the major gave his blessing for Gina to marry the young man. I guess her marriage has been a pretty sad and lonely one, seein' as how her husband's been gone most of the time."

"But where is she . . . Gina? In Ohio with her parents?"

"Oh, no. She's stayin' at Bardstown with an aunt, waitin' for Lieutenant Hampton. They say it nearly killed Senator Slayton when she married the boy, him bein' a Confederate and all." He hesitated and looked at her apologetically. "Beggin' your pardon, Leanna."

"No . . . no, it's all right."

"I'm goin' to go tell the rest of the men. I don't know what the major will do, or if he will go to his sister. But as soon as you're ready we'll go on out to Pleasant Hill. It ain't far, and we need to get there before dark."

"I'll only be a few minutes."

Once in Alex's bedroom, Leanna went directly to the silver-framed picture of Virginia Slayton and her young Confederate lieutenant. She felt such sadness, as if she'd lost someone she knew.

Leanna was hardly aware of bathing or dressing. All she could think of was those black eyes filled with pain and those lips compressed in grief. She supposed she'd never been this close to such sorrow, except for when Mrs. Macky's husband had died. Yet even that was different, as Mr. Macky had been old and sick. This young man . . . this hurt Leanna, stunned her. Most unbelievably of all, it made her ache to hold Alex in her arms.

Once she was dressed, she stood at the window and gazed far out toward the western horizon, searching futilely for a glimpse of him. As the wrenching pain gripped her heart, she brushed the tears from her eyes. The deep sense of longing and sadness within her was something she could not explain. She leaned her head against the cool windowpanes and gave in at last to tears.

"Alex," she whispered. "Oh, Alex, I am so sorry."

Within half an hour, accompanied by Jimmy and Trey, she was on her way to the Shaker village. When she first saw the rolling hills, crisscrossed by mile after mile of gray stone walls, she was surprised.

The land was well kept and prosperous, like any good farmland. Somehow, she'd expected the people living here to be more concerned with the spiritual and less with an earthly aspect of tending the land.

To the left, on a slight rise above the road, sat two large houses surrounded by huge old trees. One house was brick, and the other wood painted in a pale, cool yellow. The houses were some distance from the rest of the village, which was visible through the trees ahead of them. The road to Harrodsburg ran straight through the line of houses and outbuildings.

The village seemed surprisingly large, and many fat cattle grazed in the meadows beyond the clusters of houses. On the opposite side of the road was a smaller pasture surrounded by the stone walls. This pasture contained several dozen sheep with thickly matted wool, dirtied now by winter mud and debris.

Jimmy and Trey had been especially quiet on the ride, and she knew they were thinking of Alex. Leanna had tried not to think of him or wonder when she might see him again. There was such an ache within her chest and a longing to comfort him that she wondered if it would ever go away.

"I can smell the cookin' already," Jimmy said, sniffing the air.

Trey nodded, and his lips moved slightly—the closest thing to a smile Leanna had seen from him.

"So," she said. "You came for the famous cooking? And I thought the two of you wanted to spend just a bit more time with me."

"Why, we do, Miss Leanna," Jimmy drawled. "We surely do."

Trey laughed aloud at Jimmy's poor imitation of a Southern gentleman, and, despite her sadness, Leanna joined in.

"But I do hope they invite us to supper while we're here," Jimmy said.

"The Shakers welcome everyone, don't they? I'm sure they will invite you for supper."

"Oh, remember, Leanna," Jimmy said. "They don't call themselves Shakers. That's a word the rest of the world has given them."

"I'll remember."

The closer they came to the center of the village, the greater sense of apprehension Leanna felt. She didn't know how she would manage here in such a foreign place. How would she adjust her playful spirit to these staid, religious people? And what about her father? How could she ever help him if she became a virtual prisoner here?

She was not conscious of the worried look on her face or that she had begun to chew her lip nervously.

Jimmy reached out and took the reins of Leanna's mare to pull her to a halt. "Before we go in, I want to say something," he said. "I know this ain't your kind of place, Leanna. But they're good people, there's no need to be afraid. I mean, they don't believe in punishment or bein' hurtful to anyone. Just give 'em a chance for a while, 'cause like the major says, this is probably the best place for you right now, until he can find out what's happened to your daddy."

"Alex . . . the major is trying to find my father?"

"Why, yeah, sure he is. Didn't he tell you that?"

"No, he didn't." Why was it she was always the last one to know anything?

"It might be hard at first, stayin' here. But don't forget we're right over the hill, and if you need me or Trey, here, just come runnin' across that meadow right back there and you'll come out at the Sutton place."

Leanna smiled at his sweetness and the serious look on his face. "I will, Jimmy. But don't worry. I don't intend to be here long enough for it to matter whether I like it or not."

Jimmy's eyebrows lifted, and he looked toward Trey. They exchanged a glance that Leanna did not particularly like, but she brushed her doubts aside. Then she leaned across and kissed Jimmy quickly on the cheek. She smiled at the startled look in his pale blue eyes.

"Thank you, Jimmy . . . and you, Trey, for helping me."

The black man only nodded, still solemn and unreachable as far as she was concerned. The young private blushed and reined his horse on toward the large brick house ahead of them.

It was almost dark when they stepped down from their mounts in front of the house that Jimmy said was the office and guesthouse. The white picket fence in front gleamed softly in the waning twilight, and the yellow lamplight fanned out from the uncurtained windows of the lower floor of the house.

As they walked up the wide steps to the arched door, Leanna noted the warm faded brown bricks and dark green shutters at the windows.

They knocked and then stepped into the hallway, where they were greeted immediately by a man and woman, each of them dressed solemnly in brown. The man looked to be in his midsixties, tall and spare, with thin brown hair that grew past his collar in the back.

The woman looked even older than the man. She was tiny, with a wizened little face and dark, deep-set eyes. She wore a white bonnet set back on her head, revealing an almost hairless pate.

They introduced themselves as Sister Jane Baldwin and Brother Levi Wilhite. Both of them were trustees, who, as they explained, dealt with the public and made guests comfortable.

Leanna could see that they were trying to welcome her, but something kept them from giving her all their attention. There was an urgency about them as they looked at the two soldiers.

"We are relieved to see our brothers," the old man said. "There have been problems here and throughout the countryside."

Jimmy stepped forward. "What happened, Brother Levi?"

"Renegades, several of them. They went right down the road out there, shooting as they went." The tall man shook his head.

"Was anybody hurt?" Jimmy asked.

"No, thank the Lord. But several windows were shot out, and they took a few cattle with them. I'm afraid it will only get worse. I don't know what we're to do. You know, Private Anderson, that we don't agree with war for any reason, and we've tried to offer food and assistance to all who need it."

"I know that, sir. Did you get a look at these men? Could you tell anything about them?"

"Brother Limuel at the post office saw them. But I can tell you they were only drifters, most likely not associated with either side."

"You're probably right."

The tiny woman spoke for the first time. "It would be a blessing if you men and the major were closer to us."

Jimmy nodded. "Well, I'll mention it to Major Slayton soon as I get back."

The brother stepped forward, took Jimmy's hand, and shook it fervently. "Thank you, son. Thank you. Now, brothers, if thee would like to step into the dining room there, one of the sisters will gladly provide food."

The invitation was what they had been waiting for. Both of them, with hats in hands, stepped toward Leanna.

"Well, good-bye for now, Leanna," Jimmy said. "And don't forget what I told you before, if . . ." His voice dropped. "If you need anything."

"I won't forget. And thank you Jimmy for all you've done for me. Good-bye, Trey," she added, looking past Jimmy.

After they left Leanna felt a pang of homesickness, as if she'd known them for years instead of days.

"The soldiers are good friends," Brother Levi said. "We tend to their horses and keep them shod."

The man indicated that Leanna should step into a parlor just off the hallway. She noticed the gleam of bare wood floors partially covered by plain rag rugs.

The furniture, what there was of it, was simple and modest, almost austere. In one corner was a small black stove that sat far out into the room. But even the large, high-ceilinged parlor felt warm and cozy.

They motioned Leanna to a small rocking chair near the stove. She sat, noting the chair's slender, delicately curved arms and rockers. Then she waited for Brother Levi to speak, feeling more uncertain than ever about staying in such a foreign place.

"Do you often have guests like me?" Leanna asked.

"Yea," Sister Jane answered in a small voice. "Though not so many now since the war."

The man stepped forward and looked down at Leanna with a frown. "But I did not understand that thee would be a guest."

"Oh," she said, shrugging her shoulders. "I didn't ask what arrangements were made for me."

"Of course, thee may stay here as a guest for a few days, if that is thy wish. But if the stay is to be longer, perhaps thee should consider our society and our beliefs for thine own life. It is the usual order of things." He looked at her kindly, with a slight smile.

"Well, I . . . I don't know. My father wanted me to come here for shelter until the war is over, I suppose. But if that is a problem . . ."

"Nay, 'tis not. It will be no problem. It's just that we have no provision for such a visit, much as we would like to make our home available to everyone. To stay longer thee must become a member of the United Society of Believers."

"I see," Leanna said. She had not counted on this. She supposed she could pretend an interest for the time being, until she could find her father or return to Lexington anyway.

"Of course I will consider what you've said," she said. "And if I may I would like to learn more about your society."

The old man and woman looked at one another and smiled with satisfaction.

"After supper I will take thee to a guest room for the night," Sister Jane said. "And tomorrow thee will be assigned to a family house and to an eldress who will instruct thee in our ways."

After a simple but delicious meal, Leanna followed the little woman into the hall and up a beautiful curving stairway that spiraled all the way to the third floor. She thought she'd never seen such a beautiful one, and to find it in a society that decried beauty and elegance seemed even more unusual.

She was placed in a room on the second floor, which was not much different from the parlor downstairs. Everything was of the simplest and plainest of designs. The walls were all white, and the wide baseboards and heavy doors were stained a dark blue color. All around the wall of the room were pegs—for hanging clothes, Leanna supposed, since there was little furniture for storage. There was another small black stove, and it seemed to keep the room very warm.

Leanna was not overly concerned with the appearance of her surroundings, however. Once she saw the narrow little bed and its immaculately clean sheets and quilts, she could think of nothing else except sinking her tired body into it for at least twelve hours' sleep.

She bathed quickly at the washbasin Sister Jane had provided. Then she pulled Alex's white cambric shirt from her bag. She had brought it with her on impulse, for some reason she could not explain. Slipping it on, she took a deep breath, inhaling the same clean fresh scent she'd noticed before. Now it brought with it the unbidden thought of Alex so clearly that she felt as if he were actually in the room with her. Oddly, she was comforted.

Quickly she blew out the candles and crawled into the small bed. The cold wind whistled around the house and rattled the long windows. She felt grateful to be inside, where it was warm and cozy—something she'd always taken for granted before.

The fire popped in the black stove and cast flickering patterns through the cracks around its door. Leanna watched the moving shadows sleepily as she thought of Alex and wondered where he was and what he was thinking.

Had he even thought of her at all? She supposed that was a selfish thought given his own sad news. Still, the thought of him would not go away, nor would the vision of his dark flashing eyes and sensual lips.

Only yesterday she had said she hated him and couldn't wait to be away from him. Now, here, in the strange room among these quiet people, Leanna found that Alex Slayton was an indelible thought on her mind as she fell asleep.

13

Somewhere deep in Leanna's sleep-dimmed mind she heard a ringing, like a church bell. It was a loud, clear sound that echoed across the rolling countryside and into the room where she lay.

Finally she opened her eyes. It was still dark outside, but the firelight from the little stove no longer moved on the walls. She felt warm and sleepy beneath the quilts. She turned over and pulled part of the pillow over her ear. Soon she no longer heard the bell, and with a small, contented sigh she drifted back to sleep.

"Leanna," the voice insisted. "Wake up, Leanna. It's morning and thee has much to do today."

"I'll be sleeping late, Mrs. Macky. Have cook bring a tray around noon." Leanna did not open her eyes as she mumbled the words.

There was a surprised chuckle of laughter. "The child thinks she's at home," the voice whispered.

Leanna reluctantly opened her eyes. The tiny woman called Sister Jane stood near her bed, and there was another woman with her, also dressed in the Shaker garb. What were they doing in her room at this hour of night? It was still dark outside.

"Did thee not hear the bell?" Sister Jane asked gently.

"Bell? I . . . I heard a bell, but—"

"The great bell is rung at five for rising. It sounds throughout the day for different duties and for prayer."

"Five . . . in the *morning?*"

"Yea, child," the woman said with a smile. "There's plenty of time for dressing and cleaning thy room before breakfast and prayers."

Leanna turned back over, feeling so tired and sleepy that she could hardly speak. "I don't want any breakfast, thank you."

"But thee must eat a hearty breakfast to prepare for the duties of the day." For the first time Sister Jane frowned at the girl in the bed. She did not wish to be harsh with her, but this behavior could not be tolerated.

"Go ahead to thy breakfast, Sister Jane," the other woman spoke. "I will attend to our new sister."

When the door closed behind the older woman, Leanna gave a great sigh of relief and snuggled back down under the covers. But suddenly the quilts were thrown back and the cold air swept over her, shocking her bare legs.

"Wha—?" Leanna sat up immediately and gazed into the cool green eyes of the woman beside her bed.

"The Believers will not tolerate a slacker!" The woman's voice was shrill and sharp, grating on Leanna's ears. "Be up with thee and prepare thyself for the day's work."

"Who the devil do you think you are?" Leanna asked angrily. "Barging into my—"

"Silence!"

The woman before Leanna had fire in her eyes. She was not what Leanna had expected. She looked nothing like the sweet, gentle Sister Jane, nor was she what Leanna thought the other women here would be like. She was probably not past thirty, and the hair that peeked out from beneath her bonnet was curly and very blond. Her skin was a lovely peach color, giving her startling green eyes a strange, doll-like appearance. On either side of her perfectly formed heart-shaped face were two beguiling dimples.

Her lips were curled now, obviously disapproving of Leanna. "I am Sister Emily. Emily McGrath. I am the eldress of the West family dwelling where thee will be living."

"But I . . . I thought I might have a day or two to . . ."

"To what? To lie abed and contemplate the evil sins of the worldly? Nay, sister, the sooner thee learns, the sooner thy soul shall be free."

Leanna pulled her feet from beneath the quilts and swung them over the side of the bed. She was wide awake now.

"Look," she began, certain that she could convince this woman of how tired she was. "I told Sister Jane last night that I would like to think about staying here for a while. I did not say I would become a member of your society."

"Fine." The woman shrugged. "And I suppose thy

father's enemies will be happy to welcome thee back to Lexington."

"What do you know of my father?" Leanna demanded, her eyes suddenly as dark as a stormy sky.

"I am an eldress of the church and as such am in charge of the spiritual welfare of our members. And I serve as a supervisor for other officers. So it is not unusual that I should know thy background, especially as I shall serve as thy instructor in faith."

This woman called Sister Emily was obviously proud of her position and the authority that allowed her such power. Evidently she was not above using that power to force someone to do as she wished.

"And as an eldress you would threaten me in order to keep me here?"

"There was no threat intended, Sister," Emily said. "And I personally do not care if thee stays or goes."

"But you just said my father's enemies—"

"I only wanted thee to be aware that thy safety is secured here. But it cannot be if thee leaves our boundaries."

Leanna did not believe her. She had seen women like her before, women whose husbands were wealthy or politically powerful. The only difference was that the sister hid her ambition behind the cloak of religion rather than the glitter of society.

Leanna also sensed that the woman meant every word of her veiled threat. If she wanted to stay here, she would have to give in. "Thank you, Sister Emily, for making that clear. I will be dressed in a few moments."

The woman's green eyes sparkled with triumph. Now that she was satisfied of winning, her lips curved into a dimpled smile. "Good."

Leanna watched the woman leave, noting the swing

of her narrow hips beneath her staid Shaker gown and the toss of her head as she walked. Leanna wondered how this attractive young woman fit in here, and why she would choose such a life for herself. It was obviously not her sweet, peaceful nature that brought her here.

Leanna quickly made her bed and hung her few items of clothing on the pegs around the wall. Then she walked down the stairs to where Sister Emily was waiting impatiently.

"We must hurry to breakfast or we shall be late for morning prayer," she said, turning to lead the way outside in the frigid predawn air.

Leanna followed the woman out into the darkness and down the frozen road. All the large houses along the way were brightly lit, and she could see through some of the windows the bustle of the occupants as they went about setting their rooms in order for the day.

Sister Emily walked quickly, and Leanna had to struggle to keep up. At the far end of the street Emily turned without speaking and walked up several steps to a large house fashioned out of the same brown brick as the trustees' house. There were two white doors at the center of the house, and Sister Emily chose the one on the right.

Turning to Leanna, she said, "Women always enter the house through the right door and use the stairway on the right of the house."

"How odd," Leanna said, more to herself. "But what's the purpose?"

Emily stopped and looked at her haughtily. "A symbolic separation of men and women. There is no cohabitation here. Even those who come to us as a family are separated. The Believers practice a doctrine of celibacy."

Leanna's mouth flew open, but she quickly clamped her lips together, attempting to suppress the words that threatened to tumble out.

"By being celibate, one places oneself in a position of absolute surrender to God's will."

She motioned for Leanna to follow her down the wide hallway toward the back of the house. There were bare wood floors, white walls, and the same deep blue molding and doors as in the trustees' house.

"He that soweth to the flesh, shall of the flesh reap corruption; and he that soweth to the Spirit, shall of the Spirit reap life everlasting," Emily quoted.

Out of Emily's view, Leanna rolled her eyes at the woman's religious zeal.

There were two doors into the large dining room. Positioned in the hall between the two doors was an enormous grandfather clock which now chimed the half hour. The men and women were being seated at the long gleaming pine tables, with the men on the left and the women on the right.

The delicious aroma of bacon and hot bread drifted from the kitchen into the dining room. Soon women came through the doors carrying platters of food, which they placed on each table.

There were no children in the West family house, and only a small number of people altogether—no more than six or eight men and about the same number of women.

The women glanced at Leanna with shy welcoming smiles. Even some of the men gazed at her curiously, although they quickly turned their attention back to their food. There was little talking, and the only noise was the sound of tableware against the plain white dishes and sometimes a polite, whispered, "Pass the salt, please, Sister."

Leanna sat across from Sister Emily. Leanna was hungry, but watchful as well, for she did not want to breach any etiquette and insult the family at her first meal.

There seemed to be a great abundance of food, which was unusual now in some parts of the South. Leanna knew that these people were well known for their industrious nature, though. They raised beautiful, well-tended crops, and their fat, healthy livestock was always in great demand. She could see that they had profited well by their hard work.

Leanna found the food delicious. She could certainly understand why Jimmy and Trey had been so anxious to eat here. There were bacon and eggs, grits, gravy, several kinds of baked fruit, and hot biscuits and butter. Leanna ate until she was a bit embarrassed. No one seemed to notice; all the women at her table were hearty eaters. It made her wonder exactly what arduous chores were to follow.

After breakfast she again followed Emily back out onto the road. This time they were accompanied by the others of the house. Ahead of them she could see other residents walking from their houses down the roadway and sidewalks toward a large white frame building in the center of the village. Its many windows were aglow with lamplight.

Leanna moved with the others into a large room that took nearly the entire lower floor of the building. There were rows of wooden benches, two sets separated by an aisle, facing the front of the room. Everyone seated themselves quietly, and Leanna took a moment to look around the room and study the people there. They looked no different from those in any other church, except for their dress and for the fact that, again, the men seated themselves on the left side and the women on the right.

Emily went toward the back of the room, and Leanna found a seat. She soon became aware that someone was watching her. She glanced to her right and into the curious gaze of a small woman, perhaps sixty years old. Leanna smiled and looked away, not sure what was permitted here in the way of conversation, or if she should even approach another person first. She certainly had a lot to learn.

She turned slightly and looked behind her, noticing for the first time two small windows high above each side of the room. Behind one window sat a man, and at the other a woman. Leanna was surprised to see that the woman was Emily McGrath who nodded down at her, as if she should be impressed by the woman's position.

When Leanna turned back to face the front, the little woman beside her giggled beneath her breath.

"The watchdogs," she whispered.

"What are they doing?" Leanna asked.

"Just what I said . . . watching us." The woman did not turn toward Leanna but looked straight ahead. "Brother Jackson watches the men, and Sister Emily watches us."

There was something different about this woman. For one thing she did not seem to favor the quaint speech that Leanna had heard Sister Jane and Sister Emily use. And there was a definite mischievous twinkle in her brown eyes, which made Leanna smile. In fact, she felt an urge now to giggle as she did when she was a child in school.

"I'm not sure how I should act," Leanna whispered.

"Mornin' prayers are usually quiet . . . no shenanigans this early. They sorta have to build up to that. Just watch me and do what I do."

As the tiny woman said, the service was simple and quiet, with a short song that was lovely and soothing, and several prayers that seemed to drag on endlessly.

Before dismissal, Brother Levi Wilhite, the trustee who had greeted her last night, stepped to the front of the room.

"I am happy to announce the arrival of Brother Andre Bomberg from Sweden, who will take charge of our orchards. Brother Andre is a horticulturist of great skill, and he will no doubt bring our trees to great fruition. For this we give thanks to God."

The Swede stood and made a small stiff bow. He was an older man, though strong and hearty looking. His thinning hair was silver, as were his bushy eyebrows.

The room resounded with amens, and then Brother Levi continued.

"I am also pleased to announce the arrival of Sister Leanna, who has been assigned to the West family dwelling." Brother Levi nodded toward Leanna as many of the members turned to greet her with smiles.

"I am also saddened to announce that Lydia and Mary Sechrest have gone back into the world, and ask that we pray for the silly lambs lest they come unprepared upon wolves."

Leanna was puzzled. What did he mean, gone back into the world? Were they dead?

"They run off," her seat mate whispered as if she'd

read her thoughts. "Last night, both of 'em run off with a travelin' medicine man."

Brother Levi looked directly at the woman beside Leanna. "If thee will cease thy chatter in the house of God, I shall continue."

The woman beside Leanna grew instantly still.

"It is with sadness and joy that I inform you that Sister Rebecca Green passed this morning in the Center family infirmary, where she has been for the past week. Her funeral will be celebrated tomorrow morning. You are now dismissed to go to your duties."

Leanna followed the others outside and stood for a moment on the steps, unsure if she should wait for Sister Emily or not. It was cold, and her breath made little clouds of vapor in the air. She sensed someone at her side and looked down to see the tiny woman who had sat next to her.

Leanna noted again the twinkling brown eyes and softly lined face. The hair that peeped from beneath her bonnet was thick and wiry. She could tell that it had once been black but was now streaked liberally with gray.

"How do you do?" the woman said. "I'm Polly Wilhite."

Leanna smiled at her, grateful for someone to talk to. Then the name the woman had used registered in her mind. She looked at her for a moment. "The man who just spoke, Mr. Wilhite. Are you? . . ."

"His wife? Yes, I'm sorry to say I am." The woman's lips tightened, and she seemed angry.

"Oh," Leanna said, thinking to herself that the two did not seem to suit each other. "He seems like a very nice man."

"He's an old fool!" the woman said. "I swear I

reckon the man's grown senile in his old age. We gave up the prettiest farmland God ever made, over on the Kentucky River. Bottomland, good pastureland." Polly gave a small grunt and clucked her tongue, looking off into the distance thoughtfully.

"How long have you been here, Sister Polly?"

"Goin' on five years now. We came here in fifty-eight. And you don't have to call me Sister. Just because I live here with these people don't mean I've taken up their silly ways."

Leanna smiled, knowing she'd been right in her assessment of the woman before. She didn't belong here any more than Leanna did.

"Here comes your keeper, honey," Polly whispered.

Leanna turned to see Sister Emily walking from the meetinghouse toward them.

"Sister Polly," the blond woman said, "I'm glad thee waited. And I'm happy thee has met Sister Leanna, for she will be moving into thy room. I'd like thee to teach her the sewing chores."

Polly turned to Leanna, looking genuinely pleased. "Good."

"Please accompany Sister Leanna to the trustee's house and help her gather her belongings. I will wait for thee at home."

Leanna felt an immediate lifting of her spirits, just for the freedom from Emily McGrath's company. She had always done as she pleased with her time, and this forced observance of all her activities was not going to be easy.

Leanna and the diminutive Polly wrapped their capes closely around themselves and started off into the winter wind. The older woman's step was quick and nimble, and Leanna was barely able to keep up.

"Levi told me of your father, lass. I'm sorry. This war's an ugly thing."

"I'm going to find him," Leanna said, her lips pressed together with determination. "I don't believe he's done what they accused him of."

"Well, you just be careful. There are a lot of men who do foolish things when they begin to argue about the war. And they will regard your father as an enemy whether he's guilty or not. And that, little lady, puts you in danger, too."

"That's what I've been told is the reason for my being here although I can't see the sense in it."

"Ain't no sense! Some men don't need no reason to do the things they do. Besides, you're alone now, and that in itself should be enough to make you cautious."

"I will be. I intend to stay here until I find out where my father is. One of the officers stationed at the Sutton place will help me, I think."

"Major Slayton?" Polly asked, her eyes twinkling up at Leanna.

"You know him?"

"'Course I know him. We take care of his horses. And he's a friend. He's here often, as a matter of fact, and well thought of too, I might add."

"I see." She followed Polly up the stairs and gathered her belongings.

"If you had a lick of sense, girl, you'd leave this place, latch onto your major, and never let him out of your sight."

"He's not *my* major!" Leanna said. "I hardly know him, except as a friend of my father's."

Polly smiled and turned her head to one side, studying Leanna's face closely.

"That may be. But just remember, the war's took

many a young man away never to return. Be a shame if you never got to know a man like him, just because of bein' on two different sides of the war.''

Leanna stared at the woman, wishing she weren't quite so nosy or so perceptive.

"Well, anyone who would let such a thing stand in the way of a man and woman would have to be a mighty silly girl. Don't you think?'' Polly said.

"There's more than that standing between us, I think,'' Leanna said. "I have my pride. Besides, there's a possibility that Major Slayton had something to do with what happened to my father.''

"Oh, I doubt that, girl,'' the older woman said. "Yes indeed, I doubt that. He's a man of honor. You just remember I told you that, eh? And as for pride, well, pride is a mighty lonesome bed partner.''

Leanna blinked her eyes at the woman. She didn't think anyone had ever spoken to her so bluntly before, not even Mrs. Macky. But she was not offended. If anything, she found the woman's spirit invigorating.

"Well, we'd best be goin','' Polly said. "Sister Emily will be in a real snit if we keep her from her high and mighty duties.''

They were in the trustees' house now, and Leanna looked around the room where she'd found warmth and comfort last night. She wasn't sure what would happen now, but she knew she'd never been so alone or so unsure in her life. In only a few short weeks her life had changed from one of parties and carefree days and nights to this—to the staid Shaker existence, with people she did not know and could not trust. She knew, with a sudden, burning pain in her heart, that she could not go back. Her life would never be the same again.

14

As Leanna and Polly hurried back along the road toward the West family house, the sun began to brighten the sky to the east. Now Leanna could see the heavy frost that sprinkled bright little stars upon the ground and the trees.

"Oh," she whispered, her steps beginning to slow as she took in the beauty of the scene.

The sun touched the highest limbs of the bare trees and turned the frost to sparkling gold. It glistened on the grass and fence tops like a tinsel decoration on a Christmas tree.

Polly smiled at the girl and slowed her steps to match. This was a morning worth seeing, and it pleased her that her new roommate appreciated it.

"Pleasant Hill is indeed a beautiful place. There's no denying that," the older woman said.

"I don't think I've ever seen anything so lovely," Leanna whispered almost reverently.

"Remember that in the weeks to come, dear," Polly said. "If we learn to see the beauty around us then we are never alone and we're never bored."

Walking through the right-hand door of the house that would now be her home, Leanna felt the warmth of the dwelling surround her. Emily was there, as promised, sitting on a long wooden bench beneath the staircase.

"Ah, thee has returned. Good, we have much to do today. Polly, please direct our new sister to her room."

With a roll of her eyes at the woman's stilted formality, Polly opened the first door to the right of the hallway and motioned Leanna inside.

The room they entered was large and airy, with long windows and wide windowsills. Everything was spotless, and there were no extra touches to make it appear homey. But it was not a cheerless room. In fact, Leanna found it quite pleasant.

Instead of the small black stoves she had seen in the other rooms, this one contained a small fireplace with an arched top. There were still hot coals burning, and Polly went immediately to place more wood in the opening until the embers began to crack and snap into life once more.

There was one small bed in the room, and near the large windows were several dress forms, one with a man's jacket on it. On a nearby table sat head forms on which bonnets and white cotton prayer caps were perched.

Polly motioned her toward another door and pointed out a separate bedroom, much smaller than the one they were in. "This was Mary Sechrest's room," she told Leanna. "And in the closet there are several of her dresses. You'd be about her size, so if you like, you can have them."

Leanna felt a great deal of relief at having her own bedroom. She had not expected it. The room was tiny, hardly big enough for anything other than a bed and small dresser. There was one large window, which looked across the yard to the next dwelling.

"This room gets cold at night, so you'll need all those quilts there in the cupboards," Polly said. "I know it's not what you're used to, child."

"No, it's fine, really," Leanna said with a smile. It was a change from her own luxurious bedroom, but she had not even thought of that at first. Macky would never believe it.

Emily followed behind them. "For the time being, Sister Leanna, thee will be an apprentice to Sister Polly. She is the most skilled seamstress at Pleasant Hill and can teach thee much. After a while thy duties may change. And when spring arrives, all the women and men help with the planting, the gardening, and later the gathering of crops. Have you any questions?" The woman's green eyes were cold and clear as glass.

"No, ma'am. No questions," Leanna said. She only wondered why Emily did not like her.

"Good. Work hard and God will reward thee with His blessing. Thee may ask Polly about our community, but in spiritual matters thee must come to me."

"Yes, ma'am," Leanna replied, remembering Macky's words of caution about behaving herself.

With a curt nod, the woman left. Both Polly and Leanna breathed a sight of relief as the door closed behind her.

"Come and sit before the fire for a moment," Polly

said. "I have the best job in the village because there's no one to look over my shoulder as I work."

"I think that will suit me as well," Leanna said, settling herself into one of the small, delicate rocking chairs.

Polly took a basket of sewing and began to work as they rocked before the fire. "I suppose this is very different than you're used to?"

"Oh, yes, much different," Leanna replied, watching the flames thoughtfully.

"One does get used to it," Polly said. "But I still miss my home, especially the kitchen. Oh, how I loved my old kitchen with its big black stove, the hiss of the kettle in the wintertime. There was a big porch right outside, and I could hear Levi come and tramp around in his boots before he came into the kitchen. He even built a big cupboard in the kitchen for me, where I kept staples and my churn. I always loved to churn." Her voice had grown wistful and quiet, and Leanna could hear the longing in it.

"I suppose I've never learned to do very much," Leanna admitted. "Other than study. I was good at that. But I never learned to do chores. We had servants for that." She looked at Polly rather apologetically.

"Nothin' wrong with that, child. There's many a chore I'd give over to someone else if I could." She continued to rock. "No, living here ain't all bad. There's plenty of good food, and women are treated the same as men. I suppose you've already noticed that with Sister Emily and Sister Jane. Women here have the same rights as a man. Can even have the same position in the church. Now, that ain't something you see out in the world."

"No."

"Negroes, too," Polly continued. "The Believers have been known to buy slaves just for the purpose of settin' 'em free. Why, they were doin' that while that tall, skinny Abe Lincoln was still a lad at his mama's knee."

"I didn't realize that."

"Oh, yes," Polly said, intent on her sewing. "Don't be put off by the likes of Sister Emily. She's a rare one. The Believers are good people, the kindest, hardest workin', most God-fearin' people you'll ever meet. Yep, you'll be treated good here. 'Course a young, pretty girl like yourself might want somethin' better than to be treated good, huh?"

"Right now I don't know what I want, or what I'll do next."

"Give yourself time, child. Give yourself time. Your world will tilt back to the right again soon."

Leanna smiled. She was lucky even to have found this feisty, wise little woman.

That evening, after prayers, several people stood outside the meetinghouse, talking. They were obviously worried about the renegades who had shot up the village.

"Haven't thee heard?" one of the women asked another. "The soldiers are moving here from the Sutton place, moving tomorrow, as a matter of fact."

Forgetting that she hardly knew these people, Leanna walked over to them and joined the conversation. "Are you sure?" she asked.

"Yea, Sister," the woman replied. "Brother Levi told us earlier. He seemed to think our worries will be over once they're here."

Leanna's heart was beating furiously. She had tried not to think of Alex and his men, or of how much she missed them. But now she felt joyous, as if part of her family were coming back to her.

Her feet barely seemed to touch the ground as she walked back to the West family house. Polly, who went with her, glanced at the girl from time to time, and a big smile lit her face as she recognized the reason for Leanna's happiness.

The next morning, snow was falling heavily, blanketing the tall houses and the rolling land around them under a white, sparkling stillness. But even the snow and frigid temperature could not keep Leanna from walking to the meetinghouse.

After prayers she looked across the village toward a small yellow house. Polly had said that the soldiers' new headquarters would be there. Leanna's heart skipped a beat as she saw the men on horseback just coming into sight from across the meadow. The snow was so wet and thick that she could not make out their features, but she recognized the big gray horse at the front and the tall man sitting on its back.

"We'd best get out of this weather, child," Polly said, her gaze following Leanna's to the string of riders.

As they hurried home, Leanna's eyes moved time and again to the small yellow house and the men that surrounded it until finally she could no longer see them. Even if she could, what made her think that Alex would want to talk to her? After the way he'd acted at the river, she was certain that he had been happy to be rid of her.

The snow continued on and off for days, hindering outdoor work and activities. Leanna saw Alex only from a distance, and even then she wasn't sure if he recognized her.

The next week was a difficult one for Leanna. The

work itself was not so demanding, but she was not used to rising at five in the morning and going to bed at dark. By the third day, though, she began to adjust and grow tired shortly after supper.

She learned a lot from Polly about sewing, and about the village. Since the woman was an admitted gossip, she also learned about the residents at Pleasant Hill.

Leanna had become acquainted with several of the women in the West family house. One was a young woman, not much older than Leanna. Her name was Rachel Harris, and she was expecting her first child. Rachel told Leanna that her husband had gone to join the army, hoping to use the money he received to help with their expenses. But she had not heard from him since he'd left and she feared that he had died on some battlefield, alone and unnoticed.

So Rachel came to Pleasant Hill. Other than that initial time, Rachel never mentioned her husband again. Leanna suspected the girl and her husband had had problems, and that perhaps Rachel had even run away from him.

There was much talk of the war, and it made Leanna fear for her father and how she was going to find him. She thought several times of going to Alex, but she hesitated, afraid he might reject her.

One morning, when Leanna woke, she found Polly huddled before the fire. A shawl was wrapped around her shoulders, and a quilt lay across her knees. She was shivering nonetheless, and her face was pale and drawn.

"What's wrong?" Leanna asked, going to her knees before the older woman.

"Oh, nothing, child," Polly replied in a scratchy voice. "Just a cold, I think. I'll be fine."

Leanna touched the woman's forehead. It seemed hot, as if she might have a touch of fever.

"Shall I go to the infirmary for medicine?" Leanna asked.

Still shivering, Polly glanced at her and then nodded with a tight little smile. "Maybe so," she said. "Maybe some of Sister Charity's elderberry tea would be just the thing."

"I'll go right after prayers," Leanna said. She knew what reprimand she would receive from Sister Emily if she missed them.

As Leanna turned to go, Polly called to her. "And maybe a few of the sister's horehound candy drops for my throat."

Leanna smiled at the woman, knowing how much she liked sweets of any kind.

"All right. I'll be back as soon as I can. You sit right there before the fire and keep warm."

She could hardly wait till morning prayers were finished. She had worked hard since coming to Pleasant Hill and had had little time for herself. Just being outside alone would be a pleasure. She remembered Polly's words about the beauty around them, and she knew the truth of it.

The snow still lay in deep mounds on the ground, but today the sky was clear and she thought they would see the sun later. It was hardly light enough yet to tell.

Leanna left the meetinghouse and cut across the road to one of the stone pathways. All the walkways had been cleared, and this one led directly to the huge Center house, where Sister Charity's infirmary was.

Leanna had no idea that anyone else would be out in the cold so early and was paying little attention to anything except the snow. Suddenly, as she turned a corner behind one of the outbuildings, someone loomed in the dim light before her. It was too late to stop, and her feet continued to slide across the icy walkway until she collided with the man.

Her bonnet fell to the ground, and flame gold hair spilled down her back. In her haste, Leanna had not pinned her hair, knowing that she would be back in her room soon. She felt strong hands grip her shoulders to steady her as she looked up with stunned surprise into the intense black gaze of Alex Slayton.

"Alex," she whispered breathlessly, unable to believe that he was finally here before her, as real and strong as she remembered.

In one quick movement he swung her around until her back was against the building and they were both out of the stinging wind. And out of the sight of the ever-watchful Believers.

Leanna felt as if all the breath had left her body, as if her bones had simply melted away. She leaned back against the wooden siding of the building, letting it support her as she gazed up at him.

He seemed stunned as he continued to look down at her, his breath coming quickly. Alex knew that he should break away and try to appear cool and unmoved by the sight of her. But he simply couldn't. It had happened too quickly for him to pretend indifference.

"How are you?" he asked, his voice hoarse with emotion.

"Fine . . . I'm fine. . . ." She wasn't even aware of what she was saying, and neither of them could seem to look away.

Alex had missed her. He'd never have imagined how much. She'd been here only a few days, and already it seemed like months. Many times he had regretted his coolness to her that day at the river crossing, and he had wanted to come to her. But how could he?

Now, finally, he was able to drink in every inch of her lovely face and the sparkling golden red hair that fell about her shoulders. Her pink lips were parted as she watched him, her green eyes searching his own as she continued to stare at him. There was no anger on her face now, no resentment toward him. He thought for a moment that he detected even a welcoming light in her eyes.

There seemed suddenly to be no one else around them. He thought nothing of where they were or who might be watching. For as he stepped closer and his body pressed hers against the building, he didn't care about anything or anyone except Leanna and the temptation of her lips.

With a low murmur of pleasure he took her face between his hands. She was breathing in short little gasps that pushed her breasts against him. And without knowing why, he was kissing her, tasting with shocked delight the sweet warmth of her mouth and hearing with elation her own sighs of pleasure.

His arms moved downward of their own will, touching the soft curves of her body until his hands found her waist beneath the cape. His hands tightened, nearly encircling her as he pulled her against him. He had to remind himself of how small she was, lest he hold her too tightly. He could not seem to get close enough to satisfy his need to touch her, to feel every delicious inch of her body.

Leanna moved her arms round his neck, reveling in the feel of his body against hers, in the intensity with which he held her and caressed her. There was a hunger in him that she always suspected and yet never dreamed she would know. With that same hunger her fingers tangled in his thick black hair as she pulled his head down harder, returning his kiss with abandon.

The cold wind of winter melted away, and Leanna felt as if every inch of her were on fire. Never in her wildest dreams would she have imagined the way she felt. She would have done anything he asked, would have lain with him in the snow without question if only he asked it.

When Alex finally pulled away, his black eyes reflected the heat Leanna felt. She marveled at such a thing, that a man like Alex could want her as much as she did him.

They studied each other for a moment, not speaking, as Alex caressed her face with something akin to awe. He had been right about her, about the wildness hidden inside her. She was like the wind, the raging spring rains or the turbulent Kentucky thunder, and she was just as dangerous.

"Someone will see us," he said softly, pulling back, all too aware of the danger for her.

"I don't care," she whispered.

"God," he murmured, moving back against the warmth of her deliciously soft body. She was looking at him in a way he had never dreamed possible, and it was burning away all the resistance he'd managed to build between them. His mind told him it was dangerous, being this close to her, touching her, but his heart told him something entirely different. And he found that the danger only made it more exciting and more impossible to resist.

He wasn't sure later what would have happened if they had not heard footsteps coming toward the outbuilding. He only knew that at the moment he didn't care, and neither did Leanna. That realization left him feeling dazed and surprised.

He moved away from her as two of the sisters came around the house onto the walkway near them. They nodded and smiled at Leanna, but their smiles widened when they saw Alex. He and his men were heroes in the village now and considered to be the Believers' own protectors.

"Good morning, Major," the women said together.

"Sisters," Alex said with a polite smile.

He and Leanna watched as the two women walked on toward another part of the village. It was just long enough for Alex to compose himself and remind himself of his responsibility to Senator McNairy and his beautiful daughter.

When he turned to Leanna, her face was sweetly open and full of expectation. It was the happiest he'd ever seen her. It made him hate himself all the more for doing what he knew was right.

"I'm sorry, Leanna. I should never have let that happen," he said quietly, hardly able to look at her.

When he saw the light fade from her lovely jade green eyes, it was like an arrow to his heart. He clamped his teeth together, shutting off the words he longed to say to her.

"But . . . I . . . I don't understand," she said, her lips trembling slightly.

"There's nothing to understand. You looked so beautiful, falling into my arms that way and . . . I'm just a man, after all."

"Oh," she said, her eyes shooting sparks at him. "Just a man. And by that I'm supposed to assume you simply can't control yourself around a woman?"

"Something like that. . . ."

"Oh, really? Then why didn't you drag one of the sisters behind the building and kiss her? Can you tell me that? And don't look at me as if I'm a child! You can't tell me I mean nothing to you, Alex, not after today, not after the way you—" Her voice broke as her small body trembled with fury.

"Leanna, don't do this."

"No, I want you to tell me. Go ahead, tell me you don't care about me."

"I can't," he said, stepping further away from her. "I do care about you, a great deal. I promised your father that I—"

"Oh, don't! Don't you dare use my father as an excuse between us, Alex. I can't bear it."

Alex took a deep breath and clenched his fists, lest they reach for her and pull her once more into his arms.

"All right." Why would the girl never listen to reason?

"Have you learned anything about my father?" she asked suddenly as if it were an accusation. "Or is there some reason you don't want to help him?"

"What do you mean by that?" He was annoyed with himself as much as he was with her. He should never have let his emotions bring him to this point.

"I think you know perfectly well what I mean." Leanna hardly knew why she was doing this. It was not the way she had meant to go about it, but somehow her anger and pain made her want to lash out at Alex, and this was the only way she knew how. "I think you had something to do with my father's arrest."

"You what?" His jaw tightened visibly, and he put his hands on his hips, taking a long, deep breath and expelling it slowly. "I swear to you, I had nothing to do with your father's arrest. And I've already sent a message to headquarters. As soon as I hear anything I'll let you know."

She stared at him for a long while, as if she wanted to say more. Alex saw the pain in her eyes, and it made him feel like the lowest kind of bastard. He cursed himself for giving in so quickly to his instincts. It was not something he could afford to do, not with this girl.

"Leanna, I'm sorry."

"For what? For my father? For kissing me today? For what?" Her lips trembled as she spoke.

"For kissing you. It was impulsive. I . . . I had no intention of letting you think—"

"It was nothing," she said quickly, blinking away her tears. "Nothing. After all, it was only a kiss."

She turned and ran toward the Center house, unmindful now of the icy pathway or of the drifts of snow.

She had made a fool of herself, had acted like an impulsive little girl. And his only explanation was that he had not meant to lead her on. He actually felt sorry for her!

But he *had* held her tightly and whispered her name as if he couldn't bear to let her go. He had looked into her eyes and felt the spark between them, just as she had. He had felt all the things she had, hadn't he?

Alex watched her run way and shook his head trying to catch his breath. He hoped the effects of the cold air would calm the unsteady pounding of his heart and cool the desire that still burned deep within him, but he was afraid it would never go away.

"Damn it!" he muttered as he watched her run into the huge house.

15

Leanna brought the elderberry tea and the horehound drops back to Polly and spent the next few days caring for the woman, taking it upon herself to complete the sewing that Polly was so anxious about. She told no one about her encounter with Alex, not even Polly.

Only Leanna knew how often he was in her thoughts. She was almost certain now that he had not been involved in her father's arrest, for his eyes had filled with such pain when she accused him. Perhaps she had not believed it all along. She had only said it that morning as a reflex to strike out at him.

She had not even offered him her condolences on the loss of Lieutenant Hampton. She'd been too busy, as usual, thinking about herself. She remembered with guilt how her friends had often teased her about her selfishness. Was it true? It was something she'd never given much thought to until now.

Leanna and Alex saw each other often, but they barely spoke, and only then because they were usually in the company of someone else and needed to pretend politeness. He looked at her with sad, brooding eyes, and it irritated her that he could make her feel so guilty for simply wanting him.

She still found herself searching for his tall, handsome figure whenever the soldiers were out, and after she spotted him she would come back to the sewing room and throw herself into her work.

Polly was amazed at the change in the girl and swore she'd never seen anyone do better needlework than Leanna.

Several days later, as Leanna was leaving the meetinghouse after morning prayers, she dropped her prayer book on the front steps. Before she could retrieve it a man's hand reached down and scooped it up. She straightened and looked into the brown eyes of the man she'd seen upstairs with Sister Emily. The watchdog, Polly had called him.

He was short, only a couple of inches taller than Leanna's five foot three. His face was wide with round, heavy contours, his body stocky. His thinning hair was dark, almost black, as was his thick, heavy beard. Round wire-rimmed glasses almost hid his small, close-set eyes.

As he handed her the book, there was an odd look on his face, one she did not immediately recognize. His round cheeks had turned a dark crimson.

She'd seen the man before, many times. He, too,

lived in the West family dwelling. She had seen him staring at her from the men's table at supper, but he had never approached until today.

"Thank you," she said, smiling politely as she took the book from his hand.

Before he turned to walk away, his broad, callused hand touched hers and lingered as he gazed directly into her startled eyes. It was then that she recognized the look on his face, and it brought a sick feeling to the pit of her stomach. His eyes were hot and hungry, even ugly as he stared at her and allowed his gaze to roam quickly over her body. Leanna shuddered.

"Brother Jackson," a voice called from behind them.

The bearded man turned then, and just for a moment Leanna saw him smile at someone, the lustful look fading from his heavy face. Now his eyes were directed up the stairs to the woman who'd called his name, Sister Emily McGrath.

Some alarm sounded deep within Leanna's head. She remembered now that the two of them were often together. Then again, he was an elder and well respected in the village.

She couldn't be sure what it was that bothered her. Perhaps it was the furtive way his eyes had moved over her, or the way he quickly disguised his look when Sister Emily appeared. Now, Emily's resentment and anger were obvious as she stared at Leanna. Leanna thought she even saw a spark of hatred in the depths of those cold, green eyes.

By the next day she had forgotten the incident. She didn't even mention it to Polly. They were both very busy making the lightweight summer clothes that the Believers would be needing by spring.

As they sat before the fire, Leanna thought it was the

most pleasant morning she'd had. She felt almost happy here with Polly, and even though she had to abide by the strict rules, she did not mind so terribly.

"The Union army attacked Fort Henry, I hear," Polly said as she rocked back and forth.

Leanna did not reply, but a worried frown appeared between her brows. "What do you think will happen now?"

"Well, Levi says there's been a buildup of Confederate forces that want to regain the State. And the Union will have a show of force, no doubt. Maybe that's all it will be—just show, no fighting."

"Do you really think so? Or are you only trying to make me feel better?"

"And why would that make you feel better, child? Your father is no longer here. I'm sure they have taken him to one of the Confederate prisons. So you're not worried about his safety. And I don't think you're the kind of girl to worry unduly about your own." There was a question in her sparkling brown eyes as she looked across at Leanna.

"I grew quite fond of Jimmy and the . . . the other soldiers," she replied.

Polly laughed. "Well, then, you might be interested to know that Jimmy and his friends are still safe, and still here. They didn't leave in the middle of the night or anything."

"How do you know?"

"Why, because I saw them taking the horses toward the blacksmith shop just before we came in this morning."

Leanna's hands fell to her lap, the bonnet she was stitching forgotten as her eyes sought the window toward the road.

"Well, you won't find 'em standin' outside."

Leanna laughed self-consciously. She had not intended to be so obvious. It was Jimmy she longed to see, she told herself, even as she tried to banish the vision of black eyes and ebony hair from her mind. She had not seen any of them in days, and she would love to talk to Jimmy. She often thought of how much better he could make her feel about Alex. After all, he and Trey seemed to know him better than anyone.

"You know, my dear," Polly began in an innocent voice. "Brother Jackson, the blacksmith, is a member of this household."

Leanna frowned and glanced at the woman. "Yes, I know that."

"I just remembered that I've lost his shirt size. I don't suppose you would care to walk over to the barn and inquire about it?"

Leanna frowned at Polly. She wasn't sure if the woman was unusually perceptive or if Leanna herself was only too transparent. Regardless, Polly seemed to know exactly what was on Leanna's mind.

Impulsively, Leanna stood up and dropped her sewing into the chair. Then she frowned, picked up the bonnet again, and sat back down.

Polly looked at her oddly. "Well, whatever's the matter, child? You look like you've lost your best friend."

"I just hate to go looking like this, wearing these clothes."

She ran her hands down the drab gray woolen dress and plucked at the white muslin collar that was tied primly at her neck.

"I don't know what else you'd be wearing, since that's all you've got."

"I know."

"Besides, I thought you were gettin' over that kind of thinkin'."

"What do you mean?"

"I mean," Polly looked at her pointedly, "that when you were a belle in Lexington and wore all those fancy clothes, did it make people like you better? From what you've told me, your friends deserted you soon as they heard about your papa anyhow. So what reward does dressin' nice have? Makes a woman feel good, I know that."

"But—"

"Don't make people like you no better. Jimmy liked you, and the major, too, and you probably looked pretty ragged those two days from what you've said."

Leanna smiled. "Pretty bad, yes."

"You look nice now, and you look healthy. What's better than that?"

Leanna sighed. "How did you get to be so smart, Polly?" She stood up again and turned to get her cape.

Polly snorted. "Well, it weren't livin' with Levi Wilhite, that's for sure. That man ain't got the sense God give a goose!"

Both of them laughed. Leanna knew that Polly still missed her farm and had not given up hope of returning to it one day. The woman still resented her husband for having brought her here to live.

Leanna looked back from the doorway at the tiny woman and wished with all her heart that she had the power and the money to return Polly to her beloved farm on the wide Kentucky River.

"I won't be gone long," Leanna said as she left.

Polly did not look up but nodded and continued her work. "It's a lovely day for a walk. Take child. Take your time."

16

Leanna walked up the stone sidewalk beside the picket fence that ran past the houses. She felt an eagerness that she had not felt since that day with Alex. The morning was almost balmy, with a hint of sweetness in the breeze that made her think of spring.

She turned to walk by the small yellow house where Alex lived now. The road leading to the barn was narrow, just wide enough for a wagon. Neat white fences ran along each side of it.

It felt good to be outside enjoying a little freedom. She passed a cluster of smaller buildings that included the granary, the meat house, and the icehouse. Beyond a row of trees she could see the washhouse, where the families of the great Center dwelling did their laundry.

The large black barn was well away from the village, far from the other buildings. Across from it were the toolshed and wagon house. Leanna's heart began to pound with anticipation as she approached.

Would Alex be there? How could she let him know that she wasn't still angry about the day he had kissed her? Suddenly she felt shy and self-conscious—a feeling she'd rarely experienced in her life at Lexington.

There were several horses outside in the corral, but she did not see the big gray stallion that belonged to Alex.

Just as she started to go into the barn, she had a vision of someone coming around the corner. Actually he was only a blur as he almost ran into her.

"Jimmy!" Leanna exclaimed, backing away to look into the startled blue eyes of the young soldier. "Oh, Jimmy, I'm so happy to see you." Without thinking she reached out her arms to him and was welcomed by his delighted laughter as he swung her off the ground in an exuberant embrace.

"Oops," he whispered, setting her back down on the ground. "I forgot you're a Shaker miss now and not given to hugs from young men."

Leanna laughed, so happy to hear his bantering, "Oh, I've missed you Jimmy."

"I've missed you, too," he said, grinning. "Been wantin' to ask how you like it here. Are they treatin' you well? Do you have to work hard?" He reached for her small hands and turned them up to see if she'd grown calluses.

Leanna laughed at his concern. "The only calluses I have are from pushing a needle through cloth. I'm a seamstress."

"Yeah, I know, the major told me. I was only teasin' you. Well, at least now I know who I can come to when I need buttons replaced or patches on my trousers."

"Any time," she said, turning serious. She would do anything to help her dear young Jimmy.

He stepped back and looked at her. His eyes surveyed the dark gray gown that accented her lovely white skin and the bright golden red hair that curled from beneath her bonnet. "Well, you certainly look well," he said with a glint of admiration in his eyes. "You look rested, not so worried as before."

Leanna pointed toward a bench beneath the overhang of the barn roof. "Let's sit and talk for a while before someone finds me and sends me back to my chores." She hesitated for a moment. "You don't have to go already, do you?"

"Oh, no. I'll probably be here most of the day." He walked with her to sit on the wooden bench.

In their happiness to see each other, neither Leanna nor Jimmy noticed the man who stood by the toolshed across the road. He watched them now, his black eyes glinting with envy as Leanna looked up into Jimmy's smiling face. And he had not missed the poignancy of their embrace or Jimmy's clasping of her hands as he turned them over to look at her palms.

Alex had tried his best to avoid Leanna, but he should have known that he could not do it forever while they lived in the same village. Looking at her, he thought she was more beautiful than ever. Even the drab Shaker dress could not dim the creamy loveliness of her complexion or hide the soft, luscious curves of her body.

He remembered the feel of that body even now. He felt an odd lurch in his chest, just as he had when he'd seen her approach the barn earlier. Without thinking he had stepped forward to greet her, but before he could speak Jimmy had come outside, and now Alex did not

have the heart to spoil their obvious delight in each
other.

Besides, how would she react to him after the way
they had parted? They had hardly spoken since that
morning in the snow.

Leanna needed someone like Jimmy to talk to, he
told himself. A young man who still retained his ideal-
ism, who seemed carefree and happy, even in the midst
of a war. Yes, Alex decided, Jimmy Anderson was just
what Leanna needed at the moment.

He stepped back into the shadows of the toolshed,
intent only on finding the hammer that the blacksmith
had sent him for.

Leanna and Jimmy leaned against the black boards of
the barn, enjoying the warmth that the dim winter sun
had left there.

"Is . . . is Alex here today?" Leanna asked.

"Oh, sure. He's here. Want me to get him for you?"

"No, no, don't do that. I was just curious."

"He's changed, you know . . . quieter. I guess he's
worried about Gina."

"I'm sure he is. It must be very hard for him, being
separated from her right now." Leanna looked down at
her hands thoughtfully.

"Bound to be," Jimmy said, reaching down to grasp
a sprig of hay that lay on the ground. "But the major's
not one to complain, or to talk much about his personal
problems. Keeps to himself most of the time."

"I wonder if he's heard any more about my father."

"I don't know. Hasn't mentioned it to me."

"Perhaps you could ask him for me when you see
him again, that is, if you don't mind."

"Well, why don't you ask him yourself?" Jimmy
smiled at her in his teasing way.

She looked at him and saw him pointing across the road toward the toolshed. "He just went across the road there, right before you came." He watched her with a knowing expression on his face.

Leanna looked across the road, her heart already beating heavily at her throat. Just the thought of his being so near was all it took. Her face felt warm, even in the cool air that drifted to them from across the meadows.

Then she looked at Jimmy with doubtful eyes. "Oh, I don't think . . ."

"Go on," he said, pushing lightly against her shoulder. "Gosh, you women can sure get balky on us poor fellows sometimes."

She smiled at him. "I hope we can talk again soon Jimmy."

"Me, too. I'll be close by." He waved the stalk of hay toward her.

Suddenly Leanna felt alive and acutely aware of everything around her—even the sound of her shoes on the sandy road and of the birds flitting about in the meadow.

She hesitated outside the door of the toolshed, rehearsing what she would say, how she would offer her sympathy for Lieutenant Hampton. Should she apologize for her accusations about her father? No, perhaps that was too much.

For a moment she considered turning around and going back to the barn, but only for a moment. He was so close, so accessible, and the thought of not seeing him was worse than her agony over what to say.

The door creaked loudly as she opened it, and a shaft of light fell across the wooden floor. It was dim inside, and she stood there for a second, letting her eyes adjust to the dark.

Alex turned at the sound of the door and looked at Leanna's figure outlined against the light.

"Alex?" she called softly.

He moved from behind a partition, and she saw him vaguely in the shadows.

"I'm here," he said, moving to within a few feet of her.

Tiny particles of dust floated around in the shaft of light from the door, moving between Leanna and Alex like fireflies. She could see his tall outline in the dim room and the play of light across his prominent cheekbones, but his eyes were hidden from her by the shadows.

"Jimmy said you were here," she said, instantly chiding herself for sounding so stupid.

"Yes," he answered with a slight smile. He found her new shyness fascinating and wondered how long it would last.

"How are you?" she asked, moving away from the door and into the shadows with him.

Alex felt as jumpy as a cat, something he could not quite explain. As she approached him, he felt the need to step away from her. But he stood his ground, watching her with shadowed eyes, waiting for her to tell him why she came.

"I . . . I'm sorry about your sister's husband," she said softly. "I meant to tell you before. That day in the . . . when we . . ."

"Thank you." He knew his words sounded more curt than he intended. How could he explain to her the incredible anger he felt at John's death?

A quiet, burning fury made Alex want to shout to the

heavens of the futility of war and the horror of what it did to families, but now was not the time to explain it to Leanna. He doubted she would understand, anyhow. Despite her bravado, what did this young innocent know of war and death?

He turned away from her and picked up the toolbox.

"I understand your sister is still at Bardstown, not far from here." Leanna wondered at the coldness in his voice and the sudden closed look on his face.

"Yes, that's right," he said, stepping to the side to avoid her and to make his way out the door.

"Alex, wait." Leanna placed her hand on his arm. "What's wrong? Are you still angry with me?"

"No," he said quickly. "No, I'm not angry."

The touch of her hand burned, even through the thick sleeve of his jacket. He could smell her clean, sweet scent and see the tiny gold flecks in her emerald eyes as she looked at him.

"I shouldn't have accused you that day . . . about my father. I know you would never do anything to hurt him."

Alex thought he'd never experienced anything like this, the feeling he had whenever she was near. Standing in the darkened room with her so close, he found himself wanting to reach out for her, to pull her against him and kiss her until she was breathless. He felt an actual ache inside for the taste of her again.

He had been holding his breath, and now at his treacherous thoughts he expelled the air from his lungs with a soft grunt.

"Let's step outside," he said. "It's so dark in here I can hardly see you."

If he thought seeing her outside would make him feel better, he was wrong. The morning sun filtered down through hazy clouds and gleamed on her soft skin. The sight of her left him momentarily speechless, and he silently damned himself for his weakness where she was concerned. He had the will and courage to do anything in battle, and yet this petite red-haired girl scared him senseless. He reminded himself that there could be no place in his life for a woman—any woman. Most especially not this one.

"Well?" she asked, looking up at him with a hint of impatience. "I know you have reason to be angry with me. But I am sorry I accused you of betraying my father. I want us to be friends, Alex, but I still feel your anger."

"No, you're wrong," he said. "And if I made you feel that way then, I'm sorry. I was angry, but not with you, never with you, Leanna."

She blushed at his softly spoken words and at the tenderness in his eyes. "Oh," she said, the sting suddenly gone from her eyes. "I thought you were."

"No." He smiled at her, doubting that she knew how he struggled to keep himself in control.

"Alex, I hate to keep asking, but . . ."

"Ask me anything."

"Is there still no word about my father? If only I could write to him."

"I was in Harrodsburg late last night." He withdrew a piece of paper from inside his jacket and handed it to her.

With trembling fingers Leanna opened the folded piece of paper. It fluttered in the wind as she read the short terse message.

Senator Andrew McNairy has indeed been charged with treason by the Confederate States of

America. He was taken by train to a prison near Richmond, Va., which houses spies, deserters, and other prisoners of war.

Leanna looked up at Alex with troubled eyes that brimmed with tears, then continued to read.

Major Slayton, you asked about the facility. I understand it is spacious, since it was an abandoned tobacco factory. The food is abundant and conditions good.

It was signed by the adjutant general for President Jefferson Davis.

Leanna clutched the letter to her breast and gave a small sigh. "It . . . it doesn't sound so terribly bad. Do you think they're telling the truth?"

"Yes, I believe we can trust this man. This prison is probably as good a place as he could have been sent." He looked at her and smiled. "I'm sure that's not much consolation to you right now."

"Actually it is," she said. "More than I would have expected. My life has changed so completely and father's, too, that now even the smallest thing can give me hope. And this message does that. I thank you for your help."

Alex stared at her, wondering at the softness in her voice. What had happened to his little green-eyed spitfire? He had said that she needed discipline, but he found now that he did not want her to become like so many young women, unwilling or unable to speak their own minds and hearts.

"It's nothing," he said softly. "I'll keep in touch with

this man and let you know if your father is moved any-place else."

Alex suddenly looked away from her, and Leanna followed the direction of his gaze. She saw Brother Jackson standing at the barn, watching them. A cold chill ran up the back of her neck and caused her to shiver.

"Brother Jackson is waiting for me," Alex said, looking down at her with some concern. He had seen her reaction to the man and wondered at it. Were they unkind to Leanna? It was something he would have to check into.

Leanna found that she could hardly bear to say goodbye to Alex. She told herself that it was because she had no one else to talk to who understood about her father. She blinked away tears in her eyes and found a familiar lump in her throat, much as she had had as a child when her father would leave for Washington.

Alex walked toward the barn, then suddenly he turned and came back to stand very close to Leanna, almost touching her.

"I've been invited for supper at the West family house," he said, quickly glancing toward the barn.

Leanna's heart threatened to burst with joy, but she tried to look as if his words meant nothing special.

"There are things your father asked me to tell you. Can you meet me directly behind the house at nine o'clock? Do you think you can manage it?" The look in his eyes held a command, even as he asked.

"Yes," she whispered. "I will manage it."

"Good." Then he was gone, walking across the road and into the barn with Brother Jackson Cole.

Leanna had seen the look on the blacksmith's face. It was one of anger and disapproval. She wondered what kind of trouble the Believers would make for someone who broke their rules—especially something as serious as meeting a person of the opposite sex after curfew.

Leanna didn't care what the penalty would be. She only cared about the excitement that burned within her. She would be able to see Alex alone tonight, and nothing would stop her from meeting him. Nothing and no one.

17

Leanna waved to Jimmy before she left and told him that she'd probably see him at supper. He was leading one of the horses from the corral, and he gave a little salute and grinned. She thought she'd never met another young man in her life as good-natured as Jimmy Anderson.

She didn't bother to ask Brother Jackson his shirt size, because she was too embarrassed to go into the barn and ask such a ridiculous question in front of Alex. So she walked slowly back down the narrow road, taking note of every detail around her, delaying the time when she would be back in her room engaged with her sewing duties.

When Leanna came in, Polly did not even bother to ask if she'd seen Major Slayton. She could see it in her dazed green eyes. The girl was practically on a cloud.

Polly smiled and remembered for a moment how it was to be young and attracted to a man for the first time, and the difference it made when it really was a man and not a boy. From what Polly could see, Alex Slayton was certainly that.

Leanna thought she'd never spent a longer day in her entire life. She must have looked up at the little clock on the mantle at least a hundred times.

"Do you think the clock's stopped?" she asked once. Polly only laughed and shook her head, not even missing a stitch.

Finally it was time to put away their work and prepare for supper. Although for Leanna there was not much preparation to be done, considering that powder and rouge were not allowed, and her other dresses were exactly the same as she one she was wearing. But, she told herself, Polly was right: Clothes were not what was important. Alex had not seemed to mind today when he'd looked at her with his glittering dark eyes. He had not even seemed to notice her attire.

She heard the great bell at the Center house begin to ring, echoing down the streets and into every dwelling.

She and Polly were already seated when the blacksmith arrived with his guests. They were made welcome at the men's table with a minimum of fuss. The women at Leanna's table barely glanced across at the men, with one exception.

Sister Emily was watching Jackson Cole and the two men with him. For once her face was open and unguarded, and Leanna saw with surprise that she looked quite beautiful. There was a softer look about her, an admiring look in her green eyes and dimpled smile. She looked almost normal, Leanna thought—or, as the Believers would put it, a woman of the world.

Leanna hardly knew what she was eating, for she was keenly aware of Alex's gaze upon her. No matter how he tried to deny his feelings, Leanna knew that the look in his eyes tonight was only for her. She could feel it, an intimacy that made her skin tingle and her pulse flutter at her throat.

After supper she spoke briefly with Jimmy in the hallway and pointed out where her room was. The young man looked around curiously, glancing up the stairway and beyond to the second floor.

"It's really very nice here, Leanna," he said.

"Yes, it is," she replied. "And I'm not complaining."

"Well, I know it's not the same as home. And I guess they're mighty strict here—no fun or anything."

"Yes," she said, smiling at him.

"Well, who knows? One of these nights when the weather's warm, I might come knockin' at your window and spirit you away for a midnight ride." He had lowered his head, and his voice was but a whisper.

"In that case, I should tell you that my window is the second one." Her voice was equally conspiratorial. "I wouldn't want you to surprise Polly instead."

They both laughed aloud. They could not help it. The vision of Jimmy knocking on Polly's window in the middle of the night was too much to resist.

"Sister Leanna!" Emily McGrath's voice rang out behind them. "Thee knows it is unseemly to entertain a man and to share spirited laughter with him." Emily was no longer smiling but exuded that air of authority she seemed so proud of.

"Yes, I know, but—"

"There can be no explanation. Go to thy room immediately."

"Jimmy is only a friend. Surely I'm allowed to have friends."

"I will decide what is allowed! Thee will do as I say."

"I am not your slave! And I will not—"

"Please, Leanna," Jimmy said. "I'm leaving anyhow. Don't make it hard for yourself." He spoke softly, but there were two bright spots of color on his cheeks. His blue eyes, usually so tranquil, burned with resentment and humiliation.

Leanna's mouth opened and then closed when she saw Jimmy's wink at her. "Just remember what I told you," he whispered. "It might happen sooner than you think."

He was trying to make her feel better by referring to their fantasy midnight ride. She glanced beyond Jimmy to where Alex and Jackson Cole stood talking in the dining room. She did not want to do anything to spoil her chances of meeting Alex later. So she put a bright smile on her face and with a slight curtsy toward Jimmy, said, "Good night, then, Private Anderson."

"Good night," he said with a nod before turning to walk away.

Leanna stared for a moment into the cold green eyes of Sister Emily. Then, with a toss of her head, she turned and let herself into her room. She could feel the animosity of the woman's stare even as she closed the door.

Polly was waiting. "What in the world was that all about?"

"Sister Emily was upset because we were laughing. Can you believe it? Laughter, it seems, is forbidden here! She embarrassed poor Jimmy to death. Oh, I could strangle that hateful woman with my bare hands."

"I'd be careful of Emily if I were you. She's jealous, and she has a lot of power here. In fact, she can seem to do no wrong in the eyes of the elders and the trustees. I swear, I never saw anything like it. She is certainly not the smartest woman I ever met, yet one twinkle of those green eyes and a dimpling of her cheeks and they're ready to hand her the moon." Polly was breathing heavily as she stoked up the fire and moved wood into the fireplace.

"Why do you suppose men are such fools?" she suddenly asked Leanna.

"I don't know. But if all the men here are celibate and supposedly above all that, why then should her looks influence them?"

"Don't ask me, child. I don't understand it. But I'll tell you one thing. You can bet your last dollar that no matter what a man tells himself or even what he tells his God, when it comes to women they're all the same. Now, I'll admit there are many good men here who would not break their covenant of celibacy, but I'll bet you they think about it an awful lot! And women like Emily know how to use that weakness in men, whereas people like you and me, well, we just never learn the knack."

"It's pride," Leanna said. "Any of us could act the way Emily does. It's not a failure to learn, it's just a fierce pride that won't let us behave that way simply for a little authority."

"Why, child, I do believe you're right." Polly nodded her head with approval toward Leanna. The girl was growing up.

Leanna looked at the clock. It was only eight. She had another hour to wait—a long, interminable hour before she could see Alex again.

Both of them sat without talking in front of the warm fire.

"Ah, it's people like Emily that make me long for my own home," Polly said. "I'm gettin' too old to have to worry about everything I say and everything I do. Now, I'm a hard worker, always was. Ain't afraid of work. But there are times when I'd give a pretty penny just to be alone, or to lie upon my soft feather bed in the quiet of my own house and take a nap, even in the afternoon if I've a mind to."

"You really miss your home, don't you?" Leanna asked.

"Yes, I do, child. Yes, I do." Polly began to rock and hum, her bright eyes riveted on the fireplace.

"Who lives there now?"

"Lives there? At the farm, you mean?" Polly stopped rocking.

"Yes. Do you suppose they'd ever sell it back?"

"No one lives there!" There was a flare of anger across Polly's face as she said the words.

"No one? Then? . . ."

"It belongs to the Believers now. Didn't I tell you that? Oh, yes. They believe in what is called community possession of property. They say the Bible teaches the sharing of everything in common."

"You . . . you gave your beautiful farm by the river to the Shakers?" Leanna was stunned.

"I didn't give nothin'! Levi Wilhite, the old fool, he's the one done the givin'." Polly began to rock again, and her lined face crumpled with pain and anger.

"Oh, Polly, I'm sorry. I didn't realize."

"Well, I appreciate your concern. But if sorries would help, I'd have been back home a long time ago. Men rule this world, child. They can do with their wives as they please, and there ain't nobody to gainsay them. So here I am, an old woman with no home and at the mercy of people like Emily McGrath."

"Polly, if I ever go back home, I want you to come with me. The house is outside of the city, and we have enough acreage for horses and gardens. I think you would like it. At least you wouldn't have to answer to anyone."

Polly looked at Leanna, her clear brown eyes brimming with tears. "Well, bless your heart, child. Ain't nobody ever offered me so much before."

"Well, I am. And I mean it." Leanna's own eyes were stinging with tears.

"I know you do," Polly said. She reached across the short span and patted Leanna's hand. "Yes, I know you do. And I'll never forget it."

Leanna stood and glanced impatiently at the clock once more. It was finally nearing nine o'clock.

"Polly, I'm going out at nine. To . . . to meet someone."

Polly looked surprised. "Oh, child, you must be careful. If Emily or the wrong one sees you, they'll send you away for sure. Then where would you go?"

"I don't know. I have nowhere else to go," Leanna said. "But I'll be careful. I won't let anyone see me."

"Listen, have you noticed the big dormer windows on top of the Center dwelling? And the trustees' house?"

"Yes," Leanna answered, picturing the beautiful windows high on the rooftops.

"That's where they watch from. To see if anyone leaves or wanders about at night. You steer clear of those places!"

"Yes," Leanna said. "I will."

"But they could be watching from any of the houses, especially if they suspect you might leave or you might be meeting a young man."

"I'm only going close by, behind the house here."

"Well, you can bet Sister Emily has a watchful eye on you, lass. You're much too pretty not to be watched. It's best if you go out your window and stay close to the house. And come back in the same way."

"All right. And don't worry about me, I'll be fine. If worse comes to worst, I can always go back to my home in Lexington whether papa wishes it or not."

Polly nodded and walked with her to the back bedroom, where they quietly raised the window. Leanna gathered up her skirts and slid smoothly from the windowsill down to the ground.

"I'll leave it unlocked, so you can come back in," Polly whispered. "You just be careful."

The house was big, and it went back for several yards, past other bedrooms, the dining room, and the kitchen. There was still a light on in the kitchen and several lights in the upstairs windows that spread faintly across the lawn. Leanna hugged the brick walls, stooping beneath windows, until she finally reached the rear corner.

She glanced around quickly, and there, beneath the huge cedar tree, was the shadow of a man. The shadow moved, coming toward her until she could make out the hawklike features of his face.

Silently he pushed her gently against the house. Leanna found that she was already trembling from his touch and from the feel of his thigh pressing against her body as he held her still.

"Alex?" she whispered as she saw him peer around the corner.

"Shhh," he said, cupping the palm of his hand lightly over her mouth.

Then she became aware of what he had already heard. It was the sound of voices as two men walked along the sidewalk in front of the house. Soon they heard the closing of a door as the men went inside the house.

Alex slowly withdrew his hand from her mouth, although his body was still pressed against hers. "We need to talk," he said softly, his lips close to her hair. "But not here. What's that building just beyond the cedar tree?"

"It . . . it's the washhouse," she stammered. She was finding it difficult to speak, even to breathe with him so close.

"Come on." He pulled her along by the hand.

They ran across the yard, stopping for a moment beneath the thick brushy limbs of the cedar. Then he pulled her again toward the small washhouse.

The door squeaked as he pushed it open. "Hello?" he said quietly. "Anyone here?"

Leanna sighed when there was no answer and quickly stepped inside. Alex closed and bolted the door.

The pleasant smell of laundry soap and fresh linens surrounded them. Warmth lingered in the room from the boiling pots and the fireplace, where hot coals still burned brightly.

There were two rooms in the small building. The first was for boiling water and washing clothes, and it was also used for dying wool, as evidenced by the long skeins of yarn drying on a wooden rack.

Alex looked into the second room, where various articles of clothing hung, freshly ironed. It also contained a fireplace, and beside it a small flat-topped stove where the irons were heated.

He didn't know why he felt this growing excitement within himself. He'd only come to talk to Leanna about her father. He'd promised the senator that he'd tell Leanna, and he had put it off long enough.

Alex could not let her go on believing that the man was loyal to the Confederacy, for he had no idea what would happen to the senator. He felt that Leanna should be completely aware of what could happen. She had matured some during the past few weeks, and he thought now she could understand.

"Sit here," he said, taking a sheet from one of the laundry baskets and placing it on the floor before the fire.

Leanna had hardly taken her eyes away from him. She had thought so much about this meeting. It was the first time she'd been alone with him, completely alone, since that day in his tent when he had so gently brushed her hair. She removed her cloak and seated herself in front of the fire, where the glow of the coals cast an orange light around them like small flickering candles.

Alex removed his jacket and then the black leather holster she'd seen him wearing that day at the river. Only for a moment did she feel apprehensive about what might happen. What if she were caught here alone in the night with a man? She tried to force her conscience to warn her, to tell her she shouldn't be here, but she could not. Whatever was to happen, whatever his reason for asking her to meet him, she knew she would not say no. That realization set her heart and hands to trembling, even her very soul.

Alex sat with his long legs drawn up and one arm across his knees. He looked at Leanna and saw her shaking, and he thought he'd never seen any woman so beautiful or so appealing.

"Leanna, I need to talk to you about the senator, about your father."

She frowned. This was not what she expected. "What is it? Was there something you didn't tell me today? Is he hurt?"

"No, no, nothing like that. As far as I know the message I received from the adjutant general is correct, and your father is fine."

"Then what?"

"Do you remember the night of your party, the night I was in the study with your father?"

"Yes, of course I do." She watched him carefully. How could she ever forget that night?

"He had called me there to confess what he had done, and to ask me to help you if the Confederates came for him. He wanted me to tell you—"

"No!" she said, pulling back from him. "I told you before, my father has done nothing wrong. There has to be some mistake. He would never betray our neighbors, never!" Her eyes blazed at him in the light of the dying fire.

"Leanna, can't you see . . . would it be so wrong if he fought for the Union, for the country that he loves so well?"

"I don't want to hear this." She came to her feet and reached for her cloak.

But Alex was faster than she, and he, too, was on his feet, catching her from behind and turning her to face him.

"You're not leaving here until you listen to me."

"No, I won't. Why are you doing this, saying these things to me? Do you still think you can make me see how wrong I am to be loyal to the South? All right, I'll admit, I was wrong about some of it, about you and Jimmy, and Trey. But I . . ." She looked away from his dark eyes, not wanting to admit that what he was saying could be true.

She pushed against his chest with her fists, trying to free herself from the grip of his hands. In the struggle her breasts brushed against him, tingling even as she struggled to pull away. She was angry with him, and afraid. Yet her body still responded, betraying her as she fought against him.

"Leanna," he warned, shaking her, trying to ignore the touch of her body against his. "Damn it, Leanna, stop this. I thought you had grown up enough to listen to reason. Stop behaving like a spoiled brat and listen to me."

Instantly she went still, looking straight into the black depths of his eyes. She was struggling to regain her breath and her composure, but she was all too aware of some strange force that she could not fight. It made her want to cling to him, to touch his lips, even in her anger.

"Please," she whispered. She was caught, captivated by his stormy eyes that held her as surely as his hands.

She was afraid of the feelings within her. They were so strong. The warmth that spread through her body left her breasts feeling oddly full and set her legs to trembling. When she licked her dry lips nervously she had no idea how seductive the action appeared to the man who held her.

Alex's mind was in a whirl as he tried to reason with his own emotions, tried to fight the desire that her squirming body had aroused. He reminded himself again that she was an innocent, and in his charge. He told himself that those incredible emerald eyes were not liquid with desire, that every warm, beautiful inch of her body was not trembling for his lovemaking.

But it didn't work. Nothing worked except the instinct that drove him, that had invaded every part of his body since the first time he saw her. He knew now that whatever he'd told himself before, whatever reason he had given for meeting her tonight, it was a lie. *This* was the reason, this need for her, so hot and all-consuming. It had been even more apparent all day, since she'd come to him at the barn.

Slowly, as they gazed into each other's eyes, Alex's hands moved from her wrists. One arm slid around her small waist while the other buried itself in the warm fragrance of her flame gold hair. She did not move or protest as he lowered his dark head and covered her soft trembling lips with his.

18

Leanna thought she had never felt such exquisite pleasure. Alex took her lips hungrily, kissing her with a desperation that she also felt. His mouth was hot and searching, torturously sweet as it moved on hers.

Leanna moved closer, wanting without knowing why to feel every inch of his body against hers. Slowly her arms moved upward, encircling his neck as she returned his kiss. Her lips parted beneath his, and she returned the long, hot kiss with a passion that surprised even herself.

Alex slowly pulled his lips from hers, gazing into her eyes with a stunned expression. He had not expected this to happen again, and the response he felt was even stronger than before.

He could not think, could not move as Leanna's hands explored the black hair that curled over his col-

lar. She pulled her head back and gazed at his lips with
eyes grown soft and honeyed with desire.

Alex's hands moved to grasp her hair, and with a
groan proclaiming his surrender covered her mouth
again. He could feel her heart pounding against his
chest, matching the thunder of his own.

Leanna's heart told her how right this was as she
savored the taste of him, the feel of his hands upon her
body.

And Alex was fighting against it as if it were death.
This was the last thing he had intended, even as he
tasted her sweetness and felt the smooth silkiness of her
skin beneath his fingers. His mind was at war with his
senses, and he did not want to admit which was winning.

"Alex . . ." Leanna whispered, moving her lips to
his neck and burying her face against his burning skin.

He wanted her. God, how he wanted her. Right here,
right now on the floor, if necessary. It wouldn't have
mattered if someone stepped through the door. He
couldn't stop; it was too late. He was lost in her, in the
feel of her body against his and the sweet intoxication
of her passionate response.

Leanna's trembling fingers began to unbutton his
shirt, and one small hand crept inside to caress his
chest.

In the back of his mind, Alex knew that this was his
last chance to stop what was about to happen.

His slender fingers grasped her wrist and pulled her
hand away. Leanna moaned a soft protest and reached
to kiss him once more.

Alex was gasping for breath. "No, Leanna," he managed to whisper.

She was still for a moment, and then her head came

up with disbelief. He looked into her eyes and saw the pain he had caused there again, and he cursed himself.

"We can't . . . I can't do this."

For a moment she only looked at him, stunned. Then she stepped away. As Alex looked into her eyes and at her moist, swollen lips, he thought he must have lost his mind to push her away from him for the second time. It went against every inclination he felt and every instinct of his male being.

"I'm sorry," he said, his deep voice husky.

Her eyes flashed at him, and her voice too was rough with emotion. "Why do you keep doing this to me, Alex —to us?"

"Leanna, sweetheart," he whispered softly, wanting to touch her.

"What? Tell me what terrible thing in you keeps us apart. That first time you kissed me, I doubted my very being, wondering why you didn't want me. And then I swore I'd never give you a chance to hurt me again."

Her accusation hurt more than he wanted to admit. Even though he kept telling himself that he was doing what was best for her, he had to face reality. He was the one who kept reaching out to her and then pulling away. She had never wavered in her expression of need for him.

"I don't want to hurt you, Leanna. I meant only to tell you about your father. He wanted you to know the truth."

"The truth?" she snapped. "I doubt you would admit the truth if it hit you in the face. Do you want me to tell you the truth? The truth is you're afraid, Alex, afraid of becoming involved. Is it just me, or is it any woman? Obviously you had no problem relating to

Maggie that day at the river." She stopped suddenly, knowing that she was saying too much.

She didn't want this. All she really wanted was for him to take her into his arms and tell her he loved her. That admission made her turn from him and from the puzzled look in his black eyes.

Alex knew exactly what he had made her think. She thought he didn't want her, and she was afraid she'd made a fool of herself by being so ready, so willing to surrender to him.

In her feelings of guilt and shame, she had no way of knowing how much it cost him to resist her. Perhaps now, seeing her so hurt and vulnerable, it would be best to let her continue to think that. It had to end here, tonight.

"It's not you Leanna, it's me. And you're right, I am afraid, afraid for you. Can't you see how impossible this is right now, with the war? No, I guess you can't."

"You don't have to explain," she said, staring at him with glittering, cold eyes.

"You're so beautiful, and I . . ." He reached out to touch her cheek, not knowing what to say to her.

She flinched and moved away. She bit her lips to still their trembling, and with a lift of her chin, she stood straighter and smoothed the white collar of her dress.

That endearing little movement made Alex's arms ache to reach for her again, to pull her close to him and tell her how much he wanted her. He wanted to forget all his vows of protecting her. But he was a man schooled by discipline, and he only clamped his lips together firmly and watched helplessly as she reached for her cape.

"If you will excuse me, Major Slayton, I have a long

day tomorrow." Her air of dismissal would once have amused him, but not now.

Why was she so damned difficult to talk to?

"So, it's Major Slayton again?" he asked, studying her soft lips.

"I would think you'd be happy about that. It's what you want, isn't it? I've caused you nothing but trouble since you came for me that night. You've reminded me of that often enough. I could do nothing to please you, even then. I don't know why I thought we might ever be anything other than enemies. And don't worry, I shan't bother you again, and I release you from all responsibility you feel toward me. Obviously that's all there's ever been for you."

He closed his eyes for a moment. The glow from the fireplace cast a shadow across his face. Leanna thought he looked even more savage than before.

"Damn it, Leanna. Don't you ever listen?" His voice lowered to a husky whisper. "I do want you, more than I've ever wanted anyone. And my feeling responsible has nothing to do with it."

"Then what?" she asked with a pleading voice. "Are you afraid I'll expect marriage, or expect your faithfulness?"

He turned away from the pain in her beautiful eyes. "Marriage," he said softly, "is not something I could offer anyone, not as long as we're at war."

"So," she whispered, "we seem to be back where we started." She turned to leave.

"Leanna, wait."

"No!" The tears she'd been holding back threatened to splash from her eyes. "No, I don't want to hear anything else you have to say, Alexander Slayton. You've deceived me from the first. You know, I thought you

were everything a man should be, brave and coura-
geous. And now I find you've changed. You're not that
man anymore. You're too afraid of feeling, afraid to let
anyone get close to you, and I can't beg you to love me
Alex, I won't."

With a muffled sob she turned and ran to the door.
Alex did not follow as she struggled with the latch. He
did not call out when she ran out the door and disappeared across the darkened yard.

He turned and, with a deep, wrenching frustration,
kicked a basket that sat on the floor.

"Jesus," he muttered as he ran his fingers through
his hair.

He walked to the door and stared out into the darkness. His very soul urged him to go after her, to carry
her away somewhere and make love to her. To hell with
the consequences. He began to pace, knowing that he
could not.

He couldn't afford emotional attachments to anyone.
It wouldn't be fair to expect someone like Leanna to
wait until the war was over, for who knew when that
would be, or even if he would come home at all? No, he
told himself again, it was better for her this way. Despite the pain she felt tonight, he knew it was for her
own good.

With a soft muttered curse he strapped the gun holster back around his hips and plunged his arms into the
sleeves of his jacket.

As he closed the door of the washhouse behind him
and walked out across the yard, he felt as if he could
still smell her fragrance and taste the sweetness of her
lips. He stopped for a moment and looked up at the
winter sky that sparkled with stars.

"Fool," he said to himself.

He'd been playing with fire, knowing the dangers when Leanna's eyes had first flashed at him in the senator's study. He'd known when he danced with her just how tempting she was, and how dangerous. He had declared that no one would intrude into his mind or his heart. And now he was a fool, for that was exactly what he had let Leanna do.

Leanna slipped back through the window of her room. It was totally dark inside, and there was no light burning beneath the door to Polly's room. Quietly, she changed her clothes and climbed up into the narrow bed, pulling the covers over her. She pulled a shirt from beneath her pillow and held it to her lips as she breathed the scent. She imagined that she still held Alex as she touched the cool white material.

As soon as she closed her eyes, the tears came, running hotly down her face and onto the pillow. She had never known that a broken heart could hurt so badly. When Alex had pulled away from her again, she felt an ache that began in her heart and moved through her until she felt sick from the pain.

She could not help remembering how his black eyes had gazed at her there in the dim light of the washhouse, or the desire she saw in their depths. And his lips, oh, she could never forget their touch or the fire they stirred within her.

It seemed only minutes until she heard Polly stirring in the other room, stoking the fire and putting her room in order for the morning.

Leanna slowly dragged her legs over the side of the bed and slid to the floor. When she stood up her head throbbed painfully with sharp little stabs behind her eyes. She knew that it was from crying and she felt a new wave of humiliation wash over her.

Never again, she swore silently. She would never give Alex Slayton the opportunity to hurt her again.

As she joined Polly, Leanna ignored the woman's look of concern. Leanna supposed it was not hard to tell that she had cried most of the night. Her eyes were swollen and her nose stuffy, and she did not possess enough energy even to speak.

Both of them silently put their rooms in order and within moments were ready for breakfast. Just then they heard a noise in the hallway outside their door, the sound of several people walking, their steps ringing in the empty hall. They were singing.

A knock sounded at the door to the hallway. Polly and Leanna exchanged curious looks, wondering who could be calling at such an early hour. It was not even five-thirty.

Polly opened the door, and Leanna looked past her at the people gathered there. There were six men and one woman: Emily McGrath. Upon their solemn faces were looks of condemnation and disapproval. Had they found out about last night?

Brother Jackson stood at the forefront of the group, his arms outstretched toward Polly as he gazed into the room.

They stopped singing, and Brother Jackson began to speak. Leanna noted his nervousness, the brightness of his dark eyes behind the glasses and the way his lips twitched slightly as he spoke.

"Stand aside, Sister Polly, Sister Leanna. We go this morning about the Act of Cleansing."

Polly stood aside to let them enter.

"But wait," Leanna began, "what does this mean, this Act of Cleansing?"

Sister Emily's voice rang from the hallway. "It is not thy place to question our coming, Sister." She was angry and spiteful. Yet there was more than that in her words and the way she stared at Leanna. This was personal, as if the woman hated her.

"Thee will be silent, Sister Emily," Brother Jackson said, moving to stand within inches of Leanna. "I will instruct our new sister in the ways of our committee."

Leanna looked nervously at the others, who stood waiting as if for orders. She did not recognize any of the men except Brother Levi, Polly's husband, and he acted as if he did not even know the tiny woman.

There was something about Jackson Cole that morning that made Leanna very uneasy. It was the way his eyes behind the wire-rimmed glasses darted quickly from her face to her breasts. There was a sheen of perspiration on his brow and beneath his mustache. It was the air of perverse satisfaction about him.

Leanna had been the target of that sick, lustful look only once before, on that day at the river. This seemed much worse, though, for she'd somehow expected a brother of the church to be different.

He moved closer to her and began to speak. His foul-smelling breath rushed across her face, and she caught the scent of a beard not meticulously kept. She took a step backward, and his eyes glinted, but he did not pursue her further.

"There is no need for alarm, Sister," he said, his voice low and conciliatory. "It is our duty to search thy room for any articles considered unsuitable. I assure thee it is done often and we have not singled thee out for any particular reason."

Leanna was still not convinced, but she made no protest. Instead, she let the group enter the room. She saw the arch of Sister Emily's brow and the look of satisfaction in her eyes as she entered the room last.

Leanna moved with Polly to stand near the windows. She placed her arm around the woman's shoulders as they watched the group begin their search. She could only imagine how humiliating it was for Polly to have to accept this treatment from her own husband.

Levi Wilhite, without once glancing toward his wife, stripped the newly made bed and lifted the mattress to look underneath it. His right arm swept back and forth beneath the mattress, and when it emerged he held a small handmade linen sack in his hand. Still not looking at Polly, Levi threw the sack into the middle of the floor. The contents jingled with a metallic ring as it struck wood.

Leanna could feel the trembling in Polly's body and hear her shallow rapid breathing. She whispered near her ear, "It's all right, Polly. Don't let him upset you."

They tore everything apart, even the sewing that lay in the baskets and hung from the tailor's forms. Leanna felt such sympathy for Polly that she had not even considered what they might be doing to her own room. Then again, she had nothing to hide, or so she thought, until she saw Emily McGrath emerge with a dimpled smile.

Emily walked purposefully to Leanna and held out a small book under her nose. "The work of the devil," she said before turning to toss it on the floor with the small bag of coins Levi had found.

Leanna stepped forward but was stopped by Brother Jackson, who caught her by the arm and pushed her gently back toward Polly. Leanna was certain that no one else in the room saw how his arm brushed so casually against her breasts or how it lingered there until she jerked free of his grip.

"It's only a book of poetry," Leanna protested, pointing toward the book on the floor. It contained her favorite selections by Elizabeth Barrett Browning.

"It is the book of a sin-filled world!" Emily stated. "Thee knows that celibacy is the perfect state, necessary to a well-ordered and orthodox life if thee wishes to obtain spiritual distinction!"

"But I—"

"Thee wishes to remain here with the Believers?" Emily asked.

"Yes, I . . . I have no choice. But I . . ."

The blond woman bent to retrieve the book from the floor. In one swift movement she tossed it into the fire, where its velvet covering smoldered and its gold-edged pages caused the flames to turn blue.

"No," Leanna cried, moving futilely toward the fire.

"The committee declares that this book of poetry is sexual in content and has therefore been censored," Jackson Cole said quietly. His arms were flung wide, as if he addressed a great crowd of important people.

Leanna's shoulders slumped, and she moved back to the window. She told herself it did not matter. As soon as she was away from here she could get another copy of the book. But humiliation burned within her and angered her almost to the point of madness. Her face was hot, and she could not calm the shaking of her body. She fixed her eyes on the face of Emily McGrath and felt as if she could actually kill her.

Sister Emily only smiled, and again Leanna thought how strangely incongruous the dimples and sweet smile were upon the face of so evil a woman.

"Thy conduct will be taken into consideration, Sister Leanna," Brother Jackson said. "We will consider also that thee are an infant in the ways of our church, and the penance will be ordered accordingly." He looked at her almost apologetically, and his voice was not unkind.

But Leanna was not cajoled by his words or his solicitous manner. She watched him warily, her lips clamped together in resentment.

He continued to talk, this time to Polly. "Sister Polly, thee knows the ways of communal living. The hoarding of money for personal good is condemned. This money shall be placed in the treasury, and since this is thy third time, thy punishment may be more severe."

"Yes, brother," Polly muttered.

It broke Leanna's heart to see Polly's bent gray head and the look of surrender in the slump of her shoulders. How dare these people treat her this way! She was worth twenty women like Emily McGrath.

After the committee left, Leanna wrapped her arms around Polly. "Are you all right?"

"Yes . . . yes child, I'm fine. I should have known better than to try and save money. Levi always knew I kept a few coins under my mattress at home, and now he's betrayed me again. I'll never be able to leave here, never!" She sank wearily into the rocking chair.

"Oh, yes we will, Polly. I swear I'll take you away from here. Don't worry about the money. I'll think of something. I won't stay here and be subjected to such treatment, and neither will you."

But Polly was lost in her own dazed thoughts and sat looking dejectedly into the flames, where the book of poetry had now turned to a small pile of ashes.

Polly even refused to go to breakfast. "You go, I'm

not hungry," she said to Leanna, her voice soft and defeated.

Leanna pressed her lips tightly together. She would go, and she would look them all straight in the eye. They would not defeat her as easily as they had this poor defenseless little woman.

With that thought firmly in mind, she marched out into the hall and toward the dining room with a purposeful stride. When Emily McGrath looked smugly at Leanna, expecting to see a broken girl, she was surprised.

She saw instead the furious glare of Leanna's deep green eyes. Emily's smile faded quickly, and this time it was her own eyes that were forced to look away.

19

Leanna's small victory did not last long, however. Several times during the day she saw Sister Emily and Brother Jackson with their heads together in serious conversation. That night, after supper, they and others from the cleansing committee met in the little parlor just beneath the stairway.

Leanna told Polly what she'd seen, and together they sat by the fire, hardly speaking, waiting for the knock on their door that they knew would come.

When it did there was only Brother Jackson, the apparent head of the committee, come to deliver their penalties.

"It saddens me to say this, Sister Polly, but thee are not a good example for our new convert here. The committee has decided that for the time being thee may remain in the same rooms, but that is likely to change soon."

Leanna knew that Polly would not want to be separated any more than she did. They had grown very close in the short time they'd been together.

"But we do not deem it appropriate that Sister Leanna work with thee any longer. Sister Leanna is a strong, healthy young woman, and Sister Emily says we have need of such a person to help with the washing and ironing." His next words were directed to Leanna. "First thing after prayers tomorrow, Sister, please report to our West family washhouse. Thee will likely work long and hard. It is unlikely that Sister Polly's ways will influence thee again."

"But she didn't—"

He raised his hand. "Silence. Thee has much to learn about our ways, and thy first step is to listen and attend to what your elders say."

Polly shot Leanna a look, and in her tired eyes was a warning not to argue anymore. Leanna became silent, even though her heart raged and her head had begun to pound at the unfairness of this treatment.

"And, Sister Polly, since thee are no longer a young woman, our penance for you is mild. Working alone in your room day after day with no companionship is all we shall require at this time. But mark my words, thee will be watched closely."

"Yes, Brother," Polly said quietly, bowing her head.

Leanna fumed as she saw the man's smug look. He apparently enjoyed the power he wielded over others as much as Emily did.

After he left she paced before the fireplace. "We have to get out of this place, Polly. I can't stand to see the way they treat you. And I'm sure my father never knew there would be people like Emily and Jackson Cole here.''

Polly looked up, a spark of hope in her brown eyes. The poor woman had aged ten years.

"Maybe you could get the money to buy back the farm," she said. "I wouldn't ask that it be mine, only that you let me live there. Then when I'm gone it would be yours . . . a good investment and . . ."

"That's not such a bad idea," Leanna said. "I could live there with you, at least until Father is released. It is isolated, isn't it? No one would know me there."

"Why, yes," Polly said. She clasped her small hands together. "Oh, that would be splendid, truly splendid."

"Yes, it just might work. Papa surely would not object. I will explain that you are a, uh, widow, living alone, and a suitable companion for me." She turned to Polly and smiled for the first time in days.

Polly's eyes were aglow with hope. "How will you do it? And when?"

"I'm not sure. I don't want you to get your hopes up, but I'm going to try to find a way. Don't worry."

Polly relaxed noticeably, and the troubled look faded from her lined face. She began to rock and to stare into the fire, humming as she did.

That night Leanna lay for a long while thinking about what she should do. Finally, sometime near midnight, she decided. She would mail a letter tomorrow to her father's lawyer, asking him to purchase the farm from the Believers at whatever price they required. She would tell him to use his own name, so that the Shakers would not guess what Leanna was doing.

Having formed a plan, Leanna turned toward the window, watching the thin sliver of moon move slowly across the winter sky. The black sky, with its glittering sparks of light, was so like the black eyes that she dreamed of when finally she slept.

Early the next morning Leanna wrote the letter and gave it to Polly to mail. After breakfast and morning prayers she headed to the back of the house for her new job.

The sight of the small washhouse caused her pulse to race unexpectedly. She was actually apprehensive about entering the room where she and Alex had met, dreading the smell of soap and starch that would bring those memories flooding back.

She was right. The pleasant scent hit her with a force that left her shaken. It was almost as if Alex was still there, waiting, his arms strong and hard, his lips moving against hers. It did not help that her sleep last night had been disturbed by vivid dreams of him.

She took a deep breath and squared her shoulders. There was nothing like familiarity to help chase away disturbing thoughts and memories, and soon she would become so familiar with the washhouse that she would no longer associate it with Alex. She would not mourn for him, not yet. For somewhere in the deepest recesses of her heart, she knew he would be back.

Leanna was pleased to find Rachel working there, and glad that the two of them worked alone in the ironing room. The two older women in the washroom were quiet and pleasant, nothing like Emily, and for that Leanna was grateful.

For all her enjoyment of working with Rachel, Leanna soon discovered that her new job was a thankless, backbreaking one. It was not made any easier by the fact that Sister Emily supervised the work, often stopping in at the warm little house several times a day.

"Is she always so diligent?" Leanna asked Rachel after one of Emily's visits.

Rachel lowered her brown eyes, and a wisp of dark hair fell over her forehead. She looked tired. "Well . . ." she began. "To tell the truth, I don't think she takes to thee, Sister Leanna."

"Oh, that's no secret to me."

"I'm sure if we work hard and make no trouble, she will soon come around." The girl's subservience and her shy, apologetic ways irritated Leanna, but she reminded herself that the poor girl could not afford to have Emily angry with her. Still, she wished Rachel would not be such a willing stepping-stone.

The last few days of February flew, and March followed just as quickly. With it seemed to go the last remnants of winter.

Leanna saw Alex almost every day now, but it was usually from a distance. He made no move to approach her, nor she him. She was still smarting from his rejection of her, although that did not seem to prevent her heart from pounding each time she saw him.

After prayer meeting there was talk that winter was indeed over, and many predicted a long, mild spring.

Leanna prayed that this was true, for she found winter among the Shakers hard and bitterly unrelenting, more so than she could ever have expected. After all, it was a season she'd never given much thought to. Her previous winters had consisted of winter balls and long, pleasant afternoons of tea and sleigh rides.

Leanna was becoming afraid. She had not thought to be at Pleasant Hill so long, and she still had heard nothing from her father's lawyer about the farm she asked him to buy, and no further word about her father.

Her job in the washhouse seemed unending. The

more she accomplished, the more Emily assigned for her to do. Leanna swore that she would not give in and let the woman know how truly miserable she was, nor how tired she felt.

When she was not sweating over the hot iron she had to carry heavy baskets of wet clothes outdoors. Now that mild weather had come, everything was hung outside to dry. The one advantage was that it gave her a few moments outside in the clean, fresh Kentucky air. Who would ever have thought that the highlight of Leanna McNairy's day would be a short trip outside alone?

But as time went on, she found the work almost more than she could bear. Her hands had grown red and chafed and her nails torn away by the heavy wet clothes. Her skin was pale from fatigue, and she had lost so much weight that her dresses hung from her body.

Polly worried about her. She told Leanna that no one had to work that hard at Pleasant Hill and begged her to speak with Sister Jane about it. Leanna refused, though, stubbornly vowing not to give in to Emily McGrath.

One morning in early March, Leanna was standing outside hanging clothes when she saw Alex. It was nearing lunchtime, and he rode with Brother Jackson around toward the back of the house, where they tied their horses beneath a maple tree.

Leanna felt a familiar lurch in her heart at the sight of him and his dark hair ruffling in the warm breeze. Seeing him looking so tall and strong, with his uniform neat and trim, made her feel even more ragged and unattractive in her fatigue. She found herself dreading the noon meal, ashamed for him to see her this way. He had accused her often enough of being spoiled and pampered. She imagined it would give him quite a laugh to see how hard she worked now and how truly miserable she was.

Alex could hardly eat the delicious meal the Shakers had set before him. He could not keep his eyes from wandering to the next table and Leanna.

What in hell had happened to his spirited little rebel with those defiant green eyes? She kept her head bent and would not even look at him. Her lovely oval-shaped face was drawn, and there were hollows in her cheeks and dark circles below her eyes. Even her beautiful flame gold hair had lost its luster.

Alex felt a quick tightening in his chest, an angry protectiveness he'd never felt for anyone except his sister. Could he have prevented this? Was she grieving because of his behavior? God, the last thing he ever wanted was to see her like this, with the vivacious spark gone from her and the tired, worn look in its place.

He continued to stare at her, but she would not lift her head to meet his look. Damn, he muttered to himself. How had this happened? And what could he do about it? As it was, he had some bad news for her, and it made him feel even more guilty. He should already have checked on her, but he'd been protecting himself, he supposed. It had taken all his willpower to stay away.

As soon as the meal was over, Leanna disappeared. Alex searched with his eyes among the gray dresses and white cotton caps, but she was not there. He had to find her, had to know if she was all right and if there was anything he could do to help her.

He quickly shook hands with Brother Jackson and, without pausing to speak to the rest as he usually did, exited through the side door. He walked to where his horse was tied, and it was then that he spotted Leanna, hurrying toward the washhouse.

"Leanna!" he called.

She turned around and then went on inside the small house.

"Still stubborn, I see," he muttered to himself. He tied the horse to the small tree and walked quickly to the washhouse, taking no notice of the scent of spring in the air or the sound of birds singing cheerfully all around him.

He did not bother to knock but instead stepped just inside the door. One of the women looked up and smiled kindly at him.

"Anything we can do for thee, Major Slayton?" she asked.

"Yes. I wondered if I might have a word with Miss McNairy?"

Leanna heard his voice from the ironing room. She could hardly have missed it, the place was so small, and his voice, deep and masculine, seemed to ring through the house. She felt her knees begin to tremble as she lifted a tired hand to her hair that straggled from beneath her cap. Lord, she had not wanted him to see her this way.

The woman Alex had spoken to, Sister Charlotte, came to Leanna's door. "Did thee not know? Major Slayton is here."

"Yes . . ." Leanna said, pausing for a moment to take a deep breath before going to meet him.

Alex's eyes narrowed as she came toward him. She saw the disapproval, the anger in his gaze, but she supposed she could not blame him for it. She said nothing in greeting but walked past him out into the yard. They stood at the front window within view of Sister Charlotte. She didn't want yet another penance added to the ones she had already accumulated.

"My God, Leanna," Alex murmured. "What's happened to you? Have you been ill?"

Her face burned, and she felt tears spring to her eyes. "I've been working hard, that's all."

"Too damned hard. You look exhausted." He was angry, more angry than he'd been in quite a while.

"Well, that should make you happy," she said with a touch of her old fierceness. "Spoiled rich Southern girl finally soils her hands and learns what real work is. Why, I would think it gives great satisfaction. It's exactly what you think I deserve."

There was a hard, angry glint in his black eyes as he shook his head slowly. She was surprised at the pain upon his handsome face.

"No, Leanna, you're wrong. I never wanted that. I hate seeing you so unhappy."

She looked away from the intensity of his eyes. "I guess I didn't realize how bad I look," she said, looking down at her dress and running her red, worn hands down the skirt.

Suddenly he wanted to pull her into his arms and hold her, protect her from pain. He couldn't stand seeing this vulnerability in her eyes.

His eyes moved down her body, taking note of the way her dress hung loosely. The bones in her face were more prominent, emphasizing her eyes and full lips.

"You've lost weight," he said.

"It won't hurt," she said, attempting to smile. "I was entirely too round as it was."

"No . . . you weren't," he whispered. "You're tired and pale, it's true, but there's something . . . you're even more beautiful than ever." He stared at her as if he could not believe his own words.

He stepped back and allowed his dark eyes to rake her figure, taking in the diminutive waist, the lean, smooth curves of her hips, which exaggerated her full breasts even more. Damn, she was more beautiful than ever, even with her gaunt look. It gave her an angelic purity that had not been there before.

Leanna hardly knew what to say. He must have only said that she was beautiful to cheer her. "That's impossible," she said, shaking her head.

"That you could grow more beautiful? Yes, I would have thought so, too." He was smiling crookedly down at her.

She blushed, feeling awkward and shy at his teasing and unable to think of one clever word of reply.

How easily, with one smile, he could melt away all her resentments, even make her forget how afraid she was of being hurt again. Was she so starved for attention that she had forsaken her pride?

She was so sweet that Alex could not bring himself to tell her what he'd come for—not now, after seeing her this way, so fragile and pale.

"How would you like to come to a party?" he asked, smiling at her again with a devilish glint in his eyes.

Her face lit up for a moment before she looked quickly through the window at Sister Charity.

"I'd love it. But I'm afraid there's no way—"

"Oh, yes, my little one. There is always a way. You forget my specialty." He looked at her pointedly as he spoke.

She stared at him blankly for a moment. "Of course,

the Nighthawk can see in the dark, as I've heard. Can find his prey even when it's hidden in the dark depths of the forest."

"Exactly," he said. "But you, Miss McNairy, are hardly my prey."

She looked at him boldly, becoming more confident with his bantering and feeling for the first time in weeks a hint of her old fun-loving self. "Oh, I'm not so certain about that."

"Hmmm," he murmured, looking at her eyes and her softly parted lips. "Those wicked eyes hardly belong to a proper little Shaker miss." He looked back through the window and saw Sister Charlotte watching them with an anxious look on her face.

"You should go," Leanna said.

"Listen for the Nighthawk," he whispered as he moved away from Leanna.

"The Nighthawk," she repeated, as if in a daze. She stood still, unable to move until he had mounted his horse and ridden away, turning once to look back at her with a wave of his hand.

It was amazing how he brought life and energy back to her, how her heart began to sing at the thought of seeing him again. She had not forgotten how he'd hurt her before, but this time, she told herself, she would not push him. And she would be more careful of her own heart.

20

Leanna was relieved that for once there was no extra work to be done after supper. She took a towel and a change of clothes and walked across the wide lawn toward the communal bathhouse. There was no one else there, and the kettle sitting on the small stove was still hot.

She prepared the tub and spent a long while lying in the warm water, thinking about all that had happened to her the past few weeks. Most of all, she thought of Alex and the way she felt when he looked at her so steadily.

She bathed, letting the warm soapy water run down her shoulders and between her breasts. Just the thought of seeing him again made her body tingle with pleasure, made her feel warm and alive with feelings she could not explain.

"Stop it," she scolded herself quietly, shaken and surprised by the way her body reacted whenever she thought of him.

She washed her hair until it squeaked with cleanliness and then dressed and made her way back outside. The sun was beginning to fall behind the long rolling meadows beyond the village, gilding the tops of the bare trees with gold.

Leanna took a deep breath and flung her arms wide, almost dancing as she moved across the cool grass. She suddenly felt happier than she had in a long while, and there was a delicious feeling of anticipation in the pit of her stomach.

She walked by the herb garden, bending to brush her fingers across the new green shoots rising from the rich black soil. Back home the crocuses would be blooming, and soon the daffodils. But here in the Shaker village there were no flowers except the ones that bloomed on herbs and vegetables. Nothing was grown for pleasure or beauty; if there was no practical use for it, it was not planted.

Leanna felt a shiver run along her arms. The sun was behind the trees, and there was a nip of frost in the evening air. Something else had caused the chill to course down her body, though. She felt as if someone were watching her. She looked up at the large dormer windows of the Center house, but it was too early for anyone to be at the post yet. She didn't know what it was, but something made her feel uneasy.

She hurried her steps, going away from the towering shrubs of the lawn and out into the clear roadway. When she glanced back over her shoulders she saw no one. By the time she arrived in the warm interior of the West family house her intuitive feeling of danger had passed, and she was again filled with happy feelings of anticipation.

Jackson Cole stood hidden behind the bushes in the shadow of the great Center house. He watched Leanna until she reached her dwelling and only then did he breath out the air in his lungs. He slumped back against the stone wall of the house and groaned softly in the darkness.

His hand moved slowly downward to the swelling at the front of his trousers. Watching Leanna always gave him such exquisite pleasure and pain. The red-haired girl aroused him as no one ever had, not even the cruel Sister Emily.

He couldn't decide what was so different about Leanna McNairy. Even the hard work of the past few weeks had not defeated her or diminished her beauty. He should not have gone along with Emily's plan for the girl, he knew that. It was only a matter of time before one of the other elders noticed and put a stop to it.

It had been the only way to stop Emily's jealous rantings, though. Not that he really cared, but he was a man of passion, and not willing to forego his clandestine meetings with the blond sister. Oh, she was as willing and compliant as any of them in private. He took her whenever he wished.

That sinful worldly desire was the one thing that kept him from being the true and obedient Believer that he longed to be. It was something he could not control, and had never been able to. It was as if some gnawing, aggressive creature took control of his mind and body when the desire struck him. There was simply nothing he could do except give in to it.

There had been other girls, other innocent recruits who had soon bowed to his authority and submitted to his demands. He always managed to intimidate them into doing as he pleased and frightened them afterward into silence. Most of them left the village after a while, although a few still remained. Rachel Harris and her expected brat was proof that. God, but he could hardly stand to look at the girl anymore. The way her sad dejected eyes followed him all the time was sickening.

He needed a challenge, and this one, this beauty with the golden red hair, was special. He had watched and coveted her for a long time. She turned him inside out and made him stammer and tremble like a young colt. And she was exciting, a pleasure worth waiting for.

She had an independence that was unusual in women, and something he normally did not like, but in her it made him desire her all the more. The way she looked at him defiantly from the depths of those green eyes, the fury he sometimes saw when he touched her breasts. What exquisite pleasure it would be to tame her.

"I can hardly wait, Leanna," he whispered. His forehead shone with perspiration, and his breathing was ragged.

He looked across the way to the West family house. The light from Sister Emily's room shone brightly now, like a signal guiding him. He hurried from behind the bushes, glancing around to make sure that no one saw him there. His eyes glittered, never leaving the window where he knew Emily waited.

"Time for a conference, my dear Sister Emily," he

whispered with a laugh. "And you are so going to enjoy this one!"

Leanna hugged Polly briefly as she entered the room and told her about seeing Alex. She warned her that one night, perhaps even tonight, she might leave through her window as she had before.

Polly smiled and nodded, warning her that she should be careful.

Later, in her own room, Leanna found that she could not sleep; she was far too excited. She told herself that he might not come tonight. He had not actually said when it would be, but only, "Listen for the Nighthawk." She smiled into the darkness, thinking of his fierce good looks and how appropriate sounding the name was. His reluctance to discuss it seemed charming to her now.

It was only eight o'clock when she heard the first light tap at her window. She was not even certain of what she heard, but the house was quiet except for a few noises from above her room. Sister Emily must be restless tonight, she thought.

She sat up in bed. The noise sounded again at the window. She tiptoed to the window and threw back the curtains to see Jimmy Anderson crouched outside.

Leanna felt only a moment's disappointment that it was not Alex. Still, she was happy to see Jimmy. Quietly she raised the window and slid softly to the ground, with his hands about her waist guiding her. He took her hand and pulled her around the house, past the large cedar and beyond the washhouse.

He did not speak until they were well away from the dwellings and the fence that separated the village from the pasturelands. Once in the meadow he turned, still holding her hand.

"I left the horses under the big chestnut tree in the meadow."

"Where are we going?" she asked.

"It's a surprise." She could hear the smile in his voice. "Major just said to bring you."

"He told me to listen for the Nighthawk. I thought perhaps he would . . ."

Jimmy gave a low grunt of laughter. "Hate to disappoint you, but I guess you could say you heard it. They call us all Nighthawks sometimes."

When they reached the horses, Jimmy helped her into the saddle and then untied the horses and pulled himself up, too.

"The major was called Nighthawk first," Jimmy said as they moved carefully across the meadow. "It was right after our first assignment in Kentucky. There were large numbers of Confederates scattered about, most of them raiders, not regular army men. But they were causing a lot of problems. Major Slayton, he just had a knack for finding their hideouts, and we'd raid them in the middle of the night. No matter where they went or where they hid, he always seemed to be one step ahead of them. The ones we didn't capture we sent scampering back down to Tennessee."

"Some of the stories now are exaggerated," Jimmy continued. "Seems like every night raid around is done by the Nighthawk, even when we're all sound asleep at Pleasant Hill."

Leanna laughed with Jimmy. She'd forgotten how much she liked being with this young man, and how much she needed to be with someone her own age.

As they rode Leanna could feel the tension building

within her. She was so close to Alex that she could feel
it, and she wondered exactly what he had in mind for
tonight. She'd sensed today that he wanted to cheer
her, help her forget for a while the drab life she was
forced to live with the Shakers. For the first time since
she'd left home she felt a true sense of excitement wash
over her, right down to her toes.

She saw the tents in the pasture far in the distance.
Campfires flickered all around them. Jimmy rode to
Alex's tent and reined the horse to a stop beneath the
hanging branches of a willow tree.

They did not have to knock, as the tent opened immediately. But instead of Alex, as Leanna had expected,
she saw a woman silhouetted in the doorway.

"Come in, Leanna," she said, her voice soft and
quiet against the stillness of the night.

Leanna glanced at Jimmy, who only nodded and
smiled. "I'll be back," he said. "I believe we're all invited to this party."

The dark-haired young woman stood aside and motioned Leanna inside. Being in Alex's tent again with its
familiar scent of canvas and candlewax sent a wave of
bittersweet memories through her. It was still the same,
with maps and books lying on the desk, but a small
stove had been added, and there was a warm blaze
burning brightly.

Leanna was unsure of what to do next, but the
woman soon put her at ease.

"I'm Gina, Alexander's sister."

Leanna's eyes widened with curiosity. She had seen
the picture Alex had, the one of Gina and her husband,
but she looked different now, even more beautiful in
person. She was taller than Leanna, with hair almost as
black as Alex's, and her skin had a touch of warm glow

to it, like her brother's. They were very much alike, except for the eyes. Gina's were a deep, dark blue.

Leanna smiled with genuine pleasure. "I'm so happy to meet you."

"And I, you. Alex has spoken of you many times."

"He has?" She wanted to ask what he had said. Had he spoken of their many disagreements, or the way she'd defied him and considered him an enemy at first? Her cheeks burned at the thought of her sometimes hasty words.

Gina saw the troubled look in the other woman's eyes. "He had only nice things to say." Her teasing smile was so much like her brother's.

Leanna relaxed immediately and sat down on the cot where Gina motioned. "It's just that your brother and I seem to be at odds about so many things," she said.

"Well, I certainly know how that is. He and I have had our share of disagreements as well. He is so certain of himself and his decisions that he sometimes leaves no room for any other opinions."

Leanna nodded. She knew that Gina's marriage to a Confederate had caused problems between her and Alex.

"I . . . I was terribly sorry to hear about your husband."

Gina's eyes darkened, and she glanced toward the fire. "Thank you. It is still so painful I can hardly speak of it."

"I know." Leanna placed her hand on Gina's. "It is so hard to understand why things like that happen."

Gina smiled at her as she wiped a tear from her eyes. "You are very kind." She rested a hand on her waist. "At least I have a part of John with me forever."

Leanna's eyes followed the hand. With a soft intake of breath she whispered, "A baby?"

Gina's wide smile banished the tears from her eyes. "Yes, isn't it wonderful? A gift from God, I told Alex."

Leanna was so moved that she found herself unable to say anything. In fact, she was not even aware when the tent opened behind them and Alex came in.

"Now, you ladies are going to have to be a bit more spirited than this if we're to have a party," he said when he saw the wistful look on Gina's face. The reason he'd decided so spontaneously to have a party had everything to do with these two women.

Leanna's heart skipped a beat as she turned to see him standing there. He looked so tall and handsome in his blue uniform, with the light reflecting on the gleaming buttons and braid. His teeth flashed at her in a smile as genuine as any she'd seen him give. He was obviously happy to have his little sister with him.

Gina stood up and put her arms around his trim waist. "We'll have plenty of spirit, my darling brother," she said. "But first I have a little surprise for Leanna. So why don't you just go on outside, and we'll join you in a few minutes."

Alex looked at Gina so tenderly that Leanna thought her own heart would bust out of her chest. With a smile he turned to go, tugging gently at Gina's dark hair as he did. "Don't take all night, Gin," he warned.

"Quick," Gina said after he was gone. "That bag behind the cot. I took the liberty of bringing one of my dresses for you to wear." She stood back and looked at Leanna with a twinkle in her blue eyes. "Unless of course you'd prefer that lovely frock you're wearing."

Leanna looked down at her dreary gray dress and laughed, feeling young and carefree. It seemed so long ago since she had dressed for a party with another girl. Suddenly she couldn't wait to see Alex's reaction to her wearing something pretty.

Gina lay out her dress with its skirt spread across the wool blanket on Alex's cot. Leanna held her breath and reached one hand out to stroke the rich blue velvet material. It was simple but elegantly beautiful, and she knew the color would complement her fair skin and bring out the gold in her hair.

With trembling fingers she slipped the dress over her head and fastened the jet buttons up the front. The fit was almost perfect, except for a snugness in the bust that was hardly noticeable.

The dress had a high neck with a fall of white lace at the throat. The long sleeves were puffed at the shoulders. Streamers of black ribbons were stitched down the seams of the flaring skirt to hip level where they fell loose to the hemline.

Leanna twirled around, watching the yards of material and black ribbons flare out gracefully and settle back just above her toes. It made her feel special and young again, and helped her forget the backbreaking work she'd done lately and the quiet solemn life she was forced to live.

When she turned to the other woman she could see the glint of approval in Gina's eyes. She knew the dress looked as lovely as she hoped it did.

Gina had draped a fringed shawl over her shoulders, and she handed Leanna another one that was embroidered with dark roses. Then they walked eagerly outside and toward the meadow where the campfires burned.

They could hear a fiddle and the twang of a Jew's harp as they approached the others. A huge bonfire burned brightly, illuminating all those around it and throwing sparks and pieces of burning ash toward the dark sky.

Alex stood with his back to them. Following the looks of his men, he turned slowly to the two women. His eyes met Leanna's, and even in the darkness she sensed that they rested on her alone. In the light of the fire she saw his gaze move over her, then rise to look at her face in quiet admiration.

Alex's men greeted her exuberantly, making her feel as if she'd returned home from a long, lonely trip. Even Trey smiled at her faintly.

Bales of hay sat stacked around the fire, and nearby was a smaller fire over which slabs of meat roasted. They sizzled and spat, throwing a delicious aroma into the evening air.

It was a night Leanna thought she would never forget. The men played songs and sang, even Confederate songs and ones familiar to Leanna. She knew they did it in honor of her, and it brought a warm feeling to her chest. Sadly, it made her think of her father as well.

Gina seemed to enjoy herself, dancing and singing with the men. They treated her with respect, as they did Leanna, almost like a sister.

As Leanna sat watching them, Alex came to sit beside her on one of the hay bales.

"You look very beautiful tonight," he said.

Leanna's eyes lowered, and she ran her work-worn hands across the velvet material. "Gina's surprise," she said with a wistful smile.

"So, you are enjoying yourself, little Rebel?"

She laughed, finding that his words no longer offended her.

"More than you can possibly know," she said, looking at him with gratitude.

"Good."

"It was kind of you to ask me here," she said, almost shyly.

He glanced at her again, his black eyes reflecting the sparks that flew into the dark night.

"Kind?" he said, smiling at her. "If it's kind to want to look at you and see you smile, then yes, I suppose you could say I'm kind."

"I once asked if you ever laughed," she said, remembering the day at the river. "Now I'm wondering if you're ever serious." She watched his face closely as he caught the meaning of her words.

He turned to her and slid one hand behind her back to encircle her waist. He bent his dark head close, dangerously close, and she could feel the whisper of his breath upon her cheek.

"We'll be moving out tomorrow, to join Buell's army. So I suppose it might be safe this one night for me to be serious."

A small line appeared between her eyes. No, she wanted to cry, but she held her lips tightly together. What would she do if anything happened to him? For a moment she thought of Gina's husband, and she felt a terrible sense of foreboding move over her that threatened to wring the very breath from her body.

"The truth is, my Southern beauty," he said softly, "I cannot afford to be serious where you are concerned. I need all my senses to help these men survive what's ahead."

"What do you mean? What is ahead?" She couldn't hide the alarm in her voice. She ran her hands over her arms, feeling the chills that covered her.

"That's just it. I have no idea. But I do know the war is coming closer to Kentucky with each passing day."

"You're frightening me."

"I don't mean to. But I want you to know full well what could happen. And I want you to have this night to remember. Have you danced with Jimmy yet?" he asked, his voice taking a lighter tone.

"Don't try to change the subject, Major," she said.

He smiled wryly at her in the flickering light of the fire. "I hurt you before. I don't intend to do it again."

"Well, I can hardly believe my ears," she said. "An apology from the impenetrable Major Slayton?"

He winced and smiled. "Yes, I'm afraid so. That is . . . if you will accept it." He looked away, then quickly back into her eyes, a gesture she found enchanting.

"I will," she whispered. "If you will accept mine." She was so drawn to him that the words would hardly come. In her heart she laughed at how easily he had won her over again, but she knew that she would risk being hurt time and again if there was only the smallest chance that he might someday care for her as she did him.

She felt a quick catch in her chest at the thought. Her heart had just told her something that she had not even admitted to herself. She didn't hate him or resent him, as she had so often said. No, what she was feeling for him at this moment was anything but hate.

"What is it?" he said, seeing the stunned look in her eyes.

"Nothing," she said, turning her eyes from his. "Only a thought." She paused for a moment. "Alex, could we go for a walk before supper?"

His thigh was touching hers as they sat with his arm

around her waist. Now she could actually feel the tension in him, and she wanted to laugh. For suddenly she had no doubts that he was as affected by her as she was him. That knowledge made her want to sing and dance around like a child.

"Not afraid, are you, Major?"

"Deathly," he said, pulling her closer.

"I won't bite." she whispered, deliciously aware of the effect her words had on him.

"Leanna, I'm serious. Nothing's changed between us, and I don't think . . ."

"Shhh," she said, placing her hand on his mouth. "Don't say it, not tonight." She gasped softly as he kissed her fingers and she felt the flick of his tongue upon her skin. All the while his dark eyes never left hers.

"I think this time it is the Nighthawk who must be wary," she whispered. Then she rose to her feet and pulled his hand, urging him with her eyes to come with her into the velvety darkness of the perfect spring night.

21

Leanna walked unhurriedly, enjoying the tingling feel of her hand in his. She pulled the shawl close around her shoulders, for the night wind had begun to blow across the open meadows. She glanced up at the sky and saw that the moon was now covered by swiftly moving dark clouds.

When they reached the shadows of a huge elm tree that stood alone in the middle of the meadow, the sounds of the singing and laughter behind them were distant.

"I didn't realize how much I missed music and laughter until tonight." She stopped and looked up at Alex. "I'm glad you came to the village today and that you asked me here tonight."

"So am I," he said with an odd catch in his voice. He took both her hands in his and stood for a moment looking at her, breathing in her clean fragrance. "You've changed, you know."

"Have I?" she asked, slightly surprised by his words.

"It's a good change," he said quickly. "You're quieter, more serious than before." He did not add that he was finding her totally irresistible.

"Perhaps so," she said. "I've learned about a way of life I never knew existed."

"It's been hard."

"Yes." Her voice was only a whisper in the wind. "Very hard. There's a woman at the village who seems to hate me . . . Emily McGrath. And she's made it almost unbearable these last few weeks."

Alex laughed softly. "I'm not surprised."

"Well, I am. Most of the people there have been kind to me, as they're kind to one another. Yet this woman . . ."

"Emily McGrath is not a fair test of the Shakers' kindness. She's a user, Leanna, a manipulator. Being an eldress in the Church of the Believers does not change that, I'm afraid. I'm just sorry you're her present target."

"It's all right, you know," she said, with a hint of her old rebelliousness. "She won't break me."

"You don't have to tell me that."

"Alex . . . what do you know about the blacksmith, Mr. Cole?"

"Not much. Why?"

"I don't like him. I don't really know why. He's treated me decently enough. But something about him, the way he looks at me . . ."

"How?" he said quickly. "How does he look at you?"

Leanna could feel the tensing of his body as he moved closer, protectively so, she thought.

"I don't know, perhaps it's only my imagination. But his eyes . . . something makes me feel very uncomfortable when he's near."

"Damn," Alex muttered. He would not even be here to watch over her now. "Be very careful of him, Leanna," he said.

"I will."

"I don't want anything to happen to you."

"I know." she said, looking at him hopefully. "You promised my father."

"It has nothing to do with your father." He'd said it without thinking and immediately realized it was true. He moved away to lean against the tree and looked at the ground as if studying his boots.

"But speaking of your father, there is something I have to tell you. It was the reason I came to supper at the West family house tonight." When he looked at her, she could see the frown that creased his brow. "But after I saw you, how tired you were, I decided to wait until tonight."

"What is it?" she asked, her heart suddenly filled with dread.

"Your father is well. I received a letter from him today, and in it he enclosed one for you." He reached inside his jacket. She could hear the crackle of paper as he handed it to her. "But I also received a letter from Mr. Barnes, your father's attorney."

"Oh, yes, I told him to contact you when I wrote to him a few weeks ago."

"I'm sorry to have to tell you this. There's no easy way. But your home has been confiscated by the Confederates."

"What? But . . . but they can't do that. Can they? Without even proving that my father has done anything?"

"Leanna, sweetheart." He stepped closer. "That's what I've been trying to tell you. What I wanted to tell you that night at the village. Your father has already confessed, to them and to me. There is no doubt that he was a spy for the Union. And yes, the Confederates can confiscate the property of someone being held for treason."

"Treason," she whispered, her head reeling with the implications of the word. "But what about Thomas . . . Mrs. Macky?"

"They're all right. I sent word to Mrs. Macky that they are welcome at my aunt's at Bardstown. Gina will be staying here with Mr. and Mrs. Sutton for a while after we leave. Mrs. Macky will contact her when she wishes to go to Bardstown."

"I can't believe this is happening. This . . . this changes everything." She began to pace restlessly, holding her father's letter to her breast as if it were a rare treasure.

"I'm sorry," he murmured. "I know you must feel there's nowhere else to go now. But I wanted to tell you there is. If you find it impossible to stay with the Shakers, I want you to promise me you'll go to my mother in Ohio."

"I couldn't do that," she said quickly. She felt him stiffen and realized he thought she had refused because his mother lived in Ohio. "Oh, Alex, no . . . I . . . I have nothing against Ohio, if that's what you think. I only want to remain here near my home in case Father . . ."

She heard his sigh of exasperation and broke off.

Was she only fooling herself? Could her life ever really be the same again? The possibility of her father's guilt was something she had put from her mind until now.

She smoothed the letter into the pocket of her dress, thinking that perhaps it held an answer. She knew that for now, her reality was the hard life at the village, and it was something she had to adjust to if she wanted to survive.

"I know what you think, Alex," she said, her voice full of sadness. "But I know my father. There must be an explanation for what he's done, and I simply wanted to hear it from his own lips."

"I can understand that," he said softly.

The limbs of the great elm swayed in the wind. In the distance a flicker of lightning appeared.

Alex looked toward the storm front. His news and her father's letter had certainly cast a pall on the evening. It had made Leanna forget about luring him so enticingly into the darkness.

"We'd better go back. Looks like it might storm before morning, and I'd hate to spoil the supper the men have prepared."

She did not argue but went with him quietly, all the spirit seemingly gone from her.

Back at camp, the men had settled on the bales of hay to eat. Gina sat with Jimmy and looked up as Leanna and Alex came back into sight.

"You'd better hurry, big brother," she called. "The food is delicious."

After Leanna had received a plate and found a seat, Alex moved away. He'd been foolish enough to take a chance on being alone with her. He'd almost made a mistake that he knew he would regret.

Leanna found Trey sitting nearby and turned to talk to him. "How are you, Trey?"

"I'm fine, ma'am," he answered in his deep voice.

"I understand you will be leaving in the morning."

"Yes." As usual, his words were few.

"Is there anyone you left in Georgia, a girl, perhaps, who worries about you?"

He was silent for a long while, looking steadily down at his food. Then he gazed into her eyes with heat and anguish.

"Not any more," he said.

"What happened?" she asked, forgetting to be cautious with him.

"It's not something I want to talk about."

"Trey . . ." she began. How was she to ever to understand what his life had been like if he would not talk to her?

"I said I don't want to talk about it, miss." His eyes snapped angrily. "Besides, how could someone like you ever understand?"

"Someone like me?"

"Rich, white, born into privilege and class."

"You're right, I can't understand if you won't give me a chance."

He stood up and moved away from her. Leanna thought she'd never seen one man so full of bitterness. She found that she wanted more than anything to understand him, to help him if she could.

Jimmy came to sit on the seat beside her. "Trey just don't trust nobody, Leanna."

"But why? I don't want to be the kind of person he thinks I am. Some rich little snob who's above any kind of suffering, beyond understanding pain. I'm not like that, am I?"

Jimmy grinned and reached to take her hand. "No, you're not," he said. "Now, I admit at first we might have had our doubts about you, but underneath I knew you were a kind person."

"Tell me what happened to the girl Trey loved."

Jimmy shifted uncomfortably beside her. "Can't do that, Leanna. It ain't my business to tell something Trey don't want told. Just give him time. He'll come around."

Leanna's eyes sought Trey in the darkness around the edge of the campfire light. She found herself as curious as she was hurt. She had never had anyone treat her the way Trey did.

The men had all quieted down and now sat around the dying fire, feeling pleasantly full.

One of the soldiers picked up a fiddle and began to play. Its plaintive sound, slow and soul stirring, moved across the meadow and seemed to become one with the sighing wind. It was a song of love and parting, a song of battles and lost causes. Leanna thought it was the most mournful sound she'd ever heard.

Suddenly Alex stood and walked over to where Leanna sat. "I should get you back to the village. It's going to rain."

"I'll walk with you back to the tent," Gina said.

Impulsively Leanna turned to embrace Jimmy, feeling the tears that welled up in her eyes. She prayed desperately in her mind. Please, don't let anything happen to any of them.

"Take care, now, Jimmy," she managed, her tears roughening her voice.

"Don't you worry about us," he said with a weak smile. "All of us will be all right. Shoot, we'll be back before you know it."

Leanna thought she detected a note of dread in his voice, and it frightened her. The war was becoming so real, so personal. First her father and now these men— boys, really. Knowing Jimmy, Trey, and the rest had made her doubt her own stubborn loyalties. She'd discovered that the side you fought for had little to do with how important each individual life was. And now she was terribly afraid for Alex's young men, and for him.

She told the others good-bye and they each mumbled to her, some of them shuffling their feet shyly, some meeting her eyes boldly with confident winks. She looked for Trey, but he had disappeared into the night.

She and Gina walked silently back to the tent so that Leanna could change back to her Shaker garb. In the dim lamplight Gina saw Leanna's trouble eyes and frightened expression.

"Oh, Leanna, honey," she said, putting her arms around her and hugging her close. "I know exactly how you feel, and I wish there was something I could say to make your worries go away. But there isn't. It's something women have always had to bear." She was crying again.

They clung to each other for a moment, taking comfort in the comradeship of sisters, of women in love. Both of them cried, and Leanna felt thankful at that moment for Gina's presence.

Gina held Leanna's shoulders and smiled bravely. "They will be all right," she said. "Alex will see to it. And like Jimmy said, they'll be back before you know it."

Leanna nodded silently as Gina went outside. As she changed back into her own clothes, she allowed herself the luxury of a few private moments in Alex's tent to think of him and his men, and to say a quick silent prayer. Then she straightened her shoulders, took her father's letter from the blue velvet dress, and placed it inside the one she now wore.

When she went outside Alex was there, speaking quietly to his sister. He looked up at Leanna and smiled, holding out his hand to her.

"I'll come to see you before I go back to Bardstown," Gina said as she embraced her.

Alex had not bothered to bring two horses, but placed Leanna in front of him on the big gray that he rode. He made no excuses for himself, knowing exactly why he'd done it. He simply wanted to have her next to him this one night, to hold her tightly in his arms for the long, slow ride across the meadows to the village.

22

By the time they left the campsite the storm clouds had moved closer, swirling against the black sky in changing patterns. The wind came in hard gusts, making them duck their heads low against its fierce blasts.

The night reminded Leanna of another ride they had taken together, the night he had come for her at her home. So long ago, it seemed, almost a lifetime ago. She was a different person now.

All the revelations of the night came together with such poignancy that Leanna thought she could not bear it. Alex was leaving, and she had no idea when she would see him again. Her home was gone from her, perhaps forever. And her father . . . She did not even like to think of how he was faring in prison, or if she'd ever see him alive again.

She had no idea how she'd managed to survive during these past months. She could remember those first days and weeks as if through a fog. The sadness she felt now was like a heavy burden on her, threatening to bury her under its weight.

She leaned back against Alex, needing the feel of his arms about her, the security of his strong chest against her. She wanted to store up this moment and everything about him for when he would be gone. She wanted to be able to recall the feel of him holding her so firmly, the touch of his chin against her hair.

Most of all, she wanted to remember the excitement that raced through her just being near him. She knew with a woman's instinct that he felt it, too.

"Are you all right?" he asked.

She turned slightly so she could look up into his shadowed face. "Yes, you don't need to worry. I will be fine."

She saw the glitter of his black eyes in the flash of lightning that lit the countryside, and she wondered what he was thinking, what he was feeling.

"I'm sorry about your home," he said quietly.

"I was shocked," she said. "And now I'm just disappointed. Not so much for myself as for the sweet little woman with whom I share a room."

"What do you mean?"

Leanna quickly related Polly's story to Alex as they rode. The concern in her voice touched him. It was more proof of her changing. Alex had never thought to see her more concerned for another person than she was for herself, but he could feel her sincerity, hear it in the determined ring of her voice.

"Her farm must be to the west, behind the Sutton place," Alex said.

"I have no idea. I only know she speaks of her beautiful farm on the Kentucky River. I wanted to buy it for her, for me as well. We would both be happier living there. I had also thought of taking her back with me to Lexington. But now, with what you've told me, that's impossible. Polly's afraid she will die here and be buried in one of their peculiar ceremonies, far from her home and her beloved river."

"You care about her," he said softly, his lips near her hair.

"Of course I do. I've grown very fond of her, and I want to help her live the rest of her life as she wishes, in her own home. I can't bear seeing her hurt any more.

"We'll see," he said.

She did not ask what he meant, for she found herself terribly distracted now by the sound of his deep voice, the touch of his breath against her hair. She leaned against him, feeling almost as if she could melt into him and become a part of him. It was a feeling like none she'd ever experienced.

Alex felt it, too, that special blending of body and mind that happens so rarely between a man and a woman. Despite the cool wind, he felt his body burning, and the muscles tensing in his body. He found his mind playing tricks on him, making him believe there was no war, no suffering. There was only him and the desirable woman in his arms.

He pulled slightly away from her body and the swell of her hip against his thighs. A tremble coursed through him. This ride had definitely not been a good idea, he told himself, taking a deep breath of cool air into his lungs and slowly exhaling it.

The storm intensified quickly, at first with large heavy drops of rain blown by the raging wind. Then suddenly the lightning was on top of them, striking fiercely all around them. The big gray horse rode steadily onward but flinched noticeably at each new attack of lightning and thunder.

Soon the rain became a deluge, hitting them with an unexpectedly hard force and making it almost impossible to see.

"We're going to have to stop somewhere," Alex shouted against the noise of the storm.

Leanna only nodded, and huddled tightly against him as he urged the horse on.

Alex knew they weren't far from the village, although he could not be sure exactly what area. In a blinding flash of lightning he thought he saw the outline of a building ahead. As the total darkness engulfed them again he could not be sure he'd seen anything, but he nudged the horse in that direction.

As they grew nearer he saw the building again. It was the old tavern and pump house, near what the Shakers called the summer spring. When they reached the small house he pulled the horse beneath a shed outside the building.

Without speaking he pulled Leanna from the horse and carried her quickly out of the pouring rain into the shack. There was only one room inside, with a small loft that extended halfway across the top. He struck a match and saw a small stove in one corner. On the opposite side of the room was a small stone waterwheel, motionless now and obviously no longer in use.

He lit another match and lifted the iron lid from the stove to peer inside. Just as he expected from the diligent Shakers, there was kindling laid for a fire. He dropped the match into the dark hole and watched it flare into bright flames.

Leanna stood by the door, shivering, not moving or speaking. She was overcome by tingles of anticipation that ran across her chilled skin. It was almost as if this was meant to be. A chance to be alone, totally alone with Alex. Neither of them could run tonight, and Leanna didn't feel ashamed at her thoughts. It was what she wanted, with all her heart.

Alex could feel the tension in the small room that was suddenly generated between them. The flickering light from the stove and the cozy drum of rain upon the roof did nothing to help matters.

He looked across at Leanna, his black gaze catching hers and holding it. He saw the look in her eyes, the hunger and the surrender lying so quietly in their green depths. If he was to stop what was about to happen, he knew he should while he still had the presence of mind to do it.

He stepped toward the door, intending to go around her. "I'll see to the horse," he said.

"No," she said, placing her hand on his arm. "Don't go." She moved closer, sending the aroma of freshly laundered clothes and sweetly scented soap toward him.

"Leanna," he said with a hint of warning in his deep voice.

"Are you running away from me again, Alex?"

He closed his eyes and swayed slightly toward her. God, how his arms ached to reach for her. The violence of his feelings made him feel weak and unsteady.

He made a low sound of laughter, of self-derision. "If I had any sense, yes, that's exactly what I would do."

"What will I do if anything happens to you, Alex?" Her voice broke, and she could no longer maintain her calm outward appearance. Her bright eyes slowly filled with tears.

"Nothing will," he said, wanting to hold her and reassure her.

She moved closer, so close that he could see the light from the fire reflected in her eyes. She placed her hands on his chest and slowly moved them up to his shoulders and ran them through his hair.

"Promise me," she whispered.

As if in a trance, Alex was drawn by her eyes, by her lips. "I promise." Almost without knowing he reached out to place his hands around her slender waist inside her cape. "Nothing will happen to me," he said. He moved his hands lower, outlining the flare of her hips as he pulled her tantalizing body against his.

He watched her close her eyes. Her breath was coming in small gasps, and her pink tongue darted out to moisten her lips.

"Leanna," he whispered, making one last effort to stop the storm within them before they did something he knew they would both regret. He reminded himself that she was a virgin and that he alone was responsible for her welfare. He couldn't let himself take advantage of her.

But even as he cautioned himself he knew he could not stop. She was too close, too real, and the nights of wanting her had taken a heavy toll on his resistance.

How many nights had he lain awake thinking of her, seeing the vision of her in bed with the candlelight shimmering across her face? Her aloof looks at him on the dance floor and her taunting, feisty arguments with him. Those months of denying his feelings, of pushing her away, had all been in vain. They meant nothing now. He was lost, and he knew it.

Leanna gave in to all the emotions she felt for this man, all the longing she'd felt for so long. She felt giddy and strangely out of control. And here, alone with him, she found she was so excited by his presence and his touch that she was oblivious to everything else, even the noisy rage of the storm outside.

She opened her eyes to see his beautiful face, his black eyes hot with desire, and the shadows from the fire playing across his hawkish features. Leanna could hardly wait to feel his lips on hers again.

Rising up on her toes, she placed her mouth against his and felt the instant fire between them. Her heart fluttered as she felt a tremble sweep over his strong body. She knew how much he wanted to resist, how he wanted to do what was right for her. But it pleased her that he was losing the battle, and it filled her with an exuberant sense of pride and power.

She placed quick, light kisses on his mouth, trailing downward to nip at his chin. His breathing was hard, a low rasp in the quiet of the room as she buried her face against his neck, kissing him again and again.

His hands were still at her hips, and he pulled her closer, pushing his thigh between hers. Instinctively she pressed against him, moving in an unpracticed seductive way. It was more than Alex could withstand, and he found his self-control completely routed beneath her sensual onslaught. He was amazed at her innocent expertise, at her lack of inhibition. And he gasped when he felt her sharp little teeth nip at his neck.

His hands tightened around her, moving to the small of her back where he could feel the slight undulation of her hips. His dark head lowered to catch her open mouth and he kissed her hard, grinding his lips against hers, allowing himself all the privileges he'd wanted to take all along. He felt all the wildness in her release for him, as if it were the most natural thing in the world. Her obvious enjoyment thrilled and excited him more than any woman he'd ever known.

Now it was Leanna who trembled as he kissed her hotly, leaving her breathless and weak. His hands moved quickly and expertly over her, eliciting moans of pleasure from her lips. The initiative was his, and he took full advantage of it, moving his body against hers until they almost melted together.

At first the feel of their bodies through clothing felt sensual and tortuously sweet, but now both of them wanted to be free of all restraints, free to touch and feel with no barriers between them.

Alex moved her toward the corner and, hardly glancing away from her, pulled several grain sacks from a nail on the wall. He threw them on the floor and began to unfasten the tie at the neck of her cape. It fell slowly from his fingers and slid to the floor.

They continued to hold each other, swaying in an almost dancelike way as he kissed her even more passionately. She clung to him, returning his kisses feverishly until they were both on fire, until their legs trembled beneath them.

It had been a long time since Alex had made love to a woman. Never could he remember feeling this way, this out of control. He wanted to make Leanna happy, make her feel all the pleasures that sexual desire could bring to a man and woman. But she was young and inexperienced and needed time, and he was afraid his eager body would betray him.

He pulled away and looked down into her eyes, giving her one last chance to stop, to turn back from him and what they were about to do. Her look was so trusting as she moved to the floor and held her hands up to him.

Alex knelt before her and untied the white scarf around her shoulders. Slowly he unfastened the buttons of her dress, pushing the material aside and placing kisses on her skin with each new opening. He could feel the tension in her, the trembling of her body that grew stronger.

"Please, Alex," she said, urging him to love her, to fulfill this new yearning that swept over her.

"Soon, my love," he said softly as he pushed the dress from her shoulders and down to her hips. Then he helped her free of the garment.

He couldn't take his eyes away from her. Still on his knees, he began to unbutton his own jacket, aware of her eyes bright with desire, her lips parted and moist. He bent to kiss her and felt her small hands at the buttons of the white shirt he wore beneath his jacket.

He reached to push the plain cotton camisole from her shoulders, revealing for the first time her lovely full breasts. Alex thought his heart would explode inside his chest as his eyes moved over her soft creamy skin. He fairly ripped away his own shirt and moved to her, wanting more than anything to feel her bare breasts against him.

Leanna reached out and ran her hand lightly across the muscled contours of his chest, feeling the taut smoothness of his skin. Then slowly, tentatively, her hand moved lower to the rippled surface of his flat stomach.

Alex closed his eyes and took her hand, pulling it away. She laughed softly, a teasing, triumphant sound. Quickly Alex tore the chemise away, sliding it down her long slender legs and tossing it aside. And just as swiftly his own clothes followed.

Leanna had never seen a man undressed, and she found him as beautiful as any Greek statue. But he was no cold, lifeless statue; he was real, a warm flesh-and-blood man.

Alex smiled at her look of awe and quickly pulled her against him. He began to kiss her hungrily, and his hands moved to her hips to pull her beneath him.

Leanna gasped, a bit afraid now of what was about to happen. His lips on her neck, her ears, caused her to shiver uncontrollably.

"You're so beautiful," he murmured against her skin. "I've never wanted anyone the way I want you, Leanna, never." His voice was husky and breathless.

Her entire body felt hot, burning as she arched to feel the touch of his mouth on her breasts. Then quickly he moved between her legs, nudging her thighs apart.

Leanna gasped with surprise as a sharp burning sensation seared through her body when he entered her. She stiffened and looked up at Alex with a frightened look.

"It's all right, baby," he said, moving to kiss her softly, his hands touching, moving over her again slowly and sensuously.

Alex thought he might die from the pleasure of feeling her sweet fire surrounding him. But he forced himself to go slowly.

Leanna surrendered to his kisses and the touch of his hands, and soon a liquid heat moved through her. She began to move against him instinctively. The pain was receding and in its place was a glorious, exciting pleasure that grew, filling her with wild delight as she gripped his shoulders and felt her world spinning around.

She wanted all of him. It was as if she had known the ways of love all her life. She moved with him, lifting, urging his strong body to do as it wished.

And when she thought she could stand no more of the exquisite pleasure that was building within, she felt a strange, throbbing warmth move down her body. She was afraid she might actually faint as she finally seemed to explode with a pleasure that was wilder and more wonderful than she had ever dreamed possible.

"Alex . . . Alex," she cried, even as she reveled in the power of his own fulfillment.

Alex pulled her against him, fiercely raining kisses upon her face and neck. "Oh, love . . ." he whispered, his voice husky with astonishment. "My own darling little Rebel."

Leanna's heart was pounding with joy and delight in her newly discovered bond with this man. She knew that from this night until the end of her life she would never forget it, would never be the same. She also knew she would never feel this exquisite pleasure with any-one else, never love another man than Alex Slayton, her beloved Yankee, her own Nighthawk.

23

The spring storm continued to rage outside the small shack, buffeting the walls and rattling the sheets of tin roofing. Inside, the fire burned low in the stove, and the air became filled with a chilling dampness.

Alex was not sure how long they had slept on the pile of burlap. He had been awake for a while now, propped up on one elbow as he watched the woman who lay curled against his side. She slept quietly, peacefully, and there was a tiny smile that flickered at the corner of her beautiful lips.

Alex reached out one finger and brushed back a golden red curl that was still damp from the rain. Leanna stretched and then opened her eyes slowly to look up at him. She smiled and, with a move that he thought made her even more dear, pushed her face shyly against his chest, hiding her eyes from his searching gaze.

He laughed softly and reached down to kiss her cheek. When she finally lifted her head, she placed her hands gently on Alex's shoulders, enjoying the feel of his smooth brown skin and the hard flex of muscles beneath. When she felt the long slash of scar, she looked closer and saw the wide white swath that branded his shoulder.

The smooth skin of her brow furrowed, and she looked back into his eyes. He did not move as she leaned forward and slowly, gently touched her lips to his shoulder, kissing the ragged scar.

She felt and heard his hushed intake of air as her lips moved over his skin.

"I hate whoever did this to you," she said in a vehement little whisper.

He smiled, so sweetly she thought. His black eyes crinkled at the corners as he gazed at her with tenderness.

"It was a long time ago."

Her hands continued to run over his shoulders and down to his chest. "You were protecting Trey."

There was a quiet flash of surprise in his eyes. "Did he tell you that?" He brushed a kiss lightly against the hollow of her throat.

She couldn't speak as his lips moved slowly along her throat and to her ear, but closed her eyes and grew limp against him, allowing him free access as his lips moved against her skin and his teeth nibbled at her ear.

"I want . . . want to know . . ."

He laughed softly against her rose-scented hair. "Yes?" he whispered into her ear. "What is it you want to know, little Rebel?"

"To . . . to know . . . about Trey. Oh, Alex . . ." She could hardly remember what she'd been saying, able now to concentrate only on his mouth and the rasp of his whisper against her ear. "What . . . are you . . . doing to me?"

He smiled at his own response as much as hers. He was elated at her reaction to his touch and his kisses. He wondered if she had any idea what the touch of her hand did to him, or how he'd felt when her soft lips kissed the scar on his shoulder.

She was a rare, wonderful combination of woman. The blending of wild, carefree abandon with such sweet, warm compassion was an unbelievable one, and it was driving him crazy.

"Which question shall I answer for you first?" he teased. His lips hovered lightly over the pulse at her throat, savoring the warm sweetness of her skin.

He was ready for her again, tingling with excitement, his pulse racing even faster than before. He gave a low grunt and pulled her fully into his arms, delighting in the feel of her naked skin against his.

"Never mind," she whispered.

Leanna smiled as her face pressed against Alex's chest. Never in her life would she have expected to feel such wild, joyful abandon in the arms of a man. She was surprised to feel the small, nagging little flutter in the pit of her stomach again so soon after their lovemaking.

Until tonight she had been only a song without words, waiting for something she never knew existed. Now she knew what completeness was, and why so many women dreamed and longed for a lover. It was everything.

Their lovemaking this time was even more perfect

than before. Alex delighted in the trust she gave him, in her willingness to go wherever he led her. He reveled in slowly, carefully bringing her to the point of an almost frenzied need before deliberately making love to her with a tenderness he had not realized he possessed.

Afterwards she lay in his arms, marveling at how perfect he was and trying to forget that he was leaving tomorrow. She decided it was all the more reason to be happy about what had happened between them.

"Will it always be this way?" she asked.

"Will what always be this way?" he murmured against her hair.

"This . . . what just happened . . . being together this way." She suddenly felt self-conscious.

"Well, I hope next time we have a bed," he said lightly.

She nudged him with her arm. "Don't tease me about this, Alex. I'm serious."

"I know you are, love," he said quietly. How could he explain to her how special, how perfect they were together? It was a rarity he was not sure he could convey to someone so innocent as Leanna. "We were perfect, weren't we?" he asked softly.

Leanna knew that he had not really answered her question. Did that mean it would never happen again between them? Mrs. Macky had often told her about fast girls who gave themselves so foolishly to men, only to find that the man was no longer interested after the initial conquest.

She looked at Alex, watching the play of light in his black eyes. Suddenly she was afraid, more afraid than she'd ever been in her life. For she knew, swiftly and surely, that all her suffering, all she had lost, was nothing compared to the thought of losing this man.

"I'd better get you back to your room before morning," he said, reaching across her to gather his clothes.

"What time is it?"

"Late."

Quietly she moved away and pulled her own clothes back on. She swallowed hard, trying not to cry, hoping to hold back the tears until she was in the privacy of her room.

She felt Alex's arms slip around her from behind. He pulled her back against him, kissing her cheek and the corner of her mouth. She shivered and found her legs feeling weak again.

"We'll never get home," she said with a lightness she did not feel.

"I know," he said, smiling with surprise at himself. "Are you ready?"

She turned and looked deep into his eyes. "One last long kiss for remembrance."

His eyes softened as he cupped her face tenderly in both hands. He kissed her slowly and deliberately, with all the emotion she could ever hope for.

They stood for a long moment, bodies pressed close, lips only inches apart. Then Leanna turned quickly and walked out before she could give into the impulse to cry and beg him not to go.

The first fury of the storm had passed, leaving only a soft, pleasant sprinkle of rain. The wind had died, and the air now felt cool and clean, fragrant with the scent of wet grass and leaves.

Alex seemed to hold her closer this time as they rode the last distance to the West family dwelling. He left his horse well away from the house and walked silently with her through the wet grass to the large cedar tree behind the kitchen.

Leanna turned and wrapped her arms around his waist, burying her face against his wet coat. "Oh, Alex," she cried. "How can I stay here now without you? How will I get through the days without seeing you or touching you?"

He held her tightly as his hands caressed the mass of damp curls about her face. He lifted her chin toward him and slowly, tenderly kissed her eyes, her nose, and the corners of her lips as she stood breathlessly still. His kiss of good-bye was long and slow, without the impatient hunger he'd exhibited earlier. But there was such a wealth of feeling in his touch this time that she told herself the kiss said what he could not.

"I'll be back before you know it. You'll manage very well without me."

"I'm afraid."

"You are a strong woman, Leanna. Much stronger than I ever would have thought."

"Am I?"

"Yes, my love, you are." He shook her gently for emphasis. "I'll write to you as soon as I can."

She nodded, unable to speak now that the time had come for him to go.

"And if you need anything, if there are any problems, you've only to send word to Gina and she'll come for you."

"Yes," she said. Her smile became a grimace as she tried to be brave for him. "Be careful, Alex. Take care of Jimmy and Trey and the rest, and . . ."

"I will," he said gruffly, turning quickly to leave. He couldn't bear to stay longer and see the sadness on her lovely face or feel the ache in his heart.

"And come back to me," she whispered to his retreating shadow. "Please, come back to me, my darling."

Leanna hardly realized how she got from the back of the house to her room. She was crying so hard that she was sure she would wake everyone inside.

She had almost forgotten her father's letter until she felt the thickness of the envelope in her discarded dress. She quickly changed into a dry nightdress and climbed into bed, sliding her cold feet beneath the heavy layer of quilts.

She opened the damp envelope and unfolded the paper. Her heart leapt at the sight of her father's small, neat handwriting.

My dearest daughter,
I hope by now you are settled safely with the Believers at Pleasant Hill. Have faith, darling. It is the best place for you until I am free. I cannot tell you how lucky we were to have a man like Alexander Slayton helping us. There are many not so fortunate. Trust him, do as he asks.

Leanna closed her eyes and clutched the letter to her breast, marveling at the words. A few months ago they would only have angered her more, but now she saw the truth in what her father said. She did trust the man that her father had picked, more than anyone in the world.

She continued to read.

Alex has told you by now that the charges against me are all true. I'm not ashamed to have aided my country; I am only sorry that I had to choose between it and the people who were my friends. I tried to tell you this before, but you were not ready to listen. I hope now you are. Don't worry about me, my darling. The building where we are housed is quite large, with plenty of space for privacy. The food is not bad and is plentiful, the water cold and fresh. The prison has been given a unique name. It is called Castle Thunder because of the thunderous vibration whenever the artillery guns are fired. Well, I must go. I pray that you are safe and that we will soon be together again, and I hope you might some day find it in your heart to forgive me if I have betrayed your trust.

> All my love,
> Papa

Leanna was crying as she reached out to turn down the wick of the lamp. There was relief in her tears, relief that her father was safe. His letter sounded not unhappy. She realized that as she'd come to know Alex better, she knew he had not been lying about her father. So this confession came as no great surprise to her. As her father said, she was ready now to know the truth.

She lay in the dark, praying for her father. But the vision of Alex kept slipping into her mind. It would not go away, and she could not quell the ache in her heart that he was leaving. She felt as if a part of her, her very soul, was being ripped away, and that she might die without him in her life.

"Oh, God," she cried, turning her face into the pillow. "Please help me," she prayed. "Please don't let anything happen to Alex . . . please." She was still crying and whispering small prayerful words as she fell into an exhausted sleep.

*   *   *

Jackson Cole's entire body trembled with rage. He stood beside the window in the darkened kitchen, listening to the soft sound of the rain long after the couple outside had parted.

"The little slut," he said aloud. His teeth were bared, and spittle glistened on his dark beard. His eyes moved back and forth as angry thoughts raced through his mind.

The storm had awakened him, and he'd slipped down the stairs, hoping that a glass of milk would soothe his burning stomach. He had just extinguished the lamp on the table when something outside caught his eye. Turning to the window he saw the outline of two people walking toward the cedar tree. In the lingering flashes of lightning, he'd seen the glimmer of red-gold in the woman's hair. And he'd known immediately that the man Leanna McNairy embraced was the dashing Major Slayton.

Jealously coursed through his veins. It was always this way, always the tall, handsome soldiers that the girls swooned over and gave themselves to so easily. Jackson found that he almost had to force himself on a woman for sexual favors. Of course, he often told himself, if he'd been born rich, things would have been different. Oh, yes, very different indeed.

It had only been since coming to the Believers that he'd had the power and authority to catch a woman's interest. He did not delude himself; his position was what drew Emily McGrath to him. Somehow, going to bed with a man of power and position made some women feel more important. It even outweighed good looks or kindness. He simply could not understand why Leanna remained unmoved by his position and authority.

Standing in the kitchen now, he relived the scene he'd just witnessed—the sight of her clinging arms, her submission to Slayton's lingering kiss. Something in him wanted to barge into her room right now, drag her to the floor, and tear her clothes from her.

He'd like nothing better than to make her beg for mercy before he was through with her. Then even the prim, high and mighty Miss McNairy would feel his power.

"By God!" he swore, gritting his teeth. He smashed one fist into the other palm, over and over, until finally the rage had left him and in its place was the beginning of a plan. He was determined that Leanna McNairy would belong to him one day soon. He would make her forget that Alex Slayton had ever existed.

As Alex rode away from the village, he removed his hat and turned his face up toward the rain, letting the shower cool his burning skin. It had taken every bit of strength he possessed to leave Leanna there beneath the cedar tree.

For the first time in his life he'd found something, someone who made him want to forget every responsibility, every vow he'd ever made. All he needed or wanted was this woman, this flame-haired girl who turned his heart inside out. Nothing else seemed to matter now—not the war and not even his damn responsibilities, which he'd always placed above everything.

If he could have he'd have taken her tonight and run far away, away from the war, away from Kentucky and its divided people. But something wouldn't let him, perhaps that same respect for responsibility that he could not shake, even now. That and the men back at camp who depended on him. Not to mention Leanna's father. How in hell was he going to get the senator out of that prison and back home? Somehow he knew he must find a way, for Leanna.

The light rain washed over him and with it the reality of what had happened tonight. Away from her, alone with a clearing mind, he knew it had been a mistake. A terrible and perhaps costly mistake for both of them.

He had vowed not to let emotional attachments get in the way of his duty. He'd sworn he cared nothing for the senator's spoiled daughter, that he had enough responsibilities with his young soldiers. Suddenly all the reasons he should have stayed away from her came flooding back into his mind, and he was filled with a deep, wrenching guilt.

But how could he regret the love they'd shared there in the small shack? How could he regret the sweetness of her surrender and the overwhelming fulfillment he'd felt with her? No, nothing could ever make him regret it, but he would have to forget it. He would also have to make her forget. As long as there was a war, he could not afford to let it happen again.

He didn't want anything to happen to her, and he worried even now that he could be responsible for a new life—a child. What had possessed him to act so hastily, to forget every vow he'd made?

Even as he rode through the rain, through the darkness of the early morning hours, he knew. The vision before him was proof enough—the memory of her soft lips, the mass of red-gold hair, and those incredible eyes that seemed to look into his very soul while he made love to her. And he knew he'd never be able to rid himself of her touch. She was branded upon his heart forever.

Leanna wanted to stay in bed when the great bell rang only a few hours later. She thought seriously about telling Polly she was ill, but then what? Could she spend the whole day in her room with only her troubled thoughts to occupy her time?

Reluctantly she dragged herself from bed, dressed, and straightened the room before going out to greet Polly.

The older woman glanced at Leanna, taking in her red, swollen eyes and the sad, tired droop of her mouth. She wondered what on earth had happened, but she decided to say nothing. The best thing would be to wait until the girl was ready to tell her about it.

They silently went in to breakfast. Leanna picked at the food, eating little and drinking her tea with a quiet distraction.

Jackson Cole watched her from the men's table. He noted her pallor and the sadness on her beautiful face, and he hated that the look was not for him. All the while as his eyes feasted upon her, he was thinking, planning, for the day soon when he would make her his own. On that day he would teach her about the deep spiritual love that could exist when a woman was submissive to the supremacy of a man.

24

The rain continued to fall heavily throughout the day. Its soft patter on the roof and against the windows of the washhouse only added to Leanna's melancholy. The work went slowly, and everyone seemed to be feeling the same effects of the rain as Leanna.

Rachel sat quietly, mending clothes as Leanna ironed. The dark-haired girl's time was near, and she was often plagued with backaches and fatigue. Leanna did not mind taking the more strenuous tasks; in fact, they kept her mind occupied.

"Will you stay here after the baby is born?" Leanna asked, attempting conversation to help them both stay alert.

Rachel looked up with surprise. "Of course. Where else would I go?"

"Don't you have a family you could go to until your husband returns?"

"They wouldn't want me. I would only disgrace them now."

"Why would you think such a thing? Where is the disgrace in having a child?"

Rachel looked at Leanna but did not reply.

"What about your husband's family?"

"I have no husband."

Leanna could hardly believe what she was hearing. Rachel had told her before that her husband was in the war.

"Surely you must have guessed," Rachel said quietly.

"No," Leanna said. "No, I didn't. I believed the story you told me."

"I'm sorry to have deceived you. I . . . I thought everyone here knew, and that you had probably heard."

"No," Leanna said, placing her iron back on the stove. "Then I suppose this is the best place for you. The Believers are good people. It's not such a bad life, until you can decide what you want to do."

"Oh, I intend to stay here forever."

Leanna picked up a new iron and looked at the young woman with disbelief.

"You don't understand," Rachel said.

"I don't understand why a young woman would wish to spend the rest of her life without a husband to love, or a home of her own. And what about the father of your child?"

Rachel's lips tightened, but she did not look up again and she did not defend herself further.

*   *   *

After supper and evening prayers, Leanna walked with Polly back to the West family house. She was so tired that she could hardly wait to get inside and into the soft warmth of her bed.

But that thought fled as Emily McGrath met her at the door.

"Thee has a visitor, Sister Leanna," she said, her eyes sparkling with cold disdain. "She's in the parlor."

Leanna went to the small, neatly kept parlor and was delighted to see the woman standing at the window.

"Gina!"

Gina stepped forward to embrace her. "I'm sorry I couldn't come earlier today. But the rain was so hard at times that Mrs. Sutton insisted I could not go out."

"Please don't apologize. I didn't expect to see you so soon. Beside, Mrs. Sutton is right, you must take care of yourself."

Gina smiled sweetly. "Let's sit down, I want to talk a moment."

"Is anything wrong?" Leanna asked as they sat side by side on the small wooden bench near the fire.

"That's what I wanted to ask you . . . about my brother."

"What?"

"Before he left this morning, he gave me a letter to give to you." She handed an envelope to Leanna.

Leanna's heart leapt at the anticipation she felt. She was moved that he had wanted to put words on paper about last night.

"But he was troubled, worried about something. He hardly spoke except to tell me good-bye and to ask that I take care of some business for him. I know that it was very late when he came home this morning, and I wondered . . . was there any problem between the two of you?"

"Why . . . no." Leanna wondered herself what was on his mind. Then her face became warm with remembrance of the night. "Last night with Alex was . . . was . . ." She glanced at Gina, not knowing how to explain last night and wondering at the same time if she even should.

"Oh . . . I see," Gina said softly, with a little smile. "Then in that case I suppose I know what was on his mind this morning."

Leanna smiled as a soft glow brushed her cheeks. "Was he able to tell you when he'd be back?"

"No, I suppose he doesn't know. But try not to worry, Alex has a natural instinct for this sort of thing. He'll be all right."

They sat for a moment. The hiss of the fire was the only sound in the room. Then Gina sighed and stood slowly.

"I must speak with Brother Levi and Sister Jane at the trustees' house before I go. It's almost dark, and I hate to worry Mr. and Mrs. Sutton. They've been so kind to me, allowing me to stay here in the country for a while. I really needed this time alone."

"And I'm so glad we met," Leanna said. "Please come again. Perhaps one Sunday before you return to Bardstown I shall come and bring a picnic for us to share."

"That would be wonderful."

Gina liked this lovely red-haired girl that her brother had apparently fallen in love with, and she hoped to find in her the sister she'd always wanted.

Afterward, Leanna hurried to her room. She quickly

readied herself for bed and snuggled beneath the covers to savor every word Alex had written.

She held the envelope up, noting the large scrawl across the front where he had placed her name. But the expression on her face turned to one of puzzlement and then stunned surprise as she opened the letter and read the short message.

Leanna,
I hope you believe me when I say that I had not intended to hurt you more than I already have. How can I explain to you? My actions last night were very selfish and not very responsible. As we've discussed before there can be no future for us now. I only hope that by the time I return to Pleasant Hill you will have been able to forgive me and to forget that last night ever happened.

> With affection,
> Alex

Leanna could hardly breathe for the pain that gripped her. "No future . . ." she whispered. Quickly her eyes darted back over the words, searching each one, trying, hoping to find that she had misunderstood his message. But there was no mistake about what he meant.

"Selfish . . ." she whispered. "How could it have been selfish . . . the most beautiful night of my life?" She sat up in bed and stared at the letter. "Oh, Alex," she cried softly. "How could you say these things?"

She wanted to cry and scream, to leap from the bed and run into the rainy night. In her frustration she felt as if she would explode. There was simply nothing she could do. She could not even confront him to demand why.

She read the words aloud, pausing at the end. How could she forget that last night ever happened? Could he forget it had happened? Was she just a naive fool to have thought that the love they'd shared meant as much to him as it had her?

" 'With affection, Alex,' " she read. "Affection?" She could not believe it.

Was that the key to the whole thing? What Alex felt for her was only affection, while she had not been able to help herself. She had fallen madly and hopelessly in love with the tall, arrogant Yankee, almost at first sight.

"Fool," she whispered with disbelief. "I am such a fool." She could not believe it was happening to her. She had been so certain that he was not one of those men Mrs. Macky had talked about. But now, how could she believe anything else?

Her heart ached so badly that she thought she would truly die, and her stomach twisted with agony. Suddenly, she leapt from the bed and pulled at the chamber pot from under the bed. She was violently ill, her stomach heaving until she felt weak and her face was beaded with perspiration.

The door opened, and Polly rushed in, looking at her with alarm. She wet a cloth from the washstand and helped the shaking girl climb back into bed.

Leanna lay back against the pillow, exhausted, her face pale in the frame of red-gold hair.

"Shall I get you some water?" Polly asked.

"Yes, please," Leanna whispered, closing her eyes.

She took the water and felt Polly's soft hand on her forehead. "You don't seem to have a fever."

Leanna shook her head weakly from side to side as

tears squeezed from beneath her lashes and ran down her face.

Polly frowned and then noticed the letter lying on the bed. Without reading it, she could guess at its contents. Slowly she sat down on the bed.

"Oh, child," she said. "What you have can't be doctored. A broken heart must heal itself."

Leanna's eyed opened, and her lips trembled as she nodded to Polly. She wished desperately for the ache to go away, that she would wake tomorrow and find that the letter was only a dream.

Polly patted Leanna's hands. "I know how it feels. Even as old as I am, it ain't been that long since my old heart was cracked a mite, too. But it'll mend, child. It'll mend."

She held Leanna's hand and soothed her brow with a damp cloth until finally, against her will, Leanna slept.

She woke many times during the night, coming awake suddenly as if someone were shaking her violently. She would listen to the rain, trying to concentrate on its quiet, patter. Her room was dark, and Polly had gone to bed. Leanna was so exhausted that she would drift back into a fitful sleep, only to wake again moments later.

She slept more soundly in the predawn hours, even through the ringing of the great bell. When Polly came in and found her still sleeping, she tiptoed out quietly, relieved that the girl was resting peacefully at last.

Leanna did not wake until very late in the morning, well after breakfast and morning prayers. Polly had told Sister Emily that Leanna was ill and could not go to the washhouse.

When Polly brought tea in around midmorning, the aroma mingled with the scent of hot bread and seemed to invade Leanna's mind and rouse her from sleep. When she opened her eyes she was disoriented, wondering why she was still abed at such a late hour and why Polly was pouring tea.

Then it came back to her, the full understanding of what had happened. And with it the pain returned, just as sharply as when she had first read Alex's note.

She sat up in bed, gritting her teeth. Her sadness was being replaced by anger now—anger and resentment that Alex could rebuff her so easily. She had fallen too quickly in love with a man she hardly knew, and now she was paying for her foolish naïveté.

Polly noted the new spark of determination in Leanna's eyes. She handed her a cup of tea and sat beside the bed. "You slept better near morning light," she said.

"I'll be all right," Leanna said quietly, looking into the clear amber liquid of her cup.

"Will you?"

"I can't make him love me, Polly. And I won't beg!" Only the slightest tremble of her chin betrayed her feelings.

"No," Polly said. "That would never do."

"You'll see, I'll be fine."

She turned her eyes to the window, praying silently that she could make her words come true, and knowing the almost impossible task she was setting for herself. How could any woman forget the handsome black-eyed man they called the Nighthawk?

25

After tea Leanna slept again, and finally joined Polly in the sewing room that afternoon. They sat in companionable silence, listening to the sound of the continuous rain until they heard a light knock at their door.

Leanna motioned for Polly to remain seated and she went to the door. "Sister Jane," she said, surprised to see the woman.

The sweet-faced woman came in and sat with them, rocking before the fire. "I was sorry to hear thee has been ill," she said to Leanna.

"I'm feeling much better now," Leanna said.

"Well, thee looks a bit pale. And I had noticed before how thin thee has become."

"She's been working too hard," Polly said, with a spark in her eye.

Sister Jane studied Leanna's face and frowned. "Yes, I believe she has. Why is that? I was informed that thee had asked for extra work Leanna, to . . . to take thy mind off personal problems, I believe."

Leanna was unable to disguise her surprise. "Why, no, I didn't ask for extra work."

"Just as I thought," the woman said. She looked at Leanna with concern in her eyes. "Would thee wish to move to another dwelling house?"

Leanna believed she could trust this woman, and obviously Sister Jane knew what mischief Emily had been about.

"I prefer to live here with Polly."

"That will be permitted," the woman said. "Let me explain why I asked. As thee knows, our infirmary is in the Center dwelling because it is such a large structure. We have need of someone to tend the sick and to learn the use of herbs from Sister Charity. She is growing old, and her eyesight fails her. Would thee be interested in working with the sick? Thee could still live here."

"Well, I . . . I had not thought about such a thing. But I suppose—"

"Leanna would be very good at attending to the sick. She's a sweet, caring girl," Polly said.

Leanna smiled at Polly. The woman was as proud and protective of her as a mother would have been.

"I agree with Sister Polly," Sister Jane said. "And if thee would try, Sister Charity and I would both appreciate it very kindly."

Leanna knew what the woman was trying to do, and she was grateful. Perhaps it was just what she needed to take her mind off Alex. Also, it would get her away from the authority of Emily McGrath.

"Then I will be happy to try," Leanna said.

After arranging the hours and days Leanna would work, Sister Jane stood up to leave. At the door she turned and said, "We are a fair and decent people here, Leanna. And if ever anyone treats thee unkindly, I hope thee might come to me. Brother Levi and I would put a stop to it immediately."

"Well," Leanna said to Polly after the trustee had left. "I wonder what brought that on?"

"I can't imagine. But it's plain she's on to Miss Emily. And it does my heart good to know you'll be gettin' away from that little troublemaker."

"And Jackson Cole," Leanna added.

Polly's head came up quickly, and she dropped her sewing into her lap. "Why do you say that? What has he done? Has he said something to you?"

"Why, no," Leanna answered, puzzled by Polly's sudden agitation. "There's just something about him that I don't like, that's all."

"Well, I've always believed in heeding one's own instincts." Polly returned to her work. "And I've heard rumors about that one. Nasty rumors that I didn't like at all."

"What rumors?"

"Well, I don't want to slander a man if I'm not certain. But just you be forewarned, child. Stay away from that one."

"I intend to."

Leanna threw herself wholly into the work at the infirmary. She was able to fill her days with learning new, interesting things, only to find that each night brought with it renewed misery in her thoughts of Alex.

When there were no patients at the Center house,

Leanna worked outside in the garden, picking strawberries in the spring and other fruits as they came in season. She lost the tired, worried look, and the leanness she had acquired gave her a flattering appearance of good health. The sun turned her usually pale skin to a golden apricot hue and brought out sparkling highlights in her red hair.

Away from Emily McGrath, she came to see the true goodness of the Shaker people and the spiritual way they meant life to be. The simple, prayerful life, living on the abundance of their own crops, gave Leanna a sense of peace she'd never known before.

There was something inside her, some basic instinct that told her the great importance of this kind of life. Perhaps it was as God intended life to be.

Without knowing it, she impressed Sister Charity, a hard taskmaster who had intimidated Leanna at first. The sister was a large, stern-faced woman who looked as if she'd never enjoyed anything in her life. Leanna could not imagine why this woman had chosen the vocation of nursing.

Sister Charity's nearly six-foot stature and her burly, almost manly build did indeed make her an intimidating presence. Her skin was dark and swarthy, as if she'd spent the majority of her seventy years in the sun, but there was not a speck of gray in her dark chestnut hair. Her hollow, brooding eyes were often unsmiling and ringed with dark circles.

It did not take Leanna long to see the goodness beneath her hard exterior, though, and the real tenderness she held for anyone who was ill. In the infirmary her big hands were as gentle and soft with her patients as the most feminine of women. And though she had not said so in words, Leanna knew that Sister Charity liked her and approved of her work.

Time passed, and still Leanna did not hear a word from Alex. Gina had gone back to Bardstown, telling her with a mysterious smile that as soon as some business was attended to she would be back.

Early one morning near the first of July, as Leanna and Sister Charity were gathering herbs beside the Center house, they heard the clatter of wagons moving toward the village. Soon the grass and hedges, even the sidewalks, were covered with dust from the movement of the army that was passing by.

The two women stood silently and watched the tired, ragged-looking soldiers go by and the supply wagons roll slowly past, heading toward Harrodsburg.

Leanna watched with disbelief as rows of lean, haggard men in gray shuffled together in a slow, weary rhythm. They were like ghosts drifting by. Where were her dashing young gallants, her brave, handsome Confederates?

Some of the soldiers waved as they passed, and some shouted, but most of them trudged on wearily, looking straight ahead with sad determination.

Suddenly from the group Leanna heard a shout.

"Leanna! Leanna, is that you?"

"Tyler!" She ran down the fence row and to the gate. He met her there and stopped, his face saddened by the look of horror in her eyes.

"Oh, Tyler," she whispered, staring at him as tears filled her green eyes.

He was terribly thin, and the dust of the road was heavy on his gray uniform, obliterating the gold braid and making him look like a vagabond. Almost desperately he pulled her into his arms and hugged her tightly, ignoring the whistles and shouts from some of his comrades.

"Are you well, Tyler? Where are you going?"

He only smiled, and a puzzled light appeared in his pale blue eyes. Leanna's stay with the Shakers had changed her almost beyond his imagination. There was no teasing, no impatience in her now. As his eyes moved over her sun-warmed skin, he thought she had never been more beautiful.

"I'm fine, Leanna." He glanced at the columns of men, knowing that he dared not fall too far behind. "There's so much I'd like to tell you. So much. You're beautiful." With a wave of his hand he moved back toward the soldiers.

"Tyler, wait," she cried. She wanted to hold him back forever. She couldn't bear seeing him this way and could hardly stand to think of his being in battle.

"I love you, Leanna," he shouted with a smile. "I'll be back."

Leanna walked back to Sister Charity, who only shook her head. "Such a sad sight I never thought to see in my lifetime," she said.

"Are you in sympathy with the Southern cause?" Leanna asked.

"Oh, no. Not at all. I would feel just as saddened to see the Union blue march past this place. All these young men, fighting and dying. And for what? 'Tis one reason I became a Believer. War and politicians . . . bah! I'd hoped to find peace from it here at least."

Leanna was beginning to understand more every day what Sister Charity meant. The South had suffered heavy blows in the spring, and she wondered what the long, hot days of summer would bring. There were those in Washington who had boasted of an early victory over the Rebels. But now it seemed likely that the war would continue through the summer and perhaps into winter. Leanna knew in her heart that her own loyalties were becoming painfully divided.

There was talk that the Confederates wanted to regain Kentucky, and Leanna wondered if the men who'd passed were here to help accomplish that. In any case, the war was moving closer to them each day.

Leanna and Sister Charity took their baskets filled with the sweet fragrance of herbs, and turned to go into the house. From the road there was a shout and the sound of another wagon. This driver was dressed in Shaker garb though, and he seemed to be shouting at them.

As the wagon drew nearer, they could identify the face of the driver. It was Brother Jackson, and beside him, bent over in the first agonizing pains of labor, was Rachel Harris.

Sister Charity quickly handed her basket to Leanna and went to help the woman from the wagon. By the time they had her inside the house, Rachel's face was ashen and beaded with sweat. Her eyes reflected fear and pain as she reached for Leanna's hand.

"Help me," she whispered.

"We will," Leanna assured her. "Let's get you up-stairs and out of these hot clothes. Can you make it up the steps?"

Rachel's eyes swept upward, and she slumped against Leanna. She turned with a pleading look at Brother Jackson. His dark eyes darted to Leanna before he looked away from both of them, not offering to help or even acknowledging the girl's questioning look. There was something about the two of them, as their glances met, that jangled some memory in Leanna. But in the urgency of the moment it was soon forgotten.

Brother Jackson made an excuse to leave. Then, with the girl's arms over their shoulders, Leanna and Sister Charity managed to get her upstairs quickly and without inflicting more pain. She was in a surprising amount of distress considering that her labor was just beginning.

Leanna's heart was beating heavily by the time they had her undressed and into a clean white gown. She had never witnessed the birth of a child, and she felt both a sense of anticipation and fear. At the troubled look in the eyes of Sister Charity, she felt her fear growing even stronger.

Suddenly the war, her curiosity about the passing soldiers, and even her worry about Alex disappeared and she found her every sense concentrated on the girl in the bed.

As they waited, Leanna watched the large shade trees outside that towered above the three-storied structure of the Center house. The long windows in the infirmary stood open to catch the light breeze that swept across the cleanly scrubbed wooden floors. Even so, Rachel's face was red and hot, and she kicked at the sheet that lay across her legs.

She seemed to be in such pain that Leanna actually felt an ache within her own self. Sister Charity gave the girl sips of cool primrose tea for the pain, but it hardly made a difference. There was nothing they could do except bathe her face and arms and hold her hands when the contractions gripped her.

"It's going to be a long day, dear," Sister Charity whispered to Leanna. "Try to relax."

But Leanna found relaxing difficult. As the morning

drew on, she sensed that something was terribly wrong. Rachel was in agonizing pain, yet she seemed no closer to delivering the child than she had been hours earlier.

Through the long afternoon they sat with her, comforting her and assuring her that everything would be all right. By evening, when darkness at last brought a relieving coolness through the open windows, Rachel was in a semi-conscious state, totally exhausted from her futile efforts to deliver the child.

"Sister Leanna," Charity said, "take thyself downstairs and eat some supper. Thee has eaten little all day."

"No," Leanna said. "I don't want to leave her. I promised her."

"She hardly knows thee's here, child," the woman said, looking at her sadly. "Besides, thee will need strength through the night."

"Then . . . then you think it could be all night before the baby . . ."

"Sister Rachel is small, with narrow hips. Sometimes women like her labor for two days, especially with the first child."

Leanna drew in her breath, her stomach tightening in dread for the young woman.

"Sister Leanna," Charity said as she followed her out into the hallway. "Sometimes in situations like this when the mother and child . . . when neither of them have the strength to continue . . . it could be very dangerous. Do you understand what I'm trying to say?"

"You're saying that Rachel could die?" Leanna asked, her heart now filling with fear.

The woman nodded. "If thee does not wish to come back, I will understand."

"No . . . no, I'll come back. I want to be here with her, no matter what happens."

"Then go eat. We have plenty of time yet."

Sister Charity's words proved true. Rachel writhed in pain all through the night and into the next morning. Once, near dawn, she raised herself from the pillow, her eyes wide with alarm. "Jackson?" she cried, reaching her hands out blindly toward Leanna. "Jackson . . . I'm sorry. Please don't be angry with me."

Leanna frowned at her puzzling words and looked toward Sister Charity, who sat in a chair across the bed from her. The woman's dark eyes filled with anger, and she shook her head slowly.

Finally, that afternoon, when Rachel had still not delivered, Sister Charity came to her bed with a cup of tea.

"I've made this tea from the bark of the cottonwood. It should speed up her labor. But never give it to a pregnant woman not in labor."

Leanna nodded and helped spoon the liquid down Rachel's throat.

It wasn't long until the pains began to come in continuous waves. Rachel screamed until her voice grew hoarse, and the sounds were a strange rasping yelp. Leanna gripped the girl's hands. She was crying and praying quietly that the girl's agony would soon end, one way or another. This was more than anyone should endure.

Sister Charity began to prepare for the child, laying a clean blanket in a small cradle beside the bed. Then she moved quickly and efficiently to help as the baby was born.

"A little boy," she said.

Leanna went to help, noticing the small size of the

infant and its frightening bluish color. Rachel had lost consciousness now, and her legs had become limp.

"Oh, Sister Charity," Leanna said breathlessly. "She's . . . she's not? . . ."

"She's alive, child, just barely. Quickly, another pillow beneath her head so her tongue does not block her breathing."

Leanna did as the woman asked and made sure that Rachel was still breathing. She turned to look toward the cradle. Sister Charity's face was tired and sorrowful as she pulled a blanket over the dead child's small, withered body.

"No," Leanna whispered, tears coming to her eyes.

"I'm sorry, child. There was nothing either of us could have done. The baby probably has been dead for the past few weeks."

Leanna could only shake her head as she looked at the cradle. Suddenly, it was all more than she could stand. Was there nothing in this life except pain and sorrow? Where was the happiness she once knew, the joy she had thought her own private birthright?

She ran blindly from the room and down the stairs, past the sisters who were mopping the bare wooden floors and the one sweeping the front steps. She ran past the herb garden, not even seeing the beauty of her favorite spot or smelling its sweetness.

Only when she reached the fence far beyond the houses did she stop, her breath coming in ragged gasps, tears wetting her entire face. She raised her fists helplessly into the air, hitting them against the weathered locust fenceposts, unaware of the pain she inflicted on herself. Finally, exhausted, she fell on the rich green grass and cried.

"Oh, Alex," she cried. "Where are you? Why have you left me here to endure this?"

Every sadness she felt, every painful experience of the long dreadful day seemed to culminate into one common loss. Her loss of the man she loved.

26

It was late when Leanna finally managed to drag herself up from the ground. The sun hung low on the western horizon, shimmering through a wispy haze that lay across the meadows. The light cast long, thin shadows from the trees and fence posts.

Leanna walked slowly, taking deep breaths of air as she brushed the grass from her skirts. She would not give up now. Something deep inside forced her to move, to return to the poor young woman in the infirmary. She thought she'd never felt sadder in her life, and yet there was a stubborn strength welling up within her. She had no idea where it came from, but she was glad for it.

Leanna stopped in the kitchen to splash cool water from the sink onto her burning face and wash the grime from her hands and arms. The women working there to prepare the supper meal looked at her askance but said nothing. She could tell from their manner that they'd heard about the baby's death.

As she turned to leave, one of the cooks handed her a plate of freshly baked bread and thick slices of steaming mutton. The woman touched Leanna's hand and looked into her eyes with sympathy. "Thee needs to eat, Sister," was all she said.

Leanna felt tears threatening again. She took the plate and quickly went upstairs to the infirmary.

She met Sister Charity just outside Rachel's room. The woman smiled at Leanna and said nothing about her running away. "I'm happy thee came back."

"How is she?"

"She's still alive, but she's extremely weak and has developed a fever. It might be days before her condition changes. If thee likes, thee can sit with her awhile," Sister Charity said. "After supper," she added, seeing the plate Leanna carried.

"Yes," Leanna said. "I would like to stay."

The sister moved past Leanna. Then she turned back and took something from her pocket. "Oh, I almost forget, thee received some correspondence today. The sister brought it up after thee left."

Leanna took the envelopes in her hand. "Sister Charity, about this afternoon. I'm truly sorry. I . . ."

The woman's stern face crumpled into the most tender look, and she touched Leanna's shoulder. "Thee does not need to apologize for feeling sorrow, not to me, at least. I understand perhaps better than anyone. I shall never forget the first time I saw someone die, someone I'd taken care of, just the way thee did Rachel and her baby. 'Tis a hard thing to face."

Leanna was filled with such an overwhelming rush of

love for the woman that she wanted to hug her, but she did not, uncertain of how the woman might react. Instead she only whispered quietly, "Thank you."

"No, my dear," Sister Charity said, "I thank thee. Thee has the makings of a fine nurse." Then she turned and walked away.

Leanna glanced down at the envelopes in her hand. Three letters in one day! She held her breath, hoping to see the bold, scrawled handwriting of Alex's pen. Her disappointment was softened a bit when she saw the letter from her father. Then, with further surprise she noted that the others were from Jimmy and Gina.

She ate her supper quickly and then went into the quietness of Rachel's room to read the letters.

She glanced at Rachel before seating herself in a rocking chair beside the bed. The girl's hands, folded across her breasts, were motionless and pale, giving her the appearance of death. Leanna leaned toward her until she could see the slight rise and fall of her chest. Then, satisfied that the girl still lived, Leanna sat back in the chair and leaned closer to the lamp that burned dimly beside the bed.

Her father's letter was short. He was never one to waste words. He assured her again that he was well, and he hoped she would not worry unduly about him. The end of the letter was a single, mysterious sentence: "If I am lucky, your savior will also soon be mine."

Savior? What on earth did he mean? Was he speaking religiously, or could he possibly mean Alex Slayton? Leanna frowned, not knowing quite what to make of her father's words.

She opened Jimmy's letter with trembling fingers, knowing that it was his proximity to Alex that made her react so. How foolish of her to be so moved simply on the hope that Jimmy might mention something of his commanding officer.

His handwriting was scribbled carelessly across the sheet of paper and was difficult to read.

We have been involved in some hard fighting. Skirmishes mostly, nothing big. A couple of the men were wounded but continued to ride with us. The major says we're a tough bunch for city boys. (That's a joke, as you know, 'cause we're all farmers.) We hear that McClellan has failed in his attempt to capture Richmond. But the good news for us is that Corinth, Mississippi is occupied by immense force of Federal troops. We've taken New Orleans and it is believed that the entire Mississippi River valley will soon follow. I suppose I shouldn't be writing you of all people to boast of Union victory, but I feel you are a true friend to us, regardless of your personal beliefs, or ours. You will be happier to learn that your own Confederates, despite all our efforts, still remain intact and surprisingly strong. It looks to be a mighty long and hot summer. I could not end this letter without telling you that Major Slayton is well and has come through the past weeks without a scratch. But he does not seem to be himself. Could it have something to do with you? Well, I'll ask you about that when we get back to Pleasant Hill. We're on our way back now and if we run into no problems, should be there soon. Keep safe and don't let the Shakers change that beautiful smile and spirit.

Best regards,
Jimmy Anderson

Leanna's eyes filled with tears. She was so frightened, not only for Alex, but for Jimmy and the rest as well. They were on their way back, though, and she felt a spark of hope at this news.

Finally she opened Gina's neatly written letter. Actually, it was only a short note. It read,

My dear Leanna,

I mentioned before I left some business that I needed to complete. I am happy to be able to say it has been accomplished. I hope to arrive at Pleasant Hill, within the next few weeks to share the good news with you. I believe you will be very happy to hear what I have to say.

> With love,
> Gina

Three very different, yet similarly puzzling letters. All told, they made Leanna more hopeful than she had been in weeks. Despite her vows to forget Alex, she knew that the fact that he was on his way back to Pleasant Hill was one very big reason for her hope.

Leanna sat beside Rachel, watchful for any movement or sound from the girl. There was nothing, and soon the lack of sleep the night before and the delicious meal she'd just eaten took their toll, and she drifted to sleep in the rocker.

She woke near midnight and glanced quickly at Rachel. She had not moved at all since Leanna had first arrived. Leanna got up slowly and walked across the hall, where she collapsed into one of the empty beds and slept soundly till morning.

*   *   *

Over the next few days Rachel began to improve. Once she was conscious, however, she seemed drastically changed by what had happened. She hardly spoke to anyone, and her expression was flat and apathetic. Even her dark sparkling eyes were dull and lifeless.

"What's wrong with her, Sister Charity?" Leanna asked one morning as they tried to coax Rachel into conversation.

The older woman shook her head. "It has no name, child. Grief, a broken heart . . . I don't really know. We must pray that she will soon be sound of mind and spirit once more."

The hot summer days passed, each one much the same as the one before, with little rain to cool the fiery heat of the sun. Rachel gradually grew stronger, physically at least, but Leanna was alarmed to see that there was still no significant change in her mental state.

The dark-haired girl would sit quietly in a rocking chair and look out the window. Her face was often expressionless, and she spoke little. At first she asked for her baby, and when Sister Charity gently explained what had happened, Rachel cried.

She asked nothing else about the child after that, yet several times each day she asked for Jackson Cole, her dark eyes beseeching them to tell him to come to see her.

He never came, at least not to see Rachel. Sometimes Leanna would find him standing in the shadows of the house when she left in the evening to go home. He would fall into step beside her, his eyes watching her greedily as he spoke of some meaningless subject. He never hinted of what Leanna suspected he hid in his heart: He was attracted to her, she could tell. It was the feeling a woman gets when a man looks at her a certain way, yet it was not the same kind of looks she'd seen from Alex. No, there was something in Jackson Cole's opened-mouthed stare that sickened Leanna and made her try to avoid him whenever she could.

She wondered about his relationship with Rachel, and she was certain that Sister Charity did also. She had learned that the girl had become pregnant after arriving at Pleasant Hill, not before. Now the thought that the father could be Brother Jackson repulsed and infuriated Leanna.

Several weeks had passed since Jimmy's letter. She began to watch the road each day for any sign of the small troop of men. The day they finally did arrive, though, Leanna had hardly been outside. They had several children in the infirmary, and she was too busy even to think about going out.

She heard a commotion in the large sitting room outside the hallway. There was the noise of boots ringing loudly across the bare floors and the sound of voices raised in excitement.

Leanna wiped her sleeve across her perspiring brow and went into the sitting room to see what was happening. She was stopped cold by the sight that greeted her. The first thing she saw was Jimmy's face streaked with dirt and sweat, his blue eyes dark with worry.

Alex, she thought, and her heart threatened to stop beating. But then she saw him, and the relief left her body weak and shaking.

Jimmy and Alex were together carrying one of the soldiers, whose dusty blue uniform was covered with dark stains of blood.

"Leanna," Jimmy said breathlessly, "it's Trey. He's hurt real bad."

"In here," she directed, standing aside so they could carry him down the hallway.

Alex passed so close to her that she could have reached out and touched him. His gaze slid over her face and figure for only a second before he turned his concentration back to Trey.

For Leanna, seeing him whole and well gave her an overwhelming sense of relief. Yet all the pain she'd felt came rushing back, and with it a new determination that she would not run to him this time. Perhaps he was right. Perhaps there could never be anything between them, and the night they'd spent together had been a dreadful mistake.

They laid Trey on a narrow cot. His large, bulky form dwarfed the bed, and his booted feet reached past the end.

Leanna quickly assessed him. His dark skin had a gray, ashen color, and he was very still. She went to the door and met one of the sisters carrying linens.

"Get Sister Charity, quickly please."

She took the linens and set them near the bed. Then she placed a trembling hand against the pulse at Trey's throat. The heartbeat was faint.

Alex and Jimmy stood nearby, watching her quick, efficient movements, neither of them speaking but seemingly caught up in her ministrations to Trey.

She began to loosen the buttons of Trey's jacket. The material was stiff with dried blood and covered with dirt. "What happened?" she asked as she took a pair of scissors and began to cut the undershirt from his body.

"We were in a skirmish near Paris, Kentucky. An ambush led by John Hunt Morgan and his raiders. Do you know of him?" Alex's voice was deep and quiet.

"I've heard of him," she said, still working.

"It seems lately that he and his men are everywhere we turn." He said nothing more but moved closer to watch Leanna work.

He watched in fascination her cool, skillful movements, but concern for Trey was obviously foremost in his mind.

"It happened several days ago. I don't know how Trey has managed to hold on, especially in this sweltering heat."

Jimmy stepped closer. "He wouldn't let us leave him in Lexington, which would have been better for him. He insisted we bring him here to the Shakers. He said he wanted to die in a clean bed, among people he knew." Jimmy's eyes turned to Leanna with a look of foreboding.

Leanna's hands gripped Trey's filthy shirt, and she ripped the rest of the material away.

"He's not going to die!" she said fiercely through clenched teeth. "I won't let him die."

Jimmy stepped back, surprised by the vehemence in her voice. "Yes, ma'am," he said. "Well, I'll go see to the horses, Major. I guess she don't need all of us in here, smelling up her sickroom."

After Jimmy left, Alex watched the slender girl work at removing the rest of Trey's foul clothes. She did not pause for a moment or hesitate as the dirt and blood stained her hands and dress.

Alex noted the healthy golden color of her skin and the sheen of her reddish gold hair. Wisps of her hair had come loose from the neat bun at the back of her neck. He watched with surprise as her small arms rippled with muscles as she worked. His black eyes filled with admiration at her gentle yet efficient movements. There seemed to be nothing left of the spoiled, petulant girl he had spirited away from Lexington on that frigid night in January.

Trey moaned, and Leanna bent closer. "Trey?" she said. But there was no other sound from his lips. "It's all right, Trey, it's Leanna," she whispered. "You're here with us at Pleasant Hill now. I'm going to take care of you. Do you hear me?"

Alex saw Trey's fingers move, almost imperceptibly at first. Leanna saw it, too, and reached to grasp his hand. When the dark fingers moved only the slightest bit to clasp hers, she turned to Alex with a brilliant smile lighting her face.

"He heard me," she whispered.

Alex only nodded, unwilling to speak and let her see the emotion in him as well. He was impressed. He had dreamed of this moment so many times, of seeing her beautiful face again.

He had dreamed of her and grieved for her and for himself. Not a day had passed that he did not think of her and that night in the storm. He had worried about what his leaving might do to her, but he could see now that he need not have worried, and that realization both pleased and pained him.

When he looked at her face, their eyes caught and held. In hers he saw accusation and defensiveness. Hell, he couldn't blame her. He only wished he had been strong enough to resist making love to her that last night. He should have, if he'd really wanted what was best for her. He'd told himself that a thousand times since.

But he could not have resisted her any more than he could make himself stop breathing. She was in his blood and his heart, and now, looking at the strong woman she had become, he knew she was firmly ingrained in his soul as well.

"I'll come back later, after the men are settled in."

"I'll take care of him, Alex," she said, her eyes bright with unshed tears, her beautiful lips pressed firmly together.

Alex felt an ache near his heart such as he'd never experienced. No one had ever moved him as this feisty, argumentative woman had. That was something he had been fighting since the moment he'd first seen her on that night in her father's study.

He reached out and cupped her chin tenderly with his fingers. A thrill moved through him when she didn't pull away. "I know you will," he said quietly before turning to leave.

27

By the time Sister Charity arrived, Leanna had already examined the ragged wound in Trey's left shoulder. She shuddered slightly and turned to the tall woman who entered the room.

"It's Trey, Sister Charity," Leanna said. "I think he's lost a great deal of blood, and the wound looks very bad."

By now Leanna had ripped the leg of the man's trousers and exposed another wound in his left thigh. It too was festered and red, with crimson streaks running away from the gaping hole.

Sister Charity shook her head sadly. "I'm afraid this may very likely be mortal my dear," she said quietly. "With this heat and the dirt and sweat, his wounds are already terribly infected."

"No," Leanna said as she continued to remove the

material from Trey's body. "He won't die. He can't. I promised him he'd be all right."

Sister Charity watched as Leanna worked feverishly, first tossing the filthy clothes onto the floor, then bringing a pan of water near the bed to wash her patient. Fear was in every movement and reflected on her face, and Charity knew she was acting out of desperation to save her friend.

Charity did not waste any more precious time observing the girl's movements or wondering at her motivations. She placed her box of herbs on a chair near the bed and began to look through the jars, searching for just the right medication. Finally, she took out a small tin and a bottle containing a reddish purple liquid.

"This salve is made from the root of the purple coneflower, and it's the best thing I know for infections. I'll bring hot water to cleanse the wounds and see if any metal remains, then we'll see. While I'm gone, see if thee can get a spoonful or two of the elderberry wine down him." She looked at Leanna solemnly. "But don't get thy hopes up, my girl. I doubt he'll make it through the night." She touched Leanna's shoulder and then left.

Leanna shook her head as she gently washed the grime from Trey's lifeless-looking body. All the while she spoke to him, whispering fiercely, "You will make it through the night, Trey. You're going to live, do you hear me? I won't let you die. I won't let you."

After she'd forced a spoonful of the wine into Trey's mouth, she covered his body with a cool clean sheet. She was surprised to see small stains on the cloth where her tears had fallen unnoticed as she worked. Angrily she wiped her eyes and face and turned to clean the room before Sister Charity returned. She did not have time for tears.

When the sister returned she poured a few drops of mint-scented oil into the hot water and began to clean Trey's wound. Leanna gave a prayer of thanks that he was unconscious, for the woman probed and prodded at the inflamed wound in his shoulder, causing more blood to be lost. Leanna swabbed at the sister's perspiring brow as she worked, until finally the older woman wearily leaned back into the chair, holding in her hand the small forceps that contained a bloodied piece of twisted metal.

"There," she said with quiet satisfaction. "The bullet seems to have gone all the way through the wound in the leg, thank goodness. Would thee go to the kitchen and bring some broth for him and some cool water? While thee's gone I will apply the salve and bind the wounds."

"You're tired," Leanna said. "Don't you want me to help with that?"

"No, child," the woman said with a gentle smile. "When I am soundly asleep in my bed tonight thee will be here, I suspect, watching over thy friend and willing him to live. Thee will need thy strength for that."

It was well past dark when they finished with Trey, having bound his wounds with strips of clean white cloth. Leanna forced several spoonfuls of warm broth between his lips, feeding him as one would a motherless kitten.

Before Sister Charity left she warned Leanna again of the seriousness of his condition. She sorely hated for the girl to have to grieve again so soon after the death of Rachel's child, but Leanna did not seem to heed her words. It was as if she thought that she alone could will the man to live.

Leanna opened the window to let whatever cooling breeze there might be drift into the room. She was so tired that her back ached, and she knew she was filthy. Still, she would not leave Trey's bedside.

When Alex arrived shortly afterwards he found Leanna sound asleep in a chair beside the bed. He looked at her small white hand that lay across Trey's dark arm. She had refused to let go, even in sleep. He watched her tenderly for a long while, hating to wake her yet wanting to give her a much needed respite.

He knelt beside her chair and touched her arm. "Leanna," he whispered.

She found herself gazing into Alex's black eyes. They were filled with concern, and for a moment she thought she must be dreaming.

"Why don't you go to bed?" he asked. "I'll stay with him the rest of the night."

"No," she said, glancing quickly toward the bed. "He might wake and wonder where I am. He might be afraid."

Alex was touched by her almost desperate need to stay with Trey. Was she afraid that if she left he would die? She had lost so much in her young life, and Alex could understand her fears. It was as if she had placed all her hope on keeping this man alive, as if some superstition told her that everything would be all right again if only he lived.

"I'll tell you what," Alex said. "Why don't you find something to eat, change your clothes if you'd like, and then come back. Surely I can be trusted to stay with him for a few minutes."

Leanna felt ashamed of herself. He was treating her

like a child, and perhaps it was because she was acting like one. But how could she expect him to know the fear she felt at leaving Trey? She'd seen death since she'd been here, but something told her that if someone as young and vital as Trey died, there would be no hope for any of them. How could she make Alex understand that?

"I just don't want to leave him," she said, her chin trembling ever so slightly.

"I know you don't," he said, "and I understand."

"Do you?"

"We all think sometimes that if we can be in control, everything will be all right. That we can make things be the way we want." He looked straight into her eyes, determined to make her understand. "When in reality we can only do our best and then pray for the final outcome to be as we'd like. And you've already done that."

She closed her eyes and leaned back against the chair. He was right, she knew he was, but it was so hard to let go.

"All right," she said. "I would love a bath and a change of clothes. But only if you promise to be right here with him."

"I promise."

Later, after a bath and something to eat, Leanna was surprised at how much better she felt. Her mind was still in turmoil, though, not only with worries of Trey but wondering what she would say to Alex.

It was the first time they had seen each other in weeks, and when they parted it had been so sweetly. She had felt closer to him then than anyone in her whole life. Now they were like strangers, talking politely and pretending that nothing had ever happened between them.

She wanted him to know how he had hurt her and yet, if he was the kind of man to use a woman and then forget her, would he even care? And why did the sight of those ebony eyes looking at her so intently cause her insides to quiver? Why could she not hate him and forget him?

Back in Trey's room, Leanna breathed a little sigh of relief at finding that nothing had changed. Alex stood by the window, looking across the lawn toward the West family house.

"Come here a minute," he said as she entered the room.

He motioned her to the window and pointed toward a clump of trees past the herb garden. "When you came back, did you see someone at those locust trees?"

She looked past his pointing finger, squinting into the night that was only dimly lit by a half-moon, but she saw nothing. "No. I saw no one."

"As you were walking back I could have sworn there was someone hidden here, watching you." He frowned and turned from the window. "I want you to be careful."

She laughed, and her eyes flashed at him in her old rebellious way. She was amazed at the nerve of him. He had left her, telling her they had no future, rejecting her after he'd made her fall in love with him. And now he was back, expecting to take up his old overbearing habits. Well, she would have none of it.

"I am taking care of myself now, Alex," she said with a touch of sarcasm which she could not help. "What I do or don't do has nothing to do with you. So you see, there is no longer a need for you to feel any responsibility for me."

He saw the tightening of her jaw and the defiant glitter in her eyes as she looked at him. She seemed as stubborn and foolhardily as ever where her own welfare was concerned, but she was right about one thing. She had grown into a confident, self-assured young woman since his absence.

He gritted his teeth, determined that their first night together would not be marred by quarrels. He couldn't really blame her for being bitter, but damn, the girl could be a tribulation when she wanted to be.

He raised his hands in mock defense. "Excuse me. I did not mean to offend you or to sound patronizing. And I don't want to quarrel here in Trey's room."

"Oh?" she said, aching now to do battle with him, wanting to vent all the anger and frustration she'd kept within her these past months. "Then where *do* you want to quarrel, Major Slayton?"

"Forget it," he snapped, and walking past her back to the bed.

"Oh, no. I won't make it that easy for you Alex," she said. "I won't forget it. And I won't let you forget, either. This has nothing to do with my being careful or with your concern for me, but it has everything to do with what's happened between us."

He looked down at her, determined to keep his gaze steady and calm. She was right, and as usual she would not let it go until he had explained his actions to her. That was going to be a hard thing to do, because here, so close to her, with the fresh scent of her bath clinging to her skin and the damp wisps of hair at her neck, he was so distracted that he hardly knew what he was saying.

Everything in him, every sense was focused on her, the remembrance of her lips beneath his, the touch of her soft, sweet body. And the way she had clung to him, moving with him until both of them were out of their minds with desire.

The way she looked tonight brought back every feeling, every longing he'd ever had, stronger than ever. He wanted to pull her into his arms, willing or not, and kiss her angry words away until she was no longer able to think of anything except loving him.

"You're right. There are things we need to discuss," he said, his voice barely controlled. "But not here, not tonight."

"Still running, I see, Major."

He could not help but smile. She knew him too well. "Damn right," he said. "Especially from a dangerous little Rebel like you."

"You can joke all you want, but I won't be quiet about this. Not until you've explained a few things to me."

"I didn't expect you would," he said. "We'll talk soon, I promise."

He grabbed his hat and moved out the door without giving her a chance to say anything else.

Alex walked through the sitting room to the stairway and took the stairs two at a time. He needed to be outside in the fresh air, where he could think more clearly.

But damn it! What difference did he think a few more days would make? He could try to explain things to her again, but they both knew the attraction between them burned like a torch, as hotly as ever. There was no denying that.

The war was escalating, and he knew he would be drawn further into it. The only question in his mind was whether or not he would be willing to sacrifice Leanna's future for a few selfish, happy moments. For there was one thing he could not explain to her: Every day he felt destruction moving closer to them all.

Sometimes he woke at night, sweating, with a fleeting sense of death upon him. How could he explain that to the stubborn girl with the flame gold hair? How could he tell her that he thought he would die in this war? One thing had become clear to him during their time apart: He was hopelessly and desperately in love with her. And he could not offer her a future when he knew he hadn't one to give.

28

Trey lingered near death for several days, and Leanna was with him almost constantly. When she did sleep it was only for a few hours, yet in her anxiety it seemed to be all she required. Every bit of strength she possessed was attuned to the big man lying in the sickroom.

Rachel had taken to coming into the room at times. Trey was the first person she'd shown any interest in since her baby had died, and Leanna did nothing to discourage her coming.

Another person came as well, someone less welcome. Jackson Cole was curious, she supposed, about the black soldier who had requested that he be brought to Pleasant Hill to die. If Leanna had not been quite so tired or preoccupied, she might have been more cautious.

Jackson Cole's patience was growing thin. In his warped mind he had taken it slowly where Leanna was concerned, had been gentle, even indulgent with her. Still, he'd seen no response. If anything, she'd grown even colder. To see her concerned look as she bathed the big black man's face and spoke quietly to him was an insult.

Was the girl too stupid to know that he could make her happy as no man could? Many times he wanted to shake her and scream at her and make her see that everyone she'd given her sweet attention to had abandoned her.

First her father, then Alex Slayton, that arrogant Yankee soldier. Jackson Cole was no fool. He saw the look in Leanna McNairy's eyes whenever Slayton was around or when anyone mentioned his name. Did she think he did not know how shameless she was?

It was growing more obvious to Jackson every day that he would have to be more forceful with her. Some women could never grasp the reality of what was really best for them. Obviously Leanna was one of those women who wanted the thrill of being pursued aggressively, even forcefully.

He began to watch her carefully, taking note of her daily routine. That was one of the reasons he visited the infirmary often. It certainly was not to see the moon-faced Rachel, as the pathetic creature seemed to think.

Rachel was another problem to Jackson. If only she would get well enough to leave the infirmary, Jackson knew that Leanna was often there alone at night. This was an isolated part of the huge house. He was certain that he could convince her, one way or another, of his need for her, and eventually she would grow to love him just as the others had.

*   *   *

Leanna was disappointed that she rarely saw Alex alone on his visits to Trey. She wondered if he planned it that way, but she had been busy caring for other patients as well as Trey. Then there was Rachel, poor girl, who wanted to follow her around the rooms and hallway like a frightened puppy.

It was almost a week after Trey's arrival that Leanna went into his room early one morning and saw that he had moved significantly during the night. The sheets were crumpled and pushed away from his body. Stepping closer, she saw a heavy film of perspiration on his skin.

As she bathed his face with cool water, his eyelashes fluttered and then opened slowly. Leanna felt a rush of anxiety in her chest as his eyes tried to focus on her. Then, slowly, they closed again.

"Trey?" she whispered. "Can you hear me?"

He was much cooler today, she was certain of it. And the dark, festering color around his wounds was fading away. He was going to be all right.

In a few moments his eyes opened again, and this time he was able to hold them open. He smiled at Leanna, and she thought her heart would pound right out of her chest.

"Oh, Trey!" she cried. "You're awake! How do you feel?"

"Like I been kicked by a mule," he muttered, his deep voice hoarse and ragged.

She laughed. She could hardly believe he was actually speaking to her. There had been days when she felt as if he would be in his unconscious state forever. It was almost a surprise now to find him awake and lucid.

"Do you think you could eat something?"

"Yes, ma'am, I sure could. I feel like I ain't had a meal in months." He smiled weakly at her.

"That's truer than you know," she said. "You've been here a week."

He frowned and looked around the room. "Pleasant Hill?"

"Yes. Jimmy said this was where you wanted to be."

"I don't remember it."

"Well, the important thing is that you're here. Sister Charity saved your life with her medicines, I'm certain of it."

His dark eyes wandered over her face and down to the drab dress and white apron she wore. "I'll have to thank her," he said.

"Yes, well, I'll get you some food."

"Miss McNairy," he called from the bed. "I have a feeling I should thank you as well."

"No," she said, smiling. "There's no need."

"I thought I was dreaming several times, dreaming of a woman's voice that told me I'd be all right. And I remember cool, gentle hands, a woman who was always here. It was you, wasn't it?"

Leanna lowered her eyes and nodded, uncertain of what she should say during the awkward moment.

"Thank you, Miss Leanna," he said.

For the first time since she'd met him, she felt a bond between them. It was the only time he had ever looked at her without that quiet, defensive glare in his eyes. Now there was only gentleness.

"You can thank me by calling me Leanna. Not Miss Leanna and not Miss McNairy."

Now it was his turn to look embarrassed, but he

smiled and nodded slightly before closing his eyes and lying back against the pillow.

Later she insisted on feeding Trey his softly cooked egg, much to his embarrassment. Alex came to the door and paused briefly.

"Well," he drawled with obvious pleasure. "It's about time you woke up, Private. I thought you'd decided to lie around this place until winter."

Trey smiled. "If I keep getting this kind of attention, I might be tempted."

"Leanna," Alex said, "I've brought you a surprise."

She turned just in time to see a flare of dark blue skirts and the billow of lace petticoats in the hallway behind Alex.

"Gina!" She set Trey's breakfast aside and went immediately to embrace her.

"It's about time," Leanna said with a smile. "I've been waiting for you since I received your letter. What was that all about?"

Gina grinned mysteriously and exchanged a quick glance with her brother. "If you can tear yourself away from your patient, I'll explain it all to you right now."

Leanna glanced at Trey and his unfinished breakfast.

"I'll do that," Alex said. "You two go ahead."

Trey frowned at the two women. "I ain't so sure I'm goin' to like this," he said, motioning with his eyes toward Alex.

"Well, Private," Alex drawled, "I don't think you have much to say about it."

Gina and Leanna were laughing as they left the room. Leanna was so happy to see her. She looked at Gina and noted her lovely complexion, the blush of color on her cheeks. She wore a loose-fitting dress, and it was obvious now that she was expecting a child.

"You look wonderful," Leanna said.

"Oh, thank you. I needed to hear that," she said with a laugh. "I do feel well."

They went to the large, airy sitting room and sat down near one of the windows. Gina took Leanna's hands in hers and looked steadily into her eyes as if she wanted to make sure the girl was paying close attention.

"I have some wonderful news for you and your friend Polly."

"Polly?"

"Do you remember telling Alex about Polly's farm? And how she was afraid she would have to live out the rest of her life here?"

"Why, yes." Leanna could not imagine why Alex had told Gina about Polly.

Gina's eyes were aglow with excitement as she went on. "That's the business I had to take care of, it was something Alex asked me to do for him. He's purchased the farm back from the Shakers! And he wants all of us to move there. It's where my child will be born," she added breathlessly. "And Alex feels you will be happier and safer there."

Leanna could only stare openmouthed at Gina. She would never have guessed that Alex could do something so spontaneous and so wonderful. She was so taken by surprise that she could not even respond. In fact, she felt nothing except a pleasant numbness.

"All of us . . . you mean Polly and . . ."

"Yes!" Gina laughed. "You and Polly. Me, and now Trey. Oh, Leanna, the place is beautiful. The house is large and lies on a small crest overlooking the Kentucky River. The land is rich and fertile, even in the midst of this dry spell."

Leanna stared at her speechlessly.

"Well? Say something. Say you're happy, relieved. Say anything!"

Suddenly Leanna felt a great flood of joy at what this meant. She reached for Gina and hugged her, and then jumped up. "Oh, Gina, do you know what this means? It means I shall have my freedom again! I can speak as I wish, go where I please. And dresses! I shall actually be able to wear real clothes again!"

Smiling, Gina stood up and hugged the girl, and suddenly they were both crying.

Alex entered the sitting room and watched the two women. "Does this mean you're pleased?" he asked.

Leanna turned and looked at him for a long moment, taking in every feature of his strong, handsome face. She longed more than ever to kiss his curved, smiling lips.

"Yes, I'm pleased," she said, her voice almost a whisper in the large room. "I can hardly believe you even remembered what I told you about Polly."

Alex took a step closer to her, never taking his eyes off her face. "I've forgotten nothing." His voice was as expressive as his eyes, and Leanna knew he was not speaking only of Polly.

Neither of them noticed Gina quietly slipping out of the room.

"How can I thank you?" Leanna asked softly.

"By being safe and happy, as your father wished."

For only an instant Leanna felt a stab of disappointment. Then a flicker of something else in Alex's eyes, some brief ember of sadness and regret, made her look at him more closely. There had to be an explanation for his generosity, for no matter how he tried to hide it, she knew that it was for her that he'd done this.

These past few months of living with the Shakers

and working hard had taught her to trust herself and her feelings. And she knew as certainly as she'd ever known anything that Alex's actions had nothing to do with her father's wishes. They had to do with her and how he felt about her.

But why did he keep pushing her away, only to come back and look at her with such tenderness in his fathomless black eyes?

She moved closer and placed her hands on his chest. She smiled at the look of alarm in his eyes, but he did not step away.

"You almost had me convinced, you know," she said, lifting herself to her toes to touch his lips softly with her own.

Alex closed his eyes and took a deep breath. He moved forward to clasp her arms, gripping her as if he were clinging to life itself. As always when he was near her, his resistance disappeared. Every vow he'd made over the past few months seemed foolish and crazy. He was aware only of his need to feel her in his arms, to have her soft body against his.

Instinctively he pulled her hard against him. He plucked the fragile cap from her head and swiftly pulled the hairpins free, loosening her thick tresses to spill down her back. She caught her breath as he ran his hands through her hair and pulled her head back.

When she looked up at him, he saw the surrender there in her eyes, the willingness to let him back in. She parted her lips and reached up toward him. Both of them forgot where they were, forgot everything except the familiar sweetness of being together again.

Alex bent his head toward her and took her lips in a hard, hungry kiss. And she welcomed him, whispering his name as she pressed against him and returned the kiss as avidly as he.

It was a moment full of passion and heat, one that wiped away nights of separation and longing. Leanna felt as if she would die from the rapture of his long, overpowering embrace as she welcomed him back home and back into her arms.

When Alex looked down at her she whispered against his lips, "Nothing you can say will convince me this is not right, Alex Slayton."

"Willful . . ." he said with a low grunt of laughter.

He knew that the time for pulling away from her and denying what was between them was over. With a strange feeling of elation he pressed his mouth against her neck. His arms encircled her, and he held her tightly against him, rocking her back and forth.

"I won't try," he whispered against her ear. "But there are things I need to say to you, so much that needs to be resolved."

"Anything, my darling," she whispered, reveling in the feel of his lips against her skin and the press of his strong, muscular body against hers. "You can tell me anything."

Jackson Cole watched them from the doorway, his face growing crimson with rage. He waited for a moment, trying desperately to compose himself before he stepped into the room and separated the enraptured lovers. For the first time in his life, he wanted someone dead. He could have killed Alex Slayton with his own hands, but that might only spoil his plan. Instead, he stepped back outside into the hall and made a loud noise before entering the room again.

This time Alex and Leanna moved apart. Jackson noted the rapid rise and fall of Leanna's lovely breasts beneath the gray material of her dress. The spark of desire was still hot in her green eyes. The Union officer, perhaps more used to deception, looked at him coolly, with no trace of the emotion he had displayed with the girl.

"Well, Major Slayton. It's good to have thee back home," Jackson said, smiling at the man.

"Thank you. I'm not certain how long we will be here, but for the time being, it's a needed break for us."

"Yes, I'm sure," Jackson said. "And how is thy patient this morning, Sister Leanna?"

He saw her push back the tumble of hair from her face and reach quickly to the floor to retrieve her prayer cap. "He's much better. I think he will have a full recovery."

There was a hint of breathlessness in her voice that irritated Jackson. He wondered if she had any idea how beautiful she was, how desirable with her hair falling around her flushed cheeks. He had never ached for any woman the way he did for her. It angered him that she seemed so selfishly unaware of his need, so totally entranced with the tall, confident Yankee officer.

Jackson shifted his eyes away from Alex's stare, careful not to let the soldier see his own desires and guess what he had in store for Leanna.

"I'll just step in and say hello to the young man if thee doesn't mind," Cole said.

"Not at all," Leanna said. "But only a few minutes. He needs his rest."

The blacksmith nodded toward her and the man who stood so protectively near her. Then, without another word, he walked down the hall and into Trey's room.

The black soldier was asleep. Rachel was sitting quietly beside the bed, her head lowered to the sewing she held in her hands. It angered Jackson to see her there, the mewling, interfering little bitch. Every time he saw her she asked if he had seen the child, the little boy she had borne dead. Didn't the little fool realize that someone might overhear their conversation and learn that the child was his?

He could hardly stand the way she fawned over him, touching and pulling at him, asking what was wrong as her large dark eyes pleaded with him. God, but he hated women like her who never realized when the passion was over and never knew when to let go.

He wiped a film of sweat from his brow with his sleeve. It was hot, and he felt irritable and frustrated at finding Leanna in Major Slayton's arms. Would nothing ever go right for him? Must he always pretend to be something he was not, holding back the ardor of love or hate that he always felt?

Seeing the moonfaced Rachel turn and gaze at him with adoration did nothing to relieve his dangerous, hateful mood.

29

Leanna looked up into Alex's gaze. What was the tender emotion she saw there? Did she dare hope it was the same passionate love she felt for him? And if so, what kept him from telling her?

Alex glanced at the doorway through which Jackson Cole had just disappeared.

"What is it?" she asked.

"I'm not sure—a feeling. Something about that man. He's said nothing to you or bothered you in any way?"

"No, Brother Jackson is harmless, I think. It's just that he makes me uncomfortable. Do you think he saw us just now?"

"Oh, yes. I'm sure he did. Not that it matters. You'll soon be away from here, so there's nothing he can say to you."

"When?"

He smiled down into her eyes, moved by her happiness with what he had done. But this time, conscious of where he was, he did not pull her into his arms. "Within the week, I think. Just as soon as Trey can be moved." He reached out and brushed a curl back from her ear. She shivered, and pleasure flooded his dark eyes.

"I'm sorry if I hurt you," he said softly.

"You did, terribly. I couldn't believe it. Why did you say those things to me, Alex?" The happiness he'd seen before was now gone, replaced by the old pain and feelings of abandonment.

"That's one of the things I'll explain when we can be alone." He traced a finger down the side of her face. "Did you hate me so terribly?"

"Yes!" she said with a flash of fire in her eyes.

He raised one eyebrow and smiled.

"No," came her whispered admission. "Although I tried. Believe me, I tried."

"So did I. But I think it was a lost cause. I believe you have me thoroughly defeated."

"Alex . . ."

"How much longer, you two?" Gina asked in a teasing voice as she watched them from the doorway. "Haven't I been gone long enough?"

"Oh, you must be tired, Gin," Alex said, looking at her with concern.

"A little," she said.

"You go take Gina home," Leanna said. "Will you be back tonight?"

"I'm afraid not," he said. "I'm expected at Harrodsburg. But I'll be back tomorrow. We'll talk."

He quickly bent and touched his lips to hers, not in the least embarrassed at his sister's presence. Leanna felt for the first time that he was ready to acknowledge to the world what they meant to each other.

Jackson Cole ignored the look Rachel gave him as he stepped into the room. He walked to the bed and stood for a moment, looking down at the black man lying quietly. Jackson's lips curled into a sneer as he thought of Leanna's concerned attention to this man. Soon that would change. Soon she would be his, and there would be no more room in her life for anyone else.

He glanced at Rachel, smiling more at his thoughts than at her. He liked to think of Leanna becoming adoring and pliant the way this girl had. Rachel rose from her rocker and placed a hand on his arm.

"Oh, Jackson," she whispered. "I've missed you so terribly. I know how hurt you must have been when the child died, your own son. And I forgive your not coming to me before."

Jackson looked over at the black man, who was still sleeping. "Shut up!" he whispered. "Do you want everyone to know what you've done, you stupid bitch!"

"Don't say that." Tears filled her eyes. "Please, Jackson."

He grabbed her arm and pulled her to the corner of the room, away from the bed. "You must stop this, Rachel! Do you hear me? You must forget me. Can't you see that you mean nothing to me? Neither you nor that little brat you whelped!" He shook her fiercely, the frustration he felt over Leanna making him even angrier.

Tears streamed down her face as she looked at Jackson with confusion. "No, you don't mean that. You said you loved me, you said—"

"A man says many things when he's in the throes of passion, my dear. But it's over, and I want you to stay away from me. I can hardly stand the sight of your ugly sniffling face! I only took what you offered. Are you too stupid to see that? Now get away from me!" He shoved her hard against the wall and turned to go. He wanted nothing more than to be away from this clinging, foolish woman who made his stomach turn.

Jackson heard a noise behind him and turned around to see the black man trying to lift himself up onto his elbows. He was glaring at Jackson with fury in his eyes, his breath coming in heavy gasps as he struggled to sit up.

Jackson Cole laughed, a short bark of sound that rang in the room. Then he stared into the Trey's eyes and a sneer slowly spread across his face.

"Feeling protective, boy? Perhaps you'd like her," he whispered, nodding toward Rachel. "She ain't much, but the likes of her are good enough for a nigger." He turned and left the room, exiting the house through the back way so that he would not be forced to see Leanna and her lover.

He was maddened, furious with the turn of events. He'd forgotten his vows, and now the facade he had so carefully built slowly began to crumble. He wanted to beat his fists into someone's face.

He walked from the back of the Center dwelling toward the narrow road that ran behind the houses. His short, heavy legs moved quickly, reflecting the anger he felt through his entire body.

He went quickly to where he knew Emily McGrath worked in the West family garden. Luckily, she was alone. He supposed the rest had gone in for the noon meal. Without a word, he grasped her slender arm in his hand and turned her to face him. She made a small sound of protest and looked with surprise into his angry face.

"Jackson, what are you doing?"

"Shut up," he said, pulling her away to the dense rows of corn.

He looked around as he pulled her past the stand of corn and trees and farther away from the houses to a long, narrow ditch.

"What are you doing?" she asked again. "It's daylight, someone will see us!"

"Shut up," he snapped again, jerking her forward until she stumbled across the rough surface of the ground.

He looked around once more before dragging her through the hedges that partially covered the ditch. Then he roughly pushed her down onto her knees in the grassy trench. He knew they were hidden here on both sides by the thickly growing bushes, and they were far enough away from the house so that no one would stumble upon them.

Emily looked fearfully at the man who crawled into the ditch beside her. She hated it when he was like this, with that terrible crazed look on his face. Sometimes he disgusted her with his sadistic needs and his selfish, groping ways. But there was nothing she could do about it.

It was the way of a man. They always used their power to get what they wanted from a woman. She'd always been willing to accommodate him, as much for her own needs as for anything. But today there was something terribly wrong, and it frightened her.

She pulled away as his hands groped for her, pushing

at her skirts as he began to tear at the buttons of his own clothes.

"No, wait, Jackson. We can't—"

Her words were broken by the fist that slammed against the side of her jaw. "I told you to shut up!" His look was furious. He smelled of sweat, and his eyes darted about wildly behind his glasses.

"You'll do as I say, woman," he said, moving over her as his rough hands fumbled at her skirt and squeezed her breasts.

"Jackson, please . . ." She hoped to calm him, to make him see reason. She was desperately afraid that this time he might kill her. Her green eyes filled with tears, and the dimple beside her lips quivered.

He silenced her protests with his foul-tasting mouth, his teeth gnashing painfully against hers, his unkempt beard rough against her skin. He ripped away her underclothes and with no preliminaries thrust into her roughly, immediately pounding himself against her body.

Emily grunted and moaned as he pushed her harder against the ground, causing rocks on the uneven ground to pierce the skin of her back. Tears splashed down the sides of her face as she gritted her teeth and tried to endure his punishing assault.

Jackson Cole was a rough, cruel man. She knew that well enough. But he had never treated her in this manner, and she briefly wondered why, before her mind was once again turned to the pain he inflicted.

Thankfully, it was over quickly, and he slumped against her aching body as he gasped for air. She could feel the pounding of his heart through the clothes that separated them.

Her lips curled in disgust as she shoved at his limp

body, pushing him away and trying to pull herself free from him. He looked at her now with eyes that were calmer but no less cruel.

"What on earth has got into you?" she asked as she put her soiled clothes in order.

His look was blank, and he said nothing. She saw his eyes glance quickly toward the Center dwelling and his tongue dart out to lick his dry lips. Suddenly she knew, as clearly and surely as she'd ever known anything.

"It's Leanna McNairy, isn't it?" she demanded. "You've been sneaking around again over there, watching her. And she had your blood so hot that you came and treated me in this manner! You filthy pig!" Her eyes sparkled furiously. "You can't have her, you bastard, so you come to me and use me like some whore!"

He hit her then, striking her hard with his fist, again and again until the crimson light that clouded his vision cleared. He felt the wetness on his beard where spittle had come out of his mouth, and when he moved his hand to wipe it away, there was blood on it.

He looked down at the woman beneath him. Her fair skin was red where he had hit her, and there was blood smeared over her face from her broken nose. She moaned, and her eyes fluttered open to look at him with terror. He felt a brief surge of relief that he had not killed her. That would spoil his plan.

He quickly fastened the buttons of his trousers and straightened his clothes. He stood and brushed the grass and dirt from himself, then pulled her limp, bloody body up from the ditch.

"You were in the pasture," he whispered in her ear as he dug his finger painfully into her arm. "You got too close to the bull and he came at you, mauled you . . . do you understand what I'm saying?"

She swayed unsteadily, looking at him now through swollen eyes as the blood continued to ooze from her nose. He grasped the front of her dress and shook her. "Do you?"

"Yes," she gasped. "Yes . . . I got . . . too . . . too close. Sorry . . . please . . . please, just help me . . . back to the house."

"Help you? I don't have time to help you. And I'm warning you, if you say anything to anyone, I'll kill you. You know that, don't you?" He shook her hard until she opened her eyes again. "Don't you?"

"Yes," she gasped. "Yes, please . . ."

He pulled her up against him, until her feet barely touched the ground. His voice was a low, menacing growl. "And Emily, don't ever let me hear you defile Leanna McNairy's name again. Not to me—not to anyone! You're not good enough even to breathe her name. Do you hear me?"

"Yes," she said, tears now mingling with the blood on her face. "I won't . . . say anything. I promise." She was shaking almost uncontrollably, and her green eyes darted around with fear.

He reached down and grasped her breast, squeezing it cruelly until she moaned with pain. Then he smiled. "Good," he said. "Good girl."

30

It was a while before the sisters of the West family house settled down for the night. All of them were concerned about Sister Emily's unfortunate accident, and two of them decided to stay with her in her room until morning.

It was late when Jackson Cole went to his own room. Even after nightfall, the house felt terribly hot, with no hint of a breeze stirring the plain white curtains.

His hot encounter with Sister Emily, exciting as it had been, had done little to satisfy him. Now, as he lay in bed, listening to the shuffling of women in and out of Sister Emily's room across the hallway, he grew even more restless.

It was becoming more and more clear to him that nothing and no one was going to satisfy the hunger within him—no one except Leanna McNairy. For a while he tried to envision her in the ditch beneath him, her flaming hair spread out on the ground, her lips as he devoured them, and her beautiful, slender body as he took it for his own. But he could not hold the vision for long.

He sprang out of bed. It was no use. Nothing would appease this desire that burned away inside him. Nothing except the possession of the girl who had driven him crazy these past few months. Suddenly he knew it was time.

He dressed quietly and tiptoed out into the dimly lit hallway and down the stairs. Once outside, he stopped for a moment to glance into the windows at the front of the house. He could see Polly through the open window. Leanna was with her, and they were talking animatedly. Jackson could hear soft laughter through the open window, and it made him even more impatient than ever.

He hurried to the Center house and made his way quietly up the stairs to the infirmary. He found Rachel's room and pushed open the door. The girl was in bed.

He placed a hand over her mouth as she began to protest. Then he leaned closer to her and whispered his instructions. "I need you to do this one last thing for me," he added, finally taking his hand from her mouth.

Rachel looked at him through the darkness. He could see the glint of fear in her eyes. He almost laughed aloud as he saw something else there as well—renewed hope. She was so gullible, so easily manipulated.

After the girl left, he waited. He walked down the hallway, looking into the empty rooms. The black man, Trey, was helpless, and he was the only other person in the infirmary tonight except Rachel. She obviously didn't matter. Jackson thought he might even enjoy having the black man know what was happening to Leanna. That might make it even more pleasurable and exciting.

He licked his dry lips. His heart had started to pound with anticipation as he waited for her. He made his way into the sitting room and blew out the one lamp that was burning low in the corner. Then he settled himself down to wait for the woman he would make his own.

Leanna's eyes were radiant as she related to Polly what Gina and Alex had done. "Well, what do you think?"

Polly's dark eyes were wide and bright with tears. She placed the palms of her hands together and put them to her trembling lips.

"I can't believe it," she said, closing her eyes. "I can't believe I'm actually going home, and I can't believe the goodness of your Major Slayton."

"Then you're happy?"

"Happy? Oh, child, that word don't do it justice. Why, if I was a few years younger I'd get up and dance you a jig!"

"I have no doubt you still could if you really set your mind to it," Leanna said, patting Polly's arm.

"When are we going? I can't wait to see the look on old Levi's face when he finds out why Major Slayton bought the place."

Leanna laughed aloud. "Alex says within the week, as soon as Trey is able. Actually, it might not be that long, because Trey was up this afternoon, walking about, and he's growing stronger by the hour, it seems."

"Good. That's good," Polly murmured, rocking back

and forth in her chair. "Oh, I can't wait to be in my own kitchen and sleep in my own bed. I can die in peace now," she whispered.

"Nonsense, Polly! If anything, you should think of how much longer you will live in your own home.

"Yes, you're right. And when we get home, I'm going to cook your major and all of us a dinner fit for a king."

"I'm sure he would love that," Leanna said, her eyes sparkling as she thought of Alex and how just the mention of his name could excite her.

There was a light knock at the door. Leanna opened it and looked with surprise at Rachel.

"You must come quick, Sister Leanna," she said. "Trey seems to have suffered a setback. He asked me to come for you."

Leanna's heart skipped a beat. She couldn't believe it. Trey had seemed to be doing so well this afternoon. He had been free of fever and feeling strong enough to tease her about Alex. They had even talked of going to the farm soon.

"Of course. I'll come right away."

"Want me to come with you?"

"No, that's not necessary. Perhaps his fever has returned. I'll make him some willow tea and sit with him awhile. You go on to bed and try not to worry."

Leanna and Rachel hurried through the hot, humid night to the Center house. The village lay still and quiet, with only the sound of crickets disturbing the silence.

When Leanna entered the dark sitting room, she stopped, feeling for a moment an odd sense of disquiet ripple through her. There was always a lamp burning here. When Rachel scurried away from her without a word, Leanna was more certain than ever that something was wrong.

"Rachel—" she began.

Suddenly she was grasped from behind and her mouth covered by a thick hand. "Don't you worry about her, darlin'," the voice murmured. "It's just you and me now, the way it was always meant to be."

Leanna struggled against the man who held her. She could see nothing in the darkness nor could she catch a glimpse of his face. But she knew instinctively, with a gripping sense of terror, that the man who held her was Jackson Cole.

He dragged her from the sitting room down the hallway. Leanna's eyes darted briefly toward Trey's closed door, wishing she could call to him. Then she realized with fear that no one else was here except for Rachel. No one could save her now from what this man intended to do to her.

She realized now that he had been the one stalking her, his dark, hungry eyes had watched her everywhere she went. She remembered his glances and she felt herself growing sick, nauseated by the thought of what he wanted.

She tried to scream, but the sounds came out only as a muffled cry as he gripped her more tightly, twisting her face until she thought her neck would snap. He dragged her into one of the bedrooms and as he held her with one arm, he reached up to lock the door with the other. Then he shoved her against the door and reached into his pocket, pulling out a handkerchief and shoving it into her mouth.

His hands were free now and, he pinned her against the door with his thick heavy body, letting his rough hands roam and squeeze until she thought she would die from the sheer horror of it. She could not believe this was happening to her, not now when everything was finally coming together and she had plans to leave this place.

Did Jackson Cole intend to kill her? Surely a man in his right mind would not expect her to tolerate such treatment and tell no one about it afterward.

The thought of Alex made her throat ache and brought hot tears to her eyes. She couldn't bear to think that she'd never see him again.

"Oh, don't cry, baby," the man whispered in a hungry, disgusting voice. "I promise you're going to love it, just as the rest of them did. Why, poor little Rachel is probably locked away in her room right this minute, crying her heart out, sick with envy." He laughed manaically.

Leanna began to shake her head, struggling and kicking him as his hands became more insistent.

"Oh, I do like a little spirit, honey," he whispered. "But if you'll promise not to scream, I'll take off this gag so I can kiss you properly. What do you say?"

Leanna grew very still, causing Jackson to pull back and look at her cautiously. She nodded, hoping that he would remove the gag only for a second, long enough for her to call for help.

Jackson only laughed. He was no fool, but the sight of her tempting mouth was more than he could resist. He moved his face only inches from hers, and when he removed the gag, his hot, wet lips were there to take its place, muffling the scream she intended. He laughed again when she finally pulled away and he stuffed the gag back into her mouth.

He could hardly believe the taste of her, the feel of her in his arms. It would be so much more pleasurable if he could only talk to her, persuade her that this was for the best. But he knew that in her present state of mind that was impossible. He would have to show her.

Kissing her had excited him beyond all endurance. He grasped her hair now and dragged her to the small bed in the middle of the room.

Trey was not certain what woke him. He would have dismissed it as a sound outside and gone back to sleep if not for a nagging sense that something was terribly wrong. He'd felt it ever since that ugly little man named Cole had shoved the girl against the wall this afternoon. Trey had not liked the glint he saw in the man's eyes. It reminded him of some of the soldiers in battle, with wild frenzy that was more frightening than the war itself.

Trey was still weak, but something he could not explain drove him to get out of bed. He stopped with a grimace as he waited for the pain in his leg to subside. His injured shoulder hung lower than the other, but he managed to drag himself across the room to the door.

As he quietly opened the door he heard it again, the sound that had roused him from sleep. It was muffled, but it was there. He cocked his head, trying to decide if the noise was someone's voice or that of an animal outside.

He paused outside Rachel's room, listening. "Rachel?" he said quietly. There was no answer. Then he heard what he thought was someone crying. He opened the door and saw Rachel huddled on the bed. Her hands were over her ears, and she was shaking from head to foot.

"Ma'am?" he said, afraid to enter the room. "Is anything wrong?"

She looked up at him with dark, wet eyes, and he thought he'd never seen such sorrow. She swallowed hard as they both heard a bump in one of the rooms down the hall. Trey frowned and turned in that direction. Every instinct told him that this woman knew what was wrong and somehow had a part in it.

"Answer me," he said, approaching her.

She cringed from him, and it was obvious that the authority in his voice frightened her. "It's Brother Jackson," she said quickly. "He took Leanna."

"Took?" Trey frowned, disbelief welling up within him. That was it, the thing he sensed within the man, some demented evilness that manifested itself in his treatment of women. But dear God, not Leanna.

"Stay here," he said, turning as swiftly as his injuries would allow and going down the hall toward the sound. He tried the door, but it was locked.

"Leanna?" he called, his ear against the closed door. He heard something, a moan perhaps, and then there was only an eerie silence.

Trey was weak, and his legs trembled so much he wasn't sure how long he would be able to stand. Somehow he managed to kick the door in with one powerful thrust.

He saw the outline of two people on the bed, and in the dimness he saw Leanna's frightened face. Her bare shoulders gleamed in the faint light as she struggled with the man who held her down. The man leapt from the bed now and turned toward Trey.

"Get out of here, soldier boy. This don't concern you." The sight of Trey in the doorway infuriated Jackson, frustrated him now that he was so close to the treasure he sought. He was not about to let anyone keep him from it.

"Get away from her," Trey said, his deep voice rumbling dangerously.

With a low growl Jackson spun around and leapt at the black man who came at him. Trey took the full force of the man's body in his injured shoulder with a loud grunt. For a few seconds, the room spun before his eyes as pain threatened to blot out his consciousness. He gasped for breath and grabbed blindly for Jackson Cole's shirt. As his fingers found the material, he lifted the shorter man from the floor and shook him before slamming him against the far wall.

Trey could see out of the corner of his eye Leanna struggling to take the gag out of her mouth as she watched them. She had done so much for him, he had to find the strength to help her now. He straightened, his breath coming in painful gasps as he moved toward the man on the floor.

As Jackson came up at Trey, there was something in his hand, a heavy iron shoe last that was used to prop open the door. He rushed at Trey with it, tackling him around the waist and driving him into the other wall.

Leanna saw Rachel enter the room behind Jackson. She gasped as she saw the gleam of a knife that the girl held in her upraised hand. As Jackson raised the piece of iron above Trey, Rachel's arms came down, plunging the knife deep into the man's back.

Rachel began to scream and cry, the sounds growing weaker as she continued to stab wildly at Jackson. Trey finally managed to pull himself from beneath the man's lifeless, heavy body and take the knife from Rachel's shaking hands.

Leanna watched the scene before her, stunned and unable to speak. They heard the shuffle of footsteps outside as others came rushing in to find out the cause of the noise.

"Trey," Leanna whispered finally. "Are you all

right?" She stepped to him and ran her hand down his arms, noticing his wince as she did.

"Did he hurt you?" he asked as he tried to catch his breath.

"No . . . no, he didn't hurt me," she said with a choked cry. She went to him and put her arms around his waist. He had saved her, and she didn't care what the startled sisters in the hallway thought.

Leanna leaned her head on his chest, and embraced him with a gratitude she could not express with words.

Trey stood rigidly, self-consciously allowing his good arm to touch her only lightly at the waist. He had never held a white woman before, and he almost felt as if someone would appear and strike him dead.

Then he grinned at his foolish thoughts. This was Leanna, not just any white woman. His hand tightened at her waist, and he placed a swift kiss onto her bent head before pulling himself gently from her arms.

"Here," she said, holding his arm. "Sit here until you're feeling stronger."

Rachel was still on the floor, crying quietly and looking at the man she had just killed. "I love you, Jackson," she said over and over again.

Leanna knew that the girl would never be sane again.

31

The death of Brother Jackson Cole threatened to cause a serious rift among the Believers of Pleasant Hill. Some of the Shakers could not believe he had done the things of which he was accused. Others thought Rachel had simply gone mad because of her child's death and killed an innocent man.

Leanna knew that there was nothing she could do to change those people's minds. She was still considered an outsider by some. It was a blessing that Alex had obtained the farm for them, as she was certain that they would have turned her out after what happened in the infirmary that night.

Of course, there were some who'd always had their doubts about the brother, and they were not surprised. Among them were Sister Jane and Polly's husband, Levi. They were the ones who told Leanna about Sister

Emily McGrath's confession of her relationship with the blacksmith and of what had really happened to her the day he died. Emily had been afraid that Leanna's life was in danger, but had been too afraid and too sick to warn her.

Leanna didn't know who told Alex about it, but when he returned to Pleasant Hill the next day he came immediately to find her.

"Are you sure you're all right?" he asked. "God, I blame myself for this. There was something about the man . . ."

"You are not to blame yourself," Leanna said. "I saw him more often than you did, and although I never liked the man, I certainly never dreamed he was capable of this." She shivered as Alex wrapped his arms around her and held her close.

They were all anxious now to leave the village. Alex moved his headquarters to Polly's farm. It was not much farther away from Harrodsburg than the original office at the Sutton place. He and his men worked to set the house and grounds in order before Leanna and the others arrived.

Leanna sat beside Polly in the wagon now, watching the play of emotions on the older woman's wrinkled features. As they drew nearer, Leanna was worried that the dear little woman might grow too excited.

The house, as Gina had said, was beautiful. It was a simple white two-storied clapboard with large stone chimneys at each end. It was surrounded by a stand of towering oak trees. A long, low porch ran across the front, facing the river. There was a warmth to the place that made Leanna feel secure and happy, almost as if she were coming home.

Sister Jane had insisted that they take a milk cow and

some chickens with them. As they had been leaving, Levi Wilhite had shyly presented a ewe and her two lambs to Polly. She had thanked him with polite coolness as he shook her hand and told her good-bye.

When they arrived, Polly could hardly wait to look through her house and see to the settling of the animals. Alex smiled at the little woman as she thanked him time and again.

"Now, Major, I know this is your house, and if I get too high-handed you just put me in my place. It's my nature, I guess, being bossy."

Alex laughed and exchanged a happy glance with Leanna. "Technically, you're right. But somehow I feel like a guest, so it would be my pleasure if you'd remain in charge. We'll gladly do as you wish."

Polly winked at Leanna. "This-here's a mighty fine man." She grinned. "Yessir, mighty fine, Yankee or not!"

Leanna slipped an arm around Alex's waist and looked up into his face. "I agree," she said.

"Well, if you'll excuse me, I intend to milk that cow and churn myself some butter tomorrow."

Polly left, and Alex looked down tenderly at the woman in his arms. "I never thought to hear you agree to such an outrageous statement."

"Yes, well, if all Yankees are like you and Jimmy, then I suppose they can't be so bad."

The first few days at the farm passed quickly. Trey grew stronger each day and was becoming totally devoted to Leanna. There was a strong new bond between them that she knew would never be broken. Gina adored Polly and followed her advice and instructions about the farm with willing enthusiasm.

It would have been the happiest of times had it not

been for the war that loomed over them. It grew closer every day. Alex and the men knew it, and Leanna could sense their uneasiness more and more.

Whenever Alex was gone Leanna missed him more than ever and often reminded herself of their first night at the farm. It had been the sweetest, most wondrous time they'd ever spent together. Some days the memory of it was all that kept her going, that and the anticipation of the life to come that they planned for.

One hot day in late September Leanna ventured down to the river. She missed Alex so badly that day that it caused her to be jumpy and irritable. The fact that Generals Bragg and E. Kirby Smith had moved their Confederate troops into Kentucky did nothing to ease her anxiety. There was a confrontation coming. They could all feel it in the hot, dry air.

She sat down on the cool riverbank, remembering that first night here, the sweet memory she called to mind so often lately for comfort.

Both she and Alex had felt some tension, as well as an awkwardness. They had spoken after supper, almost politely, neither of them mentioning all the things they wanted to say to each other. Leanna was determined not to push him. Finally some of the men came to sit on the porch, and when it became apparent that there would be no chance to talk that evening, Leanna excused herself quietly and went to bed.

She lay awake for a long while, after the voices of the soldiers had drifted away to their tents, even after she heard the closing of Alex's door down the hall from her. Finally she could stand it no longer. Whether out of desperation or just plain stubbornness, she knew she could not let another moment pass without trying to put things between them right for good.

She got out of bed and went to Alex's room.

He was standing in the dark, gazing out at the roadway that lead to the river. He wanted to kick himself. Why was it so damned hard to tell Leanna all the things he wanted to say? When he had learned what almost happened with Jackson Cole, he'd sworn he would not let another minute pass without telling her how precious she was to him and how much he loved her.

Then the doubts would come, and he remembered the grief his sister had been forced to endure with the death of her husband. He did not want that for Leanna. For as much as he had tried to brush it away, the dark sense of doom he felt still persisted, still woke him sometimes in the night.

Tonight he could not sleep. He needed to go to her and tell her, regardless of what might happen to him later.

He unbuttoned his shirt and pulled it off his shoulders as he stood looking toward the river. There was usually a breeze here, much cooler than anywhere else, and tonight he felt the need of it.

He heard the sound of the door opening behind him and turned slowly. There, in the doorway, Leanna was silhouetted against the dim lights from the hall. He could see the bright halo of her hair, and the outline of her body and shape of her slender legs through the long white cotton gown she wore.

She moved slowly toward him, not speaking. Alex felt the breath leave his body as a slow ache moved his heart. God, she was so beautiful. How could he not love her? And how could he not tell her?

"Alex," she whispered.

He felt the touch of her cool hand on his bare chest and tried to swallow the lump in his throat that threatened to suffocate him. He could see her clearly in the moonlight that streamed through the windows.

"What is it, angel? Is anything wrong," he whispered as he took her in his arms and pulled her close.

"Alex, I love you," she whispered. "I had to tell you before . . . before you leave again." There were tears on her face.

It was so typical of her and so endearing, this straightforward manner. And the tears made him want to hold her and never let her go. With a burning ache he knew that this was all he needed, this sweet confession of her love.

"Leanna, my love. I wanted you from the first moment you whirled into your father's study and looked at me so defiantly with those beautiful, flashing eyes."

She laughed softly and pulled away to wipe the tears from her face. "I thought . . . I thought after that night in the storm that you didn't want me anymore. I thought . . ."

"No," he whispered fiercely, pulling her back against him. "I'm sorry for that, for all the times I pushed you away. But it was never because I didn't want you. Never that."

His sweet words broke through her will to be strong, and she began to sob quietly against his chest.

"Don't, sweetheart," he said, feeling tears sting his own eyes as well. "No tears tonight. I don't want to leave remembering your tears and how I've hurt you."

"You're leaving, then, tomorrow?"

"Yes." He took her face between his hands and wiped the tears away with his fingers. "Please, love."

She shuddered and looked up at him with a tremulous smile, trying so hard to be brave for him. She was amazed to feel the trembling of his strong body as he held her, amazed to see the look of love in his dark eyes as he let his fingers move down her face to her lips.

"I love you, Leanna, more than I ever thought it possible to love anyone. You've driven away all my resistance, and I cannot imagine my life without you."

"You'll never be without me Alex, never." She was thrilled by his words. She slipped her arms around his bare waist and felt the undeniable spark pass between them.

"My angel, my own darling Rebel," he said with a hint of laughter in his voice. He bent his dark head and lowered his lips to hers. The feel of her mouth beneath his, the slight taste of tears, was almost more than he could stand after all their months of separation. He moaned softly between little kisses that he pressed to her lips, her face, her eyes. "I love you . . . love you," he said.

This night was different from the first, they both knew immediately. The separations, the doubts, the fear of what was to come had only deepened their love and made it stronger. Each of them wanted to savor every precious moment in a slower, gentler way than before.

Leanna moved her hands into his black hair, kissing his bottom lip and his chin, his throat where she could feel the heavy rhythm of his beating pulse. He had grown still, his breath coming in short groans as he relished every soft, tantalizing touch. Her warm silken lips moved downward to his chest, teasing him into a sweet aching awareness.

He smiled into the darkness, remembering how they had fought, how she had hated him. Now there was only love between them, this great overpowering love that moved him as nothing in his life ever had. She was his. The woman he loved. And with a fierce joy, he knew that she loved him.

His fingers tangled in her hair to pull her head up so that he could kiss her lips, parting them gently with his own. His hands moved easily over the smooth contours of her skin, pushing the gown from her shoulders until the material fell to the floor.

Together, in a moment of silent understanding, they both moved to the bed. This time as they came to each other there was an unspoken bond between them. This time there was no tentativeness, no holding back for either of them. The slow, easy savoring gave way to a hot, hungry need that drove both of them wild. Leanna clung to him, urging him on as she whispered her love into his ear. She felt pleasure rising up within her, higher and higher, threatening to overpower her with a joy she'd never thought possible.

"Oh, God," she cried softly, feeling his hot need and the power of what he was doing to her. Her hands gripped his shoulders as the explosion pulsed through her body, and she looked into his deep black eyes with disbelief. Whatever was happening to her was glorious, wondrous, and she never wanted it to end.

Her excitement and pleasure finally sent him over the edge and with a groan he gripped her tightly, unable to hold back any longer.

"Alex, I love you," she whispered as they held each other close, waiting together and feeling the edge slip away into a quiet surfeit of joy.

Slowly their breathing returned to normal and their heartbeats slowed. Alex knew more than ever that he could never let this woman go. She was more precious to him than his own life.

"Never—" Leanna gasped. "Never have I felt anything like that, Alex. It was . . . wonderful."

She felt his soft laughter rumble in his chest. How could she ever have accused him of being too solemn, too cruel? Now all she could think of was how perfect he was, and how necessary to her life.

They lay in the dark, holding each other and speaking of things they had needed to say for a long time.

Alex told her how frightened he'd been when he heard about Jackson Cole.

"If I ever lost you, I'd die," he said, his voice rasping with emotion.

She could not believe he was saying those words to her. "You will never lose me, darling," she said, moving her fingers to touch his face.

He pulled her tightly against him, choosing his next words with care. "Promise me that if anything happens . . . if I don't come back, you will not grieve."

She quickly came up on her elbow and looked down into his face. "No!" she cried. "I could never promise such a thing. Don't you know that I feel the same about you, that I'd die without you?"

"Promise me, Leanna," he insisted. "The fear of what would happen to you if . . . if I don't make it was what kept me away from you before. Why I tried not to love you. I can't bear the thought of your sorrow."

Leanna clung to him, his words making her desperate with fear. "Why are you saying these things?" she cried. "Please, Alex, you're frightening me."

"No, love," he said, cupping her face in the palm of his hand. "I don't want to frighten you. But neither do I want any sad surprises for you. We need to face the possibility."

She stopped his words with a kiss, unable and unwilling to hear any more. She kissed him desperately, grinding her lips against his as if she could erase his words.

"It's all right," he whispered as she pulled away and he saw the despair on her lovely face. "It's all right, darling. I won't say any more."

For the rest of the night they caressed and touched, kissed as if it might be the last, spoke quietly in the darkness, and declared their love again and again. It was as if each of them sought nothing past this moment, expected nothing more than this night.

The hot surge of passion rose up between them again, bringing them together with a wild abandon that left them pleasurably exhausted. Neither of them could bear to release this fragile moment, and neither of them wanted to think of tomorrow.

As Leanna sat on the quiet riverbank now, watching the slow drift of the Kentucky River, tears filled her eyes at the rememberance those precious moments.

Sometimes she felt such a fear grip her heart that she thought it would drive her mad. How could she live if anything happened to Alex? She knew, no matter how sincerely she promised him she'd be brave, that she could not live without him.

She heard a footstep behind her and turned to see Trey walking toward her through the tall grass.

"Are you all right?" he asked, stretching his aching leg out so he could sit beside her.

"Oh, Trey," she cried, not trying to hide anything from him. "Sometimes I'm so afraid. I don't know what I'd do if anything happened to Alex."

"Nothing will happen."

"You don't understand," she said. "You can't imagine how I feel now that I've found him."

"Yes," he said, his voice growing low and serious. "I do know how you feel."

She saw the pained look in his brown eyes and waited for him to explain.

"Do you remember you asked me once if there was someone I loved? At one time there was. Her name was Sarah, and I loved her more than I'd ever thought you could love anyone. And as hard as it was for me to believe, she loved me too."

"What happened?" Leanna asked, sensing that it must have been something dreadful to separate Trey from the girl he loved.

"There was a time when things got real bad in Georgia. There were certain men who roamed the countryside, just looking for a fight. One evening they rode into the yard of the plantation where we lived, overrunning everything and everybody in their way. Some of them jumped from their horses and dragged me away from Sarah. They beat me until I couldn't see, until everything was dark. But I could hear her crying, pleading with them to stop." Trey's voice grew hoarse as he struggled to continue. His eyes were unfocused, as if he saw the dreadful scene before him even now.

"Trey," Leanna whispered, touching his hand gently. "Don't . . ."

But he continued, as if in a daze. "Later I found her . . . her clothes torn away . . . and there was blood, so much blood that I—" A strangled cry escaped his lips, and he turned his face away from Leanna.

"Oh, Trey," she whispered. "I'm so sorry . . . so very sorry."

He shook his head, unable to look at her, trying desperately to bring himself back under control.

"I . . . I never told anyone before except the major and Jimmy," he said.

She saw the shine of tears in his eyes, and her own filled again. "I'm sorry I said you couldn't understand," she whispered.

"That's not why I told you. I needed to tell someone. Sometimes when these feelings build up inside me I feel as if I'm going to explode, just the way you're feeling. I want you to know you can talk to me if you need to. And I want you to know that I think the major will be all right."

"Oh, Trey," she said. "You are such a good friend to me and to Alex, in so many ways. I'm glad you feel you can talk to me. Well, it means a lot to me."

"Come back to the house," he said, offering her his hand. "Alex wouldn't like you worrying so about him."

"Did Alex order you to look after me, Trey?"

"As a matter of fact, he did," he said with a slow smile. "But it's a pleasure, and I'd do it even if he hadn't asked."

32

The days passed in a sweltering pattern of bright blue cloudless skies and faint dry winds. The entire state was in the throes of an unprecedented drought. It moved across Kentucky, parching everything in sight and slowing the movements of people and animals to a crawl. Dust lay two inches deep on the roads, and the once-lush green meadows lay dry and brown. Water was becoming a precious commodity.

Leanna had heard how Confederate Gen. E. Kirby Smith had marched his army of twelve thousand skinny, bearded, shoeless soldiers ninety miles in three days, sustained only by parched corn. They had hit the Federal army between Richmond and Kingston and practically annihilated them. The news struck fear in Leanna's heart.

There were stories of battles between confused

soldiers who were so dust covered they could not distinguish between friend or foe.

In early October Mr. Sutton rode to the farm to tell them that Buell's army of Union soldiers was somewhere outside Harrodsburg and that a battle between him and Braxton Bragg was now imminent.

Leanna did not sleep all night. Without being told, she knew with a horrible, sense of doom that Alex and his men were there with Buell's army.

As soon as dawn came she was outside, walking, doing anything to avoid thinking about what was about to happen.

Trey came outside and handed her a cup of coffee. He wanted to help her but was unable to calm her fears.

At midmorning he came out into the yard again and looked up into the clear sky, as blue and cloudless as ever. He turned his head, trying to catch the direction of the thundering sound he'd just heard.

"What was that?" Leanna asked, fear showing in her eyes.

"I'm not sure."

Then it began, the rumbling sound that shook the earth like thunder and reverberated in the still autumn air. Polly came outside, and then Gina, her body large and awkward as she walked.

"What is it?" Gina asked fearfully.

Leanna knew before Trey met her watchful gaze, before he acknowledged what she feared in her heart.

"Cannon fire," he said quietly.

"A battle?" Polly asked, looking toward the sky, hoping it was an approaching thunderstorm instead.

"I'm afraid so," Trey said.

"Oh, God," Leanna whispered, clasping her hands together. She wanted to fall on her knees, to scream and plead with God not to take Alex. She had the most dreadful feeling inside, a desperate fear that she could not seem to shake.

Gina put an arm around her. "He'll be all right, Leanna," she said. "Believe he'll be all right."

"I'm trying," Leanna said, closing her eyes against the nausea that struck her. "I'm trying."

Trey moved away from them toward the barn. Over his shoulder he shouted, "I'll take the wagon and ride to the Shaker village, see if I can find out where the battle is. I'll be back as soon as I can."

"Be careful, Trey," Leanna warned him.

When he returned around noon, he left the mule and wagon tied to one of the huge old trees and limped over to the women, who sat expectantly on the porch.

"The battle is at Perryville, on the other side of Harrodsburg."

"Who is it?" Leanna asked fearfully.

"Bragg and Buell," he replied, looking up at her with an almost apologetic glance.

"Oh, God," she whispered, standing up suddenly. "I knew it. Alex is there. I know he's there."

Polly came to her and took her by the shoulders. "Now, Leanna," she said, "there's nothing can be done now except wait. This ain't the first battle your Alex has been in, and it probably won't be his last. He wouldn't like to see you carrying on this way now. You know that."

Leanna pressed her trembling fingers against her lips. "I know," she said, struggling for control. "I know he wouldn't."

"All right, then. The only thing we can do is wait till it's over. In the meantime, we'll all have to keep busy."

True to her word, Polly did keep them all busy the

rest of the day, finding endless chores that needed to be done. Leanna went about hers in a trance, hardly aware of what she was doing.

Near dusk the rumbling stopped and did not begin again. The night was torturously long, never ending, it seemed to Leanna. But by dawn she knew what she must do, what she had to do for her peace of mind and for Alex's well-being.

She went to Trey. "Get the wagon. I'm going to Perryville to find Alex."

"Now, Leanna."

"He's hurt, I know it. I can feel it! And if I stay here doing nothing and he should die, I'll never be able to forgive myself. I need you to understand. But if you don't, then I'll go alone."

Trey looked at her as she stood in front of him, clenching her fists. There were no tears in her eyes now, only a fierce determination and a stubbornness that nearly made him smile. Hell, the major would probably kill him when he found out about this wild plan, but there was a nagging thought in the back of his mind that Leanna could be right.

"I do understand," he said. "I'll get the wagon. Get some quilts and medical supplies and a jug of water. And bring the rifle."

Leanna took a great gulp of air, closing her eyes with relief. She had no idea where Perryville was or how she thought she would find Alex among the thousands of soldiers there. Something inside, some confidence born of her love for him, assured her that she could.

When they drove past the Shaker village, Leanna felt a small pang of homesickness. She had learned so much there, grown up so quickly. Her gaze moved beyond the barns and meadows to the pump house as she remembered the stormy night she and Alex spent there.

All the while a voice inside her head prayed that he was all right. She would not let herself think that she had no control over his fate.

As they approached Harrodsburg the road became more crowded. Beyond the town they saw many people walking, carrying clothes and various household items. Some people drove past in wagons, whole families looking anxiously toward the west as they returned to their homes, hoping to find everything intact.

Trey stopped once and asked an old gentleman who was trudging slowly along the dusty road if he knew where the battle had been."

"Just west of town, I heard," the old man said, squinting up at them in the hot sun. "They say the hills and ravines are still covered with the dead and wounded. But some have been taken to the old Jordan Peters house, not more'n a mile from here. A terrible thing . . . terrible."

"Thank you," Trey said, flicking the reins to continue down the road.

Leanna felt hot and cold at once. Her head was throbbing, and the sun burned her face and shoulders. Her insides were wound as tightly as a watch spring. All she wanted now was to locate the Peters house. She had not even thought of what would happen after that or how she would find Alex in the mass of people.

When they found the house, she was not even remotely prepared for the sight that met them. Smoke still lingered in the hot morning air, and the smell of gunpowder filled her nostrils. There was another, more sickening smell wafting in the sultry heat: the smell of blood, and of death. Her heart began a fast, skittering beat, making her feel weak and faint.

They could hear the moans before they even reached the house. They rose up around them like the low hum of an approaching wind, sending chills down Leanna's spine.

She moved closer to Trey and touched his arm. His muscles were tensed. She saw the look of horror on his face as he looked at the bodies scattered all over the countryside and in the yard of the house.

"It's all right," he said. "If he's here, we'll find him. Even if it takes all day, we'll find him.

One of the first people they saw was a short, dark-haired Federal officer who wore the insignia of a major. Trey drew alongside him and placed his foot on the long wooden brake of the wagon.

"Sir, would you happen to know a Major Alexander Slayton?"

The man looked up at them, his eyes shaded by the dust-covered hat he wore. "Hmmm, I'm not sure. I've heard of him, I believe."

"You . . . you haven't seen him, have you?" Leanna asked.

"No, ma'am. Sorry. Would you happen to know his company?"

"The Twenty-fourth Ohio, sir," Trey answered.

The sound of wagons rattling across the ground and the cries and groans of the soldiers almost obliterated his quiet words.

The officer shook his head only the slightest bit and looked away from them. But it was enough to cause Leanna's heart to turn over with fear.

"What is it?" she asked quickly. "Do you know where they are?"

He glanced down at the sheaf of papers in his hand. "I'm sorry, ma'am. They were with Buell. They went in late. I don't think they made it."

"No," she gasped, placing her hand to her lips.

"Thank you, sir," Trey said, quickly moving the wagon on toward the house. He knew the best thing for Leanna now was action, something to occupy her time and mind until they could find out exactly where the major was.

"That don't mean he's dead, Leanna," he said more gruffly than he intended. He couldn't stand the look of grief on her pretty face.

"I know, Trey, I know," she said, trying to still the trembling of her lips and the wrenching fear that gripped her body. She was terrified. She told herself that Alex would hate this, hate to see her crying and looking among the dead for him, but it was something she had to do. If he was here, even if the worst had happened, she would not leave without him. She had to know.

When they reached the house Leanna was out of the wagon before Trey could move from his seat. She walked among the bloodied figures lying on the ground, bending to speak to the ones who held a hand toward her, offering what little comfort she could to the ones who were afraid or in pain.

Trey followed behind her, doing the same. They moved closer to the house. Blood stained the wooden planks of the front porch. Flies and yellowjackets buzzed noisily in the hot afternoon sun. Still, Trey saw no one he recognized.

Leanna stopped dead still in the yard at the corner of the house, looking at something with a sickened expression. Trey stepped from the porch and quickly moved to her. He heard a choked sound as she ran away from him to lean against the trunk of a tree, where she became violently ill. When Trey followed the path her eyes had taken, he saw why.

In the yard beyond the house stood a huge oak tree, its limbs spreading and dipping around it. The doctors had placed several tables under the branches and made it their surgery station. The tables and the ground below them were crimson with blood, as were the doctors' boots. Medics stood by with rows of men lying on blankets or in the grass, waiting their turn at the surgery tables. Beyond that was a sight that turned Trey's stomach and made him want to run away, too.

He saw on a small hillock beyond the tree what he thought at first were discarded clothes and boots. But now he saw one of the surgeons toss something on the pile, and Trey realized they were actually dismembered arms and legs.

"Oh, my God," he muttered, looking away. He had seen injuries, and he had even seen amputations, but this! Lord, he'd never thought to see such a sight.

He went to Leanna and put an arm around her trembling shoulders. She had stopped heaving and was bent over, trying to catch her breath. Trey hoped he'd never have to see the look again that he saw in her eyes.

"Let me take you away from here," he said.

She turned to him, eyes blazing. "No! Do you think seeing this—this . . ." she waved her arms, not looking again toward the mound of dismembered limbs. "This has not changed my mind," she said more calmly. "I won't leave here until I find Alex, or know what's happened to him."

"All right," he said, knowing that she meant what

she said. He only wished he could spare her this terrible chore.

Trey turned back toward the row of bodies and the men who lay waiting for the surgeons. He saw a man standing a short distance away with a dirty bandage around his head. He was watching Trey and Leanna. The man took a step toward Trey, then another, until he was running toward them, waving his arms.

"Trey!" he shouted. "Trey, it's me!"

Trey's eyes narrowed as he watched with growing disbelief the man coming toward them. Leanna turned. There was a spark of life again in her eyes as she recognized him.

"Jimmy!" she cried as she started toward him. "Trey, it's Jimmy!"

She reached him before Trey's stiff leg could propel him forward. The young man, covered with dirt and his face black from gunpowder, grabbed her in his arms with such intensity that both of them almost fell. They were laughing and crying, and when he set her back on her feet she ran her hands over his face, looking at his bandaged head with concern.

"I'm all right," he said.

Jimmy turned to Trey and extended his hand. When their hands clasped together Trey pulled the boy to him and hugged him, slapping him soundly on the back.

"God, it's good to see you, boy," Trey said.

"Jimmy," Leanna began. She wanted to ask, had to know. But now that the time had come, she was afraid of what he might tell her. She didn't even have to ask, though. He could read the question in her eyes.

"He's over here, Leanna," Jimmy said quietly. "But he's hurt . . . he's hurt real bad."

"I know," she whispered with trembling lips.

They followed him toward the row of bodies that Trey had observed earlier, those awaiting the surgeon's saw.

When Leanna saw Alex she began to run, falling on the ground beside him and touching his face tenderly with her fingers. He was pale, and his breathing was so shallow that it seemed only a whisper.

"Alex," she cried, lowering her head to his chest. "Oh, Alex, my darling. Can you hear me?"

He did not answer. Leanna glanced down at the bloodied, mangled flesh of his left leg and gasped when she saw the damage. She looked up at Jimmy and Trey, who stood above her, then over to the table where the surgeons continued to saw and hack at the limbs of the nearly lifeless men on the tables.

It was only then that she realized what was intended for the man she loved.

She closed her eyes, feeling as if she might faint, feeling the earth begin to spin and the noise to recede.

She swayed, and Trey immediately fell to his knees, unaware of any pain in his still-healing leg. But she shook her head, holding him away with her hand against his chest.

"Jimmy," she said, glancing toward the tables beneath the trees. "His leg . . . are they going to? . . ."

"Yes'm. I'm afraid so. You can see for yourself, Leanna," he said gently. "It's broke bad and full of shrapnel. The doctor said in this heat there's nothing else to be done, or he'll die of gangrene. I'm sorry, honey, but it may be the only chance he has."

"No!" she cried. "No, it isn't. We're taking him home." Her voice was firm now and full of certainty.

"Oh, Leanna," Jimmy said, shaking his head. "I

don't think that's a good idea. Moving him now, taking him away from the doctors . . . I don't know."

"Trey, please get the wagon," she said, ignoring Jimmy's protests.

"Wait," Jimmy said, frowning at Trey. "Talk to her—explain it to her."

"Jim," Trey said, "if Leanna says we're taking him home, then we're taking him home. If anybody can save him, it'll be her. Now I'm going to get the wagon. Are you coming or not?"

"No," Jimmy said with a sigh. "I need to stay and take care of the others . . . their papers and belongings." His voice was full of a terrible sorrow.

"Papers? You mean—you're saying that all of them are? . . ."

Jimmy nodded, his blue eyes filled with tears at the memory of his fallen friends. "It was awful, Trey. I'm glad you weren't there."

Trey placed a hand on the boy's shoulder and shook him gently. He was so shocked that he could not think of one consoling word.

"Will you tell the commanding officer that we've taken Alex?" Trey asked.

Jimmy nodded, watching with sad, worried eyes as Trey went to get the wagon.

33

Leanna hardly noticed the jolt of the wagon or the dust that filled the air. All her attention, all her being, was focused on the man who lay on the quilt covering the bed of the wagon.

She shaded his face from the relentless sun with her body as she watched him with an intensity that blotted out everything else around her. She listened to each shallow breath he took, noted every flutter of his long, dark eyelashes. And she spoke to him, whispering again and again that she was with him, that she loved him, begging him to hang on to his life for a moment more.

She agonized every second, afraid it would be his last, for she did not feel the confidence that she'd felt when Trey was brought to her. This time she could not say with certainty that Alex would live, and the doubts threatened to shatter her into a thousand pieces.

Trey drove as carefully as he could over the rough, dusty road. He turned many times to Leanna and his injured friend. He wanted to help her, to help both of them, but there was nothing he could do.

It was growing dark when they traveled the last long mile through the brown meadows to the farmhouse. Gina and Polly stood in the yard, hands shading their eyes from the dust as they watched the approaching wagon.

Leanna thought her heart would break at Gina's worried look. Her beautiful blue eyes filled with tears, and her face crumpled into a grieving sorrow as she touched her brother and felt the nearness of his death.

Leanna did not know what she would have done without Polly and Trey. After they'd carried Alex inside, Polly took charge, giving all of them orders. Her feisty confidence did much to bolster Leanna's hopes.

After Alex was bathed and laid in a cool, clean bed in the downstairs bedroom, Polly turned to Leanna.

"His leg is real bad, darlin'," she said gently. "The doctors might have been right."

"No," Leanna insisted. "I couldn't leave him there to be hacked on and butchered like some animal. It's not that I couldn't bear for him to lose his leg. I could stand anything except losing him. But I had to give him this chance, don't you see?"

"Yes, dearie," she said with a twinkle in her eyes. "I do indeed, and I'm going to do my best for your young man. But it's going to be long, and it's going to be painful. Thank God he's unconscious."

"What do we do first?"

"*We* don't do anything," Polly said, "because *you* are going to go to the kitchen to eat something. Gina needs your company as much as you need hers. Then you can take a bath and rest. I'll call you when me and Trey are finished.''

"No," Leanna said. "I can't leave him."

"You can and you will. You won't do him a bit of good sitting here crying over him."

Leanna knew that Polly was right. She wasn't sure that she could stand seeing the shrapnel dug out of his leg or the bone put back into place. She realized that she had not eaten all day, and despite her worry, she felt hungry.

Reluctantly she looked at Alex, lying so still and pale on the small bed. She took a deep, shuddering breath and looked at Polly.

Polly smiled. "I promise I'll take the best of care, and I'll call you just as soon as we're finished."

Leanna moved to touch Alex's strong brown hands and the rough beard on his handsome face. "You can't leave me, Alex," she whispered. Then she kissed him softly on the lips and left the room without another glance.

She found Gina in the kitchen, and they came together, clutching each other and crying for the man they both loved so much. Polly was right; they did need each other. Being with Gina in the familiarity of the big kitchen comforted Leanna more than anything had all day. She felt the slightest spark of hope move within her breast.

Leanna felt better physically after her supper, and even though she wanted to go back to the bedroom, she did not. She forced herself to move to the small shed just beyond the back porch and fill the big copper tub with cool water. Once she'd bathed and changed into clean clothes, she felt like a different person.

It was a long while that she and Gina waited. Leanna's ears were attuned toward the bedroom, listening for any sound and praying that Alex was not in pain. It was late when Polly finally came out onto the porch.

The little woman looked exhausted, and her eyes were sunken and hollow from the long hours of work. Her dress was wet with perspiration. She gave a sigh as both women rose and looked at her expectantly.

"Well, he made it through just fine," she said.

"You sound worried," Leanna said. "Is everything all right?"

"Well, there was a mighty lot of metal in his leg. But I believe we got it all out. Had to put some stitches in some of the places. His leg is going to be a sight, and he may always carry a limp." She shook her head sadly.

"But?"

"But I'm mostly worried about that broken bone. It's gonna be mighty hard to heal. Thigh bone's hard to set." She moved to one of the chairs and sat down.

The two younger women exchanged glances over Polly's gray head. "I'll get you something cool to drink," Gina said. "You sit right there till I get back."

"But he *is* going to be all right, isn't he Polly?" Leanna asked, hardly noticing Gina's departure.

Polly took a deep breath and blew the air out slowly. "Well, I think so, if no infection sets in. But in this weather and with those kinds of wounds, I'm afraid that's not something we can count on."

"I have to see him," Leanna said, moving to the door.

"You go right ahead, child, and tell Trey to come out and rest a bit. He was a sight, Leanna, working so hard. I could see he's wore plumb out."

"He loves Alex, too," Leanna said.

"Yes, he does," Polly said. "Now, Leanna honey,

when Alex wakes he's going to be in a mighty lot of pain, worse than anything he's ever experienced, most likely. You got to be ready for that."

"Yes," Leanna said, already on her way to the bedroom.

He was so still, his usually tanned face pale and drawn. Leanna could not believe how weak and vulnerable he looked. He'd always seemed so strong to her, almost invincible. Her magnificent Nighthawk. The sight of him now made her heart ache.

She sat with him through the night, holding his hand and whispering words of love, encouraging him, pleading with him to come back to her. She thought the happiest moment of her life would be when he opened his black eyes and looked at her.

She had drifted off to sleep in the chair beside the bed. Near dawn she was awakened by a low groan and looked to see Alex turning his head slowly back and forth on the pillow.

She went to him and touched his brow. He was hot, burning with fever, and when his eyes flickered open, she knew with despair that he did not recognize her.

She ran to the doorway and called toward the kitchen, where Polly was cooking breakfast. The little woman came immediately into the bedroom.

"He has a fever," Leanna said with dread in her voice.

Polly went to him and placed a hand on his brow. Then she pulled the sheet back and looked at his battered, swollen leg. "Looks a little red, but I don't think there's an infection, not just yet, anyway. I'll get some cool water to bathe his fever away."

For the next few days they all took turns sitting with

Alex. Leanna could hardly stand to see the pain etched on his face as he thrashed about or stiffened in agony.

The first time she heard his voice she felt like crying with joy, even though his words were crazed from the fever.

"Leave me, Jimmy," he muttered. "Take the men . . . take the men," he whispered through teeth clenched in pain.

Sometimes he would call Leanna's name, his eyes searching the room for her. "I'm here, darling," she would say, taking his hand or touching his face. She was glad that he could not see the tears that fell onto his bed.

On the fourth morning, Leanna sat by his bed. She had fallen asleep with his hand firmly clutched in hers. She wasn't sure what woke her, but when she opened her eyes she saw Alex's steady gaze on her face. His black eyes were alert and watchful as he studied her, looking at her as if for the first time.

She leaned forward in the chair with a start, her lips moving soundlessly as she fell on her knees beside the bed. "Alex?" she said, gazing into his eyes.

He smiled and closed his eyes, and she felt the strong grip of his hand in hers. Leanna began to cry both from relief and joy. She wanted to shout, to sing her thanks to the heavens, but she could not move. All the strength and resolve she'd held so strongly the past few days disappeared, and she could do nothing but sob quietly against his chest.

She felt his hand move to her head as he stroked her hair gently. He lay with his eyes still closed, as if he did not have the strength to open them.

"My little Rebel," he whispered hoarsely.

Leanna lifted her head and looked at him. She smiled, tears still streaming from her eyes. "Not any more, my love," she said. "There is no rebellion left in me."

He smiled, his beautiful lips trembling slightly at the corners. He turned his head slowly and opened his eyes to look at her. Leanna thought she'd never seen such tenderness as then.

"You've grown into quite a woman," he whispered. "Have I told you that? My little Rebel has turned into an exceptional woman." He ran his hand down the length of her hair and then closed his eyes again.

"Do you feel like eating?"

"Sleep," he murmured. "Just sleep."

Leanna closed her eyes and clasped her hands together at her lips. "Thank you, God," she whispered. "Thank you."

Alex continued to improve, growing stronger each day. They could hardly believe how well he had come through the terrible wounds and the excruciating pain. But he was a strong, determined man, one who practically forced himself to heal. Once he heard Leanna's voice through his fevered nightmares and realized he was home, he steeled himself against the pain. He'd had to fight with everything in him to get well, but nothing was going to make him leave Leanna now, nothing.

The mood in the big farmhouse changed drastically once they all knew Alex would recover. Trey brought fish from the river for him, and Polly cooked and served it tenderly. Gina, tired now that she was in the last days of her pregnancy, sat with Alex and tried to distract him when he thought too often of the men he had lost.

One quiet autumn evening, Leanna and Alex sat on

the front porch long after the rest had gone to bed. It was the first time he'd been able to put into words what had happened that day at Perryville.

"Are you sure Jimmy is all right?" he asked.

"I'm positive, darling," she said, telling how they'd seen him at the Peters farm the day they found Alex.

"He's so young . . . they were all so young," he said, looking off toward the river with weariness in his dark eyes.

There was a sharp ache in Leanna's heart as she, too, remembered the sweetness of those young men. Their courage, their kindness to her. She thought of Steven, the boy from Pennsylvania who had been so entranced with Southern women.

Leanna placed a hand on his arm. He turned his hand and captured hers, holding it to his chest, then to his lips. "I can't believe they're all gone," he said.

"Alex . . . sweetheart. Don't torture yourself this way. They wouldn't want it."

"I keep thinking I could have done more . . . warned them. Something." He narrowed his eyes and looked vacantly into the darkness that surrounded the house.

"Do you want to tell me about it?"

"I remember the feeling I had that day—had for a long time. I thought it was me, thought I was the one who would die." There was a wealth of agony in his deep voice.

"I know," she whispered, remembering his disturbing words to her the night before he left.

He shook his head and sighed heavily. "Something happened at Perryville, the strangest thing."

"What?"

"I've heard of it before, although I'm not sure I actually believed it. It's a phenomenon of some kind, something to do with the weather, maybe. Some of the old soldiers used to talk about it around the campfire at night as if it were supernatural. But it's real, it happened."

Leanna frowned at him, curious about his strange words and worried at the odd tone of his voice.

"We couldn't hear the sound of the battle, Leanna," he said. "We were only a couple of miles from the fighting, but we couldn't hear a sound. It was eerie."

"I don't understand. We heard the fighting here, as far as we are."

"It's not easy to understand, but it happens sometimes. Those near the battle hear nothing, while people miles away hear every shot, every blast of cannon. But we heard nothing, absolutely nothing. Buell was puzzled, thinking the battle had not commenced. If only he'd sent a scout, he'd have discovered that it had. But instead he moved us all forward. We came over a hill, and next thing we knew, the sounds were all around us, and it was too late. By then we were right in the thick of the fighting."

Leanna felt in her heart the pain reflected in his eyes. But she said nothing, knowing that this was something he needed to talk about.

"Many of the soldiers to the rear saw what was happening and retreated back toward the woods. But we were right in front. I saw my men go down without a chance, some of them with the oddest look of surprise on their faces. I saw Jimmy fall from his horse, and that's all I remember."

"It's over now, darling," she said.

"No," he said in a soft but fierce voice. "It will never

be over for me. I'll see their faces and hear their screams as long as I live."

She touched his face and felt the tears. It almost broke her heart. She bent forward to kiss him, murmuring words of love to him, wanting him to know that she shared his pain.

It was the closest, most precious moment she'd ever shared with anyone, even her father. Alex was everything to her now. And she knew that whatever happened to them in their life, this moment would always remain. Sadly, the memory of the battle would remain for Alex as well.

34

As Leanna lay in bed that night she thought of the changes that the year 1862 had brought in her life. She still had no idea when her father would be released, though she received regular letters from him that assured her he was well.

And Alex. What would her life have been like without him? She could not even imagine. Loving him had made such a difference in the way she saw things and in the kind of person she wanted to be.

Even the time she'd spent with the Shakers had changed her in many ways, teaching her patience and the discipline of hard work. It was something she had not forsaken even after she left the Believers, and she knew she never would.

Alex had said she had changed from a rebel to a woman. She smiled into the darkness. That part was certainly true. He had made her a woman, and she could hardly wait until he was well and strong again so she could show him just how womanly she could be.

She wanted to take care of him, be his friend, his lover, the woman he came home to after a day of work. She wanted to have his children, precious dark-haired children with black eyes and smiles that would melt the coldest of hearts. She wanted to be his wife, and she wondered why he had not asked her.

The next morning they were delighted when an approaching rider turned out to be Jimmy Anderson. Leanna had to caution Alex about his leg, or else he might have leapt from the porch to meet the young man.

She could see the impatience in his eyes as he waited for Jimmy to come up the steps. They shook hands and clasped each other in a fierce hug. Leanna knew that the foremost thought in Alex's mind was his men. He wanted to know everything, and so she left them alone to share their grief in private.

When she came out onto the porch later with a tray of pie and cool milk, they had both ceased talking. There was no strain between them, only a quiet, companionable silence.

"Jimmy has something to tell you, Leanna," Alex said, smiling up at her with a hint of mystery.

She set the tray down and poured the milk, looking at Jimmy with anticipation.

He pulled a wrinkled letter from his shirt pocket and handed it to her. "It took a while for me to get here with this. I was afraid he might already have written you."

Leanna frowned and unfolded the letter. "Written me? Who?"

"Read," Alex said.

It was a letter from a Lieutenant Watson, one of Jefferson Davis's aides, and it was addressed to Major Alex Slayton.

"Dear Alex," she read.

I was sorry to hear about Senator McNairy. I know him to be a good and honorable man. And I appreciate your wish to help him and his daughter. I spoke to President Davis personally about the matter. He agreed that the charges against the senator are very serious, but not indefensible. He also agreed, despite the great chasm that exists now between the North and South, that he needs to be fair. Therefore it is with great pleasure that I inform you that he will see to the release of Senator McNairy from the prison in Richmond as soon as possible. The only condition shall be that he remain in the North until the war is decided and that his loyalty to the Union will be shown openly and clearly. I trust this will not be a problem since the senator has a home in Washington. President Davis extends his personal greetings to you and your family as well as to Miss Leanna McNairy.

Leanna looked across at Alex, speechless. He and Jimmy both grinned at her, enjoying the pleasure that had transformed her face.

"Lieutenant Watson was one of my students at Kentucky Union College, and a friend of Gina's husband," Alex said.

"Oh, Alex," she said. "You did this for me?"

"Of course I did it for you. Is there anything I wouldn't do for the woman I love?"

She shook her head, amazed at this man who was so

strong and so determined and could quickly become so sweet and loving.

Jimmy cleared his throat and stood up. "Well, if you'll excuse me, I think I'll go inside and speak with Gina."

They hardly noticed him leave.

Alex stood and reached for the crutches Trey had made for him. "Walk with me to the river, Leanna," he said.

She put an arm around his waist, holding one hand lightly against his chest as she helped him down the steps and out into the yard. She glanced up at the sky, which had grown dark with clouds. Perhaps, if they were lucky, the drought would break before nightfall.

They made their way along the dusty path that led to the deep green fishing hole. Leanna went slowly, being careful of Alex's leg and that his crutches did not become entangled in weeds or caught in a hole.

Once in the shade of the trees along the riverbank, he turned to her. She leaned back against the smooth bark of one of the old sycamores that had stood there for decades.

Alex looked toward the river, watching the murky green water drift by slowly. "I've made so many mistakes," he said.

It was not what she expected him to say, not what she hoped he had come here to say. "Why do you say that?" she asked.

"If I'd known in January what I know now, I would have taken you that first night at the ball and kissed you until you were breathless. And I'd never have let you out of my sight from that moment on." He looked at her with a flash of humor in his dark eyes.

She smiled up at him. "You're pretty sure of yourself, aren't you, Major?"

He lowered his eyes. "Not as sure as I sometimes pretend."

Her face grew serious as she watched him. She knew that he had doubts now about so many things, especially since Perryville.

"I wish I had never wasted a moment of our time. Never pushed you away, thinking I was doing what was best for you. Those were precious moments tossed away, all because of my stubbornness. I could have lost you forever, because I had to insist on running your life as well as mine. But you grew up somewhere along the way and made me see that you had a mind of your own."

She reached a hand up to caress his jaw and let the other rest on his chest as she looked into his eyes. "You were never in danger of losing me. Don't you know that by now? We were meant to be together. I think I knew that from the start, and nothing you could ever do would stop my loving you."

She was shaken by the spark she saw deep in his black eyes. He bent his head and placed a kiss lightly on her upturned lips. "I love you so much, Leanna," he whispered.

His kiss made her shaky, his nearness tantalizing until she could feel the pulse throb wildly in her veins. He knew he had always had this effect on her. These doubts today had nothing to do with their love, she knew that as well.

"There's something I want to tell you," he said, pulling away from her.

She waited for his words, still caressing his arm as he spoke.

"Jimmy brought another letter today. A letter accepting my resignation from the army."

Leanna felt a huge wave of relief sweep over her. It was something she had feared, his going back. She was not sure she could stand to tell him good-bye again. She closed her eyes and leaned her head against his chest.

"Oh, Alex. Thank God."

But the look of doubt was still in his eyes as he watched her face carefully. "I know you're just about to get your father back. And if you don't want to come with me now I'll understand."

"Come with you? What are you saying?"

"I've accepted a post in Central America. The government is sending a team to investigate canal routes, and I . . ."

"Central America?" she asked incredulously.

He frowned. "I understand. It's a long way from Kentucky, and your father. If you don't want to come . . ."

She began to smile, realizing for the first time what he was trying to say. This big, strong, confident man was actually struggling almost shyly to find the right words.

She laughed, a low sound of delight. "Exactly what are you asking me, Major Slayton?"

He laughed, too. "First, I'm asking you to be my wife, and you're making it very difficult." His voice was husky as he bent to kiss the corners of her tantalizing lips. "Second, I'm asking you to come with me to Central America. And I guess third, I'm asking you to leave your father and your friends behind for a while. It won't be for long, and I've been given enough time to recover from my wounds before I go. By then Gina's baby will be born. Still I know it will be hard for you. The weather down there is hot, the conditions primitive, and God knows—"

She stopped his words with her lips, pulling away only when she heard him groan, afraid that she had hurt him. But when he pulled her back against him again, she smiled, realizing that the groan was for an entirely different reason.

"Yes," she whispered.

He straightened and stared at her with dawning joy in his black eyes. "Yes? You'll marry me, you'll come to Central America?"

"Yes, yes, yes, to all three, my darling Alex. I would go anywhere with you, do anything for you. How long will it take for me to convince you of that?"

"A lifetime, I think, if I'm lucky," he whispered.

"Oh, yes, my darling Yankee," she said with a smile. "Yes to that, too."

As they turned from the river and walked arm in arm toward the lighted farmhouse, a rumble shook the air around them.

Leanna looked at Alex with a flash of fear in her eyes. "Was that—?"

"Kentucky thunder, my love," he said with a smile. "Only Kentucky thunder bringing a wild, noisy storm our way."

She looked up into his eyes. "Do you think it will be too noisy for sleeping?"

He stopped and pulled her close, kissing her until she gasped with delight. "Yes, love. I definitely think it will."

Author's Note

The description of General Buell's inability to hear the battle noise at Perryville, Kentucky, is true. This phenomenon is called acoustic shadow, or silent battle. Mark Boatner III's *Civil War Dictionary* describes it as a phenomenon whereby sound is inaudible to persons a short distance from the source but can be heard a hundred miles away. This also occurred at the Civil War battles of Seven Pines, Gaines Mill, and Chancellorsville.

The Civil War Almanac Day by Day by E.B. Long with Barbar Long says about the silent battle at Perryville: "Due to an atmospheric phenomenon by which battle noise was not heard back of the lines, Buell did not realize until late in the day that a major fight was in progress and failed to get his full force into battle."

In the battle at Perryville on October 8, 1862, the

initial Confederate assault enjoyed brief success, but a Union counterattack drove the outnumbered rebels from the field. The battle brought little credit to either commander, however. Buell failed to initiate a pursuit of the retreating Confederates, and for this final failure he was replaced in command by William Rosecrans.

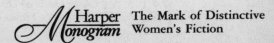

COMING NEXT MONTH

COMING UP ROSES by Catherine Anderson

From the bestselling author of the Comanche trilogy, comes a sensual historical romance. When Zach McGovern was injured in rescuing her daughter from an abandoned well, Kate Blakely nursed him back to health. Kate feared men, but Zach was different, and only buried secrets could prevent their future from coming up roses.

HOMEBODY by Louise Titchener

Bestselling author Louise Titchener pens a romantic thriller about a young woman who must battle the demons of her past, as well as the dangers she finds in her new apartment.

BAND OF GOLD by Zita Christian

The rush for gold in turn-of-the-century Alaska was nothing compared to the rush Aurelia Breighton felt when she met the man of her dreams. But then Aurelia discovered that it was not her he was after but her missing sister.

DANCING IN THE DARK by Susan P. Teklits

A tender and touching tale of two people who were thrown together by treachery and found unexpected love. A historical romance in the tradition of Constance O'Banyon.

CHANCE McCALL by Sharon Sala

Chance McCall knows that he has no right to love Jenny Tyler, the boss's daughter. With only his monthly paycheck and checkered past, he's no good for her, even though she thinks otherwise. But when an accident leaves Chance with no memory, he has no choice but to return to his past and find out why he dare not claim the woman he loves.

SWEET REVENGE by Jean Stribling

There was nothing better than sweet revenge when ex-Union captain Adam McCormick unexpectedly captured his enemy's stepdaughter, Letitia Ramsey. But when Adam found himself falling in love with her, he had to decide if revenge was worth the sacrifice of love.

HIGHLAND LOVE SONG by Constance O'Banyon

Available in trade paperback! From the bestselling author of *Forever My Love*, a sweeping and mesmerizing story continues the DeWinter legacy begun in *Song of the Nightingale*.

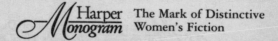

YESTERDAY'S SHADOWS
by Marianne Willman

Bettany Howard was a young orphan traveling west searching for the father who left her years ago. Wolf Star was a Cheyenne brave who longed to know who abandoned him—a white child with a jeweled talisman. Fate decreed they'd meet and try to seize the passion promised. 0-06-104044-4

MIDNIGHT ROSE by Patricia Hagan

From the rolling plantations of Richmond to the underground slave movement of Philadelphia, Erin Sterling and Ryan Youngblood would pursue their wild, breathless passion and finally surrender to the promise of a bold and unexpected love. 0-06-104023-1

WINTER TAPESTRY
by Kathy Lynn Emerson

Cordell vows to revenge the murder of her father. Roger Allington is honor bound to protect his friend's daughter but has no liking for her reckless ways. Yet his heart tells him he must pursue this beauty through a maze of plots to win her love and ignite their smoldering passion. 0-06-100220-8

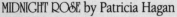